The Midwife and the Assassin

Also by Sam Thomas

The Midwife's Tale

The Harlot's Tale

The Witch Hunter's Tale

The Maidservant and the Murderer (e-book)

The Midwife and the Assassin

SAM THOMAS

MINOTAUR BOOKS ☙ NEW YORK

This is a work of fiction. All of the characters, organizations, and events portrayed in this novel are either products of the author's imagination or are used fictitiously.

For information, address St. Martin's Press, 175 Fifth Avenue, New York, N.Y. 10010.

www.minotaurbooks.com

Designed by Omar Chapa

Map by Rhys Davies

The Library of Congress has cataloged the hardcover edition as follows:

Names: Thomas, Samuel S.
Title: The midwife and the assassin : a mystery / Sam Thomas.
Description: First edition. | New York : Minotaur Books, 2016.
Identifiers: LCCN 2015042574| ISBN 9781250045768 (hardcover) | ISBN 9781466845381 (e-book)
Subjects: LCSH: Women detectives—Fiction. | Midwives—Fiction. | Espionage—Fiction. | Political violence—Fiction. | England—Fiction. | BISAC: FICTION / Mystery & Detective / Historical. | FICTION / Mystery & Detective / Women Sleuths. | GSAFD: Historical fiction. | Suspense fiction.
Classification: LCC PS3620.H64225 M52 2016 | DDC 813/.6—dc23
LC record available at http://lccn.loc.gov/2015042574

ISBN 978-1-250-09668-5 (trade paperback)

First Minotaur Books Paperback Edition: November 2016

10 9 8 7 6 5 4 3 2 1

For my mother, father, stepmother,
stepfather, and ex-stepmother

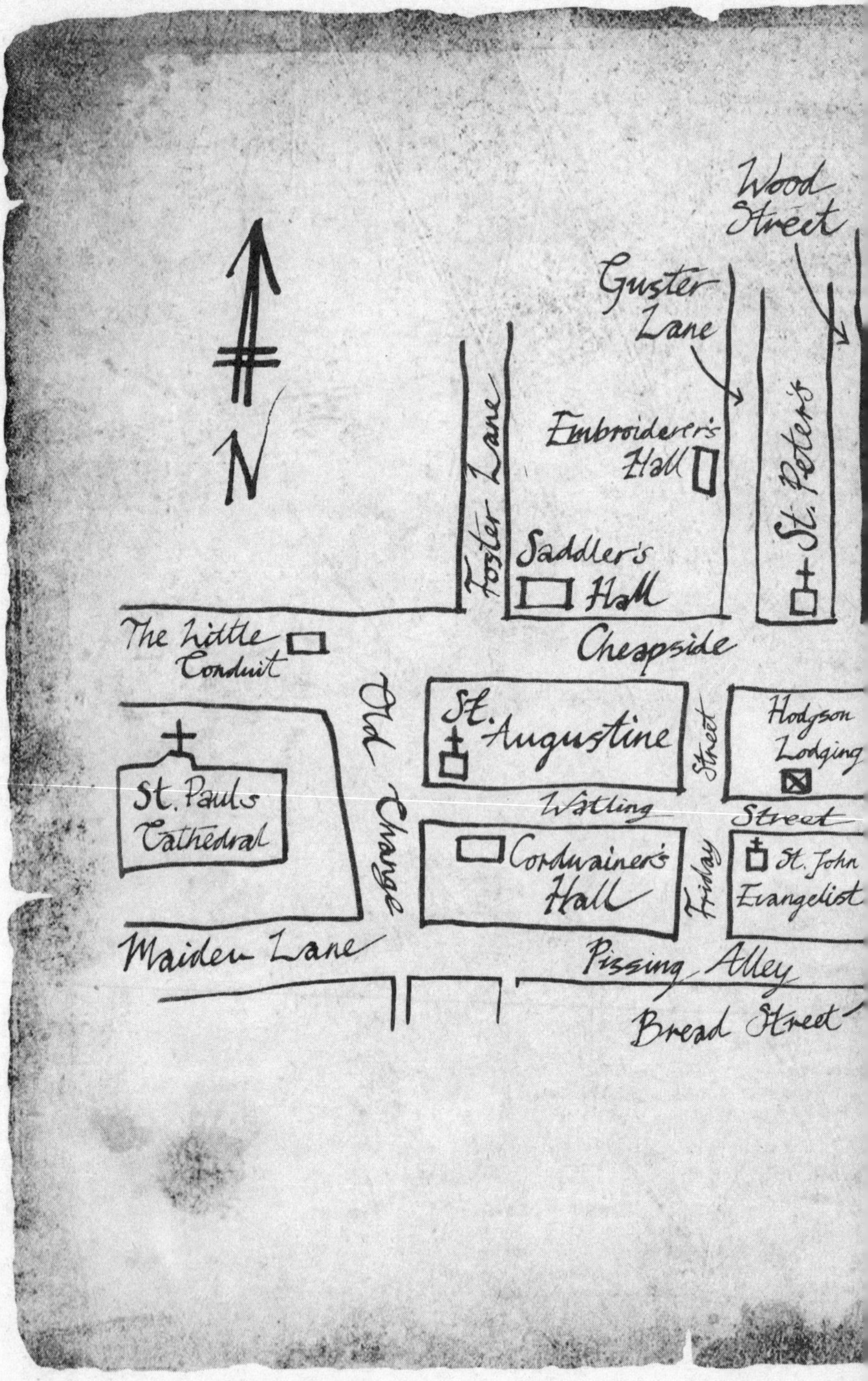

N

Wood Street

Guster Lane

Foster Lane

Embroiderer's Hall

St. Peter's

Saddler's Hall

The Little Conduit

Chespside

Old Change

St. Augustine

Street

Hodgson Lodging

St. Paul's Cathedral

Watling

Street

Cordwainer's Hall

Friday

St. John Evangelist

Maiden Lane

Pissing Alley

Bread Street

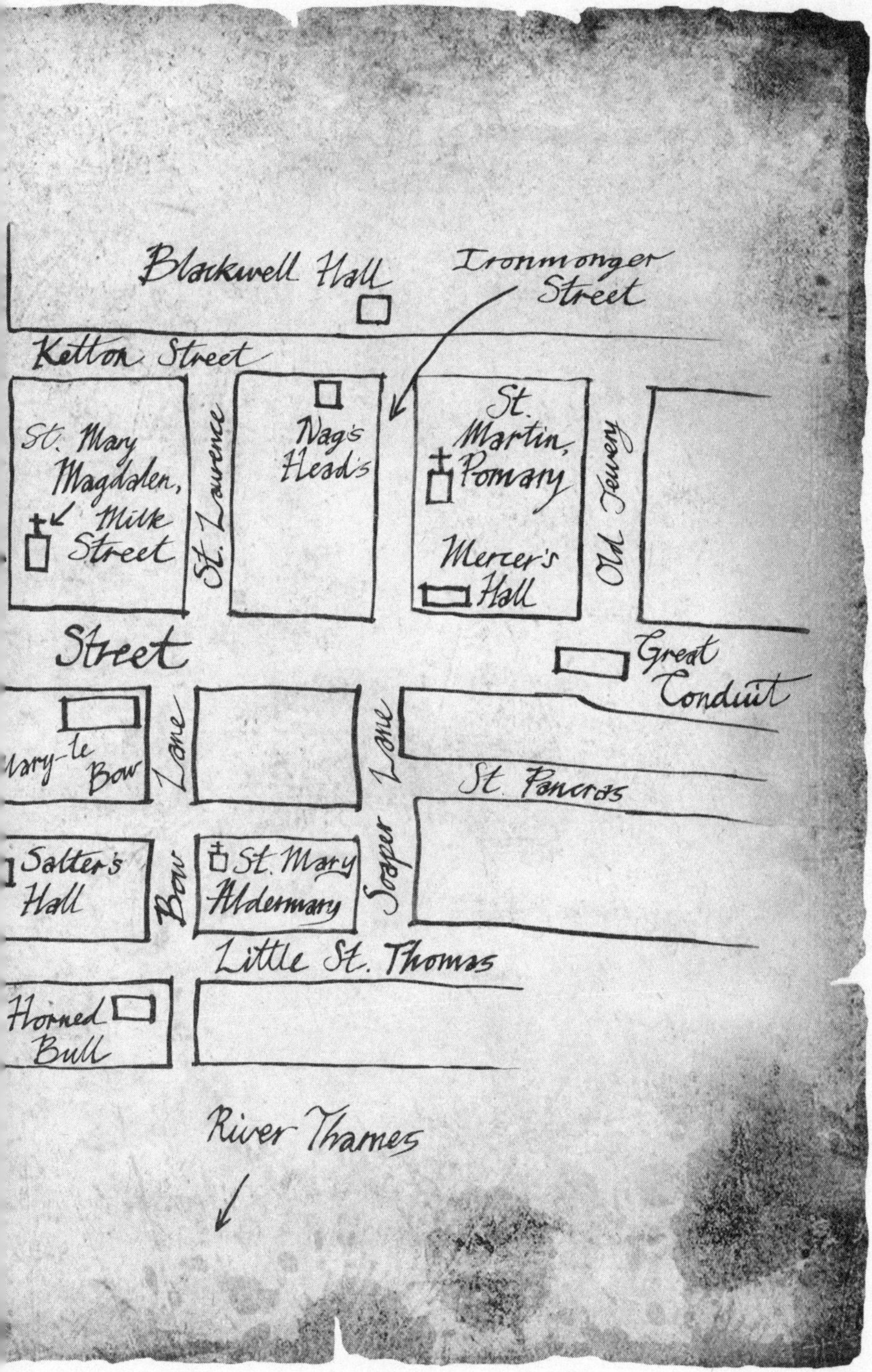

Blackwell Hall

Ironmonger Street

Kelton Street

St. Mary Magdalen, Milk Street

St. Lawrence

Nag's Head's

St. Martin, Pomary

Mercer's Hall

Old Jewery

Street

Great Conduit

Mary-le Bow

Lane

Lane

St. Pancras

Salter's Hall

Bow

St. Mary Aldermary

Soaper

Little St. Thomas

Horned Bull

River Thames

The Midwife and the Assassin

Chapter 1

The late summer sun rose with warmth of a loving mother's gaze, and I prayed yet again for the Lord to send a storm.

It was not that my estates needed the rain, for the harvest was nearly complete. What I wished for was something, *anything* to end the tediousness of life in Pontrilas. Nearly three years had passed since I'd been exiled from my beloved city of York and I now lived an all-too-quiet life on my lands in Hereford. When I first arrived, my neighbors had been eager to visit me, hoping to hear of my adventures in the north. What did I know of the witches who had been hanged? Was it true that I had sent some to the gallows myself? I had no desire to talk of such matters, but more than once I'd considered telling them the truth if only to be rid of them. If they knew the things I'd done, these kind and inoffensive women would have fled my home, never to return.

But I never said such things, of course. Instead I resigned myself to the mincing conversations of country gentlewomen. After a few months, the neighbors stopped coming so often, and I could not rouse myself to visit them. Eventually I settled into a life of reading and writing. I began to compose a book on the art of midwifery, so that other women in that office could learn from me rather than from hard experience. From time to time, my tenants would summon me to their travails, and I welcomed the distraction, but with so few women about, the calls were few and far between.

As much as my new life pained me, it was pure torture for Martha Hawkins, my maidservant and deputy. She was a bold and courageous young woman, far better suited to the life of a city midwife than a country maid. I could only imagine the horror with which she regarded the years of washing and cleaning that lay before her so long as we remained in Pontrilas. Of course, the fact that she faced a future without her beloved—and one-time betrothed—Will Hodgson only compounded her misery. My nephew stayed in York when we fled, and went into service for the Lord Mayor. He sometimes wrote to us, but with England at war with itself, letters took weeks or months to arrive, and only the Lord knew how many miscarried entirely. In his last letter, sent some months earlier, Will told us that he would be going to London. We had heard nothing since.

Even Elizabeth, my adopted daughter, had tired of Pontrilas. When we arrived, she had viewed the countryside with a sense of wonder, and I could not blame her. After years of poverty, the opulence of my estates must have seemed like heaven itself. But as the weeks and months blurred together, Elizabeth too came to miss the excitement of city life. Indeed, the only member of my household who enjoyed the change from York to Pontrilas was Hannah, my maidservant. She tolerated York for the years we lived there, but she was glad to return to Pontrilas in her old age; it was, after all, where she'd been born.

And so as fall came, Martha, Elizabeth, and I brooded around the house, wishing for something, anything to shake us out of our country languor.

To my surprise and relief, our country exile ended on an October afternoon when a letter arrived from London. A boy carried it all the way from the village—no small feat—and I had one of my maidservants reward him appropriately, with bread, cheese, and a tuppence. As I watched him eat, I was reminded of Tree, the son of sorts whom I'd left behind in York. I had just received a letter from his father, so I knew that he was doing well. Of all the things I missed about York, it was the separation from my people—Will, Tree, my gossips, and my clients—that pained me the most.

After the boy left, I opened the letter, assuming it was from Mr. Browne, the intelligencer I'd hired to send me news from the city. Mr. Browne had informed us of the King's capture and imprisonment by Parliament in 1647, and he had seen with his own eyes the riots of 1648, when the King's supporters rose up against Parliament but were quickly defeated. I knew before any of my neighbors that the King had conspired with the Scots to invade England, and of the brutal treatment that our northern neighbors received at Oliver Cromwell's hands. More recently there had been rumblings that the King should be brought to trial for the crime of making war against his own people. I could not imagine such a thing, but the world had been upside down for so long, nothing seemed impossible.

This letter, however, was not from my intelligencer. Rather, it had been sent by a jailor in the Tower of London.

To the Lady Bridget Hodgson:

I write on behalf of your nephew, Will Hodgson, now prisoner in the Tower of London. He seeks your assistance as soon as it is convenient.

Your servant,

Richard Thompson

"Martha," I cried out.

She must have heard the confusion in my voice, for her hands were still covered with flour when she found me in the parlor.

"What has happened?" she asked.

"Will has been sent to the Tower of London and needs our help." I handed Martha the letter, and she read it.

"What does this mean?" Martha looked at me in confusion. "Will has been jailed and needs our help, but only if it is convenient?"

"I don't know." If Will were an ordinary prisoner he would not have been sent to the Tower, but there was no indication of what crime—whether real or imagined—had brought him there. The letter made no sense.

Martha reread the letter and furrowed her brow. "Why didn't he write to us himself?" she asked.

"Perhaps he has been denied pen and paper," I said.

"Or he is too ill to write," Martha replied. "Gaol-fever is a terrible thing, and the Tower is a stinking, fetid place, far worse than the Castle in York."

"But surely if he were ill, his jailor would tell us to hurry," I said. "And there is no urgency about it. It is a strange thing."

"The letter is addressed to you, but we will both go, won't we?" Martha asked.

"Of course we will," I replied. "You know London far better than I do. I'd be lost by myself."

"London?" Elizabeth had slipped into the room without my

notice and now joined Martha and me in looking at Will's letter. I heard the excitement in her voice, and I knew that the coming minutes would not be easy ones.

"Martha and I must go to London to see what this letter means," I said. "You will stay here with Hannah."

Anger flared in Elizabeth's eyes. "Stay here?" she demanded. "And do what? I've ridden over Pontrilas's every inch a thousand times. It is dull and drearisome—you *must* take me with you." Elizabeth paced as she spoke, and the autumn light caught the red of her hair, giving her the glow of the sun itself.

"It is too far and too uncertain," I said. "We will not be gone for long."

Elizabeth pounced. "If you will not be gone for long, there is no reason not to take me." She looked at Martha, hoping she would prove a ready ally.

But even Martha, who usually encouraged Elizabeth's natural boldness, saw the folly in her suggestion. "London is a dangerous place," she said. "Not a city for two women and a girl."

"I am not a girl, I am twelve." Elizabeth drew herself up and looked straight into my eyes. She was long and lean, and soon she would be the most beautiful woman in Hereford. "And Matthew will be with us, for he will have to drive the carriage."

"Matthew will not be with *us,*" I said. "He will be with me and Martha. *You* will be here with Hannah."

Elizabeth continued to plead her case until well after supper, offering an endless stream of arguments and promises, each one more desperate than the last. She finally retired to her chamber, but she went so easily that I knew that the battle was not over.

Once I was alone, I thought more about our upcoming journey. I knew that leaving Elizabeth behind was the right choice, but I would miss her terribly. She had come to my home in York following the murder of her mother, and soon became not just my ward but my adopted daughter. When my enemies in the city threatened Elizabeth, they learned through bitter experience that there was nothing I would not do to protect her. And as much as I regretted the decision to leave Elizabeth behind, taking her to London would be foolhardy in the extreme.

I sat with pen and paper before me, considering all that the journey would require. Hannah would be more than happy to care for Elizabeth during our absence, but even if we were gone for just a few weeks I would have to hire another servant or two so that she would not be overburdened. The harder question was our lodging once we arrived in London. We could stay at an inn, as my father had done when he served in Parliament, but I wished we had a friend in the city.

And then I remembered Esther Cooper, one of my gossips in York. We had been friends for many years, and I'd even asked her to serve as my deputy. But shortly after Martha came to my household, Esther was arrested for the murder of her husband. Martha and I ultimately proved her innocence and saved her from burning, but her reputation within the city had been so stained that she'd fled to London to start anew. I had not seen her since she left York, but we had exchanged a handful of letters over the years. She had married a prosperous goldsmith named Charles Wallington and seemed very happy. I had no doubt she would welcome Martha and me into her home for as long as we needed. There was no time to write to her and await a response, so I composed a brief letter and sent it by one of my servants to Hereford. With any luck, it would arrive in London a day or two before we did, giving Esther at least a little time to ready her home for our arrival.

It took us two full days to prepare for our departure for London. I arranged for another midwife to work with any mothers who might go into labor, and packed the clothes I would need during our time away. These tasks were made more difficult by Elizabeth's steadfast refusal to admit that she would be staying behind. "Hannah could come with us. What does it matter whether she minds me here or in London?" Elizabeth's words were reasonable, but I could hear the frustration behind them. I tried to take her in my arms, but she ducked away.

"Elizabeth—" I started to say.

"No." Her blue eyes threw off sparks with every word. "You cannot leave me here. You and Martha will go off and have an adventure. I will be here with nothing to do, and only Hannah and my pony for companions. It is not fair."

"Fair has nothing to do with it," I said. "It is about what is best for you. You are my daughter, and I must keep you safe."

Elizabeth's face fell and her anger turned to sorrow. "But what if something happens to you? If London is as dangerous as you say, it could. I cannot . . ." Her words failed her, but I knew what she was trying to say: *I cannot be orphaned again*. I joined her in weeping and tried once again to take her in my arms. This time she did not resist.

"I love you," I said. "And I love that you want to come with us, and that you are not some sheep doing whatever you are told. But there is too much we do not know to bring you along. You will be safe here, and we will return as soon as possible. I promise." We held each other until we both had stopped crying, and then it was time to finish the preparations for our departure. A servant took the last of my chests to the carriage, and my eyes fell upon my birthing stool and the valise of oils, herbs, and tools that I took to every travail.

"I suppose it never hurts to be prepared," I murmured, and took them down as well.

After ensuring that our baggage was secure, Martha and I sat down to dinner with Elizabeth. It was a melancholy affair, and I was relieved that Elizabeth did not renew her entreaties to accompany us. I did not know if I could have held out another hour. After we had eaten, Martha and I climbed into the carriage, bid Elizabeth one final farewell, and began the journey north to Hereford, where we would find the highway to London.

We made the best time we could over the rough road. The Lord smiled on us with fair weather, so we did not have to fight the mud that sometimes took hold of English travelers and held them in place for days at a time. As we bounced our way east, Martha and I whiled away the hours trying to decipher Will's letter.

After a series of increasingly fanciful suggestions from both of us—perhaps the King was behind our call to London!—we agreed that we were doing no more than spinning cobwebs out of our imaginations. We pushed aside such questions as unknowable, and talked of more practical matters. Looking back, it is strange to think how close to the truth our most fantastical ideas had been.

As we neared London I asked Martha to tell me what she knew of the city—what more practical question could there be? She shook her head in wonder at the thought.

"It is like no place you've ever seen." Martha's voice was filled with awe, excitement, and fear. "The crowds, the noise, the filth: They put York to shame in every imaginable way. It is as if some mad architect took twenty Yorks, jumbled them up, and cast them out along the river Thames. And once the city was built, the architect filled it with every kind of person you can imagine, from every corner of the world. London is a great and terrible city, but one that offers astonishing rewards to those who learn her ways."

"And how can we do that?" I asked. I had no intention of staying in the city even one day longer than I had to, but I was entranced by Martha's description and the wonder in her voice.

"First, you'll have to forget yourself and who you were before you came," Martha replied. "Londoners don't care for the past, only the present and the future. And once you are in the city, you can become anyone you please. What is more, if you don't like who you become, you can simply transform yourself into someone else."

"What do you mean?" I asked. If I'd not been sitting in a carriage with her, I'd have thought she'd been drinking.

"When my brother and I were here, London offered endless opportunities for our trickery."

I was surprised by this admission. Before she came into my service, Martha had escaped a brutal master, only to fall in with her brother Tom, a notorious highwayman and thief. I knew they had spent some time in London, but I'd never pressed Martha for details.

"If Tom thought there was a chance we would be taken, we would simply move a half a mile, or—if things were truly dangerous—we'd cross the river. Once in a new neighborhood, where nobody knew us, we'd just start fresh: new names, new trades, new crimes. It's not one city, but hundreds, all set up together."

Martha's rapturous description was interrupted by a cry from our driver as the carriage drew to a halt.

"I'm sorry, my lady," the driver called through the window. "The cart ahead of us just lost a wheel. I'll help the driver pull his cart off the road and then we can be on our way. It won't be long, I don't think."

Martha and I climbed out of the carriage to observe the scene and ease our aching joints. A large cart filled with sacks of grain sat before us, listing precipitously to the right. A group of men had gathered around the broken wheel, surveying the damage and discussing their options. I looked past the cart and caught my breath.

We had just crested a hill—Highgate Hill, I later learned—and all of London lay below us.

"Remarkable, isn't it?" Martha asked.

I could only nod. My eyes followed the Thames as it snaked from the west until it reached the city itself. Even from this remove, St. Paul's Cathedral towered over the rest of the city, made more magnificent by the thousands of buildings that surrounded it like supplicants at an emperor's feet. To the south and east, I could pick out the spires of the city's churches, though there were so many I could not count them all. In the far distance I saw London Bridge, with its many shops and houses, and I could see the theaters in the lawless precincts south of the river. A dull blue haze hung over the entire city, produced no doubt by the thousands—tens of thousands—of hearths burning wood and sea coal to ward off the autumn chill.

By now the men had unloaded the stricken cart and dragged it to the side of the road, clearing the way for the rest of us. We returned to the carriage and, with a shout to the horses and a crack of his whip, the driver took us down the hill and into the city.

I knew that Esther Cooper's new husband, like many of the city's goldsmiths, had taken a home on an avenue called the Strand, which lay between the city and the halls of Parliament. I said a prayer of thanks that they'd chosen to live there, for it meant we would not have to pass through London itself to reach their home. If everything I'd heard was true, my carriage would have a devil of a time on London's streets, and I could not imagine how long such a journey would take.

After a time we turned south, onto a road our driver said was St. Martin's Lane, before finding ourselves on the Strand. I gazed in wonder at the riverside palaces built by England's oldest and wealthiest families. The largest houses in York would have fit inside these homes many times over. Here in miniature was the difference between York's merchants and London's nobility; it was the difference between power over a city and power over a nation. Even Martha marveled at the sight.

"I thought you already knew the city," I teased.

"My brother and I spent our time in other neighborhoods." Martha laughed. "Though if he'd found a way to rob one of these piles, he certainly would have. We'd have collapsed under the weight of all the gold they must contain."

As our carriage rolled over the roughly paved streets, I noticed that many of the shops belonged to goldsmiths. It took me a moment to work out the connection, but I soon made sense of this strange mix of noblemen and craftsmen. What better place for a goldsmith to ply his trade than a few steps from England's dukes, barons, and earls? Moreover, to the west lay the palaces of Whitehall and Westminster—the seats of King and Parliament. Within a mile of that spot one could find more power and wealth than in any other city in England. It would have been strange if the goldsmiths had settled anywhere *except* the Strand.

When I spied a sign announcing CHARLES WALLINGTON, GOLDSMITH, I called for the driver to stop. Martha and I dismounted from the carriage, hopping over the dung as best we could. We each breathed a sigh of relief that our long journey had come to an end. I told the driver to unload our luggage, and knocked loudly on Esther Wallington's door.

Chapter 2

A handsome youth answered Esther Wallington's door and peered suspiciously at Martha and me, as if deciding whether he knew us. After a moment he concluded that he did not.

"What do you want?" he spat. "Are you here to see Mr. Wallington?"

I was taken aback both by the lad's peremptory speech and his failure to acknowledge my rank. I wondered if I had become so disheveled during our journey that I no longer looked the part of a gentlewoman. Or perhaps everything I'd heard about Londoners' rude nature was true.

"We are here to see Mrs. Wallington," I announced, hoping that my carriage and dress might overcome his refractory nature. "I am Lady Bridget Hodgson."

"Oh yes," the youth replied with only the barest hint of a bow. "Come in. I will tell Mrs. Wallington you have arrived."

Martha and I followed him through the entry hall into a large and sumptuously appointed parlor. Even though we'd only passed through two rooms, it was clear that Esther had married very well indeed. Every aspect of the house—from the paintings to the ornaments to the furniture—announced the Wallingtons' great wealth. I said a prayer of thanks for this, for it meant that our stay in London would be a comfortable one, no matter how disrespectful the servants.

"If you wait here," the servant said, "Mrs. Wallington will join you presently." I glanced at Martha as she absorbed the opulence that surrounded us. She was no less impressed than I, both at Esther's good fortune and our own.

It was not long before Esther swept into the parlor, trailed by gorgeous silks and fine lace. She crossed the room and embraced me with all the warmth I could have hoped for. The years since she'd left York had done her no visible harm, or at least no more than they'd done to any of us.

"Welcome, welcome," she cried as she embraced Martha as well. "I was so pleased when I received your letter. What a wonderful surprise!" She stood back and looked me over. "And you are as beautiful as ever. It seems that country life agrees with you."

"It is quieter and cleaner, to be sure." I laughed. "But sometimes I do miss the bustle of York."

"London will cure you of that desire, I think," Esther replied. "What you've seen thus far is nothing at all. Wait until you try to travel from one side to the other!"

"How have you been?" I asked.

"Well enough," Esther replied, barely able to suppress a smile. "Did I tell you that I have a baby boy?"

Martha and I cried out in delight. Esther and her first husband had come to me when he could not get her with child, but I'd been unable to help them. At the time I'd thought the problem lay with him—she showed no signs of barrenness—and now we knew that it was the case.

"When can we see him?" Martha asked.

"He is with the wet nurse now," Esther replied. "And then he will sleep. But she will bring him down when he wakes."

I could hear the uncertainty in her voice and knew its source. I'd long counseled women to nurse their own children rather than hire a wet nurse.

"Charles insisted I hire a nurse," Esther explained. "My husband is not a young man, and is eager to have another son. He said James has a weak constitution and might not survive."

My heart sank at this. Esther's first husband had treated her very badly, and I had prayed that she would choose more wisely the second time. It appeared that she had not. I tried to hide my disappointment, but I did not believe that I succeeded.

"It is wonderful to see you," she chirped, no less eager than I to change the subject from the past to the present. I knew I could not question her choice of husbands at this late date. What was done was done.

"And you, as well," I said. "Shall I have my man bring in our luggage? I am so looking forward to renewing our friendship."

"Why don't we wait until Mr. Wallington comes home?" Esther said. "He will not be long."

I heard a measure of trepidation in her voice, as if she wanted to say more, but for some reason could not. So we sat for a time in the parlor, sipping very good wine—French, she said—and talking of York, London, and all the changes that the Lord had brought our way since we had last seen each other. Few would say that I lied about my last year in York, but none would claim that I told the truth. How would I explain my hand in so many strange deaths? So I limited myself to births and natural deaths, and omitted entirely the true reason for our departure from the city.

As afternoon began to fade into evening the front door burst open and Charles Wallington stomped into the hall.

"Tell him that one way or another I'll have my money," he shouted over his shoulder. "He can give it willingly, or he can give it by order of the court. I care not which, but he *will* pay." A young man followed close behind him, trying valiantly to scribble his master's instructions even as he walked. Wallington strode into the parlor, and all three of us stood to greet him.

Charles Wallington was a corpulent man with small, dark eyes that peered angrily out from the rolls of flesh that cascaded down his face. The elegant cut and color of his clothes accentuated his enormous girth, but did little to hide his choleric humor. In an instant I judged that Esther's choice of a second husband had been even worse than her first; at least Stephen Cooper had maintained a veneer of civility overtop of his wretched nature. Wallington did not even manage that.

"You're that York midwife." In his mouth, the words sounded like an accusation. "Did my wife not tell you?" He stared at Esther with undisguised anger and contempt.

I looked at Esther, but she refused to meet my gaze.

"She only just arrived," Esther said softly. "We were talking of other things."

"Did she tell me what?" I asked.

"That I'll not have a woman such as you in my home," Wallington replied, once again sounding more like a prosecutor than a host. "I rely on my good name for my trade. You may stay for a moment, but when you finish your wine you will be on your way."

I stared at him for what seemed an eternity, unable to find an appropriate response. As usual, Martha suffered from no such incapacity.

"A woman such as her?" she cried. "Do you mean that she is a gentlewoman by birth, or that she is among the finest midwives in England? You would be fortunate to have her in your home."

Wallington stared at Martha as if noticing her for the first time. "Do you think I am ignorant of all the things she has done? Of the trouble she caused in York before she had to flee the city?"

"Do you consider saving your wife from an unjust execution *causing trouble*?" Martha stood with her hands on her hips, chin out.

Wallington ignored Martha's question and turned to me. "When I inquired about my wife's character, I heard all about you. Disorder and tumult hover over you like a cloud, and you rain death on those around you. I'll not have you sowing such ill seeds in my home, or anywhere near it. You will drink your drink, you will leave, and you will not return."

I turned to Esther in the faint hope that she might have spine enough to defend us. Martha and I had no other friends in the city, and nowhere else to go. Her visage made it clear that I needn't have bothered.

"I sent you a letter saying as much," she murmured. "You must have left Hereford before it arrived. I am sorry."

Wallington grunted his approval at Esther's craven acquiescence and rumbled out of the room without bidding us farewell.

"You must forgive him," Esther said once he was out of earshot. "All of London's goldsmiths have suffered since the King's party fled the city and took their money with them. Things became even worse when the godly stripped the churches of unnecessary ornaments. All the goldsmiths are in desperate straits."

I looked around the room, searching in vain for some sign of suffering.

"May we at least spend the night?" I asked. "It is nearly dark, and we've nowhere to stay." I misliked the pleading tone of my voice. It reminded me of the way Esther spoke to her husband.

"I am sorry," Esther said. "Charles would not allow it." To her credit, she seemed quite unhappy at her inhospitality.

I shook my head in wonder and walked to the entry hall.

"Lady Bridget, please," Esther called after me. "You must forgive me."

I paid her no mind. Despite all I had done for her over the years, and despite how desperate I was for her help, she had proven a faithless friend. I would not soothe her conscience by saying I understood or forgave her.

I pulled open the front door and returned to my carriage.

"Load the luggage," I commanded the driver. "We'll stay elsewhere tonight."

The driver looked at me in confusion for a moment, but he must have heard the fury in my voice, for he immediately set about the work.

I climbed into the carriage and closed the door behind Martha. Thankfully, Esther did not pursue us into the street.

"My God, what a woman!" I could not contain my anger and disappointment any longer. "I saved her from burning, and this is how she repays me?"

"What will we do now?" Martha asked as the driver finished securing our luggage.

"What choice do we have?" I asked. "We'll find an inn and move forward as best we can."

We rode east on the Strand toward the city wall and, despite the gathering dark, the crowds surrounding us seemed to grow larger with every step. No less remarkable was the noise of the place. Shopkeepers, fishwives, craftsmen, grocers—all shouted their wares to the passing throngs. The chaos was made all the worse by the scores of men—and even a few women!—who cursed us in the foulest imaginable terms as our carriage forced them to the side of the road. Our driver, who was no stranger to rough language, was struck dumb by the number, variety, and vulgarity of the insults hurled his way. In some ways, the most remarkable thing about London was not its filth or its size, though these were impressive indeed, but the creativity with which Londoners swore. Perhaps they took it as a point of pride, with each swearer intending to outdo his neighbor.

"Here's an inn, my lady," the driver called out. "Shall I pull in?"

I leaned out the window to see what kind of place the driver had found. In the fading light the inn seemed adequate to our desperate situation, but who knew what secrets or dangers lay within? I felt uneasy, but I did not see any other choice. The next inn we found might be no better, and could be far worse.

"Very well," I called, adding a prayer that I'd not just made a terrible mistake.

The driver shouted to the horses and hauled on the reins, guiding the carriage into a small courtyard. Without waiting for the driver to dismount, I climbed from the carriage and went inside. To my immense pleasure I found it to be more respectable than I had hoped—the dining area was clean and the guests who had gathered for supper were well dressed.

"Now, if only they have a room for us," I muttered to myself and went in search of the innkeeper. I found him behind the bar drawing ale for one of his customers.

"Aye, we've got room," he said. "By the look of you, you'll be wanting one of our best. From Hereford, aren't you?"

"Yes, your best will be fine," I replied. "And how did you know where I came from?"

"Spend enough time dealing with travelers, and you find yourself with an ear for their accents," he said. It was only then that I noticed the hint of Cornwall in his voice. "I take it you've never been to London?" he added.

"My maid has, but I haven't," I replied. I could hear the anxiety in my voice and hated it. I was not used to being so uncertain.

"Well, welcome, then. It's not always a hospitable place, but if you keep your wits about you and don't fall ill, you'll be fine. Your room is upstairs to the left."

It took Martha and our driver a few trips to unload the carriage, but soon enough we were settled. Martha and I occupied a large second-floor room overlooking the Strand, while our driver slept above the stables with others of his kind. Martha and I ate a small supper of bread and cheese and then tumbled into bed. In the moments before I slept I said a prayer for Elizabeth's safety and begged the Lord that our search for Will would be successful.

Chapter 3

Martha and I awoke before dawn to the shouting and clatter of cart-men below our window. London, it seemed, was not a city to let even a moment of daylight go to waste.

"And now we will look for Will?" Martha asked as we began to dress.

"Immediately," I said. I paused and took her hand. I heard the anxiety in her voice and felt it myself. We had been able to keep it at bay during the journey, but now the day of reckoning had come. "Before the day is out, we will find him and see him safe and sound."

Martha nodded, but I'd not convinced her. We both knew that the law was capricious and that freeing Will from the Tower might be a Herculean task.

After we ate breakfast—more bread and cheese—we started for the door. Before we'd even left the inn, I had a sudden and disquieting realization. I knew Will was in the Tower, but I had no idea how to get there. Yes, it lay on the Thames to the east of the city, but beyond that, I knew nothing at all. I recalled how baffling York's streets had seemed when I'd first arrived there, and I felt the same way now. The only difference was that London was tenfold the larger.

"Do you know the best way to the Tower?" I asked Martha. "Should we take the carriage?" It seemed like folly to venture out on foot, but neither did I relish the idea of worming through the city in a carriage built for wide country roads.

Martha shook her head. "I don't know," she said. "It has been many years since I've tried to navigate the city, and I suspect much has changed. If we followed the river, we would get there eventually."

"Well, you'd be a true fool to take your carriage," a voice boomed behind us. "And *we can follow the river* is the worst idea I've heard in years."

We turned to find the innkeeper standing behind us. I put aside my concern that he'd been eavesdropping on our conversation, for we were in no position to refuse his help.

"If not a carriage, then what?" I asked.

"You could try a hackney," he said. "But the fastest way is by wherry."

I felt as if the innkeeper had started speaking a foreign language. He laughed at the expression on my face.

"A hackney?" I asked at last. "What is that?"

"You seen them carriages racing back and forth on the Strand? They're not so large as yours, but twice as fast. One of them could get you to the Tower without too many wrong turns, and won't get stuck on a narrow street."

I nodded. I had seen the little carriages the day before. They moved at an alarming pace and seemed no less dangerous to their passengers than to the men and women they nearly ran over.

"Well, them's hackney coaches. But like I say, you'd be better off with a wherry."

"Ah," I said, as if that made matters clear.

"A wherry is a boat that'll take you downriver and bring you back," he explained. "For a fee of course."

"And that's the surest way?" I asked doubtfully. Martha had pointed out the little boats skipping up, down, and across the river, but it had never occurred to me I might soon find myself in one of them. I cannot say I welcomed the prospect, for I'd only been in a riverboat once, riding an hour on York's River Ouse, and that journey frightened me so much that I took a carriage home.

"The surest?" the innkeeper asked. "Well, a hackney won't drown you, so *that* is the surest way. But the Tower's a long ride. I'd take the boat."

I hesitated, unsure about trusting our fate—and Will's—to so little a boat on so large a river.

"One other thing to consider, my lady," the innkeeper said. "You don't want to try taking a hackney to the Tower and returning in one day; you haven't the time. In the best case, you'll return in the dark smelling of shit from all your travels. More likely, you'll have to find another place to stay tonight and return here in the morning. You really should choose the boat."

Eventually I agreed, though without much enthusiasm. I knew that if I somehow fell in the Thames, my skirts would drag me down within seconds. Before we left, Martha and I went to the inn's kitchen and bought a capon, bread, and cheese to give to Will—who knew how well he was being kept?—and started for the river.

"Look, over there," Martha said. Stone steps led from the street down to the water. As soon as we started down, three boats swooped toward us, the driver of each crying for our attention. One was a bit quicker than the others and landed his craft on the mud immediately in front of us. The other boats veered off into deeper water, their captains cursing ours in a manner that was somehow both vile and good-natured. I supposed this was a custom of the city.

The waterman reached into his boat and produced a sturdy plank, which he set on top of the mud that lay between us. He then stepped out of the boat and extended his hand.

"Hold tight and step lightly," he said. "If you're quick enough, you won't soil your clothes." He was a tall, rangy man who seemed to be of two ages at once. His arms rippled with the tendons and muscles of a man in the flower of his youth, but his face was so badly weathered by years of sun, wind, and rain that he could have been the oldest man in England.

Martha gave him the basket of food, took his hand, and skipped across the plank to the boat. "Easy as can be," she called back with a laugh.

With one hand I lifted my skirts as best I could and stared uncertainly at the plank and mud. I grasped the waterman's hand. It was as hard and rough as a cobblestone. He smiled encouragingly—or perhaps condescendingly—and I tried to imitate Martha's agile leap. It started well enough, for I made it to the boat without landing in the mud, but I must have moved a bit *too* quickly, for I suddenly found myself leaning over the far side, my arms spinning wildly as I tried to regain my balance. For a terrible moment, I peered into the mud, imagining the humiliation of pitching face first into the river's filth. It would be days until I was clean, months before Martha would stop laughing, and years until I forgot the horror.

Just when I lost my balance entirely, someone seized my hips and pulled me back. I gasped in surprise and relief as I fell into one of the boat's narrow seats.

"There you go," the waterman said, as if saving a gentlewoman from such humiliation were a normal part of his job. "New to the river, are you? You'll figure it out soon enough. Where can I take you? Whitehall? Westminster? Southwark? The Bridge? Anywhere you'd like this side of Greenwich."

I sought my voice and failed, managing only to gabble my thanks. My heart was still pounding in my chest.

"The Tower," Martha said.

"For a tuppence," our driver replied, pulling a long pole from the boat's floor. I nodded in agreement. The waterman pushed us into the flow of the river and took his seat. He then traded his pole for a pair of oars, and with short, swift strokes began to row downriver. As we traveled, another boat pulled alongside and its rower shouted something to ours.

The waterman looked at me with a raised eyebrow. "Do you fancy a wager?" he asked. "He'll race us to the Bridge for a penny."

"I think not," I replied. Though the boat was more stable than I'd expected, I was not going to risk my life on a one-penny race.

Our captain shrugged and shouted a phrase I could not understand—the cant of the watermen, I supposed—and the two boats parted ways.

As the driver rowed to the middle of the river, we caught our first full view of London since we'd crested Highgate Hill the day before. I saw some farmland to the south, but on the north bank of the Thames, London seemed to stretch on forever. Whitehall and Westminster glowed in the morning sun, and we now could take in the full magnificence of the homes along the river. Our waterman pointed out Surrey House, York House, and Arundel House, among others. We also had a better view of the theaters—now closed by order of Parliament—on the Southwark side of the river, and ahead of us we saw the marvel that was London Bridge.

Although York had similar bridges, and I'd seen London

Bridge from a distance, I stared in open-mouthed wonder. It seemed less a bridge than a city street that had lost its way and wandered into the river. Houses six stories tall loomed over us as we approached. I caught a glimpse of a child peering down at us from a window, and marveled at his strange existence, living over water rather than on dry land. As we reached the Bridge, the river began to bounce us about, and I tightened my grip on the edges of the boat.

"Don't you worry," the waterman called. "It's just a little adventure in your day. I've been through much worse."

I nodded my thanks, not entirely trusting my voice.

After we passed beneath the Bridge, the waterman veered to the north side of the river, and the Tower of London came into view, squat and dark, intent on intimidating all who came near. As we approached the landing, I gazed at the Traitors' Gate, through which so many famous men and women had passed on their way to their executions. I noticed that the watermen steered clear of the gate, as if they feared it might pull them in.

Our driver stopped the boat next to a set of steps that led into the river itself. I said a prayer of thanks that I would not have to cross on the plank once again. I handed him two pennies.

"Do you want me to wait?" the waterman asked as we climbed out. "You'll be lucky to find another captain as skillful as me. Or one who'll save you from an early morning swim in the muck." He winked at me with a roguish grin, and once again I marveled at the liberties London's lower sorts took for granted.

My first thought was to send him on his way with a reprimand for his over-familiarity, but I could not deny that he'd handled the boat as well as I could have hoped.

"I don't know how long we'll be," I said. "It could be minutes, it could be hours."

"Fair enough," he replied. "I'll wait a bit in case it's the first, and come back around noon if it's the second."

"Thank you," I said.

Martha and I turned away from the river and looked up at the Tower.

"Do you think he's still alive?" she asked.

"Of course he is," I replied. I prayed that it was true and started up the steps to the gatehouse.

When we reached the gate, I stared up at the Tower walls in awe. I thought of the men and women who had spent their last days and nights inside: princes, cardinals, queens, lords, and—most recently—an archbishop. How had Will found himself in such a place? And how could he escape the fate that had befallen some of England's most powerful men? I took Martha's hand and gave it a squeeze.

"We will have him out of there," I said.

Even as I raised my fist to pound on the door, a window in it popped open and a guard's face appeared.

"Who are you, and what do you want?" he growled.

I gathered myself and answered as forcefully as I could. "I am here to see Will Hodgson. He is imprisoned in the Tower."

"Will Hodgson, eh?" he said. "And who might you be?" I thought he recognized Will's name, and it struck me as odd. I did not know how many prisoners were in the Tower, but it seemed unlikely a common guard would know each one.

"I am the Lady Bridget Hodgson," I replied. "I was summoned by the Tower's warden." Of course the letter had come from Will's jailor, a far less important man than the warden, but I thought the lie would ease our passage.

A shadow passed over the guard's face. I was sure that he recognized my name. He turned to speak to someone behind him and the window snapped shut. For a while nothing happened and Martha and I glanced at each other, unsure what to do. I decided to knock a second time, but before I could the door opened silently on well-oiled hinges.

To my surprise we were met not by the guard who had spoken to us through the window, but by two guards and an army colonel. The guards—including the one who had been so saucy a moment before—stood at attention, their eyes staring straight ahead. The colonel commanded their respect in a way I could not.

The officer stepped forward. He cut an impressive figure, standing nearly a full head taller than I, with a clean, crisp uniform adding to his authority. He'd cropped his hair close to the scalp in the Roundhead style, but I could see flecks of gray scattered among the brown. His eyes lit up when they met mine, and I could not help thinking that his smile seemed genuine.

"Lady Hodgson," he said with a bow. "It is good that you have arrived at last. I am Colonel Reynolds. Will you follow me?"

I glanced at Martha. Good that we had arrived *at last*? Martha shrugged, no less confused than I. With no other option available, Martha and I followed Colonel Reynolds into the Tower.

We passed through several halls and into a sunny courtyard. I was struck by how pleasant it seemed, considering the misery that surrounded us. Who knew how many prisoners the Tower held? I gazed at the stones beneath my feet. They had felt the footsteps of scores of men and women as they walked to Tower Hill, where they would be beheaded.

Martha and I had to hurry to keep up with Colonel Reynolds's long strides as he crossed to the White Tower, which lay at the heart of the Tower of London. The two guards on either side of the castle door snapped to attention when we approached. For a moment I wondered if Colonel Reynolds might be taking us straight to Will, but instead he led us to a large office. The room was occupied by a wiry man dressed not in a soldier's uniform, but in the inconspicuous garb of a mildly prosperous grocer. He sat behind a desk, leafing through a sheaf of papers, and smiled when we entered the room. Unlike Colonel Reynolds, his smile never reached his eyes.

"Lady Hodgson, it is good that you and your deputy have come so far." He rose to his feet as he spoke. "I am Mr. Marlowe."

By this time I'd had quite enough of the mystery that these men had worked so hard to create, and I was determined to put it to a stop.

"Mr. Marlowe, I am quite sure I do not know who you are, and I assure you that we came to London neither for your benefit nor for your amusement. We came here for my nephew, Will Hodgson, and I will see him immediately."

A thin smile danced across Marlowe's lips, angering me all the more.

"It is clear that you have had some notice of our arrival," I continued. "And that you view this as some sort of game. I will tell you now that I am no man's pawn. If you persist in such secrecy and uncivil behavior I will leave this place, search out Sir Robert Harley, and demand my nephew's release from him." Sir Robert was from Hereford and I knew he sat in the current Parliament. While I'd met him on several occasions, my threat was pure guilery. I had no earthly idea where in London he might be, and I doubted that he would help Will escape from the Tower.

Marlowe's smile vanished as if it had never existed. "You won't do that," he said. "Not unless you want your nephew to spend the rest of his days in the Tower. Some men have survived here for years, but I doubt he would last so long as that."

I glanced at Colonel Reynolds to see what he made of this threat, but his face remained a mask.

"The letter was from you, not Will's jailor." Martha was unable to keep silent a moment longer. "You must have had a good reason to bring us all the way from Hereford. What do you want?"

"Your maid is as overbold as I expected," he said to me. "But it is out of place in such a woman. If she wishes to see Will, she should remember who she is."

I thought for a moment and recognized the situation. Mr. Marlowe had Will in his grasp, and he would only loose his grip if Martha and I played by his rules. "It is clear that we are at your mercy," I said. "Tell us who you are and what you want."

"Thank you, Lady Hodgson," Marlowe replied. "I am glad you have seen the true state of things. As I said, I am Mr. Marlowe. I serve at the pleasure of General Cromwell, protecting England from her enemies, both within and without her borders. And you will assist me in these efforts."

"You and I might disagree as to who England's enemies are," I replied drily. "There are some—many, even—who would consider your master Cromwell to be chief among them."

"I will grant you that," Marlowe said with the ghost of a smile. "But so long as you are in my service—and make no mistake, you *are* in my service—I will decide who England's enemies are. Until I say otherwise, you will help me prevent them from overthrowing Parliament and imposing tyranny on the nation. If you care for your nephew, of course."

"And you'll keep him in the Tower if I refuse."

"Not just that," Marlowe replied. "If you refuse to assist me, you announce yourself as among England's enemies. I would have no choice but to confiscate your estates and sell them to benefit the nation."

I stared at him in astonishment, entirely unable to find a suitable response. I had heard of Royalists who had lost their lands under such confiscations. Some had noble patrons to defend them, but others had been entirely ruined, forced onto the charity of their friends and relatives. The difference between them and me, of course, was that they had taken up arms against Parliament, while I had never taken a side in the wars.

"Neutralism is now treason?" I managed at last.

Marlowe shrugged. "There is no neutralism. If you are not England's friend, you are her enemy, and you will be treated as such." He spoke the words with such dispassion, I doubted neither his seriousness nor the amount of trouble in which I had found myself.

"Why have you chosen me for this honor?" I asked. "What can *I* do?"

"You are a midwife," he replied. "You are privy to your neighbors' secrets. You enter the homes of the rich, the poor, the Roundhead, and the cavalier. What more could I look for in a spy?"

"You want me to be a spy?" I could not believe his words.

"Well, I'm not in danger of going into labor myself, so your more conventional skills would be of no use." I could not tell if he was jesting. I suspected not.

"Why have you chosen me? Surely there are midwives in London who would be eager to do your bidding. Why bring me all the way from Hereford?"

"In truth, I chose both of you," Marlowe replied. "Are you unaware of your reputations? I suppose country living will addle the mind. You and your deputy defied the Lord Mayor of York in the midst of a siege, and freed a woman who had been condemned to death. You destroyed the most powerful minister in York. And not half a year after that, you saw an Alderman hanged as a witch.

That sort of remorselessness is a rare thing in any woman, and here I have two. I cannot let you slip through my fingers."

"And we cannot refuse?"

"You can," Marlowe said. "But at great cost."

"And you do this in defense of England's liberty?" I asked. I did not think an appeal to his conscience or political principles would work—I doubted he had either one—but I could not simply give in.

"I do it to defend England against tyranny and popery," he replied. "Oceans of blood have been spilt in our late civil wars, and England's enemies want nothing more than to wallow in blood once again. I will not allow this to happen. I find it passing strange that you balk at this task. Surely preserving the peace is worth a brief time in my service. And it would save your nephew's life, as well. Do not forget that."

I considered the situation, hoping I might find an escape, but it was clear that he had set his trap well.

"What would you have us do?" I asked.

Chapter 4

Marlowe returned to his seat and leaned back, smiling broadly at my surrender. It struck me that his smile would not have been out of place on a wolf. And if he was the wolf, was I not the lamb?

"Before we discuss the terms of your service," Marlowe said, "we should bring in your nephew. He has as much an interest in these matters as anyone. Colonel Reynolds, would you please fetch Mr. Hodgson?"

My heart leaped at Marlowe's words, and I heard Martha gasp. Could it be so easy to obtain Will's freedom? And after three years apart, what would I say to him when he finally appeared?

Each moment that Martha and I waited for Will's arrival seemed to last ten thousand years. For a moment I worried that this was some sort of game, that Marlowe would raise our hopes only to dash them, and in doing so bring us entirely to our knees. I could not deny that such a ploy would work, and I prayed that he was not so cruel as that.

The Lord must have heard my entreaties, for the door opened and Will appeared. Even as I rushed to embrace him, I recognized the changes that the last three years had wrought on his frame. He still carried his cane, for his clubfoot would never be healed, but he nevertheless seemed stronger than when we'd parted ways. I also saw that he'd cut his hair in the Roundhead way, and wondered what it might mean. Had he joined that faction?

Will wrapped his arms round Martha and me, burying his face between us. Within moments all three of us were sobbing, and our tears washed away the anger and resentment that had driven us apart during our last dreadful days in York. After a time, I stepped back and let Will and Martha hold each other. I heard murmured apologies, declarations of love, and promises that they would never again spend so long apart. I prayed that this was true, but knew the world had a habit of mocking such words, however genuine they might be.

I looked to Colonel Reynolds and I was surprised to find his eyes brimming with tears. He looked to me and offered a small, sad smile, as if he had known such love, but only in some distant past. I was less pleased by Marlowe's expression, for there was no longing in his smile, only the cold satisfaction of a man who had drawn the ace of trumps and didn't care who knew it. He had already demonstrated that he would use my love of Will to force me into service, and now he knew he could do the same to Martha.

Marlowe rapped on his desk, reclaiming our attention. "Now that we all are here, we should discuss why I brought you together."

Silence fell over the room, and I felt like an accused criminal awaiting my sentence.

"As you know, these are tumultuous days for England. The King has made war on his own people, and now he is prisoner on the Isle of Wight. Parliament rules the land, but it faces threats from every quarter." Marlowe stood and began to count off Parliament's enemies.

"The most dangerous faction is the bloody-minded Royalists. They have fomented rebellions here in England and planned invasions from abroad, including from France, Scotland, and Ireland. They wish to restore the King's tyrannical rule even if it means plunging the nation back into war.

"Then there are so-called moderate men who wish to negotiate with the King. They would play Esau to his Jacob, returning him the throne in exchange for little more than a bowl of stew. If either of these factions has their way, the King once again will rule as a tyrant.

"Finally, there are the Levellers. These mad-brains accuse Cromwell and Parliament of ruling as tyrants no different from the King. They seek to overthrow the present government and to replace it with anarchy."

I glanced uncertainly around the room. I did not know what Royalists, moderate men, or Levellers had to do with me. Since leaving York I'd kept clear of the political tumult, and could offer Marlowe little help discovering the plans of any party he named. Martha and Will seemed no less confused than I, and Colonel Reynolds's face betrayed nothing.

"Before the end of the year," Marlowe continued, "these matters will come to a head and the fate of the King will be decided. These next months will be dangerous ones. It is my duty to secure the ship of state and help her to reach safe harbor. *Your* duty will be to assist me in this task."

"I told you already," I said, "I am a midwife and that is all."

"Not anymore," Marlowe replied. "You are my creature, and you will do my bidding. And it is not just you, Lady Hodgson, but all three of you. I am told you work well together, or at least you did in York. You will bring those skills to London and put them to good use."

"And if we don't, I will return to the Tower," Will said.

He had taken a step away from Martha, and now I could see him more clearly. He appeared to be in good health, and strangely clean for having lain in the Tower for several weeks. Of course, since he was bait for me, rather than a true prisoner, Marlowe would have been careful to keep him alive. If Will had died in prison, Marlowe's advantage over me would have evaporated like the morning fog.

"Liberty has its price," Marlowe said to Will. "If you wish to remain free, you, your aunt, and her maidservant will work on my behalf. It is as simple as that." Marlowe spoke as if our conscription into his service were as inevitable as the rise and fall of the tides.

"If you would have me inform on my friends, you have missed the mark entirely," I said. "Other than Sir Robert, I know only one family in London, and they will have nothing to do with me. You will have to look elsewhere for your spy."

"Oh, it's not the Wallingtons," Marlowe said. "Indeed, it's not the Royalists at all."

I was shocked that he had heard of my visit to Esther, for he only could have known of our plans by reading the letters I had sent from Pontrilas. How long had he been doing that?

"It is the Levellers," Will said. "He means for us to spy on the Levellers."

"What?" I cried. "How so? I know none of them."

I had read about the Levellers, of course, and knew their arguments to be quite mad. No matter which crack-brained fool was writing, their demands were those of lunatics. Some demanded the right to print whatever they wanted, however seditious or blasphemous. Others sought toleration of all religions, no matter how foolish or atheistic. And some demanded that all men, no matter how poor, be allowed to vote for members of Parliament. They were, as Mr. Marlowe had said, mad-brains one and all.

"I know them, Aunt Bridget," Will said. "I am why he chose you."

Martha and I looked at Will in confusion.

"Last year when I left the Lord Mayor's service, I came to London," Will said. "I fell in with some who are called Levellers. Soon after, Mr. Marlowe's men burst in upon one of their meetings. They arrested me and many others."

"Are you a Leveller?" I asked. I could not imagine Will joining up with such a mob.

He shrugged. "Do not judge them by what their enemies claim. You must hear their ideas for yourself. And whatever Mr. Marlowe might say, they have no desire to destroy the government. They simply believe the government should rule by the consent of the people, not by force of arms."

Marlowe snorted dismissively at Will's description. "Luckily for your nephew, he was taken up before he could find himself too deep in their plotting, else he would be in the low dungeon. But it was through him that I learned of you and your unusual work in York."

"I am sorry, Aunt Bridget," Will said. "When the questioners asked about my family, I told them about you. I hoped that your rank might win me my freedom. I did not mean for you to be trapped as well."

I took his hand. "You could not have known. It is not your fault."

Will shook his head in despair, unwilling to be so easily forgiven.

"Blame who you like," Marlowe said, "the fact remains that I have restored your nephew to you, Lady Bridget, and now you will work for me."

"I told you, I know no Levellers," I said. "You've wasted your time and ours."

"You may not know them yet," Marlowe replied. "But you will know them very soon. Colonel Reynolds will explain what we have planned for you."

The three of us turned to face the Colonel.

"The Levellers are scattered throughout the city." Colonel Reynolds spoke softly, as if he regretted his place in the sordid business. "There is a group across the river in Southwark, where we found Will."

"We had planned to put you with that crowd," Marlowe said. "But we discovered that their gangrenous ideas have spread to the city itself."

"Our concern now is with a group in Cheapside," Colonel Reynolds said, "not far from St. Paul's. They meet in a tavern called the Nag's Head. We watch those meetings as best we can, but we need to know what is said in private gatherings."

"We are worried about one family in particular," Marlowe said, "Daniel and Katherine Chidley. They are born Levellers and as turbulent and factious a pair as you'll find in all of England."

"Katherine?" Martha asked. "The wife as well?"

"Especially the wife," Marlowe replied. "Before the war, she was a thorn in the King's side and the Bishops' as well. Now she makes trouble for Parliament. She is opposed to all good order and authority, whatever its form."

"And she is a midwife," Colonel Reynolds added. "That is why Mr. Marlowe chose you for this task. You should have no trouble striking up a friendship." He produced an envelope from his coat pocket and handed it to me. "You and your maidservant will live in the Cheap—Cheapside—across the street from the Chidleys. We have rented an apartment for you there. Your nephew will stay with me at a nearby inn called the Horned Bull. You and I will meet from time to time and you will tell me what you have learned. You need do nothing more than watch and listen."

"An apartment?" I asked. "You don't think people will find it curious that a gentlewoman from Hereford suddenly took it into her head to move to London and occupy a tenement in Cheapside? If the Levellers are so easily gulled, they could hardly threaten the government."

"Yes, you are right, of course," Marlowe said. "And you can credit Colonel Reynolds with untying that particular knot."

Marlowe paused, relishing his words, and once again I felt like a lamb that had wandered into a wolf's den.

"Before you go to the Cheap," Marlowe said, "we will turn you from a gentlewoman into a common widow."

I can only imagine the expression on my face, but Marlowe found it delightful enough to laugh out loud. It was not a natural sound.

"Once you arrive in the Cheap, you will no longer be *Lady Hodgson,*" Marlowe continued. "You will be *Mrs. Hodgson,* or *Widow Hodgson,* or even *Midwife Hodgson,* if you like. But from this day forward you are no better than any of your neighbors." Marlowe paused. "If it is any consolation, Martha will still be your deputy."

I could not even gibber. Even Martha was shocked into silence. My mind reeled at the idea of lowering myself to such a place. *Mrs.* Hodgson? *Widow* Hodgson? It was not that there were no respectable women outside the gentry, of course. Indeed, in York many of my best gossips were common folk. But I'd been *Lady*

Hodgson for so long that I had come to rely on both the name and the title. And now Marlowe would have me walk away from that world entirely.

"You will find all you need in that envelope," Colonel Reynolds said. "You have a copy of your husband's will, and a license from the Archbishop of York allowing you the office of a midwife. If anyone should question you, they will prove your story to be true."

I opened the packet and leafed through the papers. While I'd kept my name, little else about me had survived. I now hailed from Halifax, where I'd lived with my husband, Edmund. Edmund—a clothier, it seemed—had died the previous spring, leaving me nothing except a spinning wheel, two chairs, and three pounds.

"You have a little money to help you get settled," Colonel Reynolds said. "But you will have to work if you want to eat."

To his credit, Colonel Reynolds seemed quite uncomfortable with his duties. The scheme may have been his, but he was not enjoying its execution.

"You will need new clothes, of course," Marlowe said, his eyes shining with unseemly glee. "Or rather, old ones, for a new widow can hardly wear new clothes." Marlowe actually laughed at this. "And you will have to send away your carriage. Once you look the part of a poor widow, Colonel Reynolds will take you to Cheapside."

"Will two days be enough time?" Colonel Reynolds asked.

I nodded numbly. I had no idea how long such a change would take. And then I thought of Elizabeth. "What of my daughter?" I asked. "If I am to be in your service, I must bring her here."

Marlowe thought for a moment. "She will stay in Hereford for now. I cannot have you mothering, midwifing, *and* spying. Do you have any questions?"

I stared at Mr. Marlowe, aghast that with a few words he'd deprived me of my daughter. I shook my head.

"Good," Marlowe said. "Two days it is. I look forward to your reports." With that he returned to his papers. It seemed we were dismissed.

Colonel Reynolds accompanied Will, Martha, and me to the Tower gate and then down to the riverside.

"Colonel Reynolds," I said, "You told me that you would call on us in two days' time."

He nodded.

"How do you know where we are staying? *We* didn't know where we would be staying until last night."

Colonel Reynolds smiled ruefully. "Mr. Marlowe has more spies in his employ than the three of you. He knew the road you'd be taking in from Hereford, and learned from your letters that your first stop would be at Esther Wallington's. He had a man watch the Wallingtons and follow you from there. London is growing, but a beautiful gentlewoman newly arrived from Hereford will stand out even among so many thousands."

I felt myself blush at the compliment and cursed myself for it. As far as I was concerned, Reynolds and Marlowe were comrades in the same dirty business. Once I'd regained myself, I bid Colonel Reynolds farewell.

"Good day, my lady," he replied before turning to Will. "After you've said your farewells you should come back to the Tower. We will get you a proper room rather than a cell."

Will nodded, and Colonel Reynolds started toward the Tower. Even before he'd passed from sight, Martha and Will burst out laughing.

"My Lord, Aunt Bridget, you are crimson," Will cried. "A *beautiful gentlewoman newly arrived from Hereford . . .*"

"*. . . will stand out even among so many thousands!*" Martha joined in, expertly aping the Colonel's Lancashire accent and manner of speech.

I felt myself coloring again, but this time I could not keep a smile from my lips. When *was* the last time a man's compliment had unsettled me so much? A half dozen or more country squires had certainly made their desires known—a widow with land was better hunting than a fat fowl with a broken wing—but none had affected me the way Colonel Reynolds had.

"I'll grant you that he cuts a fine figure," Martha said. "So I cannot fault you in this. And a poor widow from Halifax like yourself could certainly do worse than marrying an army officer."

Martha meant it as a good-natured jest, of course, but the mention of my new status brought us back to the business at hand.

"Yes," I said. "About that . . ."

Before Martha could reply, a cry came across the water, and our waterman steered his boat toward us.

"We will talk at the inn," I said.

"Do not worry," Martha replied. "Becoming someone else is not such a hard thing. It will surprise you."

Chapter 5

The following morning, Will came to our inn near the Strand, and we talked for hours. Martha and I told him of the wearisomeness of country living, while he recounted his many adventures in York and London.

"After a year in his service, the Lord Mayor offered me my freedom." Will smiled slightly. "I don't think he thought I'd accept. But there was nothing left for me in York, so I decided to see what I might find in London. It is as grand and terrible as I'd imagined."

"How did you come so close to the Levellers?" I asked. I still could not fathom how he'd been transformed from a wealthy merchant's son to one who consorted with such a turbulent faction.

"Luck or providence," Will replied. "If you believe in either one. I was in an alehouse and met a man with a sprig of sage in his hatband."

"Sage?" I asked. "Whatever for?"

"That's what I asked him," Will said. "Sea green is the Levellers' favored color, and they wear sage to show their support for the cause. Cromwell had recently jailed John Lilburne and put other leaders in the Tower, so those who favored the Levellers were making their feelings known in any way they could."

"By wearing sage," I said.

Will nodded. "He told me about some of their ideas and invited me to meetings to hear more."

"At the Nag's Head?" I remembered this was the tavern mentioned by Marlowe and Colonel Reynolds.

"No, the Whalebone," Will said. "It's south of the river. Lodgings were cheaper there, so that's where I'd settled."

"What did the Levellers say?" Martha asked.

I was surprised by Martha's question. I'd known her for years, but she'd shown scant interest in politics except for pointing out the hypocrisies of those in power.

"They say that no man should be compelled to worship against his will," Will said. "Nor can he be driven to take up arms in another man's fight. That neither Parliament nor King can prevent a freeborn Englishman from speaking his mind. That the poorest man in England has as much a life to live as the greatest."

"And that no man should be governed except by his own consent." I did not hide my disdain for such a fevered dream. "Will, do you not see? The Levellers would make the poor as great as the rich. If paupers ruled the nation, they would vote themselves a share of every estate. My servants would declare themselves masters and mistresses, simply by virtue of their greater numbers. Thievery would become legal. They would loose anarchy upon England!"

Will smiled sadly. "Am I not a pauper, Aunt Bridget? I have nothing but the clothes on my back. If a new Parliament were selected today, I would have no more of a voice than the lowest beggar in England. Tell me: If *I* were to vote for a Member of Parliament, would it be a step toward the anarchy you fear?"

Will's words vexed me, not least because I had no ready response. I held fast to my belief that democracy could lead only to robbery and chaos, but my principles foundered on his example. While I did not say as much to Will, I resolved to think on the matter.

After Will returned to the Tower, Martha and I packed away my silk and lace, exchanging them for wool and linen. As Mr. Marlowe had pointed out, I would not need my carriage, so I simply loaded it with my clothes and luggage to send everything back to Hereford.

While the driver prepared to depart, I wrote letters to Hannah and Elizabeth. I told them that Will was safe and free from the Tower but that we would have to stay in London for a while longer. Elizabeth would have been thrilled to hear of my work as a spy, but I knew I could not tell her. I resolved instead to make my stay in London sound as dreary as a winter in Pontrilas. I described the rudeness of the people, the slowness of the city's streets, the stench, and the smoke. I expressed my sorrow that I'd left her behind, but assured her that she was not missing anything of interest.

And so it was that two days after we found Will, I stood before a mirror and stared at a common housewife.

I fought to control the tears of humiliation that filled my eyes, even as Martha and Will fought not to laugh aloud. In my heart I knew that trading silk for broadcloth should not have driven me to tears, but I'd never seen myself dressed so poorly.

"If I'm going to don such garb, the Levellers' work is done," I said. "For now there isn't a bit of difference between rich and poor."

"Well said, *Widow* Hodgson," Will teased.

"Oh yes, *Mrs.* Hodgson," Martha added. "I could not have put it better myself."

It was all I could do not to stamp my foot in frustration, but such petulance would only encourage them all the more. Perhaps I would indulge myself when I was alone.

Around the time we bid the carriage farewell, Colonel Reynolds arrived. It was nearly time for Martha and me to begin our new lives. He'd traded his uniform for the clothes of a shopkeeper, but he looked quite handsome all the same.

When he saw me, Colonel Reynolds tried—and failed—to suppress a smile, and I felt my ears turning red. I fought down the urge to flee the room.

"You look beautiful even in plain wool," he said.

I returned his smile against my will and found myself caught up in the genuine warmth of his eyes. Martha laughed aloud and went downstairs, leaving me alone with Colonel Reynolds.

"I have drawn you a map of the Cheap," he said, handing me a sheet of paper. "Cheapside Street is the spine through the neighborhood, running from St. Paul's in the west to the Great Conduit in the east. If you become lost—and you *will* become lost—simply find Cheapside Street or the Conduit and start your journey again.

"The Nag's Head is north of Cheapside, here." He pointed to a clearly marked square on his map. "That's where you'll find the Levellers' most lively discussions. Mr. Marlowe has secured you lodgings on Watling Street, just north south of Pissing Alley."

"You must thank him for that," I murmured. "It sounds lovely."

Colonel Reynolds laughed and put his hand on my arm. My heart beat a little faster at his touch. I was appalled, not by his forwardness but by my reaction. I had reached my fortieth year, been married twice and widowed twice, yet here I was blushing like a maiden at a morris dance.

"Once you are settled," Colonel Reynolds continued, "you should put out a sign announcing yourself."

I looked at him in utter confusion. "Announcing myself?"

"As a midwife. It is a common practice in the city. Most midwives use the sign of a cradle, though I've seen some who favor a birthing stool. If you keep your eyes open on our way to the Cheap, you will see more than a few examples."

"And then what?" I asked. I had no idea how to begin the work of a spy.

"And then you listen. You are across the street from the Chidleys, so you'll have no trouble striking up a friendship with them, not least because Katherine is a midwife. If you are called to a birth, ask her to join you. What could be more natural?"

"And then what?" I persisted.

"If she talks of politics, pay attention. If the Levellers are plotting against the government, the Chidleys will be a part of it, and there will be signs. Watch for visitors at strange hours. See if either of them sneaks about at night. The more they do such things, the more dangerous they could be."

"If she is a midwife, she will keep strange hours as a matter of course. A woman's travail is no respecter of the city's curfew."

"All the more reason for you to make her your comrade," Colonel Reynolds said. "Mr. Marlowe chose you well. He is no fool."

I turned from him and looked out into the street, watching the carts flowing out of the city, bound for every corner of the realm.

"What if we flee?" I asked. "We could rise one morning, climb aboard a carriage, and be out of the city before dinner."

"I hope you do not," Colonel Reynolds said. "Mr. Marlowe

has a long reach and a longer memory. Even if you were able to escape the city, he would find you." He paused for a moment. "Lady Hodgson, look at me."

I did.

"I beg you: Do not betray Mr. Marlowe. He is a powerful man, and it is far better to have him as a friend than an enemy."

I bowed my head, and in that instant I made Martha and me into Mr. Marlowe's servants.

"Thank you," he said. "I know it pains you, but it is the right thing to do. Or at least the wise thing."

A few minutes later Will arrived, driving the cart that would take Martha and me to our new home in the Cheap. Will and Colonel Reynolds sat on the bench behind the horses, while Martha and I rode in the back with our luggage.

"This is a fitting introduction to life as a poor widow," I muttered to myself as the cart rumbled away from the inn.

We traveled east along the Strand—which became Fleet Street at the Temple Bar—and through Ludgate. With each step the buildings around us grew larger and the crowds more numerous. When I arrived in York, everything about the city—its size, the close-built houses, and the overpowering stench of its gutters—had left me in a daze for months. In every way, London made a hamlet of York. The houses were taller, and they seemed ready to tip into the street at any moment. The roads leading off Fleet Street were every bit as narrow and confusing as those in York, but there were more of them. And the smell, my God, the smell! I supposed that my time in the country had keened my nose and the stinkingness turned my stomach.

Soon we spilled into St. Paul's Churchyard, and I stared in amazement at the cathedral. It was larger than the Minster in York, an accomplishment I would never have thought possible. The churchyard itself was awash in buyers and sellers. Most prominent were the bookmen and stationers who had built dozens of stalls from which they sold books of every kind. Many were dedicated to the news of the day, and thanks to the power of the godly, I was not surprised to see scores of sermons. But Londoners would not be satisfied with such limited fare. Alongside the news and sermons were books about murders and monsters of every stripe, with ghastly pictures on the front and titles that promised even more blood inside.

After we escaped the churchyard, our progress slowed to a crawl, giving us the opportunity to bask in the noise of the city. And what noise! Fishwives cried their wares with voices harsh enough to shatter glass, and every doorway held a housewife, some gossiping, some scolding, but every one of them talking. I saw women carrying goods to the market, and others bringing their purchases home. London's women were known throughout England as an unruly mob, and now I saw what such liberty meant.

"We're now on Watling Street," Colonel Reynolds called out above the din.

"But we haven't turned!" I objected. "We are on the same road."

"Ah, this is just the start," he replied with a laugh. "At that corner ahead, Watling Street becomes Canwicke Street, and a few streets later it turns into Eastcheap. I would imagine it makes getting around York seem like a child's game."

I shook my head in wonder, and resolved to leave the Cheap only if I had to.

"This is Friday Street," Colonel Reynolds announced as we made a slow turn to the north. It will take us all the way to Cheapside Street."

I looked down at the map he had given to me at the inn. "But isn't our house on Watling Street?"

"Aye, it is," he said. "But you should see Cheapside Street itself, and know how to get from there to your lodging."

The cart rattled north until Friday Street emptied onto Cheapside; it felt as if we were carried from a tiny stream into the Thames itself. Cheapside was broader than any street I'd ever seen, and even as evening approached it teemed with life as thousands of Londoners moved in and out of its shops, or made their way to the Great Conduit for water. For the first time that day I saw a broad swath of sky above, and I realized how constricted the side streets had made me feel. It would be some time before I grew used to city living again.

"When I was a boy, my father brought me all the way to London to see the King's procession before he was crowned," Colonel Reynolds said. "They say that in the time of Queen Elizabeth, Cheapside was so overrun with goldsmiths it was the richest neighborhood in all of England."

When I gazed down the street, I could see drugsters, scriveners, girdlers, and booksellers, but never did spy a goldsmith.

"The goldsmiths are gone now," he said. "Most of them, like your friend's husband, moved to the Strand to be nearer to the court."

We approached a remarkable church—St. Mary-le-Bow, Colonel Reynolds called it—more magnificent than any in York, save the Minster itself. As we passed, the bells began to peal.

"Curfew approaches," Colonel Reynolds said. "We should take you home. You don't want to be caught out at night, not before you are known to your neighbors."

We turned back south—on Bow Lane, said my map—and soon came back to Watling Street. The cart drew to a halt, and

Colonel Reynolds pointed west toward the setting sun. "You'll be living that way, across Bread Street. Look for a haberdasher's shop owned by a widow named Mrs. Evelyn. She'll be your landlady, and she is expecting you. Daniel and Katherine Chidley live across the street, above their shop. They're coat-makers for the army."

"Mrs. Evelyn won't know who we are, will she?" I asked. "Who we really are, I mean."

Colonel Reynolds shook his head. "We conducted our business with her by letter under a false name. I pretended to be your brother, writing on your behalf. She knows only that you are called Widow Hodgson, and that in Halifax you were a midwife.

"Speaking of letters," Colonel Reynolds continued. "If you wish to send any to your daughter, you should send them to me first."

"What, so you can read them yourself?" I bristled at the presumption. "What I say to my daughter is no business of yours."

Colonel Reynolds refused to respond to my surliness in kind. "A poor widow from Halifax should not be seen sending letters to Hereford. It would raise questions that you cannot answer."

I saw his point and grumbled an apology before climbing out of the cart. Martha and I retrieved our bags, and Will joined us in the street.

"Will must come with me," Colonel Reynolds said.

"Why can't he stay with us?" I protested. "He lived with me in York. I can simply tell people the truth—he is my nephew, come to London in search of work."

Colonel Reynolds's smile revealed both warmth and pity. "Trust me, he's better off if he lodges with me. Come on, Will." Will hesitated. "Do not worry," Colonel Reynolds continued. "The Horned Bull is not far, and I marked it on your map. If you send a lad for us, we can be here in minutes."

I nodded to Will. "Perhaps it is for the best."

Will and Colonel Reynolds bid Martha and me farewell, and we watched as the cart disappeared down Bow Lane.

"Well," I said, "we might as well see what manner of lodging Mr. Marlowe has gotten for us."

Martha nodded and we began to push our way through the crowd.

Chapter 6

Mrs. Evelyn opened the door before I'd finished knocking. She was a fat, good-humored woman with an easy laugh and a warmth about her that is found only in the very best gossips.

"Welcome!" she cried. "Welcome to London. You must be Mrs. Hodgson." She took my hand and pulled me inside. "Please do come in." Mrs. Evelyn took our luggage from us and started up the stairs, utterly untroubled by the weight. Martha and I hurried after her.

"Your letters said that you are a grace-wife," she said over her shoulder. "Good, good. Such a one is always welcome in the Cheap. Good women we have."

I started to reply, but she would not allow it.

"There are others in the neighborhood, of course: Grace Ramsden, for one. But she is so great with child that her travail could start at any moment. And once the baby is born, *someone* will have to take her place at least for a time. Why not you?"

By now we had climbed three sets of stairs, passing Mrs.

Evelyn's own quarters along the way. Mrs. Evelyn stopped at a rough wood door and pushed it open.

"No lock, I'm afraid, but we have a good one on the front door, so you needn't worry. And here we are!"

Martha and I stared through the doorway, both struck dumb by the sight. Mrs. Evelyn did not notice.

"Go on in!" she cried. "There's plenty of room for the two of you. And in the back you've got a nice big bed to share." She herded us into the tenement like a garrulous, barrel-chested sheep dog. The room in which we found ourselves contained a small stone hearth, two stools, and a trestle table. The table seemed to wobble under the pressure of my gaze, and I worried that a sneeze would send it crashing to the ground. The other room—the only other room—held our bed, so this entry-room would serve triple duty as our kitchen, dining room, and parlor.

I peered into the bedroom and pasted a smile on my face. A small bed stood in the corner, one end of the frame supported by blocks of wood rather than proper legs. The thin, straw mattress promised little in the way of comfort, and the limp canvas coverlet offered even less.

"We have a second clothes chest somewhere, and one of you can use that," Mrs. Evelyn chirped. Only now did I notice a single pitifully small wood box in the corner. "When winter comes you'll be glad to have each other to keep warm, but there's no reason you should share a chest."

"This is lovely," Martha said at last. "We cannot thank you enough for your neighborliness."

Mrs. Evelyn beamed, and I thanked the Lord for her momentary silence. After a few more minutes of talk about the neighbors—none of whom I knew, of course—Mrs. Evelyn excused herself and left the room, pulling the door closed behind her.

Martha and I held our breath until her footsteps faded.

"Oh Lord," I moaned, even as Martha burst out laughing.

"For what it's worth," Martha said, "this isn't so different from the garret of your house in York, and I lived there for years. The only difference is that instead of sharing a bed with Hannah, I'll share one with you." Despite our miserable condition, Martha was entirely delighted with this turn of events.

"A straw mattress?" I moaned. "I've never slept on one."

This pleased Martha even more. "It's the *only* thing I've ever slept on, so how poor can it be?"

I could find no response that would not seem peevish, so I held my tongue.

The sun had set, and I felt a chill seeping through the ill-fitting windows and into my bones. My first thought was to start a fire in the hearth to chase away the cold. I realized then that we had neither wood nor coal.

Without warning, tears of fear and frustration welled up in my eyes. I dropped onto one of our stools, which promptly collapsed into a small pile of kindling. I tumbled backwards, crashing into the table, which tipped onto its side and fell apart at every joint. It was all too much. I looked around the dirty little room that was now my home and began to sob.

I felt Martha's arms around me and she helped me to our remaining stool. She made sure I wasn't bleeding, and then retrieved a bottle of wine from our bags. We'd only brought one, but this seemed like the time to open it. We then discovered that we had no glasses from which to drink. Even I had to smile at this final indignity.

When Martha sat on the floor and leaned against the wall, I joined her. We sat in silence for a time, passing the bottle between us, drinking straight from the neck.

"Oh, God, what have we gotten ourselves into?" I asked. We'd drunk about three-quarters of the wine, and it soothed some of the days' wounds. "No silks, no feather bed, no chairs . . . no wine glasses."

Martha laughed. "You'll get used to most of it soon enough. And we can buy wine glasses."

Once we'd finished the bottle, Martha and I—exhausted, hungry, and a little bit drunk—climbed into our bed and slept.

Martha and I awoke the next morning to a knock on our door and the consequent creak as it swung open.

"Hello? Martha? Aunt Bridget?" Will's voice rang through our rooms.

I sat up and every muscle cried out in protest. The night had been a cold one, and while I'd fallen asleep readily enough, my rest had been interrupted by frequent bouts of shivering whenever the wind made its way beneath our meager covering. I looked about the room. In the dim morning light it seemed no better than it had the night before.

"Mrs. Evelyn," Will called out, louder now. "I don't think this is right. I'm looking for Mrs. Hodgson. She is a midwife."

"We're in here, Will," Martha called as we rolled out of bed.

Will poked his head into our chamber, his eyes wide with wonder. "This can't be right. These are the quarters that Mr. Marlowe found for you?"

"It seems my husband was not much of a clothier," I replied.

"Apparently not," Will said. "You should have married better."

"If you're going to be so impudent to a poor widow, you can

get to work," Martha replied. "I'll start the cleaning, and you see to fixing the table and stool. Get those back together, and perhaps Mrs. Hodgson will bring you some breakfast."

Will was trapped and he knew it, though I doubt he minded very much. I think all three of us welcomed the prospect of a morning together, even if it was spent cleaning our little tenement. We had been apart for too long. Martha borrowed a bucket from Mrs. Evelyn and went for water, while I started for Cheapside Street. Even at this early hour the streets were thronged with people, horses, carts, and goods. I wound my way through the crowd, buying charcoal for our hearth, cheese, bread, and a few dishes from which to eat our meals. It pained me to buy the roughest plates and bowls I could find, but our new dishes should match my new rank; anything too fine would seem out of place.

I returned to find that Will had reassembled our furniture and now he and Martha were making good progress, scrubbing away the worst of the dirt. Slowly, slowly, with each passing hour, our rooms didn't seem so bad. The three of us worked through the day, cleaning and furnishing the rooms as best we could. By the time afternoon came, I'd decided I would not tolerate another miserable night. I could not buy a feather bed—Mrs. Evelyn would surely notice, and wonder where I'd gotten so much money—but there were a few things that I could do. While Martha sought food for our supper, I returned to Cheapside Street and purchased a down quilt, a coverlet of fine linen for the mattress, and two chairs for our parlor.

When I returned, Will went out for ale, and Martha and I sewed our new quilt into the filthy coverlet that came with the bed. From the parlor it looked miserable, but it would keep us warm. Martha set to roasting the fowl she'd bought, and soon enough we three were gathered around the table, pots of ale in our hands, and a fine meal before us. And on that night, except for Elizabeth's absence, London didn't seem like such a bad place after all.

Martha and I had not been asleep for long when a pounding on our door dragged us to wakefulness.

"Mrs. Hodgson! Mrs. Hodgson!" Even through my fuzzed head I knew it was Mrs. Evelyn. "You must come right away." She burst into our chamber and started pulling on my arm as if she meant to drag me from my bed. A maidservant stood behind her holding a taper, and in the flickering light I could see that Mrs. Evelyn was on the edge of panic.

"What is it? What is wrong?" I climbed out of bed and began to pull on my dress.

"It is Grace Ramsden," she said. "I was attending her in her travail and something has gone terribly wrong. Her midwife knew that you had come to the neighborhood, and sent me to find you. She needs your help."

By now Martha had rolled out of bed, and we exchanged a worried glance. While we'd encountered no problems in Hereford, the last birth we'd attended in York had ended in disaster. As we dressed I prayed that we would be able to help Mrs. Ramsden. We followed Mrs. Evelyn as she led us south to Pissing Alley and then toward Little Saint Thomas. As in York, the rough cobbled streets did their best to trip us with every step, and the shadows loomed about us menacingly.

Just before we reached Little Saint Thomas, we passed the Horned Bull. I looked up at the darkened windows, wondering which one might be Will's. As we walked, Martha and I peppered Mrs. Evelyn with questions about Mrs. Ramsden. She was around thirty-five years old, and married to a blacksmith.

"How many children has she borne?" I asked. Knowing about Mrs. Ramsden's earlier travails would make it easier for me to help her. Mrs. Evelyn's answer brought me up short.

"This is her first," she said.

"Her first travail?" Martha asked in astonishment.

It was not uncommon for a woman Mrs. Ramsden's age to give birth, but quite strange that this would be her *first* child. A husband and wife who went so long without children were most likely barren, and that did not change with age.

"Aye," Mrs. Evelyn said. "She was ever so eager for this one, too. It would be a terrible stroke if she lost him so close to her time."

I murmured my agreement. It would be an awful end to an unlikely pregnancy.

"It is here," Mrs. Evelyn said, leading us down a side street. When we reached the Ramsdens' door I noticed a pair of wood signs above it. One was an anvil and hammer; the other was a cradle with GRACE RAMSDEN painted on it. We entered the house and climbed the stairs to Grace's chamber. I said a prayer that God would protect Mrs. Ramsden and her little one and stepped through the door into the strangest travail I'd ever seen in my life.

In an instant I knew that something had gone terribly wrong, but not in an ordinary fashion. The woman I took to be Mrs. Ramsden squatted on a birthing stool next to her bed. Strangely enough she was not supported by her gossips, but sat by herself. More curious still was that she held a fire iron in both hands and waved it before her like a sword. Her gossips had retreated to a far corner of the room where they stared at her uneasily. Mrs. Ramsden moaned and lowered the fire iron as she was struck by a labor pang, but none of the women moved to help her.

"Have you all gone mad?" I demanded. Martha and I strode as one toward Mrs. Ramsden.

"You stay away," she screamed, and swung the fire iron at us with such fury it nearly pulled her from the birthing stool. "Step closer and I'll knock your brains out."

Martha and I edged slowly toward the other women.

"Who is her midwife?" I asked. "And what is happening here?"

One of the matrons stepped forward. She was a small woman of perhaps fifty years. She seemed as delicate as a sparrow but had the sharp features of a hawk. But what I remembered long after our first meeting were her eyes. At first glance they might be taken for blue, but in truth they were a piercing gray, and they flashed with more energy and intelligence than you'd find in a hundred men.

"I am Katherine Chidley," she said. "You must be Widow Hodgson."

"Katherine Chidley," I repeated, doing my best to hide my surprise. How was it that we had so quickly found Mr. Marlowe's rebel? As I looked at her more closely, I was surprised that such a slight woman had frightened him so completely. I would later learn that his fears were not entirely misplaced, for she could be a determined enemy indeed.

"Aye," I replied, gritting my teeth at my new title. "And this is my deputy, Martha Hawkins. What is happening here?"

Mrs. Chidley drew Martha and me into the hall before she spoke. "It is the strangest thing. Mrs. Ramsden has been in travail for hours but will have no help from me or any of her gossips. You saw what happens if we try. She said she's delivered many a woman, and she can deliver herself as well."

"Is she mad?" I asked the question in all seriousness, for such a decision seemed more appropriate for a lunatic than an experienced midwife.

"If so, she's hid it well before tonight," Katherine replied. She started to say more, but a gut-wrenching scream from within the chamber cut her off. We hurried back inside to find Mrs. Ramsden sitting on the floor weeping as if the world had come to an end.

"My baby, my baby," she whispered. She held a tiny gray creature in her arms; it could only be her stillborn child. Tears came to my eyes as I thought of the weeks and months of mourning that lay before her. Katherine Chidley and I stepped forward at the same time to take Mrs. Ramsden in our arms. It would be poor comfort, but at moments such as this, there was nothing more we could do.

To my shock, Mrs. Ramsden snatched up the fire iron, and once again swung it at my head, coming within inches of splitting my skull at one blow. "You will not have him away from me," she shouted. "I will hold him a bit longer, and if you try to take him I'll see you dead and buried."

Mrs. Chidley and I stumbled backward and out of the fire iron's reach and looked to each other. We simultaneously shook our heads in wonder. Neither of us had seen anything like this.

We stood for a time staring at the scene before us. Mrs. Ramsden had put down the fire iron, turned her back on us, and now cradled the child. The gossips were utterly terrified, of course, and lined the walls wanting to stay as far from Mrs. Ramsden as possible. It was a sad and strange scene, but the more I considered it, the more curious it became. I beckoned for Martha.

"I must speak with Mrs. Chidley," I murmured in her ear. "But I dare not leave Mrs. Ramsden alone with the gossips. Mind her well. You must not allow her to leave, especially with the child. If she tries, stop her at any cost and call for us. We will not go far."

Martha nodded, her eyes hard as stones. If Mrs. Ramsden tried to flee, she'd have a battle on her hands.

"Good," I said. I cast my eyes around the room and spied a bottle of sack that the gossips had brought. Understandably, they'd not yet opened it. I took it and two glasses and gestured to Mrs. Chidley. "Mrs. Chidley, might we talk?"

She nodded and followed me out of the chamber and into the Ramsdens' kitchen. A fire burned on the hearth, heating water to wash a child that now lay dead. We sat at the table and I poured two glasses of wine.

"That was passing strange," I said.

"Aye," she replied. "I've been a midwife near twenty years, and I've never seen stranger."

"And not just Mrs. Ramsden's madness, though that was strange enough."

"No," Mrs. Chidley replied. "It was a very short travail. How long were we gone from the room?"

"Not more than a few minutes," I said. "And this was her first child?"

"So she says."

"It was curious that she kept her skirts on the entire time," I said. "And that they remained dry throughout the birth."

"Nor were there any signs of the birth on the floor or on the birthing stool." Mrs. Chidley spoke with a heaviness that perfectly mirrored my own sorrow at what we had discovered.

"It was also odd that that the child had no birth string," I said. "And there was no afterbirth, at least not yet."

"I warrant we could wait all night and into the morning, and there still would be no afterbirth," she replied.

I nodded and we sat in silence as we finished our wine. Neither of us wanted to complete the circle we'd begun to draw, for it looked rather too much like a noose that would soon find its way around Mrs. Ramsden's neck.

"That is not her child," Mrs. Chidley said at last.

"No," I said. "But it is someone's child. And it is dead, perhaps at her hands."

"Ah, Christ," she moaned as she pushed back her chair. "I do not want to do this."

"I'll help you," I said. "I've done similar work, and I know that it's best done with friends."

"I'd welcome it, Mrs. Hodgson."

"Bridget," I replied. "If we're going to be friends, you must call me Bridget."

"Then I am Katherine," she said. "Now let us put an end to this bloody business."

Chapter 7

As we neared Mrs. Ramsden's chamber we heard her shouting once again, and this time Martha answered her. Katherine and I exchanged a glance and threw open the door to find Martha and Mrs. Ramsden engaged in a gruesome wrestling match, as Mrs. Ramsden tried to flee with the child and Martha tried to keep her from doing so.

"I will bury my child and none will stop me," Mrs. Ramsden cried.

Katherine and I crossed the room, seized Mrs. Ramsden by the arms, and—despite her loud and increasingly obscene protests—dragged her to the bed. She held the child's body to her breast the entire time.

"This is not your child, Grace Ramsden," Katherine declared. "And you must consider me and Mrs. Hodgson to be the finest fools in England if you thought we would be taken in by such a ruse."

The gossips cried out in surprise at this accusation, but a smile darted across Martha's lips. She had come to the same conclusion.

In the tumult that followed all the women started to talk at once, and each vied for a closer look at the child in Mrs. Ramsden's arms. This would not be a birth soon forgotten, and none of the gossips wanted to be left without some news of her own.

"Of course it's mine," Mrs. Ramsden cried, silencing the crowd. "How could it be otherwise?"

"When did you cut the navel string?" Katherine asked. "And where is the afterbirth?"

"And why is he so clean?" I asked. "You did not wash him—the water is still in the kitchen, and the child has none of the stuff and matter of birth upon him."

At this the women began to chatter once again, and one slipped out of the room. Soon the entire Cheap would have some account of what had happened.

"Give me the child, Grace," Katherine said. Her voice barely rose above a whisper, but I could hear the steel behind it.

When Mrs. Ramsden did not move, Martha and I stepped forward and held her arms while Katherine prized the child from her grasp. After a moment Mrs. Ramsden surrendered to the inevitable and released the infant. While Martha watched Mrs. Ramsden in case she tried to reclaim the child, Katherine and I stepped away from the bed to examine the corpse.

He was a baby boy, and while we could not judge how long he had been dead, his skin was cold and dry. In no wise could he have been born only a few minutes before.

"You never were pregnant, Grace," Katherine said. "Where did you get the child? You must tell us."

A deathly quiet settled over the room as we waited for her answer. Had she stolen a young mother's child and murdered it herself? None of the gossips had heard of an infant missing from anywhere in the neighborhood, but the Cheap was one small corner of London. If she had taken the child from one of the more distant parishes, they might not have heard the news. Or had she happened upon a newly dead child, and in a moment of madness taken it for her own? It was unlikely, but every explanation seemed more fantastical than the last.

Katherine continued to question Mrs. Ramsden, by turns threatening, cajoling, and begging her to tell the truth. But she never said a word. Before long, the room began to fill with other women from the neighborhood, and finally the constable arrived. As soon as he saw Katherine, he waved her over. She brought me along and introduced me as Widow Hodgson. I nearly corrected her (*Lady* Hodgson), but held my tongue. It would be some time before I became accustomed to my new name.

"Have you examined her body?" the constable asked.

"Not yet," Katherine replied. "We will not find anything of use. We know it is not her child."

"The Justice will want to know that you looked," he replied. "I'll wait outside while you do that, and then I'll have to take her to Newgate."

Katherine nodded and the constable stepped out of the room. To my relief, Grace Ramsden offered no resistance when we laid her back on the bed and raised her skirts. Of course we found no signs of a pregnancy or birth, and she certainly had not delivered a child that day. We summoned the constable and informed him of our findings, and he led Mrs. Ramsden out of the room. Two of the gossips went in search of the parish curate, while two others took the child to St. Thomas Church for burial. Slowly the remaining gossips drifted away as well, until only Katherine, Martha, and I were left.

"How long have you known her?" I asked Katherine. "Why would she do such a strange thing?"

Katherine sighed heavily. "We've worked together as midwives for years. She came to me when her husband couldn't get her with child. I tried to help, but to no good effect. Either she is barren or her husband is."

"A barren midwife?" I asked. There were no laws against such a thing, of course, but I knew that mothers would shy away from a midwife who could not have children of her own.

"Aye," Katherine said. "She was afraid that her barrenness might drive mothers to other grace-wives, but I never thought she would resort to such strange trickery."

Martha started at Katherine in astonishment. "You mean this was a ruse to win over the neighborhood women? Why would she take such a risk?"

"Look around you," Katherine said. We did, and only now noticed the decayed condition of the Ramsdens' small chamber. The furnishings were ill made and held together with little more than prayers. The bedclothes had been worn so thin in some places that the straw broke through. I then recalled how meager were the offerings in the kitchen. Despite Grace's midwifery and her husband's work as a blacksmith, the Ramsdens were as poor as could be.

"Her husband is notoriously unskilled at his trade, *and* he's prone to drunkenness," Katherine explained. "What little money he makes he pours down his gullet, and if he gets his hands on *her* money it meets the same fate. If she could no longer work as a midwife, they would fall onto parish charity and then into true poverty. She needed to be a midwife to survive."

"What will happen to her?" Martha asked. We had seen how unpredictable the courts could be in York, and we had no idea what to expect from London's.

"God knows," Katherine replied. "It will depend on what they think she's done, and what she says when they question her."

"Could she have murdered the child?" Martha asked. We all knew the fate that awaited infanticides.

"I cannot believe it," Katherine replied. "She has been a midwife for years. She cannot have become such a monster. As strange as it is, she must have somehow procured a child's corpse."

Katherine, Martha, and I walked together back toward Watling Street. By now the city had come to life, and the streets were filled with citizens going about their business. It seemed strange that the stuff of every day life went on for so many, while Grace Ramsden now sat in a stinking prison.

"You should put up a sign," Katherine said when we reached our door. "We've mothers aplenty, so a capable midwife is a welcome neighbor."

"If there is any word about Mrs. Ramsden, please let us know," I replied.

"I will."

There seemed much more to say, but we all were far too tired. Katherine embraced Martha and me as if we were long-time gossips, and we parted ways.

Martha and I awoke far earlier than we would have liked to the noise of the city below our window. It began with two men shouting, but it soon sounded like a riot. When it became clear the dispute would not soon end, we went to the window to see what the matter was. Below us Martha and I saw that two carters traveling opposite directions had turned on to our street at the same time. There was not enough room for them to pass each other and neither wished to give way, so they now busied themselves hurling oaths at one another. Of course the longer they shouted, the more people backed up behind them, and soon it was as if the civil wars had been reborn before our eyes, as those traveling west battled those going east and no man seemed prepared to talk rather than shout.

"I suppose we should start the day," Martha said. "We'll not be getting back to sleep."

"It seems not," I replied. "If you go for water, I'll start the sweeping."

With only two rooms and the both of us putting our hands to the work, cleaning took no time at all, and then the day lay before us begging to be filled—but with what? We had no friends save Katherine and no mothers to visit.

"So this is our new life," I said with a laugh. "A poor widow and her spinster servant, just passing our days in the Cheap."

"Last night was not so ordinary," Martha replied. "Do you think Katherine was right, that we could resume our business here?"

"You mean make ourselves midwives, not just in passing but as a profession?" I thought of Elizabeth, left behind in Pontrilas while Martha and I sought our fortunes in London. "I hope we won't be here long enough for that."

"But if we are to be spies, we must *act* as if we will be. And who knows what the future will bring?"

"Very well," I said. "If we are to be midwives once again, your first duty as my deputy is to have a sign made. *That* can be your task for this morning."

Martha brightened at the prospect and dashed out in search of a sign-maker.

Once I was alone, my mind returned to Elizabeth. It was too soon to hope for a letter from Pontrilas, but I could always send another. I wrote a letter making clear the drudgery of life in the city. I did not think I would convince her.

By the time I finished, Martha had returned from the signmaker and, after studying Colonel Reynolds's map for a time, we went in search of the Horned Bull. To my pleasure, we found it with only two wrong turns, but we were both disappointed to discover that Will and Colonel Reynolds had left for the day. I left my letter to Elizabeth with the innkeeper and we began the trip back to the Cheap.

"How does Will seem to you?" Martha asked as we walked. Hope and fear were woven into her every word.

"Serious," I said. "He's long been a melancholy lad, thanks to his crippled leg. But he does not seem as angry as he once did." I paused for a moment. "But that is not what you mean."

"No," Martha said.

I thought for a moment. "He is the same man we left in York, and you are the same woman. He will see that soon enough, and you will marry."

"And then what?"

I did not have an answer for that question. If Will and Martha were to marry, what would happen when the time came for me to return to Pontrilas? Would Will come with us? Would he want to? Or would they both stay in London?

"And then we shall see," I said. "I know it is not the answer you seek, but the fact is that we must wait."

We had just reached our door when a voice called out to us over the general hubbub. "Good afternoon, Mrs. Hodgson." Katherine Chidley strode across the street towards us. She had a sprig of sage pinned to her bodice. The crowd parted before her as if she were a troop of cavalry rather than a small woman. "After we left each other, I realized that I'd not formally welcomed you to the Cheap," she said.

"You did, in a fashion," I replied. "And a strange welcome it was."

Katherine laughed. "Aye. It's all the neighbors will talk about, of course. If a gossip brings up any other news, she is quickly pushed aside." Katherine paused, and her smile faded. "It was a terrible night. But the heart of man is a wicked thing, and we should not be surprised."

I knew from this that Katherine counted herself among the Puritans, and I felt my heart beat faster. While most of the godly meant well, I'd met too many from that faction—both men and women—whose holy words hid horrid deeds. I pushed that thought aside, for she'd done nothing untoward.

"Now, tell me how it is that you have come to the Cheap," Katherine said. "You are not from London, are you?"

I told her the story that Mr. Marlowe and Colonel Reynolds had concocted on my behalf, describing my life in Halifax, the death of my husband, and my decision to move to London. "I heard that a midwife in London could earn more in a week than her country cousins could in a month, so I climbed in a cart and traveled south," I said. "It was that or turn to my neighbors' charity."

"You're from Halifax?" Katherine knit her brow in confusion. "You sound like you're from the west, not the north." Her question was neither suspicious nor accusatory, but it was clear that my lie had caught her attention. My heart beat loudly in my chest as I sought a way to explain this contradiction, and I cursed Mr. Marlowe for laying this accidental trap. As was so often the case, Martha's quick mind saved me.

"Her father was a minister," Martha replied.

"Aye," I said. I could see in a moment that it was an excellent lie. "We lived in Hereford for many years, but he found a position in Bradford when I was a youth and we settled there. I moved to Halifax when I married."

"And how long have you been a midwife?"

"My husband's mother taught me the art," I replied. The pace of my heart slowed now that we'd moved on to safer ground. "Ten or more years ago—could it have been so long?"

"Time does pass." Katherine nodded. "Have you got a license from the bishop, then?"

"I do," I said. "I didn't see the need, but our vicar, Mr. Green, insisted. He was a great one for uniformity and order. If the bishop said midwives should have licenses, Mr. Green demanded it."

"And how long have you been a midwife?" Martha asked. "Some years, I imagine."

"Aye," Katherine said. "In His goodness, the Lord has given me near twenty years of service in that work."

"And you took a license?" I asked. Thanks to Mr. Marlowe I knew the answer, of course. Katherine would quit midwifing before she bent her knee to a bishop. But I could not give away how much I already knew about her.

"The day a bishop gives birth is the day I'll seek his permission to practice my craft." Katherine spat the words.

Ten years before, such words would have horrified me. I loved the Church and respected her bishops, counting them as godly men. But in the years since the wars began, I had come to see that the powerful and the corrupt were often one in the same, and that if I wanted justice to be done, *I* would have to do it. Thus, while I had no quarrel with the bishops, I found myself liking Katherine's spirit more and more.

"I hope you do not think the worse of me for craving their approval," I said.

"Of course not. Things are not so free in the countryside as they are here in London."

"Yes, I gathered that," I remarked, and we laughed together.

"How long have you been Mrs. Hodgson's deputy?" Katherine asked Martha.

"Nearly five years." Martha paused for a moment. "I suppose I shall be a midwife in my own right before too long." She glanced in my direction. The prospect of her independence surprised us both, I think.

"The two of you are what's right with England," Katherine said. "Too many of our sex would have been unwilling or afraid to move so far as you have. Too many would have been content to fall onto charity. England would be a far stronger nation if its women were not such sheep. That is why I love London so. The women here are made of different stuff; we will not simply do as we are told, whether it is kings, bishops, or husbands doing the telling."

I saw the surprise on Martha's face and imagined that it mirrored my own. I knew that the Levellers fought to overthrow the King, but I had not imagined they would seek to bring down husbands as well.

"What of silly wives who require a firm hand?" I asked. "I've met many a woman who would be utterly lost without a husband to guide her." As much as I lamented her choice of husbands, I knew that Esther Cooper—now Wallington—could not have survived by herself.

"What of silly *husbands*?" Blood rose in Katherine's cheeks as she spoke. "And what of cruel or malicious ones? Surely you've met more than a few of them over the years. If a woman relies on her husband, if she takes only what liberty he is willing to grant her, she can expect no better than she gets. And God have mercy on her for that."

My mind snapped to Phineas, my own late husband for whom the word *silly* might have been coined. And then I thought of the women whose husbands beat them without mercy. Such violence turned them—as Katherine put it—into mere sheep. Not all men were so bad, of course. My first husband had been a kind soul, and for all his faults Phineas never hurt me. But I had known too many violent men to consider them rare beasts.

"Aye," I said at last. "I have seen such men. The silly ones and the cruel ones."

"Then you see what I am saying." Katherine opened her mouth, ready to press her argument, but stopped herself. "I should apologize. We are new gossips, and I have said too much too soon."

I laughed. "It is your willingness to speak your mind and insistence on being heard that makes you a good midwife. I would be disappointed if you changed your ways once you left the birthing chamber."

"Thank you, Bridget," she said. "Now tell me: Have you any children?"

I knew she was trying to turn the conversation to more lightsome subjects, but in this she failed.

"I had two," I replied. "A son who died soon after his birth, and a daughter who lived until she was eight. My husband died before we had any others."

"Ah, no," Katherine sighed. "I am sorry for that."

"And you?"

"I have one boy, our firstborn," she said. "He is grown now. But over the years I've lost seven others."

"I am sorry," I said. I wondered for a moment which stroke cut deeper: losing two children and having none to comfort you in your old age, or burying seven but keeping one. The Lord's whip had many tails.

"The Lord tests us all." Katherine seemed to have heard my thoughts. "He tested me and Daniel just as he tested you. Sometimes, after one of our children died, I would ask the Lord for my own death, to bring an end to my trials, but He denied me. By His grace Daniel and I remained steadfast in our faith, and over the years He has lightened our burdens."

I glanced at Martha, wondering what she would make of Katherine's words. Martha had lost her faith even before we met, and she had nothing but scorn for the godly. To my surprise, rather than rejecting Katherine's premise, Martha nodded in sympathy.

"Tell me, Mrs. Chidley," Martha said. "What is the sage you have pinned to your dress? I have seen others wearing it, but I do not know the reason. Is it to ward off the stench of the city?"

I silently thanked Martha for so skillfully bringing the conversation to the Levellers. The sooner we discovered if there was a plot, the sooner we could satisfy Mr. Marlowe and return to our previous lives.

"It is a sign by which we know who among us opposes tyranny," Katherine said. "Sea green is the color of the Leveller party."

"But the King is already brought down," I said. "What tyranny is there?"

"England does not need a prince to have a tyrant," she replied, sounding more like a minister in the pulpit than a housewife on the street. "Parliament has opposed freedom with the same vigor that the King did. If you speak ill of Cromwell, he'll see you clapped in irons before the words are out of your mouth. How is that any different from when Charles ruled over us?"

"And the Levellers will stop this?" I asked. I did not imagine she would spontaneously admit to plotting against Parliament, but her ideas were so strange I wondered where they had led her.

"The Levellers want nothing more than to restore our rights

as freeborn Englishmen," she proclaimed. "We have learned that true liberty is no different from the grapes that grow in the vineyards of the Lord. If we do not attend to the vines, they shall wither and die."

"The harvest has been a meager one so far," I said. "Your leaders spend more time in prison than out."

"It is not easy work," Katherine acknowledged with a wry smile. "But the Lord and the common law of England both are with us, so victory must be ours." She paused for a moment. "If these ideas do not disturb you, I can tell you more. Come to the Nag's Head. It is north of Cheapside, not far from Blackwell Hall."

"Thank you," I said. "We might." I knew that we would—it was why we'd come to London, after all—but I did not want to seem overeager.

Katherine bid us farewell and went into her husband's shop. As I watched her go, I noticed that she, too, had chosen a cradle for the sign above her door.

That night as Martha and I lay in bed, we heard a man and woman next door shouting at each other. I said a prayer that the husband would not resort to violence, but the sound of blows and a woman's cries told me that the Lord had not heard me.

Anger rose in my breast, and I began to pull on my clothes.

"What are you going to do?" Martha asked.

"Put a stop to this," I replied. "I cannot let any man abuse his wife in such a fashion."

"And who are you?"

The question brought me to a halt. In York, I was Lady Hodgson, and with a sharp word I could stay the hand of all but the most violent of husbands. And if a man persisted in his violence, I could invite a magistrate to supper, and ask him to bring the matter to the courts. But in London I was merely Widow Hodgson, a woman of little consequence and less power. I realized then that when I'd shed my silk gown, I'd lost more than a fine set of clothes.

"If you go marching in there, he'll beat you worse than his wife," Martha said. "And then he'll beat her some more."

I sat on the bed and stared at the wall. As much as I hated it, Martha was right. As I listened to the woman weep, Katherine's words about malicious husbands rang in my ears. Perhaps the woman had acted in an untoward fashion; perhaps she had been one of the *silly wives* I'd mentioned. But did she deserve to be beaten? For the first time I wondered what I would have done if Phineas had been as violent as the man next door. Would I have fought back? Not at that tender age. Would I have fled York for my parents' house hundreds of miles away? Such a thing would never have occurred to me. No, if Phineas had been a brute, *I* would have been the wife weeping through the walls.

I tried to push such melancholy thoughts from my head, but instead my mind ran to my daughter, Elizabeth. In a few short years men would come a-courting. While I would try to find a better husband for her than Phineas had been to me, there were no sure wagers. What if I chose poorly? What would I have her do if her husband were inclined to violence? Meekly suffer whatever outrages her husband chose to visit upon her? Or demand to be treated with the loving kindness that a husband owed his wife? I knew my answer to that question, but I also knew that if I voiced such thoughts, if I said on the street, *Women should not be made to suffer at their husbands' hands,* people would call me a troublesome and tumultuous woman just as they called Katherine one. And perhaps they would be right.

Chapter 8

The following Sunday, Martha and I returned from the afternoon service at St. Mary-le-Bow to find two letters newly arrived from Pontrilas, one each from Elizabeth and Hannah. I opened Elizabeth's first, hoping that her anger at being left behind had faded. It had not. The fury of her words—*abandoned, forsaken, discarded*—mixed with the tears still visible on the paper to rend my heart in two. I cursed Marlowe for drawing me away from my daughter and renewed my vow to finish his business as quickly as I could. Hannah's letter confirmed what I'd read in Elizabeth's; she was by turns furious and morose, and spent every minute she could out of the house, riding to the eastern edge of my estates and gazing toward London.

I wrote a brief note to Hannah, thanking her for her patience, and a longer letter to Elizabeth. I told her of my love, and lamented the pain that my departure had caused her. *I promise that I will return the moment that my work here is done. You must be patient.* But I could not, of course, know when that would be. I summoned one of Mrs. Evelyn's boys, and sent him to the Horned Bull with the letters.

He'd not been gone for long when Katherine Chidley knocked on our door. "Thank the Lord, you are both here."

"What is it?" Martha asked.

"Not now," Katherine replied. "The walls are thin. Besides, I need a pot of ale."

When Katherine led Martha and me north on Bread Street, then onto Milk Street, I knew that we must be going to the Nag's Head. Women and men in the neighborhood nodded when they saw Katherine coming, clearing a path so we could pass without any trouble. Katherine was even more powerful than I'd imagined: for while I had received such courtesy in York, that was by dint of my birth; she had earned this respect entirely by her deeds. We arrived at the tavern and Katherine called for three pots of ale.

"Word has come from Newgate that Grace Ramsden will be tried for infanticide," she said. "They say that she stole the child from his mother, killed him, and then smuggled him into her delivery room."

"My God," Martha breathed. "They found the mother?"

"No," Katherine said. "Nor has she confessed."

Martha and I stared at her in confusion. "If there is no accuser and no confession, why will she be tried?" I asked at last.

I'd thought about Grace Ramsden many times over the previous week, and I simply could not believe that she had deliberately murdered a child in order to keep her clients. No midwife would do such a thing.

"They have nothing but the sheriff's suspicions," Katherine said. "But that was enough to convince a magistrate to order a trial. And what she did was so horrible, I fear the deed will be enough to see her hanged, whether she murdered the child or not."

"She hasn't told them where she found the child?" I asked.

"She's not spoken a word since they took her to Newgate," Katherine said.

"When will she be tried?" Martha asked.

"All too soon," Katherine said. "The Assizes start this week."

In my youth, I would have trusted the law to mete out justice, and simply allowed the trial to run its course. But my final years in York had showed me that the law concerned itself with power above all else. If it also offered justice, that was only by happy accident. I also knew that Katherine was of a similar mind, and I could guess why she'd sought out Martha and me.

"If we do nothing, she will hang," Martha said, speaking for both of us. "We cannot allow that, not on such thin evidence. We have to find out what happened."

"I hoped you would say that," Katherine said. "If she did not kill the boy herself, she must have found a stillborn child. But where?"

We considered the question while we drank our ale. "The mother must be a single woman, perhaps a widow, perhaps a maiden," I said. "And a poor one at that. No respectable wife would give over her child so easily, even if he were stillborn. She would demand a proper burial."

"Mrs. Ramsden might have delivered the child dead-born, and told the mother she would take it to be buried," Martha said. "If the mother had no husband to oversee the funeral, she would never know the truth, and wouldn't complain to the Justices."

Katherine considered the idea for a moment before shaking her head. "That relies too much on chance to be the whole story," she said. "Mrs. Ramsden announced her pregnancy last spring. She could not have known that she would deliver a singlewoman of a stillborn child just in time for her own travail. She planned her scheme more carefully than that."

"What if the mother's a whore?" Martha asked. "If so, the child would have no father to claim him, and the mother would be happy to avoid a whipping for bearing a bastard."

"And if Mrs. Ramsden got to know the city's doxies," I said, "they could help her find a stillborn child when she needed one."

Katherine nodded in grim satisfaction. "Grace simply waited until she reached her supposed time, and *then* found a willing mother. Once she had the stillborn child, she feigned her own travail." She turned to me. "Hold tight to your deputy, Mrs. Hodgson, else I might take her for my own."

"What do we do now?" Martha asked.

"If we have to find a harlot, the place to start is in Southwark on the other side of the river. In the morning we'll begin our search."

"Southwark?" I said with a smile. "I can provide a guide to accompany us."

From the moment they met, Will and Katherine got along like old friends. The four of us chattered amiably as we walked south to London Bridge. We fell silent, though, when we reached the gatehouse on the far end. We looked up at the row of heads that had been posted on pikes as a warning against treason. A raven sat on one man's head, croaking indignantly, as if he hungered for more executions. I looked away, and we entered the city of Southwark.

Once we passed over the Bridge, it felt as if we were in a different city, for Southwark made the chaos of London seem like a model of order and uniformity. The houses were lower built—none more than four stories tall—but the streets were ill maintained, and Southwark's residents seemed to be even less inclined to good order than London's; chapmen, fishwives and shopkeepers filled the air with a cacophony of voices. Before the war, Southwark had been home to London's theaters, as well as bear- and bull-baiting pits. While the greatest of these had been closed, many smaller disorders persisted in the knowledge that London's officers had no power south of the river. It was this gap in good government that made Southwark so attractive to London's brothel-keepers and thus drew us across the river.

"The best place to start is in the Clink." Will pointed to the west, past a church the size of a small cathedral.

"I'm afraid to ask," Martha said mischievously, "how you know where to find a brothel."

"A blind man would be able to direct you to the stews." Will laughed. "They are entirely shameless here." The four of us skirted south of the church and passed a decrepit mansion that lay further west.

"That's Winchester House," Will said. "It was home to the Bishop, when we had bishops. And those are the theaters, of course." To the west and south we could see round buildings looming over their neighbors.

"We should go first to the Holland's Leaguer," Will said.

"It is real place?" I asked in surprise. Years before I'd heard of a most scandalous play, also called *The Holland's Leaguer,* but I had not realized it existed outside the author's debauched mind.

"Aye," Will said. "In the flesh, if you will." We turned one final corner and found ourselves standing before a large and ramshackle tenement. A garishly painted quean stood at the entrance trying to lure customers with flashes of her bosom. She noticed Will's interest—in the building, I told myself—and approached him. She took his arm and whispered something in his ear that caused him to turn a deep crimson. Martha laughed at Will's state before stepping forward to take his other arm.

"Er, that is tempting," Will said once he'd regained his tongue. "But impossible, I think. In truth we are here on more serious business."

"We would like to see your bawd," Katherine said.

The quean looked us over before she answered. "He'll want to know why," she said. "You can't just walk up and ask to see him, you know."

If I were still Lady Hodgson, I could have bought an audience with the bawd no matter the price, but *Widow* Hodgson could hardly spend so freely, not in Katherine's presence.

"A few days ago a woman might have come here." Katherine paused, knowing how strange her words would sound. "She was looking for a stillborn child."

"What do you mean?" the quean asked. "You found a child and you are searching for his mother?"

"No," Katherine said. "A woman came here, to purchase a stillborn child."

The quean gasped and sputtered in response. "My God, have you gone mad?" she demanded. "Who would do such a thing?" She produced a whistle from her apron and blew three times. Two large and very ugly men strode out of the brothel. Each held a cudgel and seemed eager to put it to use.

"Get away from here," the quean hissed, her bosom heaving. "If I see you again, you'll be much the worse for it. You are lunatics, you are, buying a stillborn child!"

"*We* do not want to buy a child," I tried to explain. "We are looking for a woman who . . ." I stopped my speech when one of the men stepped forward, slapping his palm with his club. There seemed no point in arguing further, so we moved on with as much speed and dignity as we could. Once we were out of sight of the brothel we stopped to catch our breath.

"Perhaps we should try another approach," Katherine said with a smile.

"If we are following Mrs. Ramsden's trail," Martha said, "it is not the bawd we need to talk to, but the doxies themselves."

"How can we find a whore without talking to a bawd?" Katherine asked. "If the three of us try to hire a *putain,* it will surely bring attention we don't want."

"We send Will by himself," Martha said. "He can hire the doxy." While Will turned crimson again and struggled to find his voice, Martha explained her scheme. "He can go with the harlot as any man might. And once they are alone, he can give her a few pennies and ask about Mrs. Ramsden."

Katherine and I glanced at each other and looked to Will. He still seemed shocked that Martha would send him alone into a brothel.

"If you have another way, we can try it," Martha said.

None of us did.

"Very well then," Martha said. "Let us begin."

The four of us pooled our ready money and estimated that if all went well we could send Will into four or five brothels. We found another such place not far from the Holland's Leaguer, and Will entered.

"How long do you think he'll be?" I asked.

"Not long if he knows what's good for him," Martha replied.

Such was the case, for soon after the brothel door burst open and Will stumbled into the street followed closely by a young harlot.

"His pintle is as soft as an overcooked carrot, it is!" The girl crowed with unseemly joy. "But you're welcome to return any time you'd like, and I'll make it stand right tall. But for now you should go on your way."

Will rejoined us and we hurried to find an alley where we could talk.

"What happened?" Katherine demanded.

"That little play was the doxy's idea." Will had once again turned bright red. "She told me to pretend I couldn't, er, stand. That way she wouldn't have to give a share of our money to the bawd. It seemed like a kind thing to do. I didn't know she would announce my failure to all of Southwark."

"Did she tell you anything of use?" Martha asked.

"Aye," Will said. "She heard gossip about a woman searching for a doxy who had neared her time."

"Was it Mrs. Ramsden?" I asked. "It must have been."

"She never saw the woman," Will said. "And doesn't know anyone who did. But I think we are close."

"I hope so," Martha said. "If you visit too many more brothels your face might stay that color."

It took visits to two more brothels, but at last Will found a woman who said she could answer our questions.

"She can't talk right now," Will said when he returned to us. "But around supper she'll meet us in the alehouse on the corner."

I glanced up at the autumn sun, hanging low in the reddening sky. I did not know when a harlot took her supper, but I hoped she would not be long. I did not look forward to a night walk through Southwark.

The four of us crossed to the alehouse and found a table by a window from which we could see the brothel door. The ale was undrinkable and the food unfit for the city's vermin. We sat in tense silence hoping the harlot would bring us closer to the truth, but we also knew she might be lying in the hope of tricking Will out of a few more pennies.

Within an hour a woman stumbled out of the brothel and wove her way to the alehouse. She was so drunk it seemed a small miracle that she found her way through the door on the first try. Will waved her to our table as soon as she entered.

"D'you have my tuppence?" she asked as she sat. I gazed at her face in amazement. The pox had taken a terrible toll on her. If she was half so old as she appeared, she was an ancient whore indeed. I wondered what kind of man would willingly lie with such a woman. One who was no less cup-shot than she, I supposed.

I put two pennies on the table, and—as I expected—she tried to take them at once. I seized her wrist and squeezed.

"You must answer our questions first," I said. "And if we are pleased, you'll have your tuppence."

The whore's nostrils flared in either anger or fear. She pulled her hand back but did not try to take the coins.

"Just tell them what you told me," Will said. "Then you'll have your money and be on your way."

"Buy me an ale, too," the woman said. "I'm too thirsty to talk right now."

Will and I exchanged a glance. We had no choice, so Will waved his cup at the bartender.

When the slattern had her drink she drained it at a draught and wiped her mouth on her sleeve. "Very good," she said. "A woman came here a few weeks ago. She said she was a midwife and that her husband was a physician. She said the two of them, her and her husband, were trying to help mothers save their children from dying young."

"And what did she want?" Katherine asked.

"She said they needed a baby who had died. They would examine his body and learn from it." The whore shook her head in wonder at the idea. "She promised an entire shilling to the mother, and she said she'd give the child a Christian burial after they looked at it."

"Who was she?" I asked.

"I don't know," she said. "I wasn't with child, so she had no interest in me."

"Tell her the rest," Will urged her.

"This other doxy I know, Isabella Wroth, she had a child born dead. She sent for the woman."

My heart leaped in my chest, and I looked from Katherine to Martha. Could we be so close to finding the mother of the dead child? The quean saw the look in my eye and in a blink the coins on the table disappeared.

"Where is she?" Katherine demanded. "You must tell us."

I despaired to hear Katherine's tone, and a pained look crossed Martha's face. Unless this whore was a complete fool, we'd have to empty our purses to find Isabella Wroth. And from the light that now shone in her eyes, I knew she was no fool.

"That's what you *really* need to know isn't it?" she asked. "It will cost you."

I ground my teeth and reached deep into my purse. When the whore had the last of my coins she reached across the table, plucked Will's ale from his hands, and drank it down. She belched loudly and smiled at us. "Follow me."

The doxy led us into a maze of streets and alleys. Our path seemed so crazy I wondered if her goal was for us to become so lost and desperate that we would pay her to lead us back to London Bridge. If so, she would be disappointed, for she'd already taken every penny we had. Eventually we reached an aged tenement and climbed three sets of stairs to the top floor. There was just one door, and when we knocked a woman's voice invited us in.

Chapter 9

The scene within was just what I expected. The apartment contained so little that it made our rooms at Mrs. Evelyn's seem like Whitehall Palace. A bed, a clothes chest, a candle, a small unlit stove, and nothing else. Isabella Wroth lay on a small bed; two other women sat next to her. Even a penniless doxy had her gossips.

Isabella's welcoming smile faded when she saw that our guide had brought strangers with her. She could not have guessed why we had come, but she knew an ill wind when she felt one.

"These ones want to speak to you, Isabella," our guide announced before scampering down the stairs. I had no doubt that within minutes our money would be poured down her throat. Isabella and her gossips looked at us warily, wanting to know why we had come but afraid to ask. Even in the guttering candlelight I could see that she was far younger than the whore who'd brought us here. She had not been in the profession for long, and the pox had not yet begun its slow destruction of her face.

"We must speak to you alone," I said as gently as I could.

Martha stepped forward and knelt at the side of the bed. "We are here about your baby. We know what happened and must talk to you about it. You are in no danger."

After a moment Isabella nodded, and her gossips slipped out of the room, with Will close behind.

"Your friend said that a woman came to you in search of a stillborn child," Martha said. She took Isabella's hand just as she would take a mother's, comforting the girl and easing her fears. In that moment, Martha was doing the work of a midwife.

"That quean is not my friend," Isabella noted. "Not if she brought you to me for a few pennies."

Martha smiled and waited while Isabella calmed herself. "Tell me about your child."

"A woman did come here," Isabella said at last. "She was a midwife, and wife to a physician. She said that if I let her have my boy, she would find a way to save other little ones. And she promised that she'd give him a decenter burial than I could afford, with a sermon and bells."

Martha looked up at Katherine and me, unsure what to say. The truth of what had happened to her child—that he'd been used in Grace Ramsden's lunatic scheme to feign childbirth—would hurt Isabella far more than Grace's ingenious lie.

Katherine stepped forward and joined Martha at Isabella's bedside. "And Mrs. Ramsden did all that. But the sheriff does not believe her. He has accused her of stealing your son and murdering him."

"What?" Isabella cried. "He was dead-born, so she couldn't have killed him. And she never would! She was kind to me when nobody else would be."

"And now she needs your help," Martha said. "You must tell the jury that the child was stillborn. If you don't, Mrs. Ramsden will hang."

Fear swirled into Isabella's eyes. "Will I be whipped as a bastard bearer?" she asked. "I knew a whore who died of her whipping when she got a fever from one of the cuts."

Martha offered the girl a conspiratorial smile. "The child was born in Southwark, wasn't he?"

Isabella nodded.

"And Mrs. Ramsden will be tried in London," Martha said. "Another city, another law. Nobody there will have the right to whip you for something that happened here."

Isabella smiled faintly. Sometimes—not often, but sometimes—the space between what was right and what was legal could work to help the poor. "What do I need to do?" she asked.

With the trial only a few days away, it seemed best for Isabella to accompany us to London. No good could come from trying to find her a second time on the eve of the trial.

"You can stay with me," Katherine said. "There's room enough with my other maidservants, and we have coal for the stove. You will be much more comfortable there."

Isabella nodded. I supposed that leaving Southwark and losing her place at the brothel could not be counted as too great a loss. How much worse could things be north of the river? She collected her belongings and we went outside to find Will waiting on the street. The five of us began the long walk back to the Cheap. It was a hard journey for Isabella so soon after her travail, but we had no money for a hackney or a wherry so we had no choice but to walk. With such a large party we worried more about being taken by the Watch than being accosted by thieves, but the journey proved uneventful. Nevertheless, it was past midnight when Martha and I hauled our weary bones up to our room and into bed.

* * *

When the morning of Grace Ramsden's trial came, Katherine, Martha, and I accompanied Isabella Wroth to Newgate gaol. As with so many notorious cases, the scene seemed more appropriate for a carnival than a court. Victualers and ale-sellers had found their places outside the jail walls, and were doing a fine business despite the early hour. Chapmen walked up and down the streets shouting their pamphlets, and a few particularly daring whores plied their wares.

We found the room where Mrs. Ramsden would be tried and discovered that she would soon be brought to the court. We told Isabella that, as a witness, she must wait outside. It was not true, but she still did not know the truth about why Mrs. Ramsden had taken her child and I did not want to dispel her illusion. She looked nervous until Martha offered to stay by her side.

I took a deep breath as I entered the courtroom, for I knew that if we failed to prove Mrs. Ramsden's innocence she would hang before dinner. In keeping with the prison itself, the courtroom was a cramped and rank space, made all the more so by the crowds that had filled every seat and aisle. Indeed, it was hard to tell which men were there as jurymen, which were witnesses, and which were merely curious.

Eventually a guard led Grace Ramsden into the court, and she stood next to the judge's raised table; she had shackles on her wrists, but I was relieved she'd not been laid in double-irons. I also said a prayer of thanks that she seemed healthy enough, for gaol-fever took as many prisoners as the hangman.

The constable who had arrested Mrs. Ramsden spoke first, explaining to the jury what had happened on the night of her "travail." He went into great and lurid detail—far more than was necessary—and from the look in the jurymen's eyes it was clear that he'd convinced them to hang her. Katherine and I had a difficult task ahead of us.

As Mrs. Ramsden's midwife, Katherine spoke next, telling the jury *why* she had done such a terrible thing. It would not speak to her innocence, but we hoped it would make her seem less monstrous. She went on to tell the jury that the child had been born small, and had neither hair nor fingernails. These were lies, for the child had had both, but we were more interested in saving Mrs. Ramsden's life than telling the narrow truth of the matter; we would have our justice, even if it required perjury.

A few of the jurymen looked confused at Katherine's description of the child's body—what had hair and nails to do with anything?—so I stepped forward to ask her to explain.

"If he was born without hair and nails, it means he was born well before his time," she said. "And if he was born so early, he likely was born dead." The jurymen nodded, and for the first time I thought we might have a chance of convincing them.

Finally, it was Isabella's turn to appear. She was obviously frightened as she made her way to the front of the court, and I could not fault her for that. What girl would feel differently if she found herself in such a situation? Since Mrs. Ramsden had no advocate and Katherine had already spoken as a witness, the judge allowed me to put the questions to Isabella. I avoided any mention of her work as a doxy, and in the maidservant's dress Katherine had provided, there was no reason anyone on the jury would guess.

Isabella told the jury about meeting Mrs. Ramsden when she was with child, and about Mrs. Ramsden's strange and unsettling request.

"She told you she *wanted* a stillborn child?" I asked, feigning confusion.

"Aye, she told me that she would learn from his body. She said that if she could learn how my son died, she might help other children to live. I thought that giving her my son would help. She meant no harm."

Some of the jurymen nodded and looked more closely at Grace Ramsden. At least now their faces showed puzzlement rather than cold fury. I knew that justice still could miscarry, but it seemed likely that thanks to Isabella's testimony, Katherine and I had just saved Grace Ramsden from hanging.

An hour later, my hope was borne out when the jury found Mrs. Ramsden not guilty of infanticide. The judge and jury were horrified by her actions, of course, and the judge lectured her on the evil that she had done, but since there was no crime, he had no choice but to set her free.

When the judge announced his decision, Katherine, Martha, and I embraced, and immediately began to search the crowd for Mrs. Ramsden. By the time we reached the front of the room, she was gone.

"Taken to have her irons knocked off," a guard explained.

"Where will we find her?" Katherine asked.

"She'll come back here if she wants." The guard shrugged. "If she doesn't there are other doors she can use."

Katherine, Martha, and I waited in the courtroom for nearly a half an hour, but Grace Ramsden never appeared. With nothing else to do, we returned to the Cheap, our victory hollowed out by Mrs. Ramsden's disappearance. That night Mr. and Mrs. Ramsden emptied out their tenement and left the Cheap, never to be seen again.

With that, Katherine, Martha, and I became famous throughout the Cheap, now known as the midwives who had saved Grace

Ramsden from hanging. What other midwives had done *that* for a mother? In a happy coincidence, the following day a boy delivered the sign Martha had ordered for us to hang above our door. Within days, Martha and I had mothers from throughout the Cheap—including many of Mrs. Ramsden's former clients—calling us to their bedsides.

With the mothers came money, of course, as parents and friends rewarded us handsomely for our work, and we were able to purchase a few of the goods that I missed most from my life as a gentlewoman. We could not buy anything too grand, of course—I continued to dress in wool—but we purchased new linens for the bed, furniture that was less likely to collapse, and even a feather mattress. (Martha agreed that feathers were far superior to straw, and vowed never to go back.) I continued to exchange letters with Elizabeth—hers still bitter, mine as loving as I could make them. Each night I prayed that the Lord would both soften her heart and see our little family reunited.

Our friendship with Katherine Chidley grew along with our purses, but so too did my unease at the lies we told her, due to our obligations to Mr. Marlowe. I felt a sense of kinship with Katherine that even her strange ideas could not shake. While she never hid her godly enthusiasm or her curious political opinions, neither did she insist that I join in her thinking. She lived her gospel rather than merely preaching it. I had no desire to betray her, certainly not to such an ill-natured man as Marlowe. During supper one night I said as much to Martha, hoping that she could find a way out of the maze into which we had been cast.

"I like it no more than you," she said. "But if we betray Marlowe for Katherine's sake, you will feel his wrath. You risk losing all you have."

We sat in silence for a time. Martha was right, but it still did not sit well with me. In the end, I resolved to tell Marlowe about any plots I discovered, but at the same time to do my best to protect Katherine. If he would ruin me for such loyalty, so be it.

I could only see it as divine providence that the day after I came to this conclusion, Mr. Marlowe sent a letter renewing his demand that Martha and I discover what the Levellers had planned, and what role the Chidleys might play in their schemes. So Martha and I began to frequent the Nag's Head, the tavern known as a haven for the Levellers. There, we found ourselves drawn into the strangest discussions, as members of that group called for new government and new laws; one man even wished to make divorce legal. It seemed as if gossip about friends and neighbors had become a thing of the past, as all anyone wished to discuss were matters of state. I could not see the sense in some of the wilder ideas, but found myself enjoying the speeches and conversations. I wrote to Mr. Marlowe telling him what we heard, omitting any mention of Katherine, and he seemed satisfied. And as long as he was happy, we were safe.

One evening a man I'd never seen before came to the Nag's Head. Though he was a stranger to me, and none spoke his name, everyone seemed to know who he was. He stood on one of the benches and began to inveigh against the tyranny of the law. He looked at me when he spoke, and he must have seen something in my face, for he turned his attention entirely in my direction.

"You've seen it, haven't you?" he cried out. "The law, which ought to be an instrument of justice, has become a cudgel with which the rich and the powerful bludgeon the poor and the meek." Katherine—tonight accompanied by her husband, Daniel—shouted her support of the stranger's words, and others joined in.

"What fate awaits a poor man who steals bread to feed his children?" He spoke with the power and authority of the finest preacher in England, and none in the room dared look away from his face. "Time in the stocks and a whipping if he is fortunate. But what fate awaits the great man who uses the law to drive his tenants from their land? More wealth and more power are his reward. Where is the justice in that?"

The crowd cried up its approval, and Daniel Chidley climbed atop another bench to add his words to the speaker's. "John is right, of course. The law must be reformed to the benefit of *all* the people, not just those who can read Latin. In truth all men must be equal before the law. They must be free from arrest without cause, and if they are accused of a crime they must be judged by *common* men, not by gentlemen who know nothing of a poor man's life."

"Ah, but it is not merely the law that must be transformed," John replied, as if the two were players, and the rest of us their audience. "We must change the very form of government under which we live and labor. No man should live under a government *unless he gives his consent to it*—all else is tyranny. No man in England, not even the poorest, is bound to a government if he cannot vote. And every Englishman has the right—nay, the sacred duty—to protest the tyrannical rule of this Parliament." At this the crowd broke out in such tumult that I feared a revolt might begin before my eyes. In the end, however, the speeches finished without a call to arms, and all the patrons went on their way.

That night I lay awake long after Martha had drifted to sleep, thinking of what John had said about the law and justice. I thought not of farmers driven from their land under the cover of law, but of maidservants whipped for bastardy after being raped by their masters. I thought of Esther Wallington, convicted of murder because it would please the Lord Mayor of York. And I thought of my own fate as I was driven out of York because I was too zealous in the pursuit of justice. This was not the first time I had entertained such ideas, of course, but that night in the Nag's Head I realized how many others had similar doubts. Was it possible for the law and justice to be reconciled? And if it were possible, could it be done without a rising of the common folk and utter anarchy?

The next morning Martha and I awoke to find that a letter from Will had been slipped under our door. The paper had been hastily torn from a larger sheet, and he'd not taken the time to sign it.

Aunt Bridget—Colonel Reynolds will summon you today. You must tell him the truth. He knows more than you realize.

A sense of unease rose within me. What could Will mean by this? What did Colonel Reynolds know?

Will's words proved prophetic as at that instant Mrs. Evelyn appeared at our door. She brought a note from Colonel Reynolds, summoning Martha and me to a meeting at the east end of St. Paul's Churchyard.

"And who is Tom Reynolds?" Mrs. Evelyn asked. If she felt any shame at reading my letter, she hid it well.

"He is my cousin," I replied. "He has come to London to repay the last of the debts owed to my husband; when you are a widow, no penny can go to waste."

"And it is his first time in the city?" Mrs. Evelyn asked.

"Aye. We thought he'd have an easier time finding St. Paul's than Watling Street." Before Martha had come into my service, I might have stammered out a lie that not even a child would believe. But even as I taught her the art of midwifery, she taught me the art of deception—and while she was a quicker study, I was not without my successes. I glimpsed a smile on Martha's face and felt a measure of pride rising within me. What a strange friendship we had.

"What can such a summons mean?" Martha asked as we walked west on Cheapside toward the cathedral. "They've been content with our newsless notes until now."

"I don't know," I said. "But we should be careful. Clearly something has happened."

As we entered the churchyard—and utterly without warning—Colonel Reynolds fell in beside me and took my arm. I admit my heart leaped at his touch, though I cannot say whether it was from surprise or the nearness of his presence. It had been some years since any man had been so forward with me. I was equally surprised when Will swooped down to Martha's side, took her arm, and led her away from me. Colonel Reynolds and I were alone.

"Tell me what happened at the Nag's Head last night," he said.

"And good morning to you, too, Colonel," I replied.

"Quite right." Colonel Reynolds laughed. "That was rude of me. Good morning, Mrs. Hodgson. At meetings such as these, please call me Tom. The fewer people who know who I am, the better."

"Very well. Tom, then."

"So, Mrs. Hodgson, tell me how you have been these past weeks."

"I imagine Will told you about our adventures at the Assizes," I said.

"Aye. I will say that while Mr. Marlowe admires your tenacity, he had hoped you would make less of a spectacle of yourself. But if your adventure bound you to Katherine Chidley, it is for the best. After all, your job *is* to spy on her and her husband. You remember that, don't you?"

I stopped walking for a moment, startled by his directness and made uneasy by this bald and bloodless reminder that I had agreed to betray the woman who had become my gossip. The doubts and hesitations that had been nipping at my heels began to howl around me.

"She is a good woman and a fine midwife," I said. "You need not fear her."

Colonel Reynolds—*Tom,* I reminded myself—turned to face me. I saw a measure of sympathy in his eyes, and I was grateful for it.

"I know you have become her friend," Tom said softly. "But you cannot let your loyalty to Mrs. Chidley lead you to betray Mr. Marlowe. He would call it treason, and he might not be entirely wrong."

I stood in silence, hating Mr. Marlowe for putting me in such a position.

"If she is as innocent as you say, you do not need to fear for her," Tom said.

"Why not?" I asked. "Because Mr. Marlowe would not harm an innocent woman?" The anger in my voice took me by surprise.

"No," Tom admitted. "If he thought it necessary, he would hang the Virgin Mary. But if you insist on her innocence, I will do my best to protect her. I have no desire to see the innocent suffer."

"Thank you," I said. "And tell me: Why is Mr. Marlowe so afraid of a single old woman?"

Tom laughed. "If it were just a single old woman, he would not be worried. Indeed, if it were just the crowd at the Nag's Head, he would not worry. They are good talkers, but most will do little more than that."

"Then what is he afraid of?"

"Soldiers in the New Model Army have raised up the Leveller standard."

I could not help laughing at this. "Cromwell has become afraid of his own army? He is afraid that the army that brought down the King now will bring him down as well? That is marvelous!"

Tom abruptly steered us out of the churchyard and toward a cook shop that lay nearby. "Are you hungry?" he asked. "I'm famished."

Without awaiting my response, he led me into the shop and to a table at the back of the room. He sat with his back to the wall and stared intently at the door through which we'd come. When nobody followed us in, he said to me in a hushed voice, "Now we can talk in earnest."

Chapter 10

"You are afraid of being spied upon?" I asked.

"I am *wary* of being spied upon," Tom Reynolds replied with a wan smile. "But no more than a cavalryman is wary of being thrown from his mount. It is not something I dwell upon, but something I must consider."

"That is a fair distinction," I said. "Is it true that Mr. Marlowe and Cromwell are afraid of the very army that brought Cromwell to power?"

"It is Mr. Marlowe's job to be afraid. He is afraid of the army. He is afraid of the King, and he is afraid of the King's friends. He is even afraid of *Cromwell's* friends if he thinks they might negotiate with the King. His fear is why he has succeeded for so long."

"Regardless of Mr. Marlowe's fears, I do not like informing on my friends," I said.

"And I did not like the war," Tom said. "I did not like firing cannons into ranks of brave Englishmen as they trudged up some sodden hill. But the world is a harsh place—far harsher than Mr. Marlowe. It cares not for any man's wants and wishes." He paused for a moment, and I was taken aback by the vehemence in his voice.

At that moment the cook came to our table. "We've got chicken and carrots. And ale." He spoke with strange belligerence, as if daring us to challenge his words.

"That's fine," Tom replied.

The cook grumbled as he departed, as if Tom's agreeable nature had only infuriated him all the more.

"A charming man," I noted.

Tom laughed, and I caught my breath. In that moment there was something about him that reminded me of my first husband, Luke. I could not say what it was—perhaps the tenor of his laugh, or the way his eyes crinkled at the corners—but for what seemed like ages I could not hope to speak. Luke had died just a few months after we married, and I still counted his loss as one of God's most brutal blows. But when Tom laughed, it was as if Luke were there before me. This was exceedingly strange, for in most ways Tom and Luke could not have been more different: Where Luke was slight, Tom was broad and strong, and while Luke let his fair curls fall to his collar, Tom kept his cut close to the scalp. Despite these differences, there was something in Tom that made me feel the way I had decades earlier.

To my relief, Tom did not notice my condition. "I am sorry for my hard words. I know what you are doing is not easy. But we are nearing a decisive moment, and we cannot know whether the cards will fall with us or against us."

"What do you mean?" I asked. This was why he'd wanted to find a quiet corner in which to talk.

"It is the King," he replied.

I caught my breath. I knew the King lived as a prisoner on the Isle of Wight, and the great question facing the nation—indeed, the *only* question facing the nation—was what Parliament would do with him.

"A decision is near, then?" I asked.

Tom shrugged. "There are too many decision makers for me to say, but at the end of the day the problem is simple: We can defeat the King a thousand times, yet he will still be the King. But if he defeats us once, we all shall hang. If that is the case, what can we do with him?"

"Exile?" I asked.

"So we can await his return at the head of an Irish army on French ships? I cannot see Cromwell choosing such a course."

"What then?" I asked. "If he is dangerous in England and no less dangerous abroad, what can Cromwell do?"

"First things first," Tom replied. "Tell me about last night at the Nag's Head."

I sighed in resignation. "A stranger was there," I said. "He spoke of the injustice of the law, and said the people should demand a change."

"What else?"

"He said no man is bound to a government without his consent. He is for nothing but anarchy." I did not know if I believed this last, but I thought Mr. Marlowe would appreciate it.

"Did anyone else speak?"

I laughed. "Everyone spoke. It was a house of bibble-babble."

"Did anyone else *stand* and speak?"

I paused for a moment. Daniel Chidley had risen, of course, but I was reluctant to say anything that might hurt Katherine. Then I remembered Will's note. *You must tell him the truth. He knows more than you realize.*

"Daniel Chidley did," I said. "He mined the same vein as the other one, proclaiming the injustice of the law."

Tom nodded. "That first man was John Lilburne. Freeborn John, they call him."

"It was?" My mouth hung open in astonishment. I had heard his name, of course. If a group so fractious as the Levellers could be said to have a leader, it was Lilburne. I marveled that I had been in the same room with such a famous—not to say tumultuous—man. And then I realized something. "How do you know?" I asked.

"Know what?"

"How do you know the man I saw was John Lilburne? *I* didn't even know it was him."

Tom grinned. "You are not the only spy in the Cheap, Mrs. Hodgson."

"If you knew all this, then why did you ask?" Even as the words escaped my lips, I knew the answer. "You were testing me. You knew what John Lilburne said, and you knew that Daniel Chidley spoke. You wanted to be sure I would tell the truth about the Chidleys."

Tom nodded curtly. "I did not want to test you. But I had to know that I could trust you on such matters."

"What if I'd lied?"

"You didn't," he said. "So it does not matter."

"I have been in the Cheap for weeks; why are you testing me now?"

Tom thought for a moment before answering. "Two reasons. First, now you are friends with Mrs. Chidley, and we had to be sure that you had not joined her faction. You proved that by telling the truth about last night.

"Second, and more important," he continued, "we have reached the final act of our nation's bloody play. Next month the King will be brought to London. To what end I cannot say. Perhaps he will be King once more. Perhaps be will be tried for treason."

If Tom's expression had not been so serious I would have laughed aloud. I looked around the room to ensure nobody had heard him.

"You cannot try the King for treason," I whispered. Merely saying the words roiled my guts. "Who has the right to do such a thing? Parliament? He is the King."

"Whether they have the right to try him is not the issue," Tom replied. "They have the power to do so, and that is all that matters." He pushed back from the table. "I have said enough already, and have lost my appetite."

He left a few coins on the table for the food we'd never received—probably for the best, I told myself—and we returned to the churchyard. We saw Martha and Will from a distance, walking the cathedral grounds, arm in arm.

"Will has not said much of his life before coming to London," Tom said. "But he loves the two of you."

"Aye," I said. Will whispered in Martha's ear, and she threw her head back in laughter.

"What happened to the three of you?"

I looked up at Tom, wondering if this might be another test, but his eyes were open and guileless.

"When we were in York, Martha and I . . ." I paused for a moment. "We hurt Will very badly."

"The business with the witch hunts?"

"Aye," I said. "We had no choice, but Will did not see it that way. We left the city, and he stayed. Grievous wounds do not heal quickly."

When Martha leaned toward Will and bussed him on the cheek, Tom laughed. Once again my stomach wheeled in a circle. "They seem to have rediscovered each other," Tom said.

"Aye." Without thinking, I took Tom's arm in mine, and my

ears pinked at my own audacity. I did not dare look up to see his reaction, but at least he did not pull away.

As Will and Martha approached, Tom called out. "I'm sorry, Will. I have pressing business, and you must come with me."

Will nodded and turned to Martha to bid her farewell. I glanced at Tom, and found him gazing at me with the strangest expression. I looked away with the faint hope that my face did not redden too much.

After Will and Tom disappeared into the crowd, Martha turned to me, a smile on her face. "And how did you come to be holding his arm? You make a fair couple, you do."

"Oh, stop. I did nothing untoward." I knew that by now my neck was as red as my face. "Let us go home."

Martha and I started back to the Cheap.

"Will told me that they knew what happened at the Nag's Head," Martha said. "Colonel Reynolds was testing you."

"Aye," I replied. "I saw the trap just in time. I remembered Will's note and told him the truth."

"Thank God," Martha said. "I do not want to know what revenge Mr. Marlowe would seek if he thought we had betrayed him."

"Nor do I," I said.

We reached the Little Conduit, where those living on the west end of the Cheap came for water. When I arrived in London, I found the system of conduits to be nothing short of miraculous, as they carried water by pipes and troughs all the way from springs at Tyburn, north of the city wall. At nearly every hour of the day a crowd gathered there, waiting for a turn at the spigot and gossiping about the news of the town. So it was on this day, as a chapman stood on the street corner crying his wares.

"Tell me, good people," he called out. "Do I need to remind

you of the day? Surely you have not forgotten what anniversary this is?"

Martha and I glanced at each other. Neither of us had the faintest idea.

The chapman pulled a sheet from his pack and burst into song. His voice was so clear and pleasing, in a moment I found myself entirely in his thrall.

Full forty years ago it was, in sixteen hundred and five
When papists zealous for the Mass in England did contrive,
The King, and Queen, and Prince, and Lords, and every English knight,
With fire and powder, and a match, at a single blow to smite

I realized then that the chapman was singing of the Gunpowder Plot, when Guy Fawkes and his traitorous brethren had plotted to destroy the nation by blowing up Parliament while King James was inside. It was a story every English child knew: The plotters had rented a cellar beneath Parliament's meeting place, and then begun their nefarious work.

They laid their powder in this vault, full six and thirty barrels,
With one unheard-of deep assault, to end their former quarrels.

Luckily, Parliament's sergeant-at-arms discovered the plot.

The vault was searched by honest men, and then appeared quite plain,
The iron, stones, and gunpowder tubs, and all the powder-train.
At this hell-mouth, with triple match, a lantern in his hand,
Stood Guy Fawkes in dead of night, all comers to withstand.

Fawkes and his band were executed as traitors, of course, but the fear of a popish plot endured, a fact visible in the number of sheets the chapman sold once he had finished his song.

That evening I reflected on the plot, and began to see my work for Mr. Marlowe from his position. On that night in 1605, one man—the sergeant-at-arms—had prevented the destruction of both King and Parliament and captured the worst traitor in England's long history. What if the sergeant-at-arms had *not* visited the cellar, choosing instead to join his friends in an alehouse? What if he had decided to go home to his wife? In that instant, he would have condemned King and Parliament to be altogether destroyed, and God only knew what would have followed such a catastrophe. The Protestant cause had survived—indeed England herself had survived—because one man had done his job to the utmost of his ability.

Of course I did not think that Katherine Chidley could pose such a danger to the nation, but what of those around her? Tom had said that the Nag's Head mob were more talk than deed, but what of their comrades in the army? If, thanks to my neglect, they plunged the nation into civil war and anarchy, how would I excuse myself?

I resolved then to be more watchful around the Levellers, but I could not help feeling that the greater danger lay with the King's men. After all, it was they whom Parliament had defeated so recently, and it was they who swore they would die for their sovereign's sake.

As November turned to December, changes came over the city, and not merely the coming of winter. It turned out that Tom Reynolds had been right about the fate of the King, for just a few weeks before Christmas he was brought from the Isle of Wight to Hurst Castle in the south, where the army kept him under close guard until he could be brought to London. Upon this news, rumors and conspiracies raced through the city like a wind-driven fire, and nowhere did the flames burn hotter than at the Nag's Head.

There were, of course, the rumors that the King would be tried for treason, but there were plenty of others as well. Some claimed that Cromwell planned to put King Charles back on the throne, and then rule over him as if he were a child. Others hoped that the King might have been chastened by the late civil wars, and could be restored to the throne not as a tyrant but as a benevolent sovereign. Some of the wilder spirits in the Nag's Head conjured a more frightening possibility. They claimed that Cromwell so feared the Levellers that he would restore the King in order to pacify the Royalists, and then use his free hand to destroy the Levellers once and for all.

Each night I prayed that King and Parliament would find a way to resolve their dispute without shedding any more blood. The Lord, however, answered my prayers in the negative. According to the news-books that soon flooded the streets, Cromwell placed guards of the army on the stairs leading to the Commons House and seized all the moderate men from Parliament. These poor souls were carried to Queens Court, leaving behind only those who were hottest against King Charles. If Cromwell intended to restore the King, this was an unlikely crew to do the work. From that day forward, the talk against the King became ever more violent. Preachers shouted that his word could not be trusted, and that any man who spoke in His Majesty's favor was a traitor to England. I wondered at a world in which men who did nothing more than defend their sovereign could be called traitors.

The strangest thing was that even as the kingdom stumbled

toward anarchy, my life in the Cheap had never been better. My reputation and Martha's spread even beyond our neighborhood as more and more women in the city invited us to deliver them. Soon we were busier than we'd ever been in York. I wrote to Elizabeth at every opportunity, but with each passing week my promises that I soon would return rang more hollow. What good is 'soon' if that day never comes? To my relief, Elizabeth continued to send letters to me, and her anger was gradually replaced by a surliness that I entirely understood. I realized that in order for me to be a true mother to Elizabeth, either she would have to come to London or I would have to find my way back to Pontrilas. I hoped that once the King's fate was settled, one of these might come to pass.

Early that winter, one final change came over our household when it became clear that Martha was no longer my deputy, but my comrade. A woman named Mary Moffat signaled the change when she came to our home and, in my presence, asked *Martha* to attend her in her travail.

Martha fumbled for an answer before stammering out her acceptance. After Mary had gone, Martha turned to me, her eyes as wide as I'd ever seen them.

"It seems you've been my deputy long enough," I said. "Now you are a midwife. Congratulations and well done!"

Martha burst into a mixture of laughter and tears as we embraced. I thought back to the moment when, many years before, I had had the same experience. Becoming a midwife was an awesome and terrifying charge, and Martha would remember that day for the rest of her life.

And so, our little piece of Watling Street became known as Midwife's Row, for within just a few steps you could find three of us: Katherine Chidley, me, and now Martha. And the three of us became closer gossips as a result, calling each other for advice and relief in difficult or prolonged labors, and sending mothers to one another when we were overburdened by births, baptisms, and churchings.

As we traveled around the Cheap on the business of midwifery, we noticed the neighborhood's women had become no less fascinated by politics than the men had. Indeed, gossips now asked each other questions usually heard only in the halls of Parliament: What would Cromwell do with the King? If he were tried, who would sit in judgment? If he were restored, how would it be managed? Rumors and gossip changed hands faster than a well-clipped coin.

At least that was the case until January ninth—a cold day it was—when all these matters came to a head. Martha and I were walking past the Little Conduit when four ranks of trumpeters surrounded by a company of pikemen marched into Cheapside Street. Blaring horns announced the arrival of Parliament's sergeant-at-arms. Within minutes the crowd around the soldiers had grown to the hundreds, if not thousands.

When the sergeant thought the crowd large enough, he climbed atop a pulpit of sorts, produced a sheet of paper, and began to read.

"By order of the Parliament of England." His voice boomed as the crowd fell silent. "It is notorious that Charles Stuart, now King of England, has endeavored to destroy the ancient liberties of this nation, and to introduce a tyrannical government in their place. He has prosecuted this malicious design with fire and sword, and traitorously made war against his own subjects. The country has been wasted, the treasury exhausted, thousands of people murdered. All of this has been done in the name of the King."

The people stood in silence as the sergeant took a breath.

"The present Parliament hoped that the King's imprisonment might quiet the tumult that has so gripped this nation. Instead, their mercy served only to encourage the said Charles Stuart in his evil schemes, as he has raised both rebellions and invasions."

My chest constricted as I realized what could be the only conclusion of this speech.

"It has thus been ordered that the said Charles Stuart be tried before a High Court of Justice for the crime of treason."

I held my breath and waited for the crowd's reaction.

Chapter 11

Even as the sergeant finished his pronouncement, the crowd began to shout. It quickly became clear that the Cheap was no less divided than the rest of England. Cries of "Shame, shame!" and "Long live good King Charles!" vied with "God be praised!" and "Amen, amen!"

As Martha and I fled the tumult, I remembered Tom's observation that no matter how many times Parliament's armies defeated the King, he would remain King. And if Charles won but once, all his enemies would be hanged. If these propositions were true—and who could deny them?—how could our wars end with anything other than trials and executions? The only question was which party would do the beheading.

That night, Martha and I resorted to the Nag's Head, eager to hear how the news of the King's trial had been received. I assumed the Levellers would rejoice at the prospect, for it seemed to me that the King's death would bring their hopes for a new England that much closer. By the time we arrived at the tavern, the discussion—or to be more precise, the argument—had already begun. Katherine Chidley sat at a table on the far side of the room, and we crossed to join her. The main dispute was, naturally enough, over the fate of the King. Some argued that the King's mendacity—not to mention his decision to raise an army of barbarous Scots—had left Parliament with no options other than a trial and execution. Others, including Daniel Chidley, took a more difficult position.

"There is no question that the King is an evil man." Daniel's voice rang out clear and loud despite the general hubbub. He was a tall, handsome man, and when he spoke every ear in the tavern belonged to him. I could see why Katherine had married him, for the two were well matched. "And I would not deny that a true Parliament could try him for any crime it saw fit. But this is *not* a true Parliament. A true Parliament would be selected by all Englishmen. This Parliament—or *rump* of a Parliament, I should say—is made up entirely of Cromwell's creatures."

Many heads nodded in agreement, though a few seemed less pleased at Daniel's words. I looked more closely at Daniel and wondered if he might be so fervent as to rebel against Cromwell.

Daniel continued, "Oliver Cromwell would reduce us all to mere servants, quaking before the power of the sword. With Cromwell as our sole sovereign, England would become a place where the strong rule over the weak and none of us is truly free. Mark my words: If the King is tried by this unlawful Parliament, *all* of England will be reduced to a state of slavery. And we will be the architects of our own servitude."

"What then would you propose?" The challenge came from the tapster who stood behind the bar. From the lines on his face I put his age around fifty years, but a lifetime of lifting and tapping barrels of ale had left him well muscled, and every bit as strong as the youths who frequented the Nag's Head. "The King has left us no option other than to try him. If we do not, he will cobble together an army of papists—whether French or Irish, it matters not—and return England to the slaughter of the civil wars."

I leaned to Katherine and said into her ear, "Who is he?"

"Jeremiah Goodkey," Katherine replied. "He owns the Nag's Head, and is as fiery a soul as you'll find in all London. I will answer him."

To my surprise, Katherine climbed onto our table and raised her hands for quiet. "Jeremiah Goodkey, you are my friend, but in this matter you are wrong. If we are to try the King, we must have a true Parliament, a Parliament that has been elected by *all* Englishmen, no matter their wealth." She paused, waiting until the cheers and hisses faded into quiet. Then she said, "And it must also be elected by all Englishwomen, no matter *their* wealth."

For a time it seemed as if Katherine's words had begun the revolt that Mr. Marlowe so feared, for in their wake no mouth remained closed. Every soul in the tavern cried out either for or against the idea of allowing women to vote, and a few men appeared ready to cross the line from arguing to fighting. A smile flitted across Katherine's lips as she ducked a chicken leg that someone hurled in her direction, and she made for the street. I followed her with Martha close behind.

"You knew the trouble your words would cause," I cried when we were outside. "Why would you say such a thing?" She was already laughing, and I joined with her.

"I said it because I believe it, and because it is true," she said. "The Lord's prophets do not always receive a warm welcome. And they invariably bring trouble with them."

"Do you truly believe this?" Martha asked. "That women should vote?" I could hear the wonder in her voice at such a prospect.

"Of course I do," Katherine answered. "Else I would not have said it."

"But look at the trouble you have caused," I objected. "How can that be for the good? Who would allow such an idea to come to pass if it causes such divisions?"

"Nobody would," Katherine replied. "And nobody would be more surprised than me if women *were* allowed to vote. But I spoke the Lord's truth, and now everyone in the tavern is discussing the matter. Sometimes making trouble is all you can do. And sometimes making trouble is enough." She peered through the tavern window. "Things have calmed a bit. I should go back in." Katherine bid us farewell and ducked back through the door.

I shook my head. "I think I've heard enough for tonight," I said. "Let's go home."

As Martha and I neared Cheapside Street, a handful of the City Watch passed us, headed toward the Nag's Head. I wondered if the arguments at the tavern had over-boiled their pot and turned to violence.

"Will you tell Mr. Marlowe about the unrest Katherine caused?" Martha asked.

"I was wondering the same thing," I said. "I don't want to cause trouble for her, but what happens if we lie and Mr. Marlowe finds out?" I considered the question as we passed St. Mary-le-Bow and turned south on Bread Street, nearly home. How familiar the Cheap had become! Just a few months before it had seemed a maze without end, and now I could navigate its streets even in the dark. The confusion of the streets gave me my answer.

"Are you sure of what you heard at the Nag's Head?" I asked.

"What do you mean?"

"I know that Katherine spoke, but with so many in the tavern, and so much noise, I could hardly hear a thing. Indeed, with so much shouting, I cannot say for sure who started the tumult."

"Aye," Martha said. "With so many voices raised in anger, it could have been anyone."

That night I wrote a confused letter to Mr. Marlowe, describing the arguments we heard and noting the disagreement between Daniel Chidley and Jeremiah Goodkey. I mentioned that Katherine stood to speak, but said there'd been so much shouting I could not hear her words. When I finished the letter, I joined Martha in our bed. She was still awake.

"What do you make of it all?" she asked.

"Of the trial of the King?" I asked. "Or of giving every Englishman the right to vote, no matter their worth? Or of Katherine's mad plan to let women vote as well?"

"All of it."

I considered the question for a time before answering. "I do not know. I am not blind to the injustices that plague England, but I cannot countenance turning the world entirely upside down in the hope that anarchy is superior to tyranny." I thought for a moment more. "But in the end it does not matter what you or I think, for matters of state do not lie in our hands. We are sailors on a storm-tossed ship, not the captains. We must do our duty as best we can, but in the end we are at the mercy of others."

"And you are content as a common sailor?" Martha asked.

"We have done our part," I replied. "In York we saved Esther Wallington from an unjust execution and saw murderers hanged for their crimes. And do not forget the fate that awaited Grace Ramsden if we had not been here to help. A ship cannot survive a storm without her sailors. We must do our best and hope that our captains can guide our craft to a safe harbor."

But the next morning it became clear that our safe harbor

would prove elusive. Martha and I had just finished cleaning our rooms when one of Katherine Chidley's maidservants pounded up the stairs and burst through the door.

"Mrs. Hodgson, please help," she cried out. "Mrs. Chidley needs you. Her husband has been murdered!"

Martha and I hurled ourselves down the stairs and across the street to the Chidleys' shop. The room was filled with cloth waiting to be cut and sewn into coats for the New Model Army, but on this day no work was being done. We found Katherine by herself, gazing at Daniel's lifeless body. Despite the hours we'd spent together, Katherine had never said much about Daniel or their marriage, but the pure anguish on her face made clear that his death had hollowed her to the marrow.

Daniel's body lay propped against the wall, his eyes staring at the front door, as if he were awaiting a visitor—or watching his murderer leave. His coat was unbuttoned, revealing a linen shirt, unmarked except for a small hole and the circle of blood that had seeped into the fabric. A thin crimson line ran downward from the hole. He must have died quickly to have bled so little.

I went to Katherine and put my arm around her shoulders. She said nothing, but she leaned into me, accepting the support I offered. Martha crossed the room and knelt next to Daniel's body. We had examined bodies under such circumstances before, and Martha had proved most acute in her observations. If Daniel's murderer had left behind any sign of his identity, Martha would find it. She lifted his coat and carefully pulled back his shirt so she could see the wound in his chest. She then examined his hands and fingernails, looking for skin or blood. Finally, she lifted his chin, so she could see his neck. She thought for a moment, nodded, and stood.

At that moment the door flew open and the constable burst into the shop. He was followed by a small army of beadles and, finally, the Chidleys' maidservant. When the constable saw Daniel's body the blood ran from his face, and I worried he might faint. He looked around the room in a panic, as if the murderer might be lying in wait. When his eyes settled on Katherine, they narrowed, and he strode across the room.

"You've done it, haven't you, you harridan," he hissed at Katherine. "You've finally gotten that rebellion you've wanted for so long. Wasn't taking the King enough? You had to overthrow your own husband?"

I was about to intervene, but I did not get the chance, for Martha was having none of his nonsense, either.

"You cannot be serious," she cried, stepping between Katherine and the constable.

The constable started to speak, but Martha was not yet done.

"Take Mrs. Chidley to her chamber," she said to the maidservant. "She does not need to hear any of this."

To her credit, the girl did not even glance in the constable's direction, but came straight to her mistress. Katherine nodded absently and accompanied her servant up the stairs.

Martha turned back to the constable.

"How was Mr. Chidley killed?" she demanded.

"He was stabbed," the constable replied scornfully. "The worst of fools can see that."

"Correct on both counts," Martha replied. "He *was* stabbed, and we now know that the worst of fools *can* see it. But *how* was he stabbed?"

"What do you mean?" he asked. "In the chest? With a knife?"

I could see Martha battling the urge to throttle the constable. "Look at Mr. Chidley, and imagine how it happened."

"She stabbed him," the constable replied. I admired Martha for not punching him in the throat.

"Yes, you said that already. But if that is true, *how* did she do it?" She took piece of kindling from beside the hearth and handed it to the constable. "Stab me as Mrs. Chidley stabbed Mr. Chidley."

"I will do no such thing." The constable was more offended by Martha's impertinence than the dead body before him.

"Do what she says," I said. "Or the Justice will hear of it." It was an empty threat—what sway did I have over a Justice of the Peace?—but it worked well enough.

"But—"

"Mr. Chidley has been murdered, and the girl is trying to help. Do what she says."

"Very well." The constable turned to Martha and pretended to stab her in the chest.

Martha cried out and fell back, her arms flailing. After a moment she settled against the wall next to Daniel.

"There," the constable said. "Just as I told you."

"Why, then, is the shop in perfect order?" she asked. "Why has no cloth been knocked to the floor? Do you see blood anywhere except on his body?"

The constable looked around the room and shook his head.

"Then by your account, after Mr. Chidley was stabbed, he did not fight back, nor did he call for help. Rather he sat down and waited to die."

"Mrs. Chidley held him down," he replied weakly. I did not think he believed his own words.

"A woman as small as Mrs. Chidley held down her own husband while he died? All without getting a spot of blood on her, or alerting her maidservant?"

The constable looked as if he were coming down with a winter fever.

"Look at his neck," Martha said.

The constable knelt next to Daniel's body and lifted his chin as Martha had done. He stared at Daniel's neck for a few moments before standing. "His neck is marked."

"Aye, but how?"

"There are marks in the shape of fingers and a thumb," the constable muttered. "Someone held him by the throat."

"And that is why he died so quietly," Martha said. "The murderer seized Mr. Chidley's neck, stabbed him, and then held him against the wall while he died. He didn't even pull out the blade until Mr. Chidley was dead. That's why he bled so little."

"At the moment he died, Daniel was looking into his killer's eyes," I said to myself.

"Now tell me, constable," Martha continued, "do you think Mrs. Chidley is strong enough to have held Mr. Chidley by the throat, stabbed him in the chest, and kept her grip for all the time it took him die? And is she cold enough to stare into her own husband's face, even as he breathed his last?"

For a time nobody spoke.

"Perhaps you should summon the coroner and a Justice of the Peace," I murmured. "Let men above your rank concern themselves with this matter."

Relief filled the constable's eyes. He nodded to one of the beadles, who dashed off in search of help.

Within minutes more men had come to see Daniel's body, and women had come to console Katherine. Martha and I went upstairs, but Katherine was so numbed with grief that she could not hear the words of comfort that we offered. We stayed with her until nightfall and beyond, directing her other gossips and ensuring the house stayed in order. Eventually Katherine slept, and only then did Martha and I return home.

"Light a candle," I said to Martha as soon as the door closed behind us. "We must notify Mr. Marlowe of what has happened."

Martha and I spent nearly an hour crafting our letter, including every detail we could recall, from the bruises on Daniel's neck to the single wound in his chest, to the curious state of his shop. As soon as the sun rose, Martha and I delivered the letter to the Horned Bull only to find that neither Will nor Tom—how quickly I had started thinking of him as Tom—was there.

"You never know with those two," the innkeeper's wife chirped. "Sometimes they're gone for days at a time. Never say where they went. But don't think I don't ask. What is your business with them?"

Martha and I exchanged a glance. Leaving our letter with this woman would be no different than having it shouted from every pulpit in London. In the end we settled for leaving a more cryptic note, telling Will and Tom that we had important news, and that they should come to the Cheap as soon as they could.

In the days that followed, the Cheap buzzed incessantly with news of two kinds. There was Daniel's murder, of course, and the futile search for his killer. When people tired of that matter, they turned to Parliament's plan to try King Charles for treason. Curiously enough, neither Will nor Tom responded to our note, or any of the others we sent in its wake. I even went so far as to send a letter to Mr. Marlowe at the Tower, but it, too, was ignored. With nothing else to do, Martha and I concerned ourselves with life rather than death. We had our own clients, and we also took upon ourselves the care of Katherine's mothers while she grieved for Daniel.

On January twentieth, the very day the King's trial was to

begin, Martha was called to a travail, and I took advantage of my leisure to shop for a new dress. It would be wool rather than silk, of course, but I had determined to buy a more luxurious weave. As I returned home, Tom Reynolds fell into step beside me, but he gave no outward sign that he knew who I was.

"Follow me," he murmured. He passed the Evelyns' door and led me south on Bread Street toward Pissing Alley. We entered the Horned Bull, where he and Will were staying, and found a candlelit table at the back of the dining room.

"Where is Will?" I asked. "Why didn't you send him?"

"He is still away on business for Mr. Marlowe." A smile flitted across Tom's lips. "And speaking with you is not the most onerous of my duties."

I suddenly became aware of my heartbeat and hoped that the flickering light would not show the blood that had rushed to my face. "I have news," I said. "Daniel Chidley has been murdered."

"We know," Tom said. "That is why I sought you out."

"But there is much you do not know." I told him everything that Martha and I had seen on that dreadful day.

"Yes," Tom said. "Well done."

I looked at him for a moment. There was something strange in his manner. "You knew all that," I said. "You knew about the bruises, the single wound to his chest . . . all of it."

Tom smiled and shrugged. "We have many eyes in the Cheap. And that, in fact, is why I am here."

"What do you mean?" I asked.

"Mr. Marlowe was unhappy to learn of Daniel Chidley's murder."

"Unhappy?" I asked. "Daniel was as turbulent a Leveller as you'd find in London. I should have thought that Mr. Marlowe would welcome his death."

"If it had been any other Leveller, he might have," Tom replied. "But Daniel Chidley was one of Mr. Marlowe's spies."

I stared at Tom, trying to make sense of this news.

"Why would Daniel do such a thing? He lived and breathed for the Leveller cause. And why would Mr. Marlowe ask me to spy on Daniel Chidley, if Daniel was already in his employ?"

Tom laughed. "When it comes to his spies, Mr. Marlowe is nothing if not thorough. He wanted to be sure he could trust Daniel."

I remembered then that someone had spied on Martha and me on the night Daniel spoke at the Nag's Head. It must have been Daniel himself. I shook my head in wonder at the webs Mr. Marlowe wove. "Why would Daniel have agreed to be Mr. Marlowe's spy?"

"He didn't have a choice," Tom replied.

I thought for a moment and realized what must have happened. "Their son," I said. "Mr. Marlowe threatened their son in the same way he threatened Will."

"Aye," Tom said. "Their boy is in the New Model Army, and he is no less vulnerable than Will was when he was in the Tower. A parent's love is a powerful weapon."

"What threat did Mr. Marlowe make?" I asked.

Tom shrugged. "I never asked. It doesn't matter."

"No, I suppose not. Mr. Marlowe is a hateful man."

"He is effective, and in these times that is all that matters," Tom said. "It is also true that when recruiting spies Mr. Marlowe favors bribes more than threats. You and Daniel were exceptions."

"Did Katherine know that Daniel was a spy?"

"Not unless he told her. Nobody knew except Mr. Marlowe and me. At least that is what we thought."

"You think someone discovered Daniel was Mr. Marlowe's spy and killed him for it," I said.

"It would be dangerous to assume otherwise. On the day he was killed, Daniel sent me a message saying he had urgent news. We were to meet that evening. He never showed."

"That cannot be mere chance," I said.

Tom shook his head. "Someone knew about Daniel's work, and killed him for it."

"The Levellers would not be pleased to learn of Daniel's duplicity. Do you think he was killed for betraying their cause?"

"It is possible. It might also have been a Royalist who hated the democracy he preached. Daniel had no shortage of enemies."

"If someone discovered Daniel was in Mr. Marlowe's service, they might know I am as well," I said. "Did Mr. Marlowe send you to warn me of the danger?"

"I wish that were so," Tom said with a rueful smile. "But Mr. Marlowe is not so tenderhearted as that. He wants you to find Daniel Chidley's killer."

Chapter 12

I stared at Tom for a moment, struck dumb by Mr. Marlowe's audacity. "Oliver Cromwell's chief intelligencer wants *me* to find the man who killed *his* spy?" I asked. "Surely he can do such a thing himself."

Tom laughed kindly at my outrage and took my hand. A shiver dashed up my spine and back down again.

"He can't do it himself," Tom said. "An intelligencer is only as good as his spies, and Mr. Marlowe counts you as one of his. This *is* why he brought you to London."

I tried to follow Tom's words, but I found myself unable to think of anything except the fact that he still held my hand. I pulled it away so I could recover myself.

"And he has nobody else?" I asked.

"Nobody better suited to the work. Not only do you live across the street from the Chidleys, but you have more experience in such matters than anyone else in his employ. He would be a fool *not* to put this task in your hands, and, hard as he is, Mr. Marlowe is no fool."

I sat in silence considering the challenge before me. As much as I hated Marlowe and his methods, I could not forget Katherine Chidley's grief. How could I call myself her gossip if I did not do this for her? I thought then of the ease with which the murderer had killed Daniel, and of how lucky I'd been to survive my last encounter with so dangerous a man.

"Whoever killed Daniel will not hesitate to kill again," I said.

"Aye," Tom said, his face serious. "And it appears that he is very good at killing. Daniel Chidley never had a chance."

"But I cannot say no," I said.

"No, you cannot," he replied. "When it comes to Mr. Marlowe, there is only *yes*."

"Very well," I said. "Is there anything else he would have me do?"

"No, just the one murderer to catch," he said.

I laughed despite myself.

"But I can offer you some help in this matter." Tom reached into his bag and produced an envelope not unlike the one he'd given me in the Tower. "There are some people who seem more likely than others to have had a hand in Daniel Chidley's death. I have a list here, and details of what we know about them. Where you start is your business, but you should be aware of these men."

"I'll not give you my thanks, but I do appreciate the courtesy." I smiled slightly as I took the packet.

"There is one more thing," Tom said. "It is possible that you can put Daniel's work for Mr. Marlowe to your advantage."

"What do you mean?"

"If you think revealing his betrayal would help, you may do so."

"Mr. Marlowe approved this?"

Tom laughed. "It was his idea. When word gets out that Daniel was Cromwell's spy, the Levellers will wonder who else might have betrayed their cause. If they do not trust each other, they will have a devil of a time planning a rebellion."

"Very well," I said.

We stood, and Tom stepped forward to take my hand. I looked around and saw that we had the room to ourselves. "I am sorry for my part in this bloody business," he said. "You are a good woman and deserve better."

Although I knew what Tom intended to do even before he leaned toward me, his kiss somehow caught me unawares. By the time our lips parted, I could hardly breathe and felt as if I was coming down with a fever.

Martha was still out when I returned to our tenement. I took advantage of these few moments of quiet to write a letter to Elizabeth, and then I began to read the papers Tom had given me. As I finished, I heard Martha climbing the stairs. When she opened the door, all I could think about was the kiss I'd shared with Tom, for I felt quite sure that Martha would take one look at my face and know exactly what had happened. Indeed, the merest thought of that kiss caused my cheeks to turn pink and my heart to pound as if I'd just run home from the Horned Bull.

To my relief, Martha was full of gossip and good cheer, completely unaware that I'd just kissed a man for the first time since . . . my God, how long had it been? Nearly a decade?

By the time Martha had talked herself out, I thought I would be able to keep the news to myself. With forced lightness I told her that I had met with Colonel Reynolds.

"What, is he still not convinced that we are faith-worthy?" she asked. "Or did he come here to court you?"

I knew from her voice that Martha spoke in jest, but my face flushed all the same. Of course she noticed.

"What?" she cried. "He came to court you?" Her face was the very picture of devilish glee.

"Will you hush!" I cried. "Remember how thin the walls are. If any of our neighbors or—heaven forbid—Mrs. Evelyn finds out, it will be all over the Cheap by nightfall."

"Very well." Martha lowered her voice but could not stop smiling. "Where were you? Tell me what happened."

"We went to the Horned Bull—" I started.

"I imagine you did," Martha said before she burst out laughing.

"Martha!"

"Yes, yes, I'm sorry. You were at the Horned Bull. Go on."

"We talked of Daniel Chidley's murder, and then . . . he kissed me, or rather we kissed each other."

Martha stared at me. "The two of you talked of Daniel Chidley's murder, and then you fell to bussing each other. He certainly knows how to court a woman."

"Do not forget that you and Will first came together over a corpse," I said. "Indeed, much of his wooing took place as the three of us searched for murderers."

Martha laughed again. "A fair point. And what did Colonel Reynolds have to say about Daniel Chidley?"

"Mr. Marlowe wants us to find Daniel Chidley's murderer," I said.

Martha furrowed her brow. "Why does he want us to do that?" she asked. "Does he intend to thank the killer in person?"

"Not that," I said. "Daniel was in Mr. Marlowe's service. He was spying on the Levellers."

Martha sat abruptly, no less surprised at the news than I had been. It only took a few moments for her to recognize the implications of this information. "If Daniel was a spy against the Levellers, and the Levellers discovered his treachery . . ."

"Aye," I said. "The murderer could be one of the Levellers, or he could be one of the King's men. In their eyes, Daniel was a rebel whether he belonged to the Levellers or to Cromwell."

"Who knew he was a spy for Mr. Marlowe?"

"According to Colonel Reynolds, only him and Mr. Marlowe. He must have been discovered by chance."

Martha thought for a moment. "What if Mr. Marlowe was too secretive?"

"What do you mean?" I asked.

"Marlowe kept Daniel Chidley's work so secret that everyone else in London saw him as a voice against Parliament and in favor of anarchy."

"True enough," I said. "That is what *we* thought."

"What if a Parliament man grew tired of Daniel's factious nature and killed him?"

"You are suggesting that one of Cromwell's men might have unknowingly murdered Cromwell's own spy?" My head spun at the thought.

"We must consider it," Martha said. "Daniel could have been killed by any man in London!"

"Perhaps so," I said. "But Colonel Reynolds provided us a place to start." I held up the letters that Tom had given me. Martha and I spent over an hour reading through them together. As we read, I realized they contained a miniature of England's civil wars, for even if we ignored Martha's wilder ideas, every faction had a reason to kill Daniel Chidley.

"Jeremiah Goodkey," Martha read aloud. "Isn't he the owner of the Nag's Head?"

"Aye, he's old enough, but he can hoist a new keg of ale as if it's empty." The letter told us that like so many in the Leveller faction, Goodkey had fought in the wars on Parliament's side. According to Mr. Marlowe's notes, Goodkey was *a man of a noxious and rebellious spirit, bent on overturning all order, all at once. He favors nothing so much as anarchy in both church and state.*

"Of course, the King's men would say the same thing of Cromwell," Martha noted drily.

"Speaking of the King's men, there's Charles Owen," I said. "According to Mr. Marlowe's notes, he's no less dangerous than Goodkey. The only difference is that he favors the King."

Like Goodkey, Owen was a tavern-keeper, owning a house called the Crown, which lay south of the Cheap not far from the Thames. The King's men had been using the Crown as a meeting place for many years, and Royalist newssheets were freely available there. According to Tom's notes, a handful of plots had been hatched in the Crown, and Mr. Marlowe had come within a hairsbreadth of closing it down and arresting Owen as a traitor.

"If the Crown is such a nest of vipers, why would Mr. Marlowe allow it to remain open?" Martha asked. "Surely he could have arrested Owen, nailed the door shut, and been done with it."

I turned the page and continued to read. "It was kept open at Colonel Reynolds's behest," I said. "He convinced Mr. Marlowe to watch rather than act. *Better to keep the King's men in the light where we can see them than to chase such rebels into the shadows where they may be lost.*"

"He may regret that decision," Martha noted. "And what about Katherine Chidley?"

"What do you mean?" I asked.

"I think we must revisit the question of her guilt."

I gazed at Martha, my mouth hanging open. "Revisit her

guilt?" I cried. "You convinced the constable of her innocence! You saw her sorrow at Daniel's death."

"I have also seen her passion," Martha replied. "And who would be more likely to discover his treachery than his own wife? If Katherine discovered that Daniel was a spy for Cromwell, she might have killed him to protect herself and the Leveller cause."

I hated the idea that Katherine might be guilty, but I could not dismiss it out of hand. If Katherine realized that Daniel had betrayed her, her fury could have boiled over into murder.

"What about the bruises on Daniel's neck?" I asked. "She is too small to do that, no matter how angry she became. You said so yourself."

"Perhaps she told Jeremiah Goodkey of Daniel's treachery," Martha replied. "She let him into the shop, put Daniel at ease, and then Goodkey plunged the knife into his chest."

"It is possible," I admitted. "But right now we have nothing but blind suspicion. We will start with Goodkey and Owen, and work our way outward from them." I knew it might be a mistake to ignore Katherine at the outset, but she was a friend, and I would not allow myself to nurse such suspicions until we had some sign of her guilt.

That afternoon, Katherine's maidservant, the same one who had summoned us to view Daniel's body, appeared at our door. Mrs. Chidley had invited us to dinner. We agreed, of course, and accompanied the maid across the street. On that day, winter had resolved to show its strength, and even the short walk chilled us to the marrow. I wondered if the Thames ever froze the way the river Ouse had in York.

As we passed through the shop—now empty of the journeymen the Chidleys employed to sew cloth into coats—my eyes were drawn to the spot where we'd found Daniel's body. There was no sign of what had happened, of course, and it seemed as if the world had forgotten about him entirely.

We found Katherine in her parlor, talking with a man whom I'd seen coming and going but had never met.

The man rose when we entered, and Katherine introduced him as Abraham Walker.

"He was Daniel's friend," she said. "We have been in business together for many years. He supplies us with cloth. Abraham, this is Widow Hodgson and Martha Hawkins; they are midwives come of late to the Cheap."

Walker offered a warm and easy smile as he greeted us. Despite his rich clothes—he'd clearly done well for himself in the cloth trade—he was a bland and colorless man, neither so handsome that you'd want to remember him nor so ugly that you'd want to forget. I put his age around fifty, but he still retained a good measure of youthful vigor.

"I came to see Mrs. Chidley as soon as I heard about Daniel's death," he said. "I would have arrived sooner, but I was called to York on business."

The reminder of my exile from my adopted city was an unwelcome surprise, and for a moment I wondered if Walker had wandered past my house or dined with any of my friends who also were in the cloth trade. I could not ask, of course, and in truth it did not matter. I would return to York when the Lord Mayor died, but until that day I preferred not to think about it.

"I was just telling Mrs. Chidley of my visit today to the Justice of the Peace and the coroner," Mr. Walker said. "She asked me to discover what they've learned about Daniel's death. But she wanted you two to be here as well."

Martha and I looked at Walker in anticipation. "What have they found?" I asked.

"Nothing at all," he said. "They dressed it up in finer language than that, of course, but in the end they had to admit that they have no idea who killed Mr. Chidley."

I was not surprised, of course. The Justice of the Peace did not know of Daniel's spy-craft, so he would never even look to men like Goodkey or Owen.

The four of us talked for a bit more, but Walker said nothing of consequence. The one question I had—but could not ask in his presence—was why Katherine had wanted us to hear his report. As soon as he had gone, Katherine closed the door behind him.

"I am glad you are here." Her eyes shone as she spoke. "I must speak to you about Daniel's death."

Before Katherine could tell us why, her maidservant slipped into the room and announced that dinner was ready.

"Good," Katherine said. "I hope you will join me. It will be a fine meal."

We did, of course, and were well rewarded for our trouble, as roasted meats and fresh bread filled our bellies, and red wine warmed our blood. After we'd finished, Katherine dismissed her maidservant and returned to the subject of her husband's murder.

"I know I have not yet finished grieving for Daniel," she said. "But I will not let sorrow keep me from action. I intend to find Daniel's killer."

"What, by yourself?" The words escaped my lips before I could soften them. Katherine did not notice my rudeness, or at least she did not mind.

"The law has little interest in the matter," she replied. "That is clear enough. The magistrates saw Daniel as nothing but a seditionist and provocator, and consider themselves well shut of him. None will say it to my face, of course, but the men charged with finding Daniel's murderer consider his death to be a gift from God." She spat the words as if they were poison.

"Surely not," I replied, but without much certainty.

"If you don't believe me, you know neither my husband nor London's governors," she said. "If I want justice, I will have to take it for myself. You are not such a stranger to the world to think otherwise, are you?"

I thought of my last days in York and the terrible things I'd done—things I'd *had* to do—in my own search for justice.

Katherine read my face. "I've not known you long, but I know you well, Bridget Hodgson. And I know we are of the same mind. You've seen how the wealthy and the powerful use the law as a weapon; you've cursed the unjustness of their laws. And you've done what you could to put things right, no matter what the letter of the law said."

"Aye," I said. "I have."

"Why did you bring us here?" Martha asked. "What have we to do with your search for Mr. Chidley's killer?"

"Daniel was a difficult man," she said, "and one who did not shy away from an argument if he thought he was in the right. No matter what the controversy was, or how powerful his opponent might be, he took a stand and would not abandon it no matter what came to pass."

"So he had many political enemies," I said.

Katherine shook her head. "That is what the constable and Justices might say, but there is many a mile between an argument at the Nag's Head and murder." Katherine paused. "No, Daniel was killed over another matter, something more urgent than the shape of some future government."

"But what could it be?" I knew the answer, of course—his work for Mr. Marlowe—and at that moment my question felt like a lie, for I pretended ignorance of a fact that could help her find Daniel's killer. My unease at betraying Katherine nipped at me yet again, but I knew that such little pains would be nothing compared to those I would feel if I crossed Mr. Marlowe.

"I do not know why someone would kill Daniel," Katherine replied. "But discovering the answer to that question is the first step in finding his murderer. And I should like you both to help me do it."

I stared at Katherine, unable to find my tongue.

"I know it is a great deal to ask," Katherine continued. "But I must have justice for Daniel's death. And justice demands that his murderer be hanged, as surely as it demanded Grace Ramsden's release. But I cannot do this alone."

"It is one thing to see an innocent woman set free," I said, "but another to see a guilty man hanged. What is more, in Grace Ramsden's case, there *was* no murderer. If we set out in search of Daniel's killer, we could find ourselves in grave danger."

"I know," Katherine said. "This is why I will not accept your answer until tomorrow. You must make the decision on your own."

I nodded my thanks, and after saying our good-byes Martha and I returned to our rooms, once again ducking our heads against the cold north wind as we crossed the street.

"This is more than passing strange," Martha said once we were inside. We had pulled chairs closer to the hearth and huddled over the fire as it grudgingly warmed the room.

"To be asked by two different people to solve the same murder?" I said. "Passing strange, indeed."

"We shall have to tread carefully," Martha said.

"Aye, we will," I replied. "Do you still think that Katherine might have had a hand in Daniel's death?"

"It would take an audacious woman to murder her husband

and then announce her intention to find the killer," she replied. "But she is nothing if not audacious."

"But you are agreed that we will accept her request," I said.

"Aye," Martha said. "But I cannot help feeling that we have wandered into a new and dangerous land."

"That we have," I replied. "And it is home to all manner of beasts and savages. Let us hope we are able find Daniel's murderer and return again."

The next morning, Martha and I crossed the street to tell Katherine we would help her find Daniel's killer. We found her in the shop, inspecting the stitching on a pile of coats and reprimanding a journeyman for poor workmanship. The journeyman—a strapping lad who stood a full head taller than Katherine—was on the edge of tears.

When Katherine had finished, she turned to us. "You will help?" she asked.

"Aye," I said. "If a gossip will not help you solve a murder, what use is she?"

"Good," Katherine said. "Come upstairs and we'll talk."

Chapter 13

Once we settled in Katherine's parlor, we turned to the mystery of Daniel's murderer. "I assume you've thought about who might have wanted to kill him," I said.

"Aye," Katherine replied. "But as I told you, nobody comes to mind. An argument over politics does not turn easily to violence."

I considered pointing out that the English nation had just fought a war in order to bring down a tyrant: What was that but a long and bloody argument over politics? Martha spoke up before I could press my point.

"Have you looked through your husband's papers?" she asked. "Perhaps they contain some hint of what happened to him. A threatening letter, a business dispute, or some other secret."

Katherine looked at Martha, her eyes flashing. "Some other secret?" she asked. "Say what you mean, Martha Hawkins." Katherine's voice had a dangerous edge to it, and I hoped that Martha would be careful in her choice of words.

Martha was startled by the vehemence of Katherine's reaction but recovered herself quickly. "All men are sinners, and subject to temptation," she said. "Mr. Chidley would not be the first man to fall victim to his base nature, and if he did, there is no telling what might have followed."

Katherine thought for a moment and then stood. "You are right. I cannot let my love for Daniel blind me to the truth, however ugly it may be. I will take you to his office."

Martha and I followed Katherine up a flight of stairs to a room overlooking Watling Street. Daniel Chidley's shelves held all manner of books, and the desk was covered with stacks of carefully organized papers as well as a mix of notebooks and ledgers. Presumably these were where Daniel recorded cloth coming in and coats going out.

Katherine turned to us. "I snapped at you when you suggested that Daniel might have kept secrets from me. But before we start, you must promise me one thing. If you find that Daniel did indeed fall into sin, you must follow that sin wherever it took him. I do not want your love for me to keep you from the truth, however hurtful it might be."

"We promise," I said. "Now let us begin."

The three of us went to work, first leafing through Daniel's printed books. They were a mix of Leveller books—some long, some short—and religious works. If his reading was any guide, Daniel was violently opposed not just to the King but to the bishops as well. He favored allowing each congregation to choose its own priest, and would have the priests answer to nobody except their followers. Such thinking had become common during the wars, and was nowhere more prevalent than in London. Before the rebellion, Daniel would have found himself in prison for harboring such ideas.

"He was an independent spirit, to be sure," I said. "Men should choose their own governors, their own laws, *and* their own priests?"

"You disagree?" Katherine asked. "Whom would you have choose your governors and priests?"

I nearly answered that in both York and Pontrilas I had been as close to a governor as a woman could be, giving my support to candidates for Parliament, and choosing my own parish priest. But of course a poor widow could not say either of these things.

"I've known too many bad men to believe in such ideas," I said. "That sort of democracy is nothing more than anarchy primped up and calling itself *freedom.*" I glanced at Martha, hoping to find an ally in that corner. I could tell from her expression that she agreed with Katherine.

"That is where you're wrong, Bridget Hodgson," Katherine said, smiling slightly. "And someday I will convince you of it." But we both knew that this was not the time or place to debate such weighty issues. We turned back to the seemingly endless pile of papers on Daniel's desk.

The letters were no less motley than the books, covering not just business matters, but questions of religion and politics. More intriguingly, we found dozens of short, cryptic notes, many of which seemed to set the time and place for a meeting. Some meetings were to take place at the Nag's Head—if that's what *NH* meant—but others were far less clear: *SP, GC, LC, PA.*

"Have you seen these before?" I handed a few of the notes to Katherine.

"Aye," she said. "Daniel and his friends used them. I teased him that he was playing at being a spy, and that if he wanted that life he should have joined with Cromwell."

I stole a glance at Martha, but she had locked her gaze on Katherine's face.

"It's not much of a cypher," Martha said.

Katherine laughed. "And Daniel would not have been much

of a spy. *NH* is the Nag's Head; *SP* is St. Paul's; *GC* is the Great Conduit. And if he's meeting *JG* it has to be Jeremiah Goodkey. He's one of Daniel's closest friends. There's no mystery here."

As we continued our work, we found dozens of these notes scattered throughout his books and ledgers in what seemed to be a haphazard fashion. I was looking through one of Daniel's registers, this one recording coats sent to the navy, when yet another note fluttered to the ground.

Tuesd iv Nov, xii o'clock, HB, said the note. It was signed *TR*. I recognized Tom Reynolds's hand immediately, and *HB* could only be the Horned Bull. I put the note with the others, my mind racing. I knew I could use the note to our advantage—but how?

As we went through the rest of Daniel's books, collecting all the meeting papers, I puzzled at the problem, and soon I had an answer. I merely had to wait for the opportunity to put my scheme into action.

In the end we read much, but found little of interest: no bribes, no threats, and other than Tom's note, no evidence of Daniel's work for Cromwell. His profits from the New Model Army were impressive, but did nothing to help us solve the murder. By the time we finished, all we had to show for our labor were the slips of paper.

"God only knows how many other meetings there must have been," Martha said. "He can't have kept all the papers. How many did he burn? And how many did *he* send?"

"He sent as many as he received," Katherine said. "And he received many more than this. Could Daniel's murderer be somewhere in that pile?"

Now was the time to put my plan into action.

"Katherine, you go through them again," I said. "You knew him best. We will remain quiet, and you can tell us what you see."

Katherine nodded and began to leaf through the papers. "All

these places are public," she observed. "But they would be so crowded that anyone could come or go without being noticed."

"Daniel could hide in the crowd," Martha said. "He wanted to meet someplace where he could be seen but neither noticed nor remembered."

"Why would Daniel want to meet people in this way?" I asked. "Why not just have them come to the shop?"

Katherine shrugged helplessly, but I saw a degree of concern creeping into her expression. Perhaps she worried that we might discover some terrible secret after all. She turned back to the papers. When she came to the note that Tom Reynolds had sent, she set it aside without a second glance.

"Wait," I said. "*HB*. Isn't the Horned Bull an inn nearby?"

"Aye," Katherine said. "It is in Pissing Alley hard onto Bow Lane. Do you think Daniel might have met someone there?"

"It could be," I said. "Do you recognize the hand? Did Daniel ever say anything about going to the Bull, or meeting a man with the initials *TR*?"

"No, never," Katherine said. "I have no idea what that might have been about."

"Well, it gives us a place to start," I said. "Martha and I will go there and see what we can learn."

"Shall I come with you?"

"You'd best not," I replied. "If Daniel was killed by someone he knew, the murderer likely knows you as well. If he saw the three of us together he'd be on his guard, and we don't want to warn him. Martha and I will go there now."

"But you'll come back as soon as you learn something?"

"Of course we will," I said. *That is a part of the plan, after all.*

Martha and I walked to Bread Street and down Pissing Alley toward the Horned Bull.

Once we were safely away, I turned to Martha.

"Katherine's actions are not those of a woman who is guilty," I said. "If she were, she'd hardly let us search Daniel's papers."

"Unless she'd already searched them," Martha pointed out. "And burned those that she did not want us to see. Now, will you tell me why we are going to the Horned Bull?"

I told Martha of my plan.

"You'll lie to Katherine even though you think she's innocent?" Martha asked.

"We lie to her every day," I said. "And if it helps us find Daniel's killer she could hardly complain."

When we reached the Horned Bull, Martha and I sent a chambermaid to summon Will and Tom, and found a table in the inn's dining room. A few minutes later, Will appeared and walked toward us. When Martha started to laugh I realized that I was looking past Will, gazing instead at the doorway behind him.

"Who are you looking for?" Martha asked.

"What do you mean?" I replied. "I'm looking at Will." I felt my ears pink and hoped she would not notice.

Martha's laughter rang through the inn, bringing every other conversation to a halt. "If you were looking at Will with such longing on your face, I would be quite furious. You have become a better liar in recent years, but I would not count that as your masterpiece."

"Will you hush?" My mortification was complete. "If you knew who I was looking for, why did you ask?"

Will arrived, and his gaze shifted uneasily between the two of us. "What is it? What did I do?"

"Nothing," I growled. "Is Colonel Reynolds here?"

This, of course, set Martha into another fit of laughter.

"He's gone to the Tower to see Mr. Marlowe." By now, Will was confused beyond measure. "Are you laughing at me?"

"No, no," Martha managed at last. "It has nothing to do with you. We are just a pair of hens a-gossiping, that is all."

"We have news from the Cheap," I said, hoping to turn the conversation in another direction. "You should sit."

Will did, and after a few minutes Martha had regained herself enough to talk without laughing. "What is it?" Will asked.

"Katherine Chidley has asked us to help solve her husband's murder," I said.

Will raised his eyebrows in surprise. "Really! That is—convenient, I suppose. She will answer your questions without wondering why you are asking them."

"Aye," I said. "But it also means that she will be watching us more closely than we imagined."

"And we shall have to tell her what we find," Martha said. "At least some of it."

Will nodded. "I'll tell Colonel Reynolds about this. What do you intend to do now?"

I explained my scheme a second time, and Will nodded. "That could work. It will certainly throw her off balance. Is there anything you need from me or Colonel Reynolds?"

At this Martha began to laugh once again. Will shook his head in exasperation and stood. "I'll leave you be, then. Send word if you learn anything of import."

"Back to the Cheap?" Martha asked after Will had left.

"Aye," I said. "We need to tell Katherine what we 'discovered' here at the Bull."

As we walked toward the Cheap, I reflected on the lies I'd already told Katherine, and the ones I was about to tell. I told myself that

I deceived her out of necessity rather than malice, and that we both were working to discover Daniel's killer. While the facts were the facts, I could not convince myself I was entirely in the right. But what choice did I have?

When we arrived at Katherine's home, her maidservant told us she'd gone to the Nag's Head. We made our way to the tavern, where we found her deep in conversation with Jeremiah Goodkey. She seemed intent on convincing him every woman should be allowed to vote and—if she were godly enough—to serve as an alderman or even Lord Mayor. Goodkey was having none of it and argued back with admirable passion. When Goodkey noticed us, he recognized that we were waiting for Katherine and withdrew to his customary place behind the bar.

"Back so soon?" Katherine asked. "Did you find out who Daniel met with?"

"Aye," I said in a hushed tone. "But it is not news we should spread too widely."

Katherine leaned toward me so I could whisper in her ear.

"We think *TR* is a man named Thomas Reynolds," I said. "I gave a penny to a chambermaid and she told me that he is the only *TR* at the Bull."

"Do you know him?" Martha asked Katherine.

Katherine shook her head. "What does he look like?"

"We never saw him," I replied. "But the chambermaid said he'd gone to Southwark. In his absence we . . ." I paused, pretending to consider my choice of words.

"We looked about his room." Martha played her part perfectly.

Katherine's eyebrows flew up in surprise. "You burgled his room?" she whispered. "Are you mad?"

"It wasn't a proper burglary," Martha said. "We didn't take anything. We just looked through his papers."

"I'm not sure a Justice would appreciate the distinction," Katherine pointed out. "But what's done is done. What did you find?"

"You will not like the news," I said. "But you must believe us, for it is the truth."

Katherine's eyes hardened and she nodded. "Tell me."

"We found letters that were written in a kind of cipher," I said. "Some were sent to him, and some he was writing for a man named Marlowe at the Tower of London."

We sat in silence so Katherine could absorb this news. I wanted her to see the truth on her own rather than having me lay it before her.

"You think that Thomas Reynolds is in Cromwell's employment," she said.

"Who else sends ciphered letters to the Tower?" I asked.

"And if Reynolds is in Cromwell's employ, Daniel must have been as well," Katherine continued. "Why else would they have met so secretly?"

I held my breath as Katherine considered what I'd said. I could see her trying to find some other explanation for the letter and meetings, an explanation that would not make her husband a traitor to the Leveller cause.

"Perhaps Cromwell made Daniel his creature," she admitted at last. "Old 'Nol is a powerful and ruthless man."

I exhaled at last, relieved that she'd accepted the possibility of Daniel's betrayal. With that goal accomplished I could move ahead with our plan. "If someone thought Daniel was in Cromwell's service, he might have killed him for it," I said. "One of the Levellers, perhaps?"

My eyes drifted to Jeremiah Goodkey. His forearms bulged as he rubbed a cloth across the bar. He could have overcome Daniel with no trouble at all.

"You think Daniel was killed by a Leveller?" Katherine asked. "By one of his own friends?"

"If the killer thought Daniel had betrayed the cause," Martha said, "he might not have let mere friendship stay his hand."

"And once Daniel entered the world of spies, he might have made other enemies as well," I said. "After all, it is not only the Levellers who oppose Cromwell."

"You mean it could be one of the King's men," Katherine said.

"Aye," I said. "Cromwell has many enemies who would be happy to see him dead. Thus so did Daniel."

"Could the murderer be this Thomas Reynolds or Mr. Marlowe?" Katherine asked. "Perhaps they demanded Daniel's service, and Daniel refused."

My heart leaped in my chest at this suggestion. I tried to push it away, but could not. While I did not believe that Tom was behind the murder, what about Mr. Marlowe? Could he be so cunning as to kill Daniel Chidley and then ask us to solve the crime? The possibilities for deception in this matter echoed endlessly.

"I don't know," I said at last. "It is possible."

"I should like to talk to Abraham Walker," Katherine said. "And I want to tell him everything we have learned."

"The man we met at your home?" Martha asked. "I thought he was a cloth merchant."

"Aye, he is that," Katherine said, "but he is more as well. He kept himself a neutralist in the wars, and thus made himself into a man that all parties trust. He may know better who Daniel's enemies were."

"Do you trust him?" I asked.

"With my life," Katherine replied. "He has been a true friend for many years. He will not hesitate to help us."

I nodded my assent and Katherine went in search of Walker.

As soon as we were alone, Martha asked the question that was already on my lips. "*Could* it have been Marlowe?"

"I don't know," I replied. "Anything and everything seems possible now."

"But would he kill Daniel and then send us to find the killer simply to muddy the waters?"

I could only shake my head in confusion.

We sat in silence, puzzling over Marlowe's knot. And then it came free.

"If Mr. Marlowe did kill Daniel, he might be trying to fell two birds with one shot," I said. "He murdered Daniel for reasons of his own, and then sent the two of us after Goodkey and Owen. He'll hang whichever one we settle on as the killer, not caring who it is. Daniel is dead, and so is one of Cromwell's enemies."

Martha nodded. "He'd see one enemy murdered, and another executed for the crime. A good day's work even for so devious a man as Marlowe."

"Or Mr. Marlowe could be telling the truth. Perhaps Jeremiah Goodkey or Charles Owen *did* kill Daniel." I shook my head in wonder and confusion. "For a man who sewed coats, Daniel Chidley had his share of enemies."

"And if we are not careful," Martha warned, "his enemies could become ours."

"Then the sooner we finish this business, the safer we will be," I said. "Let us hope that Abraham Walker knows something of consequence."

Chapter 14

We had hoped to speak to Mr. Walker the next day, but before we had the chance, all of London was thrown into a frenzy when the trial of King Charles ended and he was sentenced to death. When word reached the Cheap, the entire neighborhood poured into the street, weeping and shouting over what had happened. Martha and I wandered alone along Cheapside Street, watching and listening to the crowd.

When we reached St. Mary-le-Bow church, a chapman—the same one I'd heard singing of Guy Fawkes and the Gunpowder Plot—was singing of more recent events.

Now thanks to the powers below
We Englishmen do reap what we sow;
The Bishop's Miter has been cast down,
And along with it has gone the Crown,
With no such thing as bishop or king,
Good order has fled the land,
So come clowns, come boys, come hobbledehoys,

Come females of each degree,
Stretch out your throats, ladies bring in your votes,
You'll make good the anarchy!

"Katherine would have him by the ears, if she heard him," Martha whispered. Indeed, some women in the crowd began to murmur against the chapman. Unfortunately, he did not realize that he had one foot on a rolling stone and would soon be tumbling downhill.

"Let's have King Charles," says John,
"Nay, let's have his son," says Hugh,
"Let England have none," says Jabbering Joan,
"We'll all be kings," says Prue.

This proved too much for one woman in the crowd, and an egg flew past the chapman's head before splattering against the wall behind him.

"What, you want to lay all this at *our* feet?" she cried. "Which of the so-called judges that sentenced the King was named Joan? Which Parliament man is named Prudence? All I see are Richards and Williams. It is you men who have brought us to this point, not us women."

By the time she'd finished her speech—and reached into her basket for another egg—the chapman had fled.

"The King was never so popular until he found himself in prison." I nearly leaped from my boots at the sound of Katherine's voice. She had slipped in behind us and now joined our little circle. "Before Charles was captured, those who hated him, hated him worse than the devil. And those who loved him, loved him not so well as their supper. But now that he is neutered, the people have forgotten his sins and long only for the order he promised but never provided."

"And what about you?" Martha asked. "Do you hate him worse than the devil?"

"I hate tyranny, whether it is the King's or Cromwell's. And I will oppose it at every turn."

"But now it seems that one tyrant will send another to the scaffold," I said. "How do you reconcile that?"

Katherine smiled broadly. "We have put ourselves in a difficult place, haven't we? In this matter, I find I must side with the King. This rump of a Parliament had no more right to judge Charles than the three of us would. I cannot complain that the law mistreats the poor and then acquiesce to its mistreatment of the rich. So, yes, last year I wanted the King brought down, and now I oppose his execution." She laughed at the contradiction.

By now the crowd had begun to disperse and Katherine began walking toward the Nag's Head. I realized that this could be a good time to speak to Jeremiah Goodkey about Daniel's death. In all the excitement about the King's conviction and condemnation, he might make a small mistake, and that could be enough. I told Katherine of my plan and her face grew pale.

"You really think Jeremiah might have killed Daniel?"

"If he discovered Daniel was working on behalf of Cromwell . . . ," I said.

Katherine breathed deeply and nodded. "I hate to think of such a thing. Jeremiah is a good friend, and I hope he is innocent of this. But he *is* of a choleric humor, and if he thought that Daniel had betrayed the Leveller cause, he might have resorted to violence. Do not let my wants and desires stand in the way of your search."

We arrived at the Nag's Head to find it full to overflowing. All the talk was of the King's fate, of course, and many an argument had already become heated. Katherine disappeared into the crowd while Martha and I edged toward Jeremiah Goodkey, hoping to catch him unawares. We found him behind the bar, arguing with a small, rat-faced man.

"So long as the King lives, there can be no freedom." Goodkey pounded the bar with so much force that the glasses rattled. "I'll not defend this Parliament, but for now, the price of freedom is the blood of kings."

The rat-faced man said something I could not hear, but his words so enraged Goodkey that he lost all semblance of control. His hand shot out and seized the man by the front of his shirt. With no apparent effort, Goodkey pulled his opponent halfway across the bar and shouted into his face, "You'll not say such things in my tavern."

The rat-faced man tried to speak, but he could not catch his breath.

"Perhaps we should return another time," Martha murmured. "He does not seem to be in the mood to answer questions."

"Aye," I said. "But where shall we go?"

"We could find Charles Owen," she said. "On this of all days, the Royalists will be more restrained in their passions."

"Let us hope," I said.

As Martha and I made our way to Charles Owen's tavern—it was aptly named the Crown—we discussed the best way to approach him, and the challenge before us quickly became clear.

"Jeremiah Goodkey at least knows our faces," I said. "But Owen is a stranger. He will not take kindly to a pair of women wandering in and questioning him about a murder."

"Let us leave the questions for tomorrow," Martha said. "Today, we can just listen. Once we have the measure of his character we will better know how to approach him when the time comes."

I nodded in agreement. While such a quiet approach would slow our search for Daniel's killer, I could not argue with her thinking. "There is one other problem," I said. "What do we do if Charles Owen proves to be the murderer?"

"What do you mean?"

"We only know of Owen through Mr. Marlowe. How would we explain our discovery to Katherine?"

"There was no *CO* among Daniel's notes, was there?"

"No," I said. "And no meeting place signified by the letter *C*."

"So he never met Charles Owen—or anyone else—at the Crown."

"Or the meetings were secret enough that he burned the notes immediately," I said.

We walked in silence, puzzling over the riddle before us, but found no solution.

"We will have to untie that knot when we come to it," Martha said.

I nodded. "But we should take this as a warning that if we are not careful, we will be caught in our own lies," I said. "We saw this trap, but there must be others."

We found the Crown with no trouble—Tom had provided a map to help us—and Martha and I stepped out of the winter wind. As we shed our cloaks I looked about the room, wondering which of the men was Charles Owen.

On the surface, the Crown had much in common with the Nag's Head; it too had rough-hewn furniture that had seen much use. A chaotic mixture of chairs and benches was scattered around tables both large and small. On this day, however, the crowd could not have been more different. While the men and women at the Nag's Head had held forth long and loud over whether the King's execution was just, the Crown's patrons had no such disagreements. At the Crown, the execution was nothing short of murder.

A few of the men who saw us enter stared at us with open suspicion. I tried to imagine Daniel slipping in here on some piece of business, and wondered if such a visit might have begun the chain of events that led to his death. Might Martha and I have begun a similar chain by our entrance?

I pointed to a large table—one that would invite company—and Martha and I crossed to it. "This place has the feel of a wake," Martha murmured as we sat.

"Aye," I said. "For them it is the prelude to one. It will be a dark day when the King is beheaded."

Martha went to the bar and returned with two pots of ale, and we sat back to wait and listen. After a time the warmth of the fire and the strength of the ale pulled me into a dull-witted state. Had I been more alert, I might not have been caught unawares by the man who slid onto the bench next to me and put his arm around my waist.

I turned in shock at such familiarity, and had to fight back a scream when I discovered Lorenzo Bacca sitting beside me. I tried to speak but could not, a malady that afflicted Martha as well.

"Words fail me, Lady Hodgson," Bacca purred. His accent raised the hair on my neck. "I have so many questions for you, I cannot think where to begin."

It had been nearly half a decade since I had last seen Lorenzo Bacca, but in no way could I have forgotten him. In the course of trying to prove that Esther Wallington had not murdered her husband,

I had come to suspect that Bacca had done so. Not only was he an assassin in the King's employ, but he had promised to kill me if I persisted in my search for the murderer. I counted my refusal to be quailed by such threats as one of my first acts of true courage.

While Bacca had proven to be innocent of that particular crime, there could be no question that he was as dangerous a man as I'd ever met. There was a striking congruity between Bacca's visage and his character, as his ruthless nature was matched with sharp features and the smile of a wolf. In the years since he'd fled York his hair had thinned a bit and there were a few more lines around his eyes, but time had treated him well.

"You simply *must* tell what brought you to . . . this." He plucked at my wool skirts as if I might be verminous with lice. As was his habit in York, Bacca wore the most colorful and expensive combination of silks and wools imaginable. Even among the King's men, who favored such clothes, he stood out like a swan among ducks.

"And once you have explained your common dress," he continued, "I hope you will tell me why you are here in the Crown, on this of all days. I cannot guess at the answer to either question, so it is with great anticipation that I look forward to your explanation." Bacca raised an eyebrow and waited.

My mind raced to find answers that would satisfy him. None presented themselves, and I briefly considered leaping to my feet and running for the street. Bacca must have sensed this, for his hand remained snug on my hip.

"We should ask the same thing of you," I said at last. "In York you were up to your ears in King Charles's business, and such work is much more dangerous now that he is down."

"The King is dead—or soon will be," Bacca replied with a knowing smile. "In which case, long live the King."

"You are serving the Prince of Wales?" I asked. "You admit that so freely?"

Bacca's laugh was not unkind, but his smile remained vulpine. "Half the men in this tavern are in the Prince's service, and the rest will be when the ax falls on his father. But that is enough about me. Now, why don't you tell my why you are dressed like a common housewife?"

I looked at Martha, hoping that she had thought of a lie that Bacca might find credible, but the desperation in her eyes mirrored my own. After a few moments, each of which seemed like an eternity, Bacca continued speaking. Like so many men of his nation, he could not keep himself quiet.

"You will not answer?" Bacca asked with a laugh. At that moment, I realized that whatever his suspicions, he was genuinely pleased to see me. "Very well, let me guess. I do not know what brought you to London, but to be dressed like this you have either fallen into poverty or you are in disguise. I know you are not so improvident for it to be the former, so you must be here as a spy of sorts. And since the Crown is favored by Royalists, you are not serving the King or the Prince. Therefore, you must be Cromwell's creature. I cannot imagine why you would join with such a bad man, but you are a clever woman and you must have your reasons."

I felt sick at the speed with which Bacca had arrived at the truth, and prayed that he could not tell how close he'd come to the mark.

"The only question that remains," he continued, "indeed the only question that matters, is why you are here and whether your business and mine will collide. That would be regrettable indeed."

"Why don't you tell us *your* business? Martha suggested brightly. "And we can tell you whether we will come into conflict."

Bacca laughed. "That is the problem, of course. Since I am with His Majesty, and you are with the traitor Old 'Nol, we can only lie to each other. What ever shall we do to escape this impasse?"

"We could go our separate ways," Martha suggested. "With neither of us troubling the other."

"I think it is too late for that," Bacca replied. "The troubling is already well under way, isn't it? You must tell me your business, or I shall have to announce who you are to all these men. I should think that they would be very pleased to get their hands on two of Cromwell's spies, especially on a day such as this."

I took a breath and released it slowly. I knew that only the most carefully crafted lie would fool Bacca. I resolved to measure out the truth drop by drop and dilute it with as many lies as I thought he would swallow. I began by mixing our search for Daniel's murderer with a mystery that Martha and I had solved some years before.

"You are right about the disguise, but wrong about the reason," I said. "We are not in Cromwell's employ. Rather, we are in search of a murderer."

Even so practiced a dissembler as Bacca could not hide his surprise.

"Really!" he cried. "What murderer? You must tell me."

"Someone has killed two of the city's whores," I replied. "Martha and I have been given the job of finding the murderer." Martha and I had solved just such a series of murders a few years before. I could only hope that Bacca hadn't heard of our exploits.

Bacca eyed us suspiciously. "Why can't the Justices find the killer on their own? Why summon a midwife?"

"You know the godly," I replied. "They have treated the whores worse than they have the actors. What doxy would trust a godly magistrate?"

"And why would they trust you?" Bacca asked.

"Since coming to London I have worked with them, delivering them of their bastards. I have done them no wrong."

"I find your story fascinating, but it does not begin to explain your presence in the Crown. There are no doxies here."

"We believe that the killer may be a man who frequents the Crown," Martha said. "We came here in hope of finding him."

Bacca looked at us, clearly suspicious. "Why did you tell me the truth so easily?"

"We have no reason to lie about this matter," I replied. "What objection could you have to our work? And as you can see, unless you are the murderer, our businesses cannot collide."

After a moment Bacca nodded. "If you are telling the truth, you have taken up a dangerous task. Perhaps I can help. Who is this man you are hoping to find?"

I had not expected such an offer and hesitated. Of course I could not refuse—what reason could I give for rejecting such courtesy? But I also knew that an invented name would not fool Bacca for long.

"It is Charles Owen," I said. "He is the owner of the Crown."

"Charles Owen," Bacca repeated. "And what evidence do you have?"

I shrugged. "The magistrate told me not to say. We are not even sure he is the murderer. But we know he frequented the women who were killed. So he may have seen the murderer." I hoped that my evasiveness on this point would make the rest of my story seem truthful.

Bacca nodded. "I know Charles. He does not seem like that

kind of man. But who can know the truth about anyone?" He stood and for a moment I thought we might be free. "I will send him here to answer your questions, and remain nearby to ensure that you are safe."

"You mustn't tell him why we have come," I said. "It is better that we catch him unawares."

Bacca paused and nodded. "Yes, you are right. Better to surprise him. I will say nothing."

Bacca strode to a man and woman standing behind the bar. They could only be Charles Owen and his wife. Bacca leaned across and whispered to Owen. He looked at us, suspicion clear on his face. When Bacca finished talking, Owen nodded and came from behind the bar. He was a tall, loose-jointed man who moved with such ease he seemed more snake than human.

"You are friends with Lorenzo," Owen said when he arrived. His accent revealed his origins in England's southwest, Devon or Cornwall, I thought. "He said that you have some questions to ask me. What about?"

When he leaned on the table I was struck by the strength in his arms. Muscles seemed to twitch beneath the skin even when they were still, as if they longed for labor to keep them occupied. I imagined his left hand grasping Daniel's throat, while his right thrust a dagger into his chest.

"We are here about the murder of Daniel Chidley," I replied.

"Are you now?" Owen's eyes flashed, and the air about us crackled with the threat of violence. "And are you truly so eager to follow him to the grave? Because that, I promise, is what will happen."

Chapter 15

I held my breath, a part of me sure that Martha and I would soon meet the same end as Daniel Chidley. I wanted desperately to signal Lorenzo Bacca that his "friend" had threatened our lives, but did not dare take my eyes off of Charles Owen.

"What do you mean?" Martha asked. Her eyes remained sharp and her voice did not quiver as I knew mine would if I spoke.

Owen stared at Martha, but after a moment his demeanor softened and he sat down. "I mean Daniel was playing a dangerous game with dangerous men, and you would be wise not to join in."

"What game?" she asked. "What men?"

Owen looked toward the door as if he were waiting for someone. I could not tell if he did so out of fear or anticipation. His eyes returned to us, but he remained silent.

"How did you know Daniel Chidley?" Martha asked. "You favor the King, and Mr. Chidley was a Leveller—there's not much common ground there."

"We both hated Cromwell, didn't we?" Owen spoke so softly

Martha and I had to lean toward him to hear. "Strange times make for strange bedfellows. Cromwell or one of his creatures must have had his fill of Daniel's agitating and killed him. As I said, that's a shame but not a surprise."

I marveled that he spoke so openly of his hatred for Cromwell, but I supposed there was no safer place in London to say such things.

"You think he was killed by Parliament men?" I asked.

"It makes the most sense, doesn't it?" Owen replied. "Cromwell fears the Levellers as much as he does the Royalists. And if he'll sentence His Majesty to death with that counterfeit trial, he'd hardly balk at putting so low a man as Daniel in his grave with no trial at all."

I considered how best to put Owen off his guard, and decided to play our ace of trumps. "Daniel wasn't killed by Cromwell," I said. "He was working for Cromwell. He was a spy."

Owen stared at me with a mixture of surprise and disbelief. "Who are you?" he asked. "Why are you here?"

"We are looking for Daniel Chidley's murderer, just as I said," I replied. "We heard that you might know something of it."

"And it seems we were right," Martha added.

"The Italian said you are midwives. Why are you sticking your beaks into such a business?"

"We are here for his wife," I said. "She doubts the Justices will do their part, and asked us to help her find Daniel's killer. Did you know that Daniel Chidley was working for Cromwell?"

"No, and I don't believe it, either," Owen said. "Whoever told you that he was, was leading you astray. Daniel and I disagreed on many things, but he was a true Leveller. As I said, you should look to Cromwell's men. But I'll warn you now. Be careful—if you come too close to the truth, they'll not hesitate to kill someone like you."

"What did you and Daniel do together?" I asked. "What was your work against Cromwell?"

Owen laughed bitterly. "Do I seem such a fool as to tell you that? I'd sooner find a rope and hang myself." He paused for a moment and peered at me through narrowed eyes. "For all I know, you work for Cromwell, and wish to trick me into a confession." He stood. "I've done nothing wrong, so finish your drinks and go. I've no desire to see you here again. You'll bring nothing but trouble on yourselves and those around you, and I've got enough trouble of my own."

I peered at Owen's belt as he walked away, wondering if he might carry a knife, but I could not catch a glimpse beneath the tails of his shirt.

"Mr. Owen," I called after him. "Where were you on January eighth? It was the day after the King's trial was announced."

Owen returned to the table and leaned over us, his jaw tight. "Are you mad, yelling that aloud? There are as many dangerous men in the King's employ as in Cromwell's, and I'd sooner not get their attention." He looked about the room before continuing in a whisper. "I had no call to kill Daniel. I told you—he and I were not enemies."

"Where were you on the eighth?" I asked again.

"Here with my wife. This place doesn't run itself. Or maybe I was at the docks looking for wine newly arrived from France. But wherever I was, it wasn't at Daniel's. I had no wish to see him dead."

"Is that your wife?" Martha nodded toward the woman we'd seen him with earlier.

"My wife?" Owen was taken entirely aback by the question. "Yes, why?"

"You said you were here with your wife, or out on some other business. If that's true, she can tell us. Let us ask her, and then we can be on our way."

Owen slammed his fist on the table. We'd asked one question too many. "You'll not speak to her. Not today, not ever. And if I see you here again, you'll be much the worse for it." He started away before turning back to us. "You would do well to learn the lesson of Daniel's death. When you take a knife by the blade, you risk being cut."

"I don't need to finish my ale," Martha whispered as Owen stalked off. The suspicion that had greeted us when we entered the Crown had become open hostility, and I said a prayer of thanks that Lorenzo Bacca had stayed nearby. A smile graced his lips and he nodded farewell as we made our way to the door.

"My God," Martha gasped as we escaped into the street. "That was an unlikely haphazard."

"Meeting Lorenzo Bacca after so many years?" I said. "It was remarkable indeed. Suddenly London seems very small. Do you think he believed our lie about the murdered doxies?"

"He seemed to. It was a story well told."

"Well told or not, he is still an assassin in the service of Prince Charles," I said. "And Daniel was both a Leveller and a spy for Cromwell. Bacca had at least two reasons to kill him."

Martha nodded. "If he is the murderer *and* he saw through the lie about the doxies—"

"Then we would find ourselves in great danger," I finished. We walked a bit faster, hoping to put more distance between us and Bacca.

"And what of Charles Owen?" Martha asked.

"He's strong enough," I said. "And he is certainly a man of violent passions. Either he or Bacca could have killed Daniel."

"Or it might have been Jeremiah Goodkey or Mr. Marlowe," Martha said.

"Aye," I said. "Or one of them. We should go to the Horned Bull. I should like to tell Colonel Reynolds of all that has happened."

"I imagine you would," Martha said with a laugh.

We found our way to the Bull with no trouble—a deed of which I was unreasonably proud—and to my pleasure we arrived at the same time as Will. I embraced him, and he gave Martha a kiss before leading us to the dining room. He seemed tired, and he was well covered with dust and mud.

"So you've been out of the city?" I asked, gesturing at his clothes. "You'll not get that dirty from cobbled streets."

Will laughed. "You don't miss much, I'll grant you that. What have you two been up to today?" He had no intention of telling us where he'd been.

"Is Colonel Reynolds here?" I asked.

Will shook his head. "He should be back shortly. We can eat while we wait."

As the three of us ate, we talked of everything except our mutual work for Mr. Marlowe, and it made for a lovely afternoon. For a time we almost forgot the troubles and dangers that lay before us.

"This is a lovely surprise." Tom Reynolds slid onto the bench next to Will. "What brings you here? Have you found Daniel Chidley's murderer already?"

I was appalled at the girlish laugh that escaped my lips. It was inappropriate for a woman to laugh in such a fashion, especially about a murder. I gathered myself as best I could before I dared reply. "Not yet. But we do have news."

"What is it?" Tom asked.

"We spoke to Charles Owen," I said.

"You did what?" Tom exclaimed. "You *spoke* to him? He could be the murderer!"

"It's a longer story than that," I replied. "And I'll get there in time if you will listen."

Tom nodded for me to continue.

"Owen had no love for Daniel," I said. "But he says had no reason to kill him, either. They both hated Cromwell."

"Did you believe him?" Tom asked.

"I don't know," I said. "There is an air of violence about him, and he has every reason to lie."

"So we have still have no idea who killed Daniel," Will said. "Owen, Goodkey, or someone else entirely."

"It is more complicated than that," Martha said. "We also met Lorenzo Bacca."

Will gasped in surprise. "What? Here in London? How?"

"Who is Lorenzo Bacca?" Tom asked. "What have the two of you been doing?"

I took a moment and thought about how best to explain our strange past and even stranger encounter with the Italian. "When I was in York, a friend was accused of murdering her husband," I said. "I tried to prove her innocence, and in doing so I made enemies of some very powerful men."

"Yes," Tom said. "We heard as much from Will. But where does this Italian come in? Who is he?"

"He is an assassin," I said. "In 1644, York was held by the Royalists, and Bacca was with the King and the Lord Mayor. When Martha and I became too dangerous, the Lord Mayor sent Bacca to threaten us." I remembered the day Bacca forced me into an alley and eased the tip of a knife between my ribs until it barely broke the skin. "He carried a knife that was long and narrow. He could have killed me in one thrust."

"Just as Daniel Chidley was killed," Martha said.

"Aye," I breathed. I'd not made the connection until that moment.

"Now he is working on behalf of Prince Charles?" Tom asked. "Why would an Italian assassin busy himself with an English war?"

"He's not a true Royalist, if that's what you mean. I think he simply found a master who was willing to pay his price. But he's no less dangerous for that."

"And you are sure he was innocent of the murder in York?" Tom asked.

"He was," I said. "But he's an assassin all the same. If the Prince paid him to kill Daniel Chidley, he would not have hesitated to do so."

"And Daniel would not have a chance against him," Martha concluded.

Tom reached into his satchel and produced paper, quill, and ink. "I'll see what I can find out about Bacca," he said, making notes to himself. "Mr. Marlowe is concerned about foreign spies, so we may have some record of him. Did you discover anything else?"

"Nothing of significance," I said. "We will talk to a cloth merchant called Abraham Walker. He was one of Daniel's friends, and Mrs. Chidley thinks he may be able to help us."

"I don't know him, but I will see what I can discover." Tom made a few more notes.

"Mrs. Chidley says he's a neutralist and avoids controversy whenever he can. He's not someone who would capture Mr. Marlowe's attention."

"The same could have been said of you," Tom pointed out with a smile. "Yet here you are."

"Aye," I said. "Here I am."

"Aunt Bridget," Will said, clearing his throat. "It has been some weeks since Martha and I have had time to speak with each other. Alone. Could we have a few minutes?"

"Of course," I said. Tom and I stood and moved toward the bar. We stood in awkward silence for a few moments watching Will and Martha. The crowd in the Horned Bull had swelled considerably since we'd arrived, so Tom and I were forced to stand very nearly nose to nose. The scent of tobacco wafted from his clothes with a pleasant warmth, and when another customer stumbled into us, Tom put his hands on my hips to steady me.

"Shall I find us a table?" he murmured. "We would be more comfortable."

I agreed, though I was unsure where we would sit, for there were no vacant chairs. Tom crossed to a table and whispered a few words to the men sitting there. They immediately stood and left. I could not help laughing as I joined him. "What did you say to them?"

"Nothing but the truth. I told them that I'd noticed their eyes lingering too long on that gentleman's purse." He nodded to a tall and very drunk man leaning heavily on the bar; his purse did seem to beg cutting. "I suggested they do their drinking elsewhere, and they agreed."

Despite the fact that robbery was no more amusing than murder, I laughed once again. At least this time it was my laugh, rather than a girl's.

"I'll get some wine," Tom said, and returned to the bar.

My mind and heart raced as Tom crossed the room. I glanced at Martha, who was looking in my direction, a mischievous glint in her eyes. I suddenly felt overtaken by drink even though I'd only had a single cup of wine with our dinner. Tom returned with a bottle of wine and two cups, and sat across from me.

"Will says he and Martha were betrothed in York," Tom said as he poured. "When do you think they'll marry?"

"They've been apart for many years," I said. "They need to get reacquainted. But it's also up to you and Mr. Marlowe, isn't it?"

Tom nodded, acknowledging the point. "What about you? You were widowed in York?"

"Once in Hereford, once in York," I said.

"Have you any children?"

My mind leaped about, from Michael and Birdy—now dead—to Tree, still in York, and Elizabeth, safe in Pontrilas. "Two died many years ago," I said. "But I now have two others, one in Hereford, one in York."

To my relief he did not ask me to explain how I could have lost two children and found two others. Perhaps Will had told him. I recalled the wistful expression on his face when he'd seen Martha and Will embrace at the Tower. "You are widowed as well?"

"Aye." He nodded. "I had a wife and a grown son. Both died when the King's men took Bolton." My heart sank at this. All England knew of Bolton's suffering when the Earl of Derby had taken the town. His men had killed hundreds without distinguishing women and children from soldiers. I recognized the regret in his eyes when he spoke of his family. It was the same regret I felt when I thought of my own lost children; he somehow blamed himself for their deaths.

"You were there?" I asked.

He nodded. "I was wounded in the fighting. I lived. They didn't." I tried to read his face, but it remained a blank stone.

"And how did you come into Mr. Marlowe's service?" I asked.

"He told me that he'd help me find Derby and see him hanged," he said.

"Is the Earl in London?" The question escaped my lips before I could stop it. Of course he wasn't. Even in Hereford, I'd heard that Derby had fled to France. "I am sorry," I said. "I did not mean it in that way."

"No, no, it is a fair question." Tom smiled ruefully. "If I am looking for Derby, why am I on this side of the English Channel?"

I nodded.

"Mr. Marlowe has a way of bringing you aboard with a promise and then diverting you to his own ends. And if you complete one task, he'll give you another, but not the one that you wanted. But you will find this out for yourself, I imagine."

"You mean on one day he might ask me to spy on the Levellers, and on the next he might ask me to solve a murder?"

Tom laughed long and loud. "Ah, yes, I had forgotten you already experienced his capriciousness." Tom's smile vanished and he looked into my eyes. "You should know that he'll not loose his grasp of you if he can help it. He'll dangle your freedom in front of you in the same way he dangles the Earl of Derby in front of me."

"Then why do you stay?" I asked.

"Because I love England, and would not have her slip into tyranny and popery. Because I cannot find Derby by myself, and someday Mr. Marlowe might." Tom paused for a moment and looked away from me. "And without a family, what else am I to do?"

I reached across the table and took his hand. Now he reminded me not of Luke, but of myself, for the sorrow in his eyes was the very twin of my own.

Tom smiled bitterly and squeezed my hand. "I am sorry. I do not know when I became so womanish."

"If love for your family is womanish, all men should be thus," I replied. "But tell me this: Would finding the Earl of Derby ease your grief?"

Tom looked at me as if I'd suggested that the sun might rise in the west. He thought for a moment, perhaps envisioning the Earl's death at his hands, and looked away. "I suppose not." We sat in silence, letting the noise of the tavern wash over us. Finally Tom spoke. "How did you survive your grief? After all you have lost—what did you do?"

"What did I do?" I repeated. I considered the years since the death of my daughter had completed the destruction of my family and left me alone in England's dark north. "I started again. I did not know I was doing it, but that's what happened. First Martha came to me, and then Will. Then there was another boy named Tree; he is still in York. And then by God's grace Elizabeth found her way to my household. When death took my family, I cobbled together another one. It was the only way I could have survived."

"And that is why you contrived to hang Will's brother," Tom said. "He threatened everyone you had."

"What else could I have done?"

Tom did not respond. I had no doubt he was thinking of the things that he might have done to save his family. If only he had sent them away from Bolton. If only he hadn't been wounded. If only—

"You know Mr. Marlowe better than anyone," I said. "How can I gain my freedom?" I hoped turning our conversation from the past to the future might lift our spirits.

"Now *that* is a delicate dance." Tom's relief at the change was palpable. "If you prove yourself too capable, he will never set you free. A general does not dismiss his best soldiers; he promotes them."

"And if I bungle the job, he will turn against me," I said.

"Aye. And since you freed Mrs. Ramsden, he knows you are no bungler."

"So what can I do?"

Tom thought for a moment. "He will not release you, but he knows that he cannot rule entirely by fear. If you were to earn some great victory, I believe he would ease the terms of your servitude."

I thought for a moment. "I could bring Elizabeth to London. In our meeting he left that door open."

"Aye, he might allow that," Tom said. "But you must give him something first."

"Like Daniel Chidley's murderer."

"I should think that would be enough."

Tom and I were so deep in conversation that we did not notice the bartender approach the table. "Finish up. Time for you to be on your way."

Martha and Will joined us, and the four of us said our farewells. When Martha and Will embraced, Tom and I took a step toward each other before remembering ourselves. Tom bowed awkwardly, and we laughed. "Let us know if you find anything more," Tom said. "I will see you soon."

Martha and I stepped out into a fierce wind that in an instant snatched away the warmth of the Bull. We walked in silence back to our home in the Cheap.

Martha and I passed the following Sabbath in peace, but awoke Monday morning to the news that work had begun on a scaffold outside the Banqueting House. The King would be beheaded in just two days' time. To my surprise, the Cheap greeted this news not with anger or celebration, but quiet resignation. With each step toward the King's death—his trial, his sentencing, and now his execution—more people bowed their heads to the inevitable. Barring some miracle—or rising by his friends—on Thursday Charles would be killed, and for the first time in its long history, England would be without a King.

Martha and I had just returned from the shops where we heard all this when there came a knock at our door. I answered to find Abraham Walker on our doorstep.

"Widow Hodgson," he said. "Katherine Chidley asked me to speak with you. May I come inside?"

Chapter 16

"Of course," I said. "We hoped to speak to you sooner, but with all the trouble . . ."

Walker shook his head in wonder as he crossed the threshold and joined Martha and me at our table. "We live in troubled times. Of that there can be no doubt."

"Katherine says you have joined in the hunt for Daniel's murderer," he said.

"She asked us to help," I said. "And she thought you might have some information that could help us in our search."

"What have you discovered so far?" he asked.

"Nothing of obvious importance," I said. "Except that Daniel had more enemies than any man ought to."

"Because he was both with the Levellers and spying for Cromwell," Walker said.

"Katherine told you that?"

"Aye. She also said that you suspect Jeremiah Goodkey."

I nodded. "There are also some in the King's faction who

might have killed him: a tavern-keeper named Owen, and an Italian called Bacca."

Walker looked surprised at this. "I count Charles Owen as a friend," Walker said. "And I'll tell you now that you are wasting your time with him."

"Why is that?" Martha asked.

"He loves the King more than is good for him, and he has an improvident tongue. But he is no murderer."

"How can you know that?" Martha clearly trusted Walker less than Katherine did. "People have secrets. People change."

"He is a man of talk, not action. He always has been. He never took up arms for the King, even when His Majesty was riding high. He would never take such a step now that the King is down. If you are going to discover Daniel's murderer, you will have to look past such a coward as Charles Owen."

"By this you mean Bacca or Jeremiah Goodkey."

"I do not know this Bacca, but Goodkey is another matter. He is a creature entirely unlike Charles Owen. During the war he was willing to spill blood for his beliefs, and if rumors are to be believed he did so by the gallon. I don't think he would hesitate to kill again if he thought it was necessary."

"We've seen his temper," Martha said.

"There is that as well. Goodkey is cunning enough to plan Daniel's murder and choleric enough to kill him on the spur of the moment. I don't know that he is guilty, but it would not surprise me in the least."

"Are there others you suspect?" I asked.

Walker shrugged. "A few, but none as much as our friend Goodkey."

"Who else?" I sensed that Walker knew more than he was saying.

"Some in Cromwell's camp, I suppose. Cromwell's spymaster is a man named Marlowe. His hands are already so bloody from killing that adding Daniel to his tally would not trouble his conscience."

I caught my breath. If Walker knew about Marlowe, could he know that Martha and I were in his service?

"Why would this Marlowe kill his own spy?" Martha asked.

"Spy-craft is a dangerous business," Walker said. "It is an easy thing to cross the wrong man and find yourself dead. If Marlowe thought that Daniel had betrayed him, Daniel's life would not be worth a cup of day-old ale."

"And if Marlowe *did* kill Mr. Chidley?" Martha asked. "What would we do then?"

"Do?" Walker laughed. "I would challenge you to find a Justice of the Peace willing to arrest Oliver Cromwell's chief intelligencer. If Marlowe or any other of Cromwell's men killed Daniel, there is nothing we *can* do. Look first at Goodkey, for he at least is vulnerable."

"I do not like it," I said. "If one of Cromwell's men is guilty . . ."

Walker interrupted. "There is no profit in stretching for fruit that is beyond your reach, and you cannot reach a man like Marlowe. Pick the fruit that is within your grasp. Jeremiah Goodkey is that fruit." Walker stood. "I should go. If you learn anything more—about Goodkey especially—tell me. I may be able to help." Walker bid us farewell and he started down the stairs. Martha and I waited to speak until we saw him on the street below.

"He seemed rather eager to guide us away from Charles Owen and toward Goodkey," Martha said.

"He knows them both," I replied. "He was simply telling us what he thought."

"I do not trust him."

"He is Katherine's friend," I said. "And if she trusts him, so should we. We cannot make every man we meet into a suspect. Let us go to the Nag's Head and talk to Jeremiah Goodkey. Perhaps he will clarify matters."

As soon as Martha and I entered the Nag's Head it was clear that we would have better luck talking to Goodkey than we'd had on our previous visit. I did not think the Levellers' passions had burned themselves out, but someone at least had banked the coals. A handful of customers—mostly men today—were scattered about the room, talking in low voices. As usual, Jeremiah Goodkey stood behind the bar.

When Martha and I sat, he came right over. He had more gray in his hair than I'd first realized, and the lines on his face would soon become wrinkles. The man was Katherine's age, at least, but there was no question that he retained the strength of his youth, for his forearms each were as thick a Christmas log.

"What will you have?" he asked. Without the overheating effects of politics, Goodkey seemed far more congenial than menacing.

"Small beers," I replied. In truth I would have preferred something stronger, but I also wanted to keep my wits about me. Goodkey returned with our drinks and set them on the table.

"And a word," I said.

Goodkey looked at us in confusion but sat down. "What word?"

"We are here about Daniel Chidley's murder," I said.

As I'd hoped, this caught Goodkey off his guard. He looked surprised for a moment and then fearful.

"What do you mean?" he asked.

"How long ago was Daniel murdered?" Martha asked.

Goodkey thought for a moment. "Weeks," he said. "A month soon enough."

"Aye," Martha said. "And have the Justices found his murderer?"

Goodkey snorted. "If they looked for Daniel's murderer, it would only be to make him a constable."

"Exactly right," I said. "Mrs. Chidley knows this, and set out to find his murderer herself."

"That sounds like Katherine," Goodkey said with a smile. "And she's enlisted you into her army? That sounds like her, too. So why are you here among Daniel's friends?"

"He wasn't killed by a stranger," I replied.

"Who then?" Goodkey asked. "Daniel talked more than most, but this is London. If talking were reason enough for murder, we'd all be murderers or murdered."

"Daniel was a spy for Oliver Cromwell."

Goodkey burst out laughing. "That is madness. Daniel would bow to a bishop before he served that tyrant."

"That may be true," Martha said. "But he was a spy all the same."

"Never."

"Katherine Chidley found letters he wrote to Cromwell's spymaster," I lied. "As well as letters the spymaster wrote in return."

Goodkey stared into my eyes, searching for some sign that my accusation was false. "It is true?" he asked.

I nodded.

"Well, that might indeed get him killed, even by a friend,"

Goodkey said. "And you think his murderer might be one of my customers."

"That is one possibility," Martha said.

"What is the other?" Goodkey thought for a moment and realized the answer to his own question. "You think *I* killed Daniel."

"You had reason enough," I replied. "And you're strong enough to hold him with one hand and stab him with the other."

"But I had no idea he was a spy, did I? So I couldn't have done it." Goodkey's denial seemed genuine enough, but I could not credit it entirely.

"That's the question," Martha said. "If you knew he'd turned against the Levellers, you'd have killed him."

"But I didn't know." Goodkey insisted, and paused for a moment. "Of course, if I did kill him, I'd deny knowing of his betrayal. How can I convince you?"

"Where were you on the morning he died?" I asked. "If you can answer that, we'll readily believe in your innocencey."

Goodkey shook his head. "I'll tell you, but it won't help: I was here, by myself. I live upstairs and spent the morning reading in my Bible. I was there when I heard of his death. I didn't go out, and nobody came in."

"Do you carry a knife?" Martha asked.

Goodkey blinked at the question and then glanced at his right hip. Quick as lightning, Martha leaned forward and snatched at Goodkey's belt. She came away with a knife in her hand. Goodkey started to object but stopped himself. I watched Goodkey's face as Martha examined the blade, but I could not read his expression.

"You might have asked," Goodkey complained. "What tavern-keeper *doesn't* carry a knife? I use it every day."

With a flick of her wrist, Martha flipped the knife so the blade was in her hand and passed it back to Goodkey. He accepted it and looked at us warily.

"It's not the blade that killed Daniel," she said. "It's too wide and has a curve to it."

"Daniel was killed with a stiletto?" Goodkey asked. "Then you can forget about any tavern-keeper. We have no use for such a knife. We're in the business of cutting, not stabbing."

"The fact that you aren't carrying the knife doesn't prove your innocencey," Martha pointed out.

"I did not kill Daniel," Goodkey insisted. "He was my friend."

"Then who did?" I asked. "He was a vocal and opinionated man who betrayed his friends. He would have made enemies faster than his shop made coats."

Goodkey's eyes darted about the room, and for a moment his unease reminded me of Charles Owen's. "Well, it would be the King's men, wouldn't it? They hate him for opposing the King, for selling coats to the New Model Army, *and* for joining in with the Levellers."

"Who do you mean?" I asked. "You have someone in mind."

Goodkey's eyes searched the room yet again, as if he feared that one of the King's spies might have slipped in when he wasn't paying attention. "There is a man," he said at last. "An Italian. He is very dangerous."

Martha and I glanced at each other. He could only have one person in mind.

"What is his name?" I asked.

"It is only rumors," he said. "I cannot be sure."

"Tell me," I insisted.

Goodkey leaned toward us, coming so close that our foreheads nearly touched. "They call him Bacca. Lorenzo Bacca. But if you trifle with him, you will regret it." Goodkey rose to his feet and nearly ran for the safety of the bar.

"And we're back to Lorenzo Bacca," Martha said. We'd left the Nag's Head and were making our way back to our side of the Cheap.

"Aye," I said. "Just before he died, Daniel told Colonel Reynolds he'd discovered a plot. Perhaps the Royalists intended a rising to rescue the King."

"That would be reason enough to see Daniel dead."

"More than enough," I said. "And if Daniel had to die, why not send Bacca?"

As we walked in silence for a few minutes puzzling over our next steps, I realized how we could use Goodkey's suspicions about Bacca to our advantage. We paused outside Katherine's shop and I explained my plan.

Martha nodded. "That should work. Let us go inside."

Katherine looked up when we entered the shop. Half a dozen young women sat hunched over tables, cutting and sewing wool cloth into coats. Katherine gestured for us to wait and returned to inspecting one girl's work. "Nicely done," she said to the seamstress. "That is what we need."

After examining a few more coats, Katherine said, "Come, let us go upstairs."

As soon as we reached the parlor, Katherine turned to face us. "You've learned something, haven't you?"

"Nothing for sure," I said.

"Tell me."

"We spoke to Jeremiah Goodkey," I said. "He denies killing Daniel, but he suggested one who might."

"Who is it?"

"One of the King's men," Martha said. "An Italian named Bacca."

Katherine thought for a moment. "You think Daniel might have discovered a Royalist scheme to return Charles to the throne."

"Bacca frequents a tavern called the Crown. Do you know it?"

"Aye," Katherine said. "It is a den of vipers if ever one existed, full of Royalists to the very top. You think Bacca killed Daniel?"

"It is possible," Martha said. "There is also the owner of the Crown. He is a man named Charles Owen. It is said that he loves the King above all else."

Katherine shook her head. "I don't know him, but if he loves the King he'd have every reason to hate Daniel. Have you learned anything else?"

"All we have are suspicions," I said.

"That is not all," Katherine said. "Now we have names. Bacca, Owen . . ." She paused. "And, though I hate the idea, there is Jeremiah Goodkey. With those three, we have a place to start, and that is no small thing. What shall we do now?"

I thought for a moment. "You can hardly frequent the Crown," I said. "So Martha and I should look to Bacca and Owen."

Katherine nodded. "And I'll see to Jeremiah. If he killed Daniel, I'll find out. He could not keep so deep a secret for long."

Martha and I bid Katherine farewell and returned to our tenement. Martha went out for our evening meal, and I wrote a letter to Elizabeth. I told her of the King's trial, and the confusion it had brought to the city. After a moment's consideration I added, *You should remain patient, but it is possible that you might soon join us in London.* I knew I was taking a risk in writing this, but I could not leave her without hope.

"Now all I need is the name of Daniel's murderer," I said to myself.

* * *

In the days that followed, London tossed itself about like a fevered patient. Every conversation was about the King's execution, and everyone spoke in hushed tones. But how else could it be, given the path England had chosen? With the death of Charles, England would have neither King nor Queen, and only the Lord knew what such events might portend. On the night of January twenty-ninth—just a handful of hours before the King would die—Katherine Chidley appeared at our door, her face a solemn mask.

"These are weighty days," she said. "And tomorrow is the weightiest of them all. In the morning I will go to the Banqueting House and witness the overturning of the old order. Will you two accompany me?"

"You are going to the King's execution?" I asked.

"Aye," she replied. "Where else is there to be on such a day?"

I considered the question and realized that she was right. If Elizabeth someday asked where I was when King Charles was executed, did I want to reply, *Asleep in my bed*? No, these were shaking days, and I too would bear witness to them.

The next morning, hours before dawn, Martha and I dressed in silence and accompanied Katherine to the Banqueting House. We walked some two miles, tracing the same route that Martha and I had taken when we entered the city. We passed through the Ludgate, over the stinking stream known—too grandly—as the River Fleet, and then onto the Strand. With every step more people joined our procession to Whitehall Palace. Although some in the crowd must have fought against the King, there was none of the jesting that all too often accompanied an execution. We all realized that in killing Charles, we were not merely killing a man. For the first time in England's history, the cry of "The King is dead!" would not be followed by "Long live the King!" The King would be dead, and that would be all.

It was still well dark when the three of us reached the Banqueting House and the scaffold came into view. At the House, King Street—how ironic the name!—became a sort of courtyard, and it was immediately clear why the army had chosen this spot for the execution. To the south lay a turreted gate flanked on one side by the Banqueting House and on the other by a high brick wall. The King would die in a blind alley. The flickering light of the torches illuminated a platform overseeing the entire yard. The army had placed cannons upon it, and pointed them into the crowd. Any attempt to free the King would result in slaughter on a grand scale. The scaffold was draped entirely in black, and even now—hours before the execution—it was surrounded by a troop of horsemen armed with pistols and swords, as well as a rank of pikemen. The army was taking no chances.

In the hours that followed, the courtyard filled to overflowing and when the sun rose we could see that every vantage point overlooking the scaffold had been taken. Faces filled each window, and some brave souls had climbed out on the roofs of surrounding buildings. All had come to witness the death of their sovereign. The crowd waited in silence for what seemed an eternity. To my relief Katherine had come prepared with enough bread and cheese to keep the worst of our hunger at bay, but by noon we were ravenous.

Sometime after that, the scaffold began to fill and we knew the final act had begun. The first to come into view were soldiers, who peered into the crowd to ensure that all was well. They were followed by men with books and inkhorns. I supposed they were there to record the King's last words. Finally came the executioner and his assistant, both disguised not just with masks, but with false beards and wigs beneath their hats. The executioner inspected the blade of his ax and then the low block on which the King would lay his head. He nodded to one of the soldiers, who went into the Banqueting House. A few moments later, the King emerged. He wore a heavy black cloak, but none of the finery one would expect from a monarch. He looked out over the crowd and nodded to himself. I later learned that he wore an extra woolen shirt under his cloak so that he would not shiver in the cold; he was loath to have his subjects think he feared death.

The King produced a piece of paper from beneath his cloak and began to read. He was so far away and surrounded by so many soldiers that we could not hope to hear him. Finally, he turned to his executioner and the two men exchanged a few words. The King removed his cloak, and then what few royal jewels he still wore. A man stepped forward and helped the King put on a cap to keep his hair from impeding the executioner's fatal blow.

At last, he knelt and placed his head on the block. The executioner bent forward and, as tenderly as any lover, tucked a stray lock of the King's hair under the cap. He then stood with his ax at the ready and waited for the King's sign. The King extended his hand and, in a blinding flash, the ax fell.

At the sound of the ax, there emerged from the assembled crowd such a groan as I had never heard before, and hoped that I might never hear again. I closed my eyes to pray, not for Charles's soul—for he had already been judged—but for England. I did not know where such a bloody stroke would lead us, but the Bible said that blood cries out from the ground for vengeance. How loud must the cries of a king's blood be, and how would the Lord answer such cries?

Even as the King's head settled into the executioner's basket, we heard men shouting and the clatter of hooves on cobblestone.

With no more warning than that, horsemen flooded the yard, driving the crowd before them. Martha, Katherine, and I linked arms and fled as quickly as we could. By the time we reached Charing Cross, the crowd had begun to thin, and it became a somber procession back along the Strand into the city proper. Martha and I accompanied Katherine to her door, where we embraced and murmured our farewells. At that moment I wanted nothing more than to climb into my bed, pull the coverlet over me, and sleep for weeks.

As soon as Martha and I crossed the street, however, a voice called out to us.

"Martha, Aunt Bridget!" Will hurried towards us. I could tell from his expression that he brought terrible news.

"What is it?" I asked.

"You must come with me. Whoever killed Daniel Chidley has killed again. Colonel Reynolds and Mr. Marlowe are with the body. They sent me to find you."

Even before Martha or I could respond, a woman called out from across the street.

"Martha Hawkins, there you are!" She hurried toward us. "Lucy Sheldon has begun her travail. She sent me to find you."

Martha's eyes darted between Will and me.

"Go," I told her. She started to protest, but I would not have it. "You see to the living, I'll look to the dead. Go upstairs, get your birthing stool and valise, and go to your mother. She comes first. If you need help, send for Mrs. Chidley."

Martha nodded and went inside.

I turned to Will. "Take me to the body."

Chapter 17

Will and I made our way south from the Cheap toward the river, and it was not long before I became thoroughly lost. As much as the Cheap now felt like home, the rest of London remained so strange and unfamiliar it might have been another city entirely.

"Who has been killed?" I asked.

"A man named Enoch Harrison," Will said. "Few people know his name, but he was among the most important men in the Kingdom."

"Who is he?"

"He owns a gunpowder-works near Greenwich. He was the chief supplier for both the New Model Army and Cromwell's navy." We turned onto a broad lane and stopped before a stately home. "Here we are."

Will led me up a set of stone stairs to the door, and we entered without knocking. We passed through an entry hall into what must have been Enoch Harrison's office. I stopped and looked at the office door—someone had broken in with such force that the frame had splintered.

Enoch Harrison's body lay facedown upon an ornately carved desk at the far end of the room. Tom Reynolds and Mr. Marlowe stood on either side, staring forlornly at the corpse. The office itself was large and well appointed, its shelves full of books, but also pistols and muskets in various states of disassembly; there was even a small brass cannon sitting in one corner.

"Good," Marlowe said when we entered. "Come around here and see what we've found."

I circled behind the desk and looked down at the corpse. It was immediately clear why Mr. Marlowe had connected Enoch Harrison's murder to Daniel Chidley's. A single wound, less than an inch wide, ruined the back of an otherwise spotless silk doublet. The hole was on his left side, just below the shoulder blade, precisely over his heart. His papers sat in neat piles around his body. As in Daniel's case, Harrison had hardly bled at all, and he'd died without a struggle. I pulled back Harrison's collar to peer at his neck. Unlike Daniel, there were no bruises, but the killer had stabbed him in the back, so choking might not have been necessary. My hand brushed the skin—it was cold and waxen.

"Do we know how long he has been dead?" I asked.

"His servant was the last person to see him alive," Marlowe said. "He left Mr. Harrison alone last night and went to bed. He thought nothing of it when Mr. Harrison did not rise for breakfast, but when he discovered the locked door he began to worry. He summoned the neighbors and they broke in."

"And nobody saw or heard anything?"

"His servant is older than Methuselah," Marlowe said, frustration dripping from every word. "The murderer could have used a cannon without disturbing the old man's sleep. Harrison's daughter was here, but she went to bed even before the servant, and didn't hear a sound."

"He died so quickly, he probably didn't *make* a sound," Tom added.

I nodded in agreement. "If he didn't live long enough to knock the papers from his desk, he could hardly be expected to cry out for help." I joined Tom and Mr. Marlowe in gazing at Mr. Harrison's body. "Why would someone kill both Daniel Chidley and Enoch Harrison?" I asked. "What did they have in common?"

"That is one question," Marlowe replied, his voice tight. "But not the most urgent."

"What do you mean?" I asked.

"The Army is preparing an expedition against Ireland," Tom said. "This week Mr. Harrison was to deliver a large shipment of gunpowder." Tom's voice trailed off, and he looked to Marlowe.

"The powder is missing," Marlowe said at last. "This morning, two men came to Mr. Harrison's warehouse with carts, horses, and a sealed letter from Mr. Harrison demanding the powder. The men took it and disappeared."

I thought for a moment, putting together the puzzle.

"The murderer forced Mr. Harrison to write and seal the letter, so his comrades could steal the powder," I said. "And then he killed Mr. Harrison to prevent him from sounding the alarm."

Tom nodded. "That is the most likely explanation."

"How much powder is missing?" I asked.

"We don't know precisely," Tom replied. "But the thieves filled four carts. Perhaps five. The watchman at the warehouse was not sure."

Marlowe looked as if he were suffering from a fever, and I understood why. He was the man tasked with securing Parliamentary rule, and someone had stolen five carts of gunpowder out from beneath him. Oliver Cromwell's chief spy had failed spectacularly.

"How did the killer know about the powder?" I asked.

Marlowe shrugged. "There are spies everywhere. How the killer found out does not matter." He spoke barely above a whisper. "The only thing that matters is recovering it."

A knock came from the door and two women entered, a maidservant and a young woman who was great with child.

"Mrs. Hodgson," Tom said, "this is Mr. Harrison's daughter, Margaret."

Under ordinary circumstances, Margaret Harrison would have been a pretty young woman, but the grief at her father's murder had left her hollow, and her red-rimmed eyes gave way to sunken cheeks and quivering lips.

"Can I take his body now?" Margaret's voice cracked when she spoke, and tears leaked from the corners of her eyes. "I can't bear the thought of leaving him here any longer."

Marlowe glanced at me, and I shrugged. Martha would have liked to see the body, but I did not know how long she would be occupied with her travail.

"Aye, you can have him," Marlowe said. "We will continue our discussion elsewhere."

When the four of us returned to the entry hall, we found a small group of men waiting—Mr. Harrison's burial party, I assumed. We nodded our condolences and found our way to Mr. Harrison's parlor. It was no less beautifully furnished than the office had been. Luxurious wall-coverings kept out the winter chill and finely woven mats covered the floors. Cromwell rewarded his powder merchants quite handsomely.

"So who would want to kill both Daniel Chidley and Enoch Harrison?" I asked again.

"That is the problem," Tom replied. "Since we don't know why Daniel Chidley was killed, Enoch Harrison's murder doesn't do much to simplify matters."

"It is possible that Royalists wanted the powder for a rising," Marlowe said. "And they killed Mr. Harrison in order to get their hands on it."

"And you think they killed Daniel because he learned of their plans?" I asked.

"It is possible." Marlowe shrugged. "Of course, what is true of the Royalists also could be said of the Levellers. If John Lilburne and the agitators in the army intended a rising of their own, they would want the powder no less than the King's men."

"What if the murders aren't so closely connected?" Will asked. "If the assassin works for pay, he might have been hired by the Levellers to kill Mr. Chidley for being a spy, and then by the Royalists to kill Mr. Harrison in order to obtain the gunpowder."

Marlowe looked as if he wanted to bite Will for making such a suggestion. The situation was already too difficult and dangerous without adding new complications.

"Perhaps we should ask how the murderer knew about the shipment of gunpowder," Tom said, hoping to deflect Marlowe's displeasure. "If we can learn that, everything else will fall into place."

When Marlowe did not reply, I spoke up: "We should pursue the assassin from two directions. Martha and I will search for connections to Daniel Chidley. And since Harrison worked so closely with the government, you should look from there."

Marlowe considered the suggestion and nodded. "Mrs. Hodgson, you will carry on as you have been. Find whatever connects the murders. Colonel Reynolds will find out how the murderer learned of the gunpowder's location." Marlowe inclined his head toward the door. It seemed we were dismissed.

As we made our way out, Marlowe called after us. "One

moment, Will. I must write to the Council about these matters. I will need you to deliver the letter immediately."

Will nodded, bid me farewell, and returned to Mr. Marlowe's side.

Tom and I stepped into the winter wind and began the long walk to the Horned Bull and beyond it, to my house in the Cheap.

"Mr. Marlowe trusts Will," I said.

"And for good reason," Tom replied. "He has proven himself as reliable as any man in Mr. Marlowe's service."

"Is it curious that I am pleased by this?" I asked. "Mr. Marlowe is a cruel man, but I've rarely seen Will so happy."

"You love your nephew. It would be strange if you felt any other way."

"Thank you," I said. "Things are so out of order. The King is dead, his son is fled, and who knows if he will return? Last autumn, my greatest concern was which of my Pontrilas neighbors to visit. Now I am no longer a gentlewoman, but a spy, and I'm joined in this by Martha and Will. Some mornings I am unsure whether the sun will rise in the east or west."

Tom nodded sympathetically. "And I take it that you realize how dangerous this matter has become thanks to the murder of Enoch Harrison."

"Aye," I said. "When only Daniel Chidley was murdered, it was a minor affair, perhaps a squabble among Levellers, or a fight between husband and wife."

Tom nodded. "And now . . ."

"Now with so much gunpowder on the loose, there is the threat of yet another rebellion."

"A rebellion, or an entirely new war," Tom said. "We cannot know how the people will react to the King's execution. If Prince

Charles were to cross the Channel tomorrow, who is to say that the people would not flock to him? And if he were to discover a ready supply of gunpowder when he arrived? We could be staring at the start of another civil war. It would be . . ." Tom's voice trailed off. The consequences would be dire indeed.

"So you do not think it was the Levellers?" I asked.

"I have not seen such violence in them. They will write their pamphlets and petition Parliament, but they are not rebels in that particular way. At least not yet."

We reached the Horned Bull, and stood outside.

"I don't know if you have food for supper in your rooms," Tom said. "But I cannot stomach the thought of another meal here. If you know where to look, there are far better places to eat, even at this hour. Would you join me?"

In truth, Martha and I had laid up plenty of bread, cheese, and pickled herring, but I welcomed the prospect of dining with Tom. I took his arm. "I would love to."

Tom guided me to an inn so brightly lit that despite the winter's cold I felt a measure of cheer. The warmth inside was all I'd hoped for, and within minutes Tom and I were enjoying a delightful meal of meats and cheeses washed down with rich red wine. We talked of our pasts, carefully avoiding any mention of the sorrows that had brought us together, but each of us knew that the other had suffered and this drew us even closer. When we ordered a second bottle of wine, I realized how the night would end if I so wished it. I thought about how many years it had been since Luke died, for that was the last time I'd felt true affection for a man. But Luke and I had been in the flower of our youth, knowing nothing of life's cruelties. Now I was older and wiser, and I knew all too well that the Lord made no promises except that death would come for all men. I could be dead in days: stabbed through the heart by an assassin, trampled by a hackney, killed by a falling roof tile. And so might Tom.

It was the thought of Tom's death that disturbed me most. I had spent the years since Luke died wondering if his was the only love I would find; indeed, I had resigned myself to it. But here was a man who saw me not as Midwife Hodgson, or Widow Hodgson, or Lady Hodgson, or even as a spy, but as all these things. He saw me and knew me, and I knew that he loved me.

"Bridget," Tom said as he refilled my glass. "I will stay the night here, and I hope you will stay with me."

I took his hand and nodded. "I will."

The next morning I awoke in a man's arms for the first time in what seemed like ten thousand lives. Gray light made its reluctant way through the windows as if it were chary of disturbing us, and I thanked the Lord for its courtesy. Tom and I each knew the other was awake, but we lay in silence for a time, unwilling to break the spell that we had cast upon ourselves. I cannot say how long our contentment lasted before a rumbling sound from Tom's stomach brought us both to laughter.

"You inspire more appetites than one, my lady," Tom said.

I nearly wept at the words *my lady,* and the love I'd felt for him the night before came rushing back. Words failed me, so I squeezed his hand, and we lapsed back into silence until his stomach roared once again. Tom laughed and rolled out of bed. "Let us find breakfast."

Tom pulled on his trousers and helped me into my clothes as lovingly as he had helped me out of them the night before. I kissed his fingers when he finished.

"Bridget," he said. "My love."

My heart thrilled at the words, and I fought down the urge to break into song. "Tom."

"We should marry," he said.

I stared at him, slack jawed, unable to speak.

"Well, then," he said at last. "I . . . suppose . . ."

"Marry?" I asked.

"Well, yes," he said. "Marry."

I found myself awash in emotions—love, fear, excitement, trepidation—and utterly without words to express any of them. "Tom . . . I . . . I don't know."

Tom laughed, and to my relief it was warm and genuine. "I know. You are a twice-widowed gentlewoman-spy, playing a poor midwife at the behest of a man you despise, who also happens to be my master. You do not know where—or even who!—you will be in a month's time. You do not know what kind of husband I would be or, after all these years, what kind of wife *you* would be. You have been your own mistress for nearly a decade, and you have no desire to become any man's woman. Yet here I am, talking of marriage."

I stared at Tom, wishing some kind of answer would come to me. I finally settled for, "Yes, that sums it up."

Tom laughed again. "And I will not have your answer today, for it is not an easy question. But know this, Bridget Hodgson: I love who you are, and I would never seek to change that."

Without warning, the most extraordinary mix of laughter and tears burst forth, washing away whatever words I might have been able to summon in response. I fell against him, still laughing and crying, and he wrapped me in his arms until I regained myself.

I looked up and found that Tom had been crying as well. I leaned forward to kiss him. "I will consider it," I said. "I love you."

Tom and I left the inn together and bid each other farewell once we were outside. I returned to the Cheap, my head still wobbling from all that had happened in the hours since I'd left Enoch Harrison's house. As I approached Watling Street I prepared myself to be interrogated by Mrs. Evelyn and Martha in case either of them realized that I'd been out all night. Indeed, Mrs. Evelyn stood in her doorway, with one eye on her shop and the other on the street.

"Good morning, Mrs. Hodgson," she called out when she saw me. "What drew you abroad last night? Were you at a travail?"

I knew better than to lie to such an inquisitive woman. If I said I'd been at a birth, she would overwhelm me with questions I could not hope to answer: Where was the birth? Who was the mother? Which gossips attended? How did they comport themselves? How is the child? I did not resent her prying, for it was the work of gossips to mind their neighbors and ensure good order. But that did not mean I wanted my night with Tom Reynolds to become the talk of the Cheap.

"Nothing so interesting, I'm afraid," I said. "I was with my nephew until late, and I did not wish to walk home at night, not by myself. It was so cold, and the city is not as safe as it once was."

Mrs. Evelyn accepted my explanation—what reason did she have to doubt it?—but I knew that any future early morning walks home would not pass unnoticed or uncommented upon.

I climbed the stairs hoping Martha had not yet returned from Lucy Sheldon's travail. The banked coals in the hearth told me she hadn't. I said a prayer of thanks, for Martha would have been much harder to fool than Mrs. Evelyn. I would tell her the truth eventually, but I wanted it to be on my own terms rather than at the end of an interrogation.

Martha arrived shortly after I did, exhausted by the travail and weaving from side to side from the drinking she must have done after. "It was nothing out of the ordinary," she said as she stripped off her skirts and fell into bed. "But it was her first child, and the gossips were very merry. They made me stay until the wine was finished."

I nodded in sympathy. Midwives were counted among the best of gossips, but such an honor came with a whole host of obligations. Within moments Martha was snoring softly. My body demanded that I join her so I might recover the sleep I'd lost the night before, but instead I settled at our table and let my mind wander over the previous day's events.

My first thoughts, of course, were about Tom, the night we'd spent together, and his suggestion that we marry. I'd spoken the truth when I said I loved him, but his description of my misgivings about marriage had been entirely correct. I'd been born Bridget Baskerville, spent a blissful year as Bridget Thurgood, and became Bridget Hodgson upon marrying Phineas. If I married Tom—if I became Bridget Reynolds—what would that mean? I believed Tom when he said that he would not try to change me, but marriages were uncertain endeavors; I knew full well what I had in my widowhood, and abandoning that certainty would be no easy thing. I buried my face in my hands and, overcome by fatigue and the future's uncertainty, allowed myself to weep. When I stopped, I crawled into bed next to Martha, closed my eyes, and was asleep in moments.

I had only been asleep for an hour or so when shouting from the street dragged me to wakefulness. I went to the window to see what was the matter, but by the time I arrived the combatants had moved on. Thanks to the wine, Martha had slept through the tumult, and I was alone. I returned to bed, but sleep eluded me.

After a half hour or so, I gave up and went to the parlor.

Thoughts of Tom pushed their way into my head, but I denied them; I did not want the tears to return. Instead, I surveyed the bloody landscape that Daniel Chidley's killer had laid before us and considered Enoch Harrison's place in it. I did not doubt that the same person had killed both men: The single knife wound was as distinctive as the Royal Seal. To my eye, it seemed likely that the murderer was a part of the Royalist faction, or at least had been hired by one of the King's men. The theft of the gunpowder would not only hurt Parliament's forces, but could supply a rising within England—a double victory for Prince Charles if he did indeed cross the Channel. If Daniel Chidley had somehow learned of the conspiracy, the King's men would not have hesitated to kill him. What was one murder if your goal was to start a war?

But what of the Levellers? If Lilburne's men in the army truly did intend to rise against Parliament's tyranny, they would need the powder as well. And they would be no less likely to kill their enemies.

So, Royalist or Leveller? Or had I missed some other murderous faction? My mind returned to Mr. Marlowe—could he have reasons of his own for seeing both men dead?

I could find no answer for any of these questions and resolved to speak to Katherine Chidley. After all, she had helped to set Martha and me on this course. I wrote a note to Martha telling her I would be across the street, then set out in search of answers to our many questions.

Chapter 18

I found Katherine in her parlor. She rose and greeted me warmly, but it took her only a moment to realize that there was more to my visit than mere friendship.

"What brings you here?" Katherine asked. "You have news?"

"Aye," I said. "Daniel's murderer has killed again."

"What?" A man's voice from behind startled me nearly out of my shoes. I spun around to find Jeremiah Goodkey staring at me, his eyes wide in surprise.

"How so?" Katherine cried. "How is it possible?"

"And how do you know it's the same man?" Goodkey seemed alarmed at the prospect. "Has he been captured?"

I stammered for a moment, trying to find a way *not* to tell Goodkey everything I'd learned, but I knew that I could not make such an announcement and then refuse to say anything more. With no other choice, I told them about Enoch Harrison: that he was a merchant murdered the day before by a single knife wound to the heart; that the murderer had killed so quickly that Harrison could not react. I finished my story without mentioning the gunpowder. If Goodkey was behind the murders, the less he knew about our investigation the better off we'd be.

"How did you learn about this murder?" Goodkey asked.

For a moment my heart ceased to beat, for I had no good answer. Why *would* someone summon me—a midwife from the Cheap—to Enoch Harrison's murder?

"A friend's husband," I said at last. "A woman I delivered is married to a constable. He knew of Daniel's murder and saw the similarity to Mr. Harrison's. He summoned me." I knew my story was as thin as year-old linen and would raise more questions than I could hope to answer. I held my breath as Goodkey considered my reply, and said a prayer of thanks when he declined to press me any further.

"It seems that Daniel's death is part of a larger and more dangerous scheme than anyone thought," Goodkey said at last. He paused for a moment. "Katherine, I am worried that if you continue mining this vein some ill might befall you. It would be safer if you left this matter to the magistrates."

"What do you mean, Jeremiah Goodkey?" Katherine asked. The steel in her voice made it abundantly clear that not only did she know what he meant, but it vexed her to no end. In that moment I almost pitied him.

"You face a practiced and expert killer," Goodkey said. He grimaced as if the act of speaking caused him physical pain. "If you pursue him too closely he could turn his attention to you. He killed Daniel and this Enoch Harrison. What chance would you have against him? You could be dead by morning."

"Are you truly such a coward?" Katherine demanded. "My husband—your friend!—was murdered, and you would simply stand aside?"

"Katherine, please listen," Goodkey said. "You must heed me.

It is for your own safety. You have no idea what this man will do if you threaten him."

"Get thee behind me, Satan," Katherine spat. "And get out of my sight."

"Katherine, you must hear me!"

"You came here to woo me, and now you betray me?" Katherine's voice had risen to a shout that, I had no doubt, was audible to her neighbors. She did not care.

Goodkey stared at her in astonishment. "Woo you?"

"What, you thought I would not recognize the true nature of your friendship?" Katherine asked. "You think a widow does not know the difference between a friend in mourning and a suitor in search of a wealthy widow? Jeremiah Goodkey, you are as subtle as a carrion kite, circling a fresh corpse. And now you are just as welcome. Get out of my house." Katherine punctuated these last words with slaps aimed at Goodkey's head.

Faced with Katherine's fury, and now her outright assault, Goodkey covered his head with his arms, scuttled to the door, and fled down the stairs. I did not know for sure, but I suspected that he left without his coat.

Katherine turned to me, her eyes still blazing. "Such a one! Can you believe such cowardice?" She took a breath and tried to recover herself. "You'll stand with me, won't you, Bridget? You will help me find out who killed my Daniel. You will help me have my revenge."

"Of course I will," I replied. Katherine was my gossip and needed my help. What else could I do?

"Good," she replied, satisfaction evident in her voice. "So what does this new murder tell us?"

"There is more to Enoch Harrison's murder than I told you," I said. "He was no ordinary merchant, and this was no ordinary murder."

"What do you mean?"

"He owned a gunpowder mill, and he was Cromwell's chief supplier," I said. "And after killing Harrison, the murderer stole enough powder to blast the Tower of London to its foundations."

Katherine thought for a moment. "But what does this have to do with Daniel's death? He was a coat-maker."

"And a spy for Oliver Cromwell," I pointed out.

Katherine winced at this reminder. "You think Daniel was killed because he discovered the plot to steal the gunpowder?"

"It is possible," I said. "The question is who did it."

"The Royalists," Katherine said. "It must have been. This Italian you mentioned, Bacca, he could be behind this."

"Aye, he could be," I said. "Or it might have been Jeremiah Goodkey."

Katherine considered this for a moment. "You think he was here not to woo me, but to find out what we had learned about Daniel's murder?" Katherine smiled wanly. "Am I so unhandsome? Truly Bridget, you do me wrong."

"I am sure his wooing was genuine," I said with a laugh. "But we must keep our eyes open to all possibilities. Cromwell has many enemies, and such a quantity of gunpowder would allow any one of them to do much mischief."

"The Levellers have no such plans," Katherine said. "If they did I would know it."

That is why Mr. Marlowe sent me here, I thought.

"Perhaps," I said. "But it would be dangerous to assume too much. And it was Goodkey who warned you to give up the hunt for Daniel's murderer, not a Royalist."

Katherine nodded. "Very well. We will keep watch on both parties. What shall we do now?"

"Let us talk about this at my tenement," I replied. "Martha should be a part of our discussion."

As we crossed the street, I realized that if Katherine and I were going to continue our search for the murderer, I would have to tell her some of the truth about my past. We reached my parlor, and I looked in on Martha. She was snoring softly, so I closed the door before joining Katherine at the table. I took Katherine's hands before I began to speak. "I must tell you something. And you must hear me to the end."

Katherine looked confused but nodded. I had earned her forbearance.

"Years ago, in a different lifetime really, it fell to me to discover another murderer."

Katherine started to respond but stopped herself. She nodded for me to continue.

"My friend was falsely accused of murdering her husband and sentenced to die. She asked for my help. I discovered the truth and saw justice done. At that time, I believed the law was good and justice was its ultimate goal.

"But in the years that followed," I continued, "I saw the innocent suffer and the guilty go free. I saw cruel men prosper, and it dawned on me that they did so not *despite* the law but *because* of the law. I realized the law was a tool like any other, a knife that could be used by a barber-surgeon to lance a boil or by a murderer to cut a throat."

"I have been preaching this for years," Katherine said.

"But unlike you, I became a part of the evil that I beheld," I said. "I used the law to my own ends, and I did so with the same pitiless heart that I condemned in others. I saw men hanged without the benefit of a trial, and used the law to murder a man who was evil but innocent."

Katherine stared at me, struck dumb for the first time since I'd known her.

"I became what I abhorred," I said. "But I will not do it again. If we find the man who killed Daniel, I will not be a part of your revenge. You will have to trust in the law."

"You are an unusual woman, even for a midwife," Katherine said at last.

"And you only know the half of it." Martha stood in the doorway. I knew from the look on her face that she'd heard everything. "But she should keep the rest of the story to herself, for your good and ours."

"If that is true, I'll not ask you to speak another word," Katherine said. "Even good gossips should have their secrets."

I nodded my thanks.

"As for the fate of Daniel's murderer," Katherine said. "You'll get no argument from me. If we find him, we will hand him over to the Justices."

"That is easy to say," I replied. "But what song will you sing if we discover the murderer is beyond the law's reach? Whoever killed Daniel may have powerful protectors."

Katherine considered the question for a time. "You are asking if I will resort to murder to avenge Daniel's death."

I nodded.

"I will not. The Levellers' goal is to remedy the law, not to destroy it. If everyone ignored the law when it did not suit them, we would have no law at all. I know it sounds cold, but Daniel would understand." She paused for a moment. "If I cannot reach Daniel's murderer through the law, I will simply redouble my efforts to reform it. And if that fails, I will rely on the Lord to provide justice in His own time."

"Then it is agreed," I said. "We will help."

Martha sat down with us, and I told them both of all that had happened: Enoch Harrison's murder, the theft of the gunpowder, and—for Martha's benefit—Jeremiah Goodkey's clumsy effort to convince Katherine to give up her search for Daniel's murderer.

"Where does this leave us?" Martha asked. "How far have we come?"

"Not far, I'm afraid," I said. "Mr. Harrison might have been killed by the Royalists—whether Charles Owen, Lorenzo Bacca, or some man we do not even suspect. Or he might have been killed by one of the Levellers, perhaps Jeremiah Goodkey. The only faction we can look past is Cromwell's, for they had no reason to kill their own gunpowder merchant."

"Can you be so sure about Cromwell's people?" Katherine asked. "What if Mr. Harrison was part of some other plot, and died for reasons we cannot begin to guess? What if the murders are not as closely connected as they seem?"

"You mean that there is one murderer but two motives?" Martha asked.

"It is possible," Katherine replied. "In these days anything is possible."

We sat in melancholy silence as we tried to find a path forward in our search for Daniel's killer. I could not see what good a new round of questioning would do us. Neither Charles Owen nor Jeremiah Goodkey would suddenly confess to Daniel's murder simply because we asked a second time. We would have to be more creative than that.

The sound of uneven footsteps rushing up the stairs announced Will's arrival even before he appeared at our door, and his hurried pace made clear he'd brought urgent news. He burst into the room without knocking.

"Aunt Bridget! Martha! You must hurry." He looked in

surprise at Katherine. "Oh, Mrs. Chidley. Three midwives? That is convenient indeed."

"What is it?" Martha asked.

"Margaret Harrison has gone into labor," he said. "She is feverish and nonsensical, but she has confessed to her father's murder."

The three of us stared at Will, slack-jawed and full of wonder. How was this possible?

"Mr. Marlowe sent me for you," Will said. "He wants you to deliver her."

Blood drained from Will's face as soon as the words passed his lips. He looked at Katherine, fully aware of his monumental blunder. "What I mean is—" he started to say.

Katherine turned to me, fury evident on her face. "*Jonathan Marlowe* sent for you?" she asked. "How is it that you know Mr. Marlowe? And why would he send for *you*?"

As I struggled for an answer, Katherine's anger boiled over. "You are one of Cromwell's spies!" she cried. "You were sent here by that tyrant to spy on me and mine!"

"And how do you know that Mr. Marlowe's Christian name is Jonathan?" Martha asked softly. "When we told you of Daniel's work for Cromwell, you professed surprise. You pretended that you had no idea who Mr. Marlowe was."

In an instant, Martha's question robbed Katherine of her righteous fury. If she knew Marlowe's name, she must have known that Daniel was in his service.

"It seems we both have some explaining to do," Katherine said at last.

"Yes, that is fine, but not now," Will insisted. "Right now you must attend Margaret Harrison. A physician is with her, and he is quite concerned."

"Very well." Katherine turned to me. "Do you have your valise and stool?"

I recognized the true meaning of her question. By offering to let me take the lead in delivering Margaret Harrison, she proffered an olive branch. "I do," I said, and bowed my head in thanks.

The four of us hurried down the stairs and into the fading afternoon light.

"Where are we going?" I asked. We were following the same route to Margaret Harrison's travail that we had taken to her father's corpse.

"To Mr. Harrison's," Will replied. "That is where she lives."

It took a moment, but I realized what Will had just told us. "A few minutes ago you called her Margaret Harrison," I said. "And she lives with her father?"

"Aye," Will said. "What of it?"

"Margaret is pregnant with a bastard?" Katherine said.

"Well, yes," Will replied. He was clearly confused by our interest in the child's legitimacy.

"Is she betrothed?" Martha asked. "How has the father not been made to marry her?" It was a strange thing for the daughter of a wealthy merchant to find herself bearing a bastard.

"I have no idea," Will replied. To his mind, the question was irrelevant.

I did not know what it meant, but between Margaret's unlikely pregnancy and her strange confession, it was clear that more was going on in the Harrison household than we had realized. The only question was whether such strange doings would lead us to Enoch Harrison's murderer.

We hurried up the steps to the Harrisons' front door and entered. Will led us up another set of stairs to a bedchamber where we found quite a crowd: Margaret Harrison, a maidservant, Mr. Marlowe, a man I took to be a physician, and Tom Reynolds. The moment I saw Tom, my stomach tilted to one side and then the other, as if I were on a storm-tossed ship. I counted it a blessing I did not cast up my dinner.

Tom and I made a show of formality in greeting each other, but I did not think it would have fooled even the most credulous child. I could only hope nobody cared enough to notice.

"Out, out, out," Katherine cried out as soon as we entered the room. "None of you men need to be here."

Will and Tom had the good sense to listen, slipping out of the room, but Marlowe and the physician looked at Katherine in confusion.

"This is women's business," I said, joining Katherine in herding them toward the door. "You'll not be a part of it."

While Mr. Marlowe bleated his objections even as he was driven from the room, the physician looked quite relieved to be removed from his post.

"Very well," Mr. Marlowe said at last, looking at Katherine and me. "But I must speak to the two of you before you begin your work."

Katherine and I glanced at each other. I nodded and turned to Martha. "Stay with her," I said.

"I will see to it," Martha said.

Katherine and I followed Marlowe into the hall. I caught a glimpse of the physician as he fled down the stairs, leaving Will, Tom, and Mr. Marlowe behind.

"What is it?" I asked. "If the girl's travail is as dire as Will said, we should see to her."

Marlowe glared at Katherine and me before responding. "For the moment I'll leave aside the question of how you *both* came to be here. But I suppose I should have expected that you would discover each other eventually."

"You have spies for your spies?" I asked.

"It is better to be sure," Marlowe said with more than a hint of pride.

"If we *hadn't* discovered it, we would be poor spies indeed," Katherine said.

Tom laughed before being silenced by a poisonous look from Mr. Marlowe.

Marlowe turned back to Katherine and inclined his head, conceding her point. "Whatever the case, you must question the girl about her father when she is in travail."

"Of course we will," I said. "But why are you concerned with the father's name?"

"I don't give a fig's end about the child's father," Marlowe replied. "You must question her about *her* father. We must know the truth about his murder, no matter the cost."

Katherine and I stared at him, lost for words.

"You want us to question her about her father's murder while she is in travail?" I asked at last.

"It is necessary," Marlowe said. "She says she is guilty, but she will not say in what way. We do not believe that she wielded the knife. Or that she killed Mr. Chidley. But she must know who did. She is the key to unraveling the entire scheme."

"You want us to threaten her?" Katherine asked. "And to abandon her if she does not confess to her part in a murder? She would be hanging herself."

"It is the only way to find the truth," Marlowe replied. "You must."

Katherine and I glanced at each other. She seemed no less uncertain than I was. I had no qualms about questioning a bastard-bearer about the father of her child, or threatening to abandon her if she refused. In my experience, even the most indocile mother chose to reveal the father's name rather than deliver her child alone. But this was a different matter. We could be asking Margaret to confess to murder. She would be putting a noose around her own neck and pulling it tight.

"I will not," I replied. "It is an evil thing to force a girl to choose between death in travail and death by hanging. I will have no part in it."

Marlowe glanced at Tom, who smiled slightly and muttered something under his breath that sounded like *As I predicted*.

"Mrs. Chidley," Marlowe said.

"You may deliver the girl yourself if you'd like," Katherine said. "But I'll not be a part of your scheme, either."

"She knows who murdered her father," Marlowe said. "And who killed your husband."

"We will ask her," Katherine said. "But if she will not confess, we will deliver her as we would any mother. We'll not be party to her execution."

"Mrs. Hodgson?" Marlowe pleaded.

"You have our answer. If you do not like it, you may do the work yourself. Or perhaps you have another midwife in your employ?"

Marlowe looked at Tom.

"What would you have me do?" Tom asked, fighting not to smile. "They are your spies, not mine."

Marlowe looked as if he had swallowed a toad. "Very well," he said at last. "Do your best."

"We will," I said.

Chapter 19

Margaret Harrison's bedchamber was large and well appointed, precisely what I would have expected from a woman of her father's wealth. This, of course, also made her unique among the bastard-bearers I'd delivered; they usually lived in tiny hovels or one-room tenements. A fire roared in the hearth, chasing away the winter chill. Margaret sat in a large bed, propped up on luxurious pillows, the very picture of a woman in the comfortable stages of early travail.

But when we approached I saw the fear shining in the girl's eyes; all was not well with her.

"Who are you?" Margaret demanded. "Why are you here?"

"Hush," I said. "I am Widow Hodgson, your midwife." I put my wrist to her forehead. I found it passing warm, but she could hardly be described as feverish.

"What fool said she had a fever?" I asked. "She's in travail and lying next to a blazing fire—she could hardly be cooler."

"The physician said it," Margaret replied, her eyes glistening with tears. "He said that a woman could not be delivered so long as she suffered from a fever. Is it true?"

"It is not true, and you don't have a fever," I replied. "You are fine."

"What about my colic? My stomach pains me. He said it was colic."

Nobody had said anything about colic, of course. *That* was a different matter. "We will see," I said. "I must examine you before I know anything."

Martha took Margaret's hand while Katherine joined me in my examination. I pressed the girl's belly, trying to distinguish the source of her pains. "Are the colic pains different than your labor pangs?" I asked. If the physician could not recognize a fever, I had no faith that he'd know colic when he saw it.

"I don't know," she said.

I pressed on the left side of her belly and the girl moaned. I waited a moment and pressed again. "Ah, God save me!" Margaret cried out.

"It is indeed colic," I said to Katherine. "And we must see to it before the child is born."

Katherine nodded. "Shall we potion her with cinnamon?"

"Aye, and oil of almonds," I said. "And we should prepare a clyster in case that does not work. We must be prepared in all events."

After Katherine departed for the kitchen, I looked back to Margaret. Fear shone in her eyes. "You will be fine," I said, taking her hand. "I have seen such a condition many times. I will see you through this."

"Thank you," she said. Tears of relief and gratitude welled up in her eyes, making my next task that much more difficult.

"We will help you, but in return you must tell us the truth about the child's father—and about what happened to *your* father."

In an instant Margaret's relief turned to fear. "He told you? That horrible Mr. Marlowe told you?"

"Aye, he did," I said. "But he said you wouldn't tell him everything that happened. You must tell us the rest. You are living under a terrible burden. Lay it on my shoulders, and you will rest easier."

Tears poured forth and within moments she was sobbing like a newly orphaned child. I climbed onto the bed next to the poor girl, and took her into my arms. She was still weeping when Katherine returned with the cinnamon water. Margaret drank a few swallows without complaint and slowly regained control of herself.

"You confessed to having a hand in your father's death," I said. "But we know that you did not kill him yourself."

Tears returned to Margaret's eyes. "It was my fault, though. I invited Bram into the house that night. He must have done it. I still cannot believe it, but it must be true."

"Start at the beginning," I said. "And tell me everything."

Margaret took a deep breath to compose herself and began to tell her story. "He started wooing me a full year ago, Bram did. He was loving and kind in a way few men are. He said I was beautiful."

At this she began to weep. It was impossible not to feel for the girl's suffering at Bram's cold-hearted betrayal. With a few soothing words and common courtesies he had won over this lonely girl. And once he had her trust, he destroyed her life, getting her with a bastard and murdering her father.

"Bram is the child's father?" I asked.

"He promised marriage," she said. "We were supposed to

marry last fall, but he was called away on an urgent matter." I had delivered countless bastards and heard countless stories of abandonment and betrayal, but I had never heard a girl sound so lost and forlorn.

"What else did he want?" I asked. "How did this lead to your father's death?"

"Bram said he was one of the King's men," she replied. "He showed me a letter with His Majesty's seal upon it. And he had some silken string that had been tied up in the most beautiful knot you have ever seen. He said these were signs that he was doing His Majesty's bidding. He told me that if he succeeded the King would make him a knight, and we would have an estate, and we would live together. He said he needed my help, that the King needed my help."

"What did he want you to do?" I asked.

"At first he wanted me to tell him all I knew about my father's business. He is a gunpowder merchant. Bram asked where the powder was made, where it was stored, everything I could discover.

"Then he wanted to know when my father was out of London, seeing to the powder works," she continued. "He said he wanted to visit me away from my father's eyes. I waited until the servants were asleep and then I opened the door for him."

"And you lay with him," Katherine said. The girl nodded.

"But that was not the only reason he came," I said.

Margaret looked away from me, and I knew we had reached the cardinal moment of her story. "Bram wanted to look through my father's books and papers to learn when Parliament was in short supply of gunpowder. He said that with that information he could better advise Prince Charles. The King's men are planning a rising, you know."

The girl was oblivious to the fact that with each word she not only betrayed her lover and his cause, but made herself party to his treason.

"And Bram murdered your father?" I asked.

"I know it must be true, but I still cannot credit it." Margaret started weeping again.

"Tell me about the night your father died."

"Bram said he wanted to speak to him. He said he would convince him both to let us marry *and* to help the King. Bram said that if my father would do these things, all would be well for us. I would be married, and my father would no longer be called a traitor."

"You let him into the house," Katherine said.

"My father's custom was to work until very late at night and then rise near noon. Bram thought it would be best if they spoke during the night when they would not be disturbed. I waited until the servants were asleep and unbarred the door. I placed a candle in my window as a sign to Bram that it was safe for him to come. Then I went to bed."

"Did you hear anything? An argument or disagreement?"

Margaret shook her head and daubed at her eyes with the edge of her sheet. "I lay there all night, wondering what would happen. I thought that in the morning, all would be right. And then I heard the door being smashed and then the shouting when the neighbors found his body." She fell forward and buried her face in my chest. I held her close and looked up at Katherine's and Martha's grim faces. It seemed we had found our murderer.

I took Margaret's face in my hands. "Margaret, you must help us find Bram. You must. Who is he? Where does he live?"

Margaret took a shuddering breath and nodded. "He is Abraham Walker," she said. "He lives south of St. Paul's."

Martha and Katherine gasped behind me. My mouth worked

for a time before I could make a sound, and even then it was a thin mewling, fit for a kitten. Even in her colic and travail Margaret could tell that she'd said something remarkable.

"What is it?" she asked. "What did I say?"

"Abraham Walker?" I repeated stupidly.

"And he lives on Knightrider Street?" Katherine said.

"Aye, that is where I sent my letters. Sometimes I would slip out and meet him there. What is wrong? What is it?" I could hear the panic rising in her voice and did not know what to say.

"What does he look like?" Katherine asked, though we all knew the answer to the question.

Margaret proceeded to describe Abraham Walker in perfect detail. There could be no mistake: Katherine's friend had murdered Enoch Harrison and—in all likelihood—Daniel Chidley as well.

Katherine sat down heavily on the bed, her face bereft of color.

"Do you know him, too?" Margaret asked.

"Aye, we know him," I said. I pushed the cup of cinnamon water to her lips. "Now finish your medicine."

After Margaret's revelation, I slipped from the room to tell the men what we'd learned.

I found Tom, Will, and Mr. Marlowe in Enoch Harrison's office. They had helped themselves to his store of wine and seemed very comfortable. Marlowe was leafing through one of Mr. Harrison's account books while Tom and Will examined the various weapons on the shelves. Marlowe rose to his feet when I entered.

"What is it?" he asked. "Did she kill him?"

"Not deliberately," I replied. "But she told us who wielded the knife: Abraham Walker."

Tom knitted his brow. "You said he was a neutralist. Why would he kill Mr. Harrison and steal the gunpowder?"

"He told Margaret that he was a Royalist intelligencer," I replied. "He proved it by showing her a waxen seal and some sort of knot woven out of silk. He seduced her so he could spy on her father."

"Was the seal genuine?" Tom asked.

"There's no way to know," I replied. "She is so blinded by her passion that he could have shown her the butt end of a candle and she would have been convinced."

"By his spying on Mr. Harrison, Walker learned about the gunpowder," Tom said.

"Aye," I said. "And then he struck. He forced Mr. Harrison to sign the letter, which he no doubt gave to one of his comrades to take to the powder works."

"And then he killed Mr. Harrison so he could not raise a hue and cry," Tom finished.

"Did you learn anything else?" Mr. Marlowe asked.

"Katherine said he lives on Knightrider Street south of St. Paul's," I said. "And that is where the girl sent her letters."

"Well done." Mr. Marlowe started to pull on his coat, and the others did the same. "Colonel Reynolds, take Will and go to the constable. Raise whatever men you can find: beadles, the trained bands, chimney sweepers, anyone who can carry a club. Find Walker wherever he is."

"Tell the men to be careful," Tom said. "Walker has already killed two people, and there's no reason to think he won't kill more."

"Careful is good," Marlowe said. "But we also should be sure to capture him alive, even at the loss of a beadle or two. It is a fine thing to catch a murderer, but make no mistake: the real prize is the gunpowder."

"We will find him," Will said as he buttoned his coat. I smiled at his earnest determination and said a prayer for his success and safety.

"See that you do," Marlowe replied. "I will go to the Tower. Bring him there when you catch him."

After the three men had left, I started up the stairs. It was only then that I realized that we four women were alone and unguarded. I went downstairs and barred the door. It seemed sturdy enough.

When I returned to Margaret's chamber I found her more relaxed. The cinnamon concoction had done its work, and confessing her crimes—however unintentional they might have been—had eased her guilt.

"Margaret," I said. "What servants are here in the house?"

"John and Patience," she said. "The others go home before dark. Why?"

"No reason," I said. "I simply wondered who else might be here." To my relief, she did not pursue the matter. Martha caught my eye. She was concerned as well, but at this point there was nothing we could do except trust that Tom and Will would catch Walker that night.

It was still well dark—perhaps three of the clock—when Margaret's travail began in earnest. She had just taken to the birthing stool when we heard a knocking at the front door. We ignored it, of course, having more urgent business before us. When the knocking turned to pounding, I realized our mistake.

I looked up at Martha. "What if it's Walker?"

"Oh, Christ," she said, and ran for the chamber door.

"Tell the servants not to open the door for anyone," I shouted.

The pounding at the front door stopped and I could feel my heart beating in my breast. Martha opened the chamber door and stepped into the hall. To my dismay we heard the bar being lifted from its braces, and the heavy creak of the front door opening. Martha stopped and looked back at us, unsure what to do.

We heard a cry of surprise, cut short by twin pistol shots.

"Close the door," Katherine said to Martha. "We must do whatever we can to block it."

Working together, Martha and Katherine quickly piled every piece of furniture they could lift in front of the door. One glance told me that it would be entirely inadequate for the job.

"What is it? What is happening?" Margaret's panicked voice reminded me that we faced two problems, not just one. "Who is at the door? Were those gunshots?"

"It must be Abraham Walker," I said. "You are the only one who knows that he killed your father. He's come to ensure your silence."

At that moment, a labor pang—the worst one yet—struck and Margaret's face coiled in upon itself as she cried out in pain.

"Be calm," I said. "All will be well." If Margaret had opened her eyes to see my face, she would have known that I believed no such thing.

The sound of heavy footsteps climbing the stairs brought me to the edge of panic. I closed my eyes and sought refuge in prayer. Then, without warning, I found myself overtaken by a sense of peace. When I opened my eyes, the world around me had begun to move more slowly. Suddenly I knew everything that could be known, and nothing was beyond my power. I had no name for this extraordinary calm, but I had felt it a few times before, always in the midst of a difficult travail. One moment I would be up to my elbows in blood and sweat, terrified that I would lose both mother and child. The next it was as if I could see the child in the mother's belly. I knew which medicines and ointments to use, and what secrets I must employ both to save the mother and to bring the child safely in to the world.

By now the footsteps had reached the top of the stairs and approached our door. Katherine and Martha leaned against it, hoping to keep us safe. They braced themselves for a crash that would signal the start of Walker's final assault.

Instead, he knocked. "Margaret," a voice called. "Are you in there? It is Bram. Open the door."

In an instant, I realized what this meant. I gestured wildly for Katherine and Martha to leave the door and join me in the far corner of the room. I turned to Margaret. "You are still some time from delivering your child. If you wish to live that long, you will have to do what I tell you."

The girl nodded.

"Good. If you remain silent, we will keep you safe." I crossed the room to Katherine and Martha. They stared at me in confusion and desperation. Why had I sent them away from the door when Walker was just on the other side?

"We must be quiet," I whispered. "Walker has no idea that Margaret is in travail, so he does not know we are here. He thinks that she is alone and will be easy prey."

The door handle rattled. "Open the door, my duck. I have come for you just as I promised." I recognized Abraham Walker's voice, but I could hear no trace of the murderous creature that lay behind it.

"Where are the neighbors?" Katherine hissed. "He fired a bloody pistol, and nobody has come to help?"

"I think I know what he did," I whispered. I crossed to the window and pulled the curtain back so the three of us could see out. The street was alight with torches and a group of armed men stood in front of the Harrisons' house. One man was talking to some of the neighbors who had braved the cold to find out what the trouble was.

"Walker knew he risked rousing the neighbors," I said. "So be brought his own men to keep the peace. They are disguised as members of the trained bands."

"Oh, God," Martha said.

"No doubt he told the neighbors that they've discovered a Royalist plot," Katherine said. "That would excuse the pistol shots. Quite clever."

"They'll kill us all and disappear into the city," I said. "Nobody will even know where to look for them."

"Margaret!" Walker demanded from the hallway. "I know you are scared, but you must let me in."

"Well," Martha said. "I'm glad we've got that sorted. But what do we do now?"

Margaret spoke before I could answer. "Bram?" she called out. "Is it really you?"

The horror in Martha's eyes matched my own. How could the girl be so foolish?

"It is, my love. I have come for you just as I promised that I would." Walker's voice was so loving that I knew he would win over poor Margaret.

I raced to Margaret's side and took her hand. "You must not do this," I whispered. "He murdered your father and now has come to do the same to you."

Margaret's eyes darted between mine and the door as she wondered who she should believe: her lover or a stranger. "What happened?" she called out. A sob caught in her throat. "What did you do to my father?"

"Oh, God," Walker cried out as if in pain. "It was the most terrible thing. It was an accident."

"Tell me what happened," Margaret insisted. She then whispered, "My love." She spoke so softly that none but I could have heard it. Tears filled her eyes.

At that instant I knew that Margaret's misguided affection for Walker had overcome her fear, and at any moment she would betray our presence in the room. If that happened, we would lose whatever slight advantage we still had.

"I came to him," Walker called out. "I asked for his permission to marry you, just as I said I would." He sounded as if he were fighting back tears of his own. "But he flew into a rage as soon as I told him of our plans. He said he would not have his daughter dishonored so horribly."

"But it would be no dishonor," Margaret exclaimed.

"I know, my sweet!" Walker cried. "But he was mad with fury. He attacked me before I could convince him. I did not mean to kill him. I only wanted for us to marry."

I leaned to Margaret. "We will open the door," I whispered. "But only if you ensure that he is by himself. Tell him he must be alone." I thought he would be, for he would not want a witness when he murdered Margaret.

In her confusion, pain, and lovesickness Margaret did not argue. "Is anyone with you?"

"I have some men downstairs," Walker replied. "And they will take us from here to the river. I have a fast ship there that will carry us to France as soon as the sun rises."

The joy that filled Margaret's eyes when she heard this lie broke my heart. The truth was that by the time the sun rose, either she or her lover would be dead. I squeezed the girl's hand. "Tell him you will open the door, but you must dress first."

Margaret looked confused, but she did as I asked. I could tell that she would not obey many more of my commands.

I crossed to the door and started dismantling the barricado that Martha and Katherine had built. Martha seized my arm but I shook her off.

"Are you mad?" she whispered. "He will kill us all."

"These sticks of furniture will not stop him," I said. "He is coming in whether we want him to or not. If we can surprise him we have a chance." I handed Martha the fire poker and took a set of iron tongs for myself. Katherine picked up a brass candlestick. We finished clearing the door and stood around it in a half circle.

Martha and Katherine gripped their makeshift weapons like swords, their faces hard as granite, ready for the battle to come.

I said a prayer and reached for the door handle.

Chapter 20

Before I turned the handle, Margaret cried out in pain. A labor pang had struck.

"Darling, what is it?" Walker called out. "Are you ill?"

"I am fine," she replied through clenched teeth. "I am in travail with our child."

Walker said nothing for a moment. While he could make his peace with killing both his lover and her father, perhaps even he scrupled at killing a woman when she was in travail with his child.

"Then I will take you to a midwife," he called out with forced lightness. "Open the door. We will go together. I know of one in the neighborhood."

I knew what Margaret's reply would be and that the time had come for us to fight or die. I looked at Katherine and Martha. They understood the situation as well as I did.

"There is no need for that . . ." Margaret called out.

I wrenched the door open and stepped back so Walker would not see me. I didn't know if he wondered who had opened the door, but he walked in without a moment's hesitation. He stared at

Margaret, so intent on his prey that he did not notice any of the rest of us until he had crossed the threshold.

Martha swung the fire iron at Walker's head with such force that I felt sure that the battle would be over with one blow. To my dismay, Walker sensed Martha's presence and simultaneously ducked beneath the blow and threw up his cloak as a sort of shield. The iron missed Walker entirely, and instead became tangled in the folds of his cloak. Martha cursed as she tried to free her weapon, but Walker was much stronger, and with a furious cry he wrested the iron out of Martha's hands.

I leaped into the affray, swinging the tongs at Walker's back. But my blow had even less of an effect than Martha's, for the handle snapped off as soon as I struck him.

Walker ignored my feeble assault and stepped toward Katherine with a heavy cudgel in his right hand.

Katherine raised the candlestick over her head and brought it down with all her strength. Walker skipped back, the blow missing him by mere inches. He darted forward, swinging his club at Katherine's head in a short, vicious arc. Katherine ducked and raised her arm, but she had no chance at all. She cried out when the club struck her arm—we all heard the bone break—and she fell silent when a second blow hit her head. Katherine fell to the ground, lifeless, blood flowing in a river from her head onto the floor. By then Margaret had begun to scream, adding even more confusion to the chaotic scene before us.

I stepped to Martha's side and we stood shoulder to shoulder between Walker and Margaret. He turned from Katherine and looked into my eyes. He gave no sign that we knew each other. He was no longer Katherine's friend, but an assassin bent on his work.

In an instant the calm that had served me so well mere moments before vanished. My heart raced, and I fought to contain the scream that clawed its way up my gullet. Walker took a deep breath as if to collect himself for these last few killings and stepped toward us. With no weapon to fight him and no hope of escape, I did the only thing I could. I lowered my head and charged him. To this day I don't know what I hoped to achieve by this. But I knew I'd rather die fighting than cowering on my knees.

Walker struck my back, but the pain seemed both distant and unimportant, something with which I could concern myself in the future. Perhaps I caught Walker by surprise, or my fear had given me some extranatural strength, but I drove him back several steps before he regained his balance. He recovered himself, and I found that my head was tucked neatly beneath his arm. As he continued to strike my back, I realized that I had found the one position where his cudgel could not kill me. Walker tried to push me away, but I wrapped my arms around his waist and held on with all my strength. I knew that if he escaped my grasp I'd be dead within seconds.

My grip began to weaken and I choked back a cry of despair. The moment before Walker would have escaped, we both were knocked to the ground. Martha had hurled herself at Walker, and she now lay atop both of us, with Walker on the bottom of our pile. By now my head was wrapped in Walker's cloak, leaving me a blind and ineffectual soldier in our deadly skirmish.

Walker fought to escape from beneath us, rolling from one side to the other, pushing and cursing all the while. I grasped and bit whatever limbs I could find, desperate to hold him fast.

I had nearly freed my head from Walker's cloak—or so I thought—when his struggles became more frantic than ever. With one desperate heave, he threw Martha and me to the side and rolled away from us. I scrabbled to my feet and turned toward him. He was on his hands and knees facing away from us, but making no effort to rise. For a moment I wondered why he stayed in so vulnerable a position. Then I saw the blood running from his neck.

He remained on his knees for a few seconds before his strength gave out and he collapsed. I circled his body until I could see his face. His eyes stared lifelessly into a distance that he would never see.

It was only then that I became aware of the room around me. Margaret's screams had turned to sobs, but I pushed them out of my mind. If she could weep, she was not yet in her final travail. I turned to Martha and found her still as a statue, staring at Walker's body. Her hand held a short and bloody knife that I recognized instantly, for I had its twin in my own apron. It was the knife Martha used to cut a child's navel string. The blade, which had been made to begin a child's life, had just ended Abraham Walker's.

My eyes fell to Katherine, whose corpse lay just beyond Walker's, and sorrow welled up in my heart. She lay exactly as she had fallen, entirely bereft of life or breath. I started across the room and saw that Margaret was crawling toward Walker's body.

Acting as one, Martha and I tried to take the poor girl by her arms and return her to the birthing stool. As soon as she felt my touch, Margaret lashed out, her fingers raking my arms like claws. I pulled back, staring in surprise at the trails of blood that welled up on the back of my hand. Even Martha thought better of interfering, and allowed the girl to take her lover in her arms one last time. I wrapped my hand in a handkerchief, and with a leaden heart crossed the room to Katherine.

I knelt at her side and began to weep. "Oh, Katherine."

"What about the men downstairs?" Martha asked. Her voice remained calm and strong despite the bloody circumstances.

"God help us," I said. "I forgot them entirely." I went to the window and looked outside. Walker's men stood in a half circle around the door, ensuring that their master would be able to finish his bloody business undisturbed. So long as they remained outside we were safe, but how long would it be before they came in search of their master? While we had bested one man armed only with a cudgel, a squad of pistols would cut us down in moments.

"How long will they wait?" Martha asked.

"Not long enough," I replied.

"There must be pistols in Mr. Harrison's office," Martha said. "We could arm ourselves and hold them at bay until help comes."

"Do you know how to charge a pistol?" I asked.

Martha's silence answered my question.

I went to the door, and with a deep sense of dread I began to rebuild the barricado. I had no expectation that it would protect us for long. Without a word, Martha joined in the work and all too soon we were done.

I cast my eyes around the room again, wondering if this might be the place that I would die. Margaret lay next to Walker, crying softly. Soon enough her labor pangs would overcome her grief and I would have to deliver her, but for now the greater danger was the armed men in the street, bent on her murder.

I heard a shout in the distance and then an answering cry from the men below our window. Martha and I pulled back the curtain. A squadron of the trained bands was racing toward us, and the men outside the Harrisons' house had drawn their swords to meet the challenge. My heart leaped when I saw Tom leading the squad. He was racing toward us, pistol in one hand, and sword in the other.

One of the men below us stepped forward, and I swallowed a cry when he raised his pistol and aimed it at Tom. I slammed my eyes shut, waiting for the shot that would shatter my heart, but unwilling to witness the death of the man I loved. In an instant I knew that losing Tom would be as heavy a blow as losing Martha or Elizabeth. I whispered a prayer, begging the Lord to have mercy on Tom and on me.

After a moment passed with no blast, I dared to look. The two squadrons had met, each one shouting at the other. The air about them crackled with violence; if one man fired his pistol or even raised his sword, half a dozen men would die. I could not understand their words, but to my eternal relief, both Tom and his opponent lowered their pistols and exchanged words rather than blows. The man said something to Tom and gestured at the front door. Tom's head whipped toward the house, and he sprinted inside as if the devil himself were on his heels.

"We should move the furnishings," Martha murmured.

"Too late," I said.

Tom thundered up the stairs and hurled himself at the chamber door with all his might. The door ripped free from its hinges and split cleanly down the middle. Had it not been for the barricado, he would have flown across the room and into Margaret's bed.

"Bridget!" Tom shouted as he clambered through the wreckage of the door. In moments he found himself mired in the pile of furniture on the other side. "What is happening? Are you in here?"

"We are fine." I called out. My eyes returned to the corpses on the floor. My heart ached with my love for Tom and my grief for Katherine. "Martha and I are fine," I said more softly.

"Thank God. What the devil is going on?" He ceased his struggles and looked about the room, taking in the destroyed furnishings, the blood, and the bodies.

Before I could answer I heard a retching sound behind me.

"Oh, God, Margaret." I turned to help the girl but found her as she had been: weeping softly at Abraham Walker's side.

It was Katherine Chidley. By some working of God, she was still alive. Martha and I dashed to her side. She was struggling to roll onto her stomach, hampered by a broken arm that lay by her side at a crazy angle. We helped her roll over, and she emptied her stomach onto the floor. When she'd finished, Martha and I carried her to the bed, taking especial care not to do any further damage to her arm. Katherine looked about the room dazedly, unaware of where she was or why she was covered in blood. She struggled to sit up, her eyes flitting between Martha and me, begging for an explanation.

"Just rest," I said. "You've been hurt, but you will be fine." I prayed that this was true. She closed her eyes and lay back on the pillow.

Behind us, Tom made his way through the wreckage of our defenses and joined us. I could only imagine what he made of the mad scene before him. "I'll send for a physician and bonesetter."

"Thank you for coming in such a hurry."

"You seem to have held your own," he replied. "I should go back downstairs. The neighbors are out, and all is bedlam."

"Tom." I took his hand. He turned to face me. "Yes," I said.

When Tom realized that I'd agreed to marry him, a smile as wide as the sun spread across his face. "Good. But I should go." He squeezed my hand and dashed downstairs.

The following hours passed in a fog, as men poured in and out of Margaret Harrison's chamber. One of the trained bands led Margaret to another room and sent for a new midwife. Then the bonesetter came and saw to Katherine's arm, while the physician peered at her head and suggested a poultice. Finally, four men arrived with a litter to carry Katherine home. Just after sunrise, Margaret gave birth to a baby boy. Mr. Marlowe arrived soon after, with Will at his side. They surveyed the scene as I explained what had happened.

Both men shook their heads in wonder.

"What brought Colonel Reynolds back so quickly?" Martha asked when we'd finished our story.

"After Colonel Reynolds and I gathered men to arrest Walker," Will said, "we sought out the churchwarden to tell us which house was his. But when we came to Walker's street, we found it already in a tumult."

"What happened?" Martha asked.

"Mr. Walker had already roused some of the trained bands himself. He told them that he'd discovered a nest of traitors and needed their help to root them out."

"So the men downstairs weren't his comrades?" Martha asked. "We were in no danger of being murdered?"

Will looked around the ruined chamber. Walker's body still lay in a pool of blood. "Not *no* danger, but the trained bands were no threat. You were safe enough once Walker was dead."

Tom crossed the room and continued the story. "When we heard that Walker had summoned the trained bands, we realized where he must have gone. Only Margaret Harrison knew his secret, so he could hardly let her live. We came back as quickly as we could, only to find that you'd taken care of the matter yourself."

"And the servants downstairs?" Martha asked. "We heard pistol shots."

"Both dead," Will replied. "Walker shot them."

"Poor souls," I said. "That's four people he killed."

"In a sense you were fortunate," Tom said. "If Walker hadn't shot them, he would have had pistols at the ready when he came through the door."

"He didn't think Margaret would put up much of a fight," I said.

"Colonel Reynolds," Marlowe said, "take Will to Abraham Walker's home and search it thoroughly. Pull up the floors if you must. Bring me whatever you find. We must unearth the gunpowder and put this matter to rest."

Tom and Will nodded and looked apologetically in our direction. They bid us farewell and were gone.

A few minutes later two of the coroner's men came for Walker's body. They rolled him onto a sheet and prepared to wrap him.

"One moment," I said. I knelt at Walker's side and looked through his pockets. I discovered a red silken cord tied into an intricate knot and held it up for Martha to see.

"That must be the knot he showed Margaret," she said.

"Aye. It would be impossible to duplicate, and thus it is a perfect sign of allegiance to the King. It is how his spies know each other." I nodded to the coroner's men, and they took Walker's body from the room.

"I'll take that to the Tower." Mr. Marlowe extended his hand for the silk cord. "It will prove useful when we arrest his comrades."

I could think of no reason to keep the knot for myself, so I handed it over. Marlowe pocketed it and followed Walker's body, leaving Martha and me alone with the wreckage and blood that were the last visible fruit of our night's work. We straightened the room as best we could, but balked at scrubbing the bloody floorboards. It had been too long a night.

We descended the stairs to find similar bloodstains by the front door. I said a prayer of thanks that it was the servants' blood rather than ours and then begged forgiveness for my selfishness. Martha and I stepped into the morning light and made our way north through the city. We had much to discuss, but neither of us knew where to begin.

"That's it then," Martha said. "Abraham Walker killed Daniel Chidley and Mr. Harrison, and now he's dead."

"So it appears," I said. "Mr. Marlowe might want the gunpowder to thwart the rising, but that's his concern, not ours. Our business is done."

"What will happen to Margaret?" Martha asked.

"It is no crime to be a fool," I said. "She'll inherit her father's estate and the gunpowder works, I suppose. It will take time, but I think she will recover. There are worse fates than being a wealthy singlewoman, even one with a bastard."

We fell silent, putting more time and space between us and the bloody chaos of Enoch Harrison's house.

"What of you and Tom Reynolds?" Martha asked. "He seemed more than usually pleased at your survival."

I laughed. "I'm surprised it took you so long to notice. Most days I felt as if I were the town crier, shouting my affairs to all the Cheap."

"And?"

I took a breath, hardly daring to reply.

Martha stopped and turned to face me. Somehow she knew. "Oh, Lord," she said. "You're not . . ."

"We are betrothed."

Martha threw her head back and burst out laughing. "You are, aren't you! I thought so; I just couldn't believe it." Martha continued to laugh, making any response on my part entirely unnecessary. "How did this happen?" she asked when we started walking again. "I never thought it would."

"Nor did I," I admitted. "At first he reminded me of Luke, but it's not that at all. He knows me as a gentlewoman, a midwife, even a poor widow, and he loves all of these parts. He does not want me to be *his*; he wants me to be *mine*. He knows why I haven't remarried, and asked me to marry him all the same. He is kind, thoughtful, and loyal. And until I met him I did not know how much I missed the affection Luke and I had for each other."

"And with this betrothal have the two of you . . ." Martha finished her sentence by raising an eyebrow.

I had no intention of answering, but the blood that rushed to my face replied on my behalf.

Martha laughed again. "Oh, that is excellent indeed."

"If we are betrothed, there is no sin," I said. Of course, Tom and I had not been betrothed when we lay together, but I had no intention of telling Martha that.

"I am not accusing you of anything," Martha said. "As I said, I find it quite excellent."

We turned onto Watling Street and with our neighbors all about us Martha fell mercifully silent. We climbed the stairs to our rooms and collapsed into bed.

When sleep came, I dreamed of Abraham Walker bursting into Margaret Harrison's chamber, cudgel in hand. I watched in horror as he struck down Katherine, just as he had the night before. But in my dream he turned on Margaret, killing her, and then Martha as well. He raised the club—now stained with three women's blood—and started toward me. I woke with a cry just before he delivered the blow that would have dashed out my brains.

I sat up and looked at Martha. She slept on, untroubled by my cry and apparently secure in her own dreams. I felt sure that if I tried to sleep my dream would return, so I climbed out of bed and dressed. With a full day before me, I resolved to visit Katherine Chidley and see how she fared.

Chapter 21

Katherine awoke as soon as I opened the chamber door. She seemed more bandages than flesh, as both her arm and head had been thoroughly wrapped in linen strips. From the lines on her face, it seemed as if she'd aged twenty years in a single night.

"There you are." Her voice barely reached above a whisper. "I hoped you would visit."

"How are you?"

"Sore," she said with a thin smile.

"Your arm is well set?"

"The bonesetter did his best," Katherine replied, shrugging her good shoulder. "He said it was a bad break and there was only so much he could do to straighten it. Time will tell."

"How much of last night do you remember?" Blows to the head sometimes robbed people of their memories, and I wondered how much Katherine might have lost.

"That's why I hoped you'd visit." Katherine's laugh, weak though it was, gave me hope that she might soon recover. "My maidservant only could tell me what the litter-bearers told her, so I am sure of nothing at all. I remember going to Mr. Harrison's, but nothing after that. They said that Abraham Walker murdered Daniel, and now he is dead. Is that true?"

"It is," I said. "You, Martha, and I were at Margaret Harrison's travail when he came to kill her. He attacked the three of us. We were very lucky to survive."

Katherine thought for a time, assembling the fragments of her memory. "Margaret knew that Abraham had killed her father," she said. "Abraham had to kill her in order to protect himself."

"Aye," I said. "He had already killed Daniel and Mr. Harrison. He did not balk at committing a third murder."

"You think the Royalists killed Daniel over a few cartloads of gunpowder?" Tears ran down Katherine's cheeks. "Over that?"

"If Mr. Marlowe discovered the plot, he'd have hanged all involved, including Abraham Walker," I said. "And of what import is a murder when you hope to start a war that will kill thousands?"

"Poor Daniel," Katherine sighed.

I paused for a moment before asking my next question, for it would bring into the open all (or nearly all) the secrets we'd kept from each other. "You knew of Daniel's work for Mr. Marlowe, but he did not tell you about the scheme he discovered?"

Katherine shook her head and sighed deeply. "He never said a word. Why would he keep such a secret?"

"To protect you," I said. "He recognized the danger he was in, and he wanted to keep you safe."

Katherine smiled sadly. "So the last thing he did was save my life. That's Daniel."

"Katherine," I said, "can you forgive me? I lied to you about my work for Marlowe, and I betrayed your confidence. That is not what a good gossip does, and I am sorry."

"I was furious at first," she said. "But I have seen for myself how Mr. Marlowe presses men into his service. When a man as powerful and ruthless as he is demands your labor, you do not deny him. How did he compel you?"

"He had Will in the Tower," I said. "He told me that if I did not spy on you, Will would die there and I would be ruined."

"Aye," Katherine said. "That is how he pressed Daniel, by threatening our son."

"I never feigned my friendship," I said.

"I know," she said. "You are not so skilled a liar as to do that." She smiled as best she could, but I could see that she was becoming weary. "What will you do now?"

"I don't know," I said. "It is Mr. Marlowe's choice, isn't it? Perhaps he will release me from his service."

"I doubt that," Katherine replied. "That would be an extraordinary kindness, and nobody has ever accused him of that particular virtue."

"No, I suppose not."

I sat with Katherine a bit longer, holding her hand as she drifted to sleep, and then I went home.

I slept through that day and the next night, awaking to a city ablaze with the news of what had happened at Enoch Harrison's house: three killings, a woman in labor, the trained bands racing through the streets in search of rebels . . . even London rarely saw such a strange series of events. The first newsbooks were slight indeed, as authors and printers had just one day (and only a few facts) with which to work. As usual, the scribblers refused to let ignorance keep them from writing their books. The result was a very strange mix of stories: Some called Walker a Royalist spy and said he was killed by the trained bands; others said he was in Parliament's employ and had been killed by the Royalists; a few ignored the politics entirely, claiming that Walker was killed by housebreakers, and by his bravery he'd saved Margaret Harrison's life. One or two claimed that a midwife had done the killing, but to my relief did not mention my name or Martha's. I knew that these pamphlets would be followed by longer and more fanciful accounts, for the story had everything that a city reader would want: illicit love, betrayal, murder, and the threat of a rebellion.

Martha and I had just finished our dinner when we heard someone climbing the steps to our rooms, and the thumping of Will's cane announced his presence well before he arrived. Martha opened the door and embraced him.

"How are you?" he asked. "Have you heard the news?"

"We've seen all manner of books," I replied. "But we know better than to credit most of them."

Will laughed. "That's probably for the best, but there's newer news than that. Mr. Marlowe sent me for you. He wants to tell you of his success. He is insufferable."

"*His* success?" Martha asked. I could hear the anger in her voice. "We handed him his murderer wrapped in woolen and ready for burial. He did no more work than the coroner's men! Less, in fact."

"Ah, he's already forgotten that," Will replied. "It is something else, but he wants to tell you himself, so get your cloaks."

I could not hide my peevishness as I wrapped myself against the cold and followed Will down to the street. The sun was already low in the sky, and it seemed likely we'd have to walk home in the dark.

"Surely you have some idea what has happened," I insisted. "Has he found the gunpowder?"

"Or has someone found it for him?" Martha asked. She sounded no less crabbed than I felt.

"I promise, I don't know," Will replied. "He sent me and Colonel Reynolds off on a wild-goose chase, and he says that while we were gone he finished the entire business."

"How can he be sure?" I asked.

Will shrugged. "He is sure enough to send a letter to Cromwell telling him as much. He would not do such a thing unless he were confident."

We trudged east, heads bowed against the swirling wind that seemed to find its way beneath our cloaks no matter how tightly we secured them. When we reached the Tower, Will pulled down his scarf so the guard could recognize him, and within a minute we were standing outside Marlowe's office. Will knocked on the door, and Marlowe bellowed for us to enter.

We found him leaning back in his chair, his feet propped up on his desk. A triumphant smile crossed his face when he saw us. Tom stood behind him, his pleasure at our arrival tempered by his obvious annoyance at Mr. Marlowe. I longed to take him in my arms and talk of our future together, but I did not think that Mr. Marlowe would approve.

"Mrs. Hodgson!" Marlowe cried out as he stood. An empty bottle of sack sat on his desk. "I am so glad you have come. Have a glass of wine. Colonel Reynolds refuses, but you three will join me. It is my will and my command."

I nodded my assent. I had no desire to antagonize Mr. Marlowe, and in truth I craved a warming glass of wine.

"Boy!" Marlowe shouted. The door opened and a youth of

perhaps twelve years peered in. "Bring another bottle and more glasses. We will celebrate my triumph."

The boy returned moments later, and once he'd filled our glasses Marlowe began to march back and forth before us, as if he were the king of all men.

"While these two," Marlowe said, gesturing at Tom and Will, "were off God knows where finding nothing at all, and you women were safe at home, *I* was preventing an assassination, a Royalist uprising, and perhaps even another civil war."

I glanced at Tom, wondering what he made of Marlowe's boasts. He refused to meet my eyes, but I could see the anger rising within him.

"We found one of Abraham Walker's accomplices in London," Marlowe continued. "And a fisherman in Rye who helped him send letters abroad. Both are taken."

"Did you find the gunpowder?" Martha asked.

Marlowe ignored her. "Walker's London accomplice was going to set the entire scheme in motion. He was to kill Cromwell as a signal to the rest of his rebellious mob. Once General Cromwell was dead, the Royalists here in England would begin a rising while those in France launched an invasion of their own."

"What about the gunpowder?" I asked.

"Shipped to France," Marlowe said with apparent satisfaction.

"We don't know that," Tom said quietly. "All we have is one man's confession. And after all he suffered, he'd have confessed to crucifying Christ himself."

"Oh, stop it." Marlowe sounded like a petulant child. "The plot is foiled, and the gunpowder is safely out of England. That is all that matters."

I could see that Tom wanted to continue the argument, but he swallowed his words. My guess was that he'd questioned Marlowe on this point many times before, and knew that once more would make no difference.

"Would you like to see him?" Marlowe asked brightly.

"See who?" I asked.

"The assassin who was going to kill General Cromwell," Marlowe said. "He's here in the Tower, and here he'll remain until we execute him." He reminded me of the rooster who took credit for the rising of the sun.

For a moment I wondered if Lorenzo Bacca might be the man awaiting execution. Stranger things had happened.

"Come on, I'll show you." Without waiting for a reply, Marlowe marched out the door. I shrugged at Martha and we followed, with will and Tom close behind. We descended a set of stairs and passed through several guarded doors before we reached our destination.

"Keep in mind that he's not the same man he was when we captured him," Marlowe said. "He used to be much stronger." Marlowe produced a key and after a few twists and turns pushed open the door.

The scene inside was both horrible and unsurprising. Two barred windows offered what little light the prisoner was allowed. The floor was covered in filthy rushes, and the walls were slimy, green, and dripping with moisture. The smell of fear, sweat, and excrement was overpowering. In the fading light I could make out a single figure, lying in a pile of straw.

"You!" Marlowe snapped. He strode across the room and prodded the prisoner with his boot. "Stand up."

When the figure did not move, Marlowe kicked him squarely in the small of his back. "I said get up."

"He can no longer stand," Tom said. "Even without the chains."

"Quite right," Marlowe said. He looked at Martha and me, smiling. "He was very frightening just a few hours ago. If I were going to send a man to kill General Cromwell, I'd have chosen him as well. It is amazing what the rack will do to even the sturdiest man's frame." Marlowe dragged the prisoner to his feet and pulled him toward us. "Ordinarily, we would not have moved so quickly. I showed him the rack, and told him what it would do to his body, but he still protested his innocence."

"The executioner broke him too quickly," Tom said. They had clearly had this argument before, and Tom had lost.

"That is true," Marlowe conceded. "But it has been years since anyone has used the rack. Nobody knew what effect it would have."

"It would have made Christ himself confess," Tom insisted. "Look at him."

Indeed, the man before us was as miserable a sight as I'd ever seen. His limbs were long and well muscled, and I had no doubt that before his time on the rack they had been straight as rods. But now they were crooked and swollen, bruised black and purple at every joint. The jailor had laid three sets of irons on him: one bound his hands, another his feet, and a third ran from his neck to his ankle, keeping him from standing entirely upright. He looked listlessly around the room, hardly seeing any of us.

"Who are you?" he asked. It was a reasonable question, but I could not think of an answer.

"Tell them what you did," Marlowe said. "What you were going to do."

"I was going to kill General Cromwell," the poor man muttered. "And that would start a rising on behalf of King Charles."

He fell to his knees and began to weep. Marlowe looked at us brightly. "You see? Just as I told you."

"I think I've seen enough." I left the cell with Martha, Will, Tom, and Marlowe close behind.

"You are sure that he is the man the Royalists chose to assassinate Oliver Cromwell?" I asked as we made our way back to Marlowe's office.

"Aye, and the plot is finished," Marlowe said. "No assassin, no assassination. No assassination, no rebellion."

"General Cromwell will be pleased," I said.

"Oh, yes," Marlowe said. "You have no idea how grateful he will be."

Once we were back in his office, Marlowe uncorked the bottle of sack. "You have two choices, Mrs. Hodgson. You can join these two hens in their doubts." He gestured at Tom and Will. "Or you can join me in another cup of wine."

When I did not reply, Marlowe laughed.

"Very well. I think you are suffering from simple envy. Colonel Reynolds and your nephew stopped nothing at all; you midwives stopped a murderer, and I give you credit for that; but *I* stopped a rebellion. The matter is over and done." He shook his head in wonder at our skepticism. "Go away, all of you, and make each other sad. You've done enough to ruin my celebration."

Marlowe's words rang in my ears, louder than any gunshot. "The matter is over and done?" I asked. "The rising is foiled?"

"Aye," Marlowe said. "Finished, ended, and expired. The Royalists had their chance, and I stopped them."

"So Parliament is secure?"

Marlowe nodded and took a swallow of wine.

"Then you will have no more use for my services," I said. "Or Martha's or Will's."

Marlowe stared at me for a moment and began to laugh. "You caught me there, Mrs. Hodgson, but no, you are not released. You have proved yourself too valuable, and the world is too dangerous. The Levellers are still a threat, as are the Royalists. Stopping one plot does not stop them all."

"Am I nothing more than your slave, then?" I asked. "Am I to do your bidding until the day I die?" Despair welled up within me. I had not expected to be set free, but I had hoped he would at least consider the possibility.

"Or until *I* die," Marlowe replied with a smile. "And no, you do not *have* to stay with me. But if you go, you will forfeit your lands. War is expensive, and Parliament is hungry for new wealth."

"What about her daughter, Elizabeth?" Tom asked. I looked at him in surprise.

"What do you mean?" Marlowe asked.

"Let Mrs. Hodgson bring her daughter to London. She has done more than you expected and deserves a reward."

My heart began to thunder in my chest at the prospect of bringing Elizabeth to London. Could it happen so quickly? I fought to keep Mr. Marlowe from seeing my eagerness, for if he knew how much joy this would bring me, he surely would demand something more in return.

Marlowe shook his head. "Things are going well as they are. Adding the daughter could cause nothing but trouble."

Tears threatened to boil forth, and I clenched my jaw to keep from screaming in frustration. I took a step forward, but Tom held up his hand.

"Mr. Marlowe," Tom said. "Jonathan."

At this, Marlowe looked up. "Jonathan, is it? This must be important to you."

"It is. And it is the right thing to do."

Marlowe shrugged as if the matter were suddenly of no importance. "Very well. I don't know how you will explain the sudden appearance of a daughter to your neighbors, but if you can think of a lie to tell them, bring her whenever you wish."

In an instant I was filled with such joy and excitement that I thought I might burst into song. Elizabeth coming to London! I started to thank Mr. Marlowe, but Tom crossed the room and took my arm.

"You have her thanks, Mr. Marlowe," he said. "We should be going."

"Very well," Marlowe said. "I am to meet with General Cromwell in the morning. I must prepare myself."

The four of us left Marlowe's office and made our way to the Tower gate.

"What is the hurry?" I whispered.

"It is better not to give him the chance to change his mind," Tom said. "He said yes. Take yes."

I started to reply, but Tom shook his head. "When we're outside the Tower we can talk more."

As soon as we passed through the gate, I could no longer restrain myself. I threw my arms around Tom's neck and embraced him with such force that he gasped in surprise. "Thank you, thank you, thank you!" I cried. Not caring who saw me, I leaned forward and kissed him on the lips.

"Aunt Bridget!" Will cried. "What . . . what?"

Even as I kissed him, Tom began to laugh. "I think your aunt has some news," Tom said when I stopped to breathe.

Will knew in an instant, of course. "Truly? The two of you?"

"Yes." I untangled myself from Tom's embrace. "The two of us."

"You are betrothed?" Will asked.

"Aye, we are," I said.

"When will you marry?"

Tom laughed. "That is a good question. We haven't had the chance to talk about that just yet." He turned to me. "What do you say? When will we marry?"

"We should wait for Elizabeth to come," I said. "I should like her to meet you beforehand. I shall write to her and Hannah immediately!" As we walked toward the Cheap, it became clear that we would finish our journey in the dark.

Tom turned onto a small street and led us to an inn. "If we are going to walk back in the dark, we might as well be well fed."

The inn's supper offerings were spare and expensive, but the wine and fire quickly warmed us and improved our already high spirits. I wished we could talk more of weddings and my plans to bring Elizabeth to London, but there was other business at hand.

"Neither of you believes that the man Marlowe tortured was the assassin," Martha said to Tom and Will.

They shook their heads.

"You saw what they did to him," Tom said. "I do not doubt that he was involved in the plot, but once they started racking him, he'd have said anything to make them stop."

Will nodded in agreement. "When he was asked where the gunpowder was, the poor wretch had no idea. But when Mr. Marlowe asked if it had been sent to France, he could not agree quickly enough. He was in such agony, he would have agreed that it was in his pocket."

"Where did Mr. Marlowe find him?" Martha asked.

"One of Walker's neighbors pointed him out," Tom said. "He

saw the two of them together, often skulking about at night. That was enough for Mr. Marlowe."

"Does Mr. Marlowe *truly* believe that he is the assassin, and that the gunpowder is gone from England?" I asked.

Tom shrugged. "You can imagine how much he *wants* this one to be guilty. Think of the pressure that the murders placed upon him. A spy was killed, then a gunpowder merchant, and the murderer escaped with enough powder to blow the Tower of London halfway to Rome. Parliament and Cromwell would have been mad with fear. They demanded an assassin, and Mr. Marlowe obliged."

"It is possible that the rising is foiled," I said. "Walker's death might have done that."

"Perhaps." Tom did not try to hide his doubts. "We'll find out soon enough, won't we?"

After finishing our meal and wrapping ourselves against the cold, our little troop returned to the Cheap. We bid Will and Tom a warm farewell before they went to the Horned Bull, then Martha and I continued on our way home.

"If you are going to live with Tom, Elizabeth, and perhaps even Hannah, you shall need a larger tenement," Martha said.

"And what of you?" I asked. "Where will you be?"

"Are you asking if Will and I are betrothed?" Martha laughed. "We were betrothed in York, and never *un*betrothed, so I suppose we still are."

"But when will you marry?"

"Perhaps the spring." Martha laughed. "The four of us could marry together, comrades one and all."

"I should like that," I said.

Martha and I arrived at our door, and I had just reached for the handle when Martha seized my arm.

She pointed to the threshold. In the dark of the stairs, I could see a flickering light under the door. We were not fools enough to have left a candle burning when we went out—someone was inside.

"Come in, come in!" a man called. "I have been waiting for hours."

There was no mistaking the voice of Lorenzo Bacca.

Chapter 22

I looked at Martha in surprise. What could a late-night visit from a man like Bacca mean?

"If he intended to do us harm, he'd hardly announce himself beforehand," Martha said.

"Aye," I replied. "And he certainly wouldn't have left a candle lit."

I opened our door and stepped inside.

Bacca sat at our table as comfortably as if he lived there himself. He'd brought a lantern, which sat before him, and he was reading a letter of some sort. As soon as we entered, he stood and folded the paper into his pocket. "I am sorry for imposing myself in such a fashion," Bacca said. "I could hardly wait outside without attracting attention. Your landlady is a watchful woman."

"What brings you here?" I asked. I allowed an edge to creep into my voice. I did not think he had come to do us harm, but that did not mean I welcomed his presence.

Bacca laughed in a kindly fashion. "You've been busy, haven't you? All the city is buzzing about your adventures."

"I do not know what you mean," I said.

"Come now," Bacca said. "The scribblers may not know your name, but it was not hard to guess. Two midwives save a mother from certain death by killing an assassin? Who could it be *except* the two of you?"

"You cannot trust such books," I said. "They cannot agree on anything at all."

"That is one thing I love about London." Bacca laughed. "There are few limits on what men can write, and none at all on what they will believe.

"But I am not so credulous," he continued. "You lied to me about the murdered doxies. And you lied when you said that your business and mine would not collide. The truth is that we are both knee-deep in government intrigues, but working for different parties."

I did not think an outright denial would fool Bacca. "How can you be so sure?"

"Your life has become a series of unanswerable questions and remarkable curiosities, and I cannot help but wonder at them. First, you came to the Crown in search of a murderer who happened to be a Royalist. Then were called to the labor of Margaret Harrison, daughter to Oliver Cromwell's powder merchant. You do not live in her neighborhood, so how would she even know your name? And why would she call for you when there are perfectly capable midwives living much closer?" Bacca seemed like a cat toying with a mouse—or rather two mice. "And while you were at the poor girl's labor, you happened to kill the assassin—also a Royalist—who murdered her father. Curious indeed!"

I remained silent.

"Or," he continued, "perhaps these are not curiosities at all. Perhaps you were sent to the Crown to spy on Charles Owen. And you were later called upon to deliver Mr. Harrison's daughter. But that leaves the question: Who sent you to the Crown and called you to Margaret Harrison's bedside?" Bacca pretended to think. He was enjoying himself immensely. "Ah! It was Cromwell! The two of you are Oliver Cromwell's creatures, just as I guessed.

"Now tell me." Bacca leaned forward, his eyes boring into mine. "Have I missed the mark? Or have I solved *your* mystery?"

When I again remained silent, Bacca laughed. "Very well," he said. "I will not insist on a confession, though it would be good for your soul."

I gazed at Bacca for a moment, trying to discern the best path forward. A denial clearly would not fool him, but perhaps I could disarm him with the truth and learn something in the process. "You did not miss much," I admitted. "Martha and I were sent to Charles Owen and called to Margaret Harrison. We both are in Cromwell's employ, though not by our choice."

"And what did you learn by your spying?" Bacca asked.

"That Abraham Walker is a murderer many times over, and that he may have been a part of a plot to kill Cromwell."

Bacca nodded. "He was a capable and dangerous man. You are fortunate to have survived your encounter with him."

"Before he died," I said, "Abraham Walker stole a quantity of gunpowder. Do you know what happened to it?"

Bacca glanced away before he replied. "I've not heard of any gunpowder. But I am sure that General Cromwell's agents are in firm control of such matters. I would not worry."

"You have more faith in Cromwell's agents than I do," I said. "Abraham Walker murdered four people, and Martha and I risked our lives to stop him. We do not want it to be for nothing. I told you the truth; now you must do the same. Do you know where the gunpowder is?"

Bacca looked at me. "I give you my word: I do not know what became of the gunpowder."

I did not know if Bacca was telling the truth, but it was clear I would not learn anything more from him. "It is very late," I said. "Why are you here? Answer me and go on your way."

"You injure me, Lady Hodgson," Bacca said. "I came here at the behest of Charles Owen's wife, Jane. She would like to see you tomorrow at the Crown."

Martha and I exchanged a glance. What could this mean?

"What business do I have with Jane Owen?" I asked.

"Come to the Crown in the morning, and you shall see." Bacca stood. "I know you are wary, so I will meet you there at ten. That way you will be sure of your safety."

"Why wouldn't we be safe?" Martha asked.

Bacca laughed. "London is a dangerous place, particularly for those who meddle in politics. Look what happened to Mr. Chidley and poor Mr. Walker. You never know what danger might befall you."

"We did well enough with Abraham Walker," Martha growled.

"You did at that," replied Bacca. "I did not mean to offend. So I will see you in the morning. Ten of the clock."

Bacca started for the door, but stopped on the threshold. He turned to me, his face as serious as I'd ever seen it. "Lady Bridget, if you do not come to the Crown, you will regret it for the rest of your days. If you believe nothing else I have said, you must believe this." Without awaiting a response, Bacca slipped out of the room and descended the stairs so softly we barely heard him go.

"What did he mean by that?" Martha asked. "Was he threatening you?"

I shook my head. "His threats are not so subtle as that. I think he was being genuine."

"So we will we go?" Martha asked.

I thought of Guy Fawkes, and of the lowly sergeant who, by simply carrying out his duties, had saved both King and Parliament. Could I do any less than he?

"Some scheme is afoot," I said. "And we must discover what it is."

The next morning I rose early and immediately wrote a letter to Hannah and Elizabeth. It would take a few days for the letter to get to Pontrilas, and a few more to arrange for Elizabeth's journey to London, but if things went well she would join Martha and me within a fortnight. My heart thrilled at the prospect, and I could only imagine Elizabeth's excitement when she read my words. I said a prayer of thanks that God had seen fit to grant me this mercy. I found a boy who would take the letter to Tom at the Horned Bull, and with that Elizabeth's journey to London had begun.

After Martha rose, we replenished our larder and stopped in to see Katherine. She was still abed and swathed in bandages, of course, but was doing her best to manage her shop all the same. Servants came in a constant stream bringing new-sewn coats for inspection and taking away either praise or reprimand.

"There you are!" Katherine smiled broadly when she saw us. "Tell me how things are in the world. I do not know how much longer I can stay cooped up like a chicken."

"You will be up soon enough," Martha said. "And the world will still be there waiting."

"But you do have news, do you not?"

Martha and I glanced at each other and then at the maidservant who remained at Katherine's side. I inclined my head toward the door.

"Leave us," Katherine said to the girl.

When we were alone I sat next to Katherine. "Mr. Marlowe called us to the Tower. They captured another conspirator. He was to assassinate Cromwell and spark a Royalist rebellion."

"Who was he?" Katherine asked.

"Nobody we knew," I said. "An associate of Abraham Walker's."

"He confessed?"

"After he was broken on the rack," I replied.

Katherine recoiled in horror. "They tortured an Englishman? By what right?"

"By Marlowe's order," I said. "Or Cromwell's."

"If that is so, why am I still in bed?" Katherine asked. "I must return to the Nag's Head and resume my work there." Her outrage grew with every passing moment. "If a freeborn Englishman can be tortured, who among us has the liberty God has granted us?"

"Cromwell hasn't got a chance against you," Martha said with a smile.

Katherine laughed. "If God be for us, who can be against us?"

"But there is good news as well," I said. "My household soon will be growing." I told her about Elizabeth and her upcoming journey to London, and of my betrothal to Tom Reynolds.

Katherine shook her head in wonder. "I've been trapped here for a few hours, and in that time you've found a husband *and* a daughter." She laughed. "But that is excellent on all fronts. Colonel Reynolds is a good man to be sure, and I shall be very happy to meet Elizabeth."

It was nearing ten o'clock, so Martha and I bid Katherine farewell and made our way to the Crown. I paused as soon as it came into view, examining the faces of the men and women outside. None looked familiar, and nobody seemed to be waiting for us. After a moment the alehouse door opened, and Bacca stepped into the street. Somehow he knew we'd arrived.

"Are you sure about this?" Martha asked. "We could have summoned Will."

"We will be fine," I said. "I don't entirely trust Bacca, but if he meant us harm he would have killed us last night."

"True enough," Martha said.

Bacca smiled—warmly, I thought—when he saw us. "Mrs. Hodgson, I am glad you came. Follow me."

We accompanied him into the Crown. It was quiet at such an early hour.

"We are here!" Bacca called out as we passed behind the bar and entered the tavern's kitchen. There we found a young woman setting ale to boil; I recognized her from our previous visit as Charles Owen's wife. She motioned for us to wait and when she'd finished stirring the brew, she crossed the kitchen to meet us. She was an attractive girl, with large brown eyes and a pleasant visage. As she approached I saw she was with child.

"You are Mrs. Hodgson," she said. "And you must be Midwife Hawkins. Signor Bacca has told me much about your work with women in the Cheap. He says you are very skilled."

I now was entirely befuddled. Had Bacca brought us to the Crown simply to meet a mother?

"As you can see," Jane continued, "I soon will need a midwife. My friends in the Cheap sang your praises, and Signor Bacca said he could arrange a meeting. You are friends from his time in York, are you not?"

I realized with a shock that Bacca had inadvertently ruined the story Mr. Marlowe had given me. If Bacca and I had met in York, I could hardly be a widow from Halifax. I could only hope this unintentional betrayal would not somehow be my undoing.

"Aye, we are," I said. "I lived there for many years. It was a large enough city, but nothing compared to London."

Jane nodded. "I came from Devon as a maidservant and met my husband here," she said. "And here we've been ever since. It's not so bad once you get used to the smell and noise."

I laughed. "Aye, but it does take time."

"You were a midwife in York?" she asked.

"For many years," I said. "I could not tell you how many mothers I've delivered."

Jane took my hands and examined them closely. "My mother taught me that you can know a midwife by her hands. *Long fingers and strong bones,* she said. She would be pleased with yours, I think."

"How long have you been with child?" I asked.

"Six months," she said. "The child quickened in November."

"And it is your first?"

"Aye," she said with a smile. "So you will have a new mother on your hands." Jane's laugh was as light as air, and soon Martha and I were laughing with her. We talked for a while longer—Martha and I suggested food and drink she should take to help strengthen the child—and then we started back to the Cheap.

As Martha and I walked home, she asked the questions that had been puzzling me. "Is Bacca as innocent as he seems? Is there nothing more to this than a woman with child?"

"I would never call him innocent," I said. "But I cannot see how he benefits from bringing us to Jane Owen."

"Nor can I," Martha said. "But we must be on our guard all the same."

For reasons I could not explain, that night I was beset by dreams of Abraham Walker. In my dream I was alone in Margaret Harrison's chamber, and Walker stood outside shouting that he would see me dead. He passed through the locked door as if he were a ghost, cudgel in hand. He ignored Margaret and came for me. I woke as he raised his arm to strike the killing blow. I did not know what such a dream could mean and was grateful when it finally left me in peace.

I passed the following week in a state of anxiety as I awaited word from Pontrilas. I imagined Elizabeth's excitement at receiving my letter, and each day I waited eagerly for some reply so I could begin to count the hours until her arrival. To pass the time, I began to search for a home large enough for my growing family. At first I would live with Elizabeth and Martha, of course, and Tom would join us after we married. I would need room for Will as well, and if I had so many in my house, I would need a maidservant or two. I told Tom that I would not leave Watling street (it was Midwife's Row, after all!), and he did not object. I soon found a house large enough for all of us not a hundred yards away; with that settled, all I could do was wait for Elizabeth's arrival.

A week after I'd sent my letter to Pontrilas, I returned home to find Martha and—to my surprise—Matthew, the driver who had brought us to London, sitting in the parlor. I bit back a wail of anguish as soon as I saw their hollowed cheeks and red-rimmed eyes.

"What has happened?" I breathed. "Oh, God, let it not be Elizabeth." But of course it was.

Chapter 23

"Elizabeth is missing," Martha said.

"What?" I cried. "How so? Missing from where? Where has she gone? Is she here in London?"

"She fled Pontrilas four days ago," Matthew said. "She'd made plans to go to your cousin Mary Baskerville's in Peterchurch, but she never arrived."

I sat at the table. "Where is she? If she's not at Pontrilas or at Mary's, where has she gone? Girls don't just disappear. In London, perhaps, but not Hereford."

"She is coming here." Matthew produced a letter written in Elizabeth's hand.

Dearest Hannah,

You will worry when you receive this note, but do not be frightened. I have had more than my fill of dull country gentlewomen, their boring daughters, and their unread sons. Since Ma and Martha left, I have been saving my pennies and shillings until I had enough to join them in

London. I know you will want to send someone after me to bring me back, but I beg you not to. I will not come back except in chains.

Your ever loving,

Elizabeth

I looked at Matthew in disbelief. "She fled Pontrilas for London?"

He nodded miserably.

"Did she not receive my letter?" I asked. "I had just sent for her! Why would she leave by herself?"

"It arrived the day after she left," Matthew said. "Hannah sent me to your cousin's house to tell her the news. That's when we discovered what she'd done."

I turned to Martha. "Send a boy for Tom and Will. We must find her."

"I already sent one," she said. "They should be here soon." Even as she spoke, we heard footsteps on the stairs, and a few moments later Tom appeared in the doorway.

"What is it?" Tom asked. "The boy said it was an emergency."

"Where is Will?" I asked.

"With Mr. Marlowe. I sent for him, and he will be here soon. What has happened?"

"Elizabeth fled Pontrilas for London."

"What, by herself?"

"Aye," I said. "And nobody knows how far she has come or where she is."

"Lord help us," Tom whispered. He took a breath and set his shoulders. "We will find her. When did she leave Hereford?"

"Four days ago," I said. "She likely will come on the same road we did, down from Highgate Hill. We must send word to all the western parishes—constables, beadles, churchwardens—everyone. We should put men at Ludgate and Newgate just to be sure. A young woman with bright red hair should not be hard to find, especially if she is by herself."

"Aye, that's the problem," Tom said. "If we announce that a twelve-year-old girl with bright red hair has come to London with no one to protect her, every pimp and bawd in the city will be looking for her."

Panic flared in my chest. I'd heard too many stories of children come to London only to be sold into brothels to ignore Tom's warning.

"Then what shall we do?" Martha asked.

"I have men," Tom said. "I'll put two at each gate, and they'll stay there from dawn until night. You should write letters in your own hand for them to show Elizabeth. No doubt she will be wary of strange men offering their help."

"In the evening we should check all the inns that lie just outside the city gates," Martha said. "If she arrives after dark she'll need a place to stay, just as we did."

Tom nodded. "I have a few innkeepers in my employ. I will send word to them."

I turned to Matthew. "Go to Ludgate and start working your way west. Stop at every tavern, inn, and victualing house you can find. Find her. Go now."

Matthew nodded and dashed down the stairs.

I found some paper and scrawled notes for Tom's sentries.

Dearest Elizabeth

These men are friends and will bring you to me in the Cheap.

Your loving mother

I took Tom's hand as I gave him the papers. "We must find her."

"We will," he said. "I promise."

I embraced him as fiercely as I ever had and fought back tears. Then he hurried out, leaving Martha and me alone.

"What else can we do?" Martha asked. "There must be something."

I thought for a moment. "Katherine Chidley. She will help."

A few minutes later we were in Katherine's shop. Somehow she had hauled herself out of bed, and she now commanded her apprentices just as she had before Walker's attack. Katherine waved with her good arm when she saw us and started across the room. She immediately saw that something was amiss. "What has happened?"

I told her about Elizabeth's mad-brained flight from Pontrilas.

"She's traveling from Hereford to London by herself?" Katherine asked. "She is your daughter indeed."

"We need your help," I said.

Katherine nodded and turned to her workers. "Put down your needles and coats and hear me, for today we have more important business than sewing." The room fell silent. "A girl in Widow Hodgson's care is missing. She is coming to London from the country, as many of you did. She is alone, and we fear she will be overcome by the city when she arrives. A girl lost in London can meet no good end, so we must find her sooner rather than later."

I stepped forward. "She is twelve years old and very tall, with bright red hair. She is likely by herself and will enter the city by Ludgate or Newgate before making her way to the Cheap."

"Where should we start?" asked one of the needlewomen.

I thought for a moment, recalling the things I'd written to Elizabeth about the Cheap in my letters. What landmarks might she use to guide her journey?

"There will be men at the gates soon enough, but if she slips past them, she will go first to St. Paul's," I said. "Two of you go to the churchyard. She loves news and will tarry among the booksellers there. Two others should walk the rest of the grounds."

Katherine chose four workers and sent them out. "Where else can we look?" she asked.

"There are too many places." I clenched my teeth to hold back the cry building in my chest. "St. Mary-le-Bow Church, the Little Conduit, the Great Conduit . . . she might even go to London Bridge. Or she could become lost and . . ."

Martha heard the hopelessness in my voice and put her arms around me. "We will find her."

"The Lord did not bring her to your household only to snatch her away," Katherine said. "He will return her to you."

I nodded even as tears ran down my cheeks. I knew Katherine meant well, but in my heart I did not believe her. After all, God had given me Birdy and Michael and then robbed me of them both. Why would He not do the same with Elizabeth?

Katherine turned to the two remaining workers, sending one to St. Mary's and the other to the Little Conduit, as it was nearest St. Paul's. That left the three of us alone in her shop.

"Someone should stay in your tenement," Katherine said. "If she's half so resourceful as you are, she could be sitting outside your door right now, wondering where everyone is."

"And," Martha added, "we must be able to find you when she is found. You go home; I'll go to Newgate and search the taverns and inns to the west."

The thought of spending the day sitting in our rooms while

others searched for Elizabeth galled me, but Katherine and Martha were right. *Someone* had to be at my home.

Katherine took my hand. "We will bring her to you."

"I know," I replied, and started home.

I told Mrs. Evelyn of the redheaded girl who might soon be knocking on her door and climbed the stairs to my tenement. For the next hour—or perhaps it was two—I stared into the street hoping for a glimpse of Elizabeth's face or a flash of her red hair. I was so intent on the world out my window that I did not hear the footsteps approaching my door.

"Midwife Hawkins!" a woman called out. "Are you here?"

I opened the door to reveal a maidservant breathing heavily from her hurried journey. "Midwife Hawkins is not here," I said. "What is it?" I looked over my shoulder, anxious to return to my post.

"She is my mistress's midwife," the girl said. "Do you know when will she return?"

"Not until evening," I said. "And perhaps not until morning."

"Morning?" The girl seemed ready to weep. "But the child is ailing now."

I caught my breath at this. "I am a midwife," I said. "Tell me what is happening."

The girl began to cry. "She was well enough when she was born, but now she is taken with a fever. We've done all we can, but . . . we need help."

The decision before me was so easy that I made it without thinking. I was doing Elizabeth no good waiting at the window, and this child needed my help. "Let me get my medicines. I will come with you."

The girl's mistress, Mrs. Claypole, lived above a haberdasher's shop on Ironmonger Lane, just north of Cheapside Street. We hurried upstairs and found her in bed holding the child. Her husband sat by her side.

"I am Mrs. Hodgson," I said. "Martha could not come, but I will do my best in her stead."

"Thank you," Mrs. Claypole said. She opened her mouth to continue, but no sound came.

"Please help," her husband said.

"I will." I took the child in my arms and could feel the fever even before I pressed my wrist against her forehead. My heart ached at what I found, for few infants could survive such a fever if it lasted too long.

"What is her name?" I asked.

"Deborah," Mrs. Claypole replied.

The child's eyes were open but glazed from the fever. "I will do my best for you, Deborah." I gave the child back to her mother. "You must unwrap her."

I turned to the maidservant. "Make Mrs. Claypole a barley soup. Use broth, but no meat. We must cool her humors."

In my valise I found oil of roses and a poplar ointment. The child wailed at the indignity of being unswaddled, and I set to anointing her limbs and chest. She soon ceased her crying and simply lay on the bed, feverish and shaking. I said a prayer that God would not take her. I wrapped the child and gave her to her mother. "When did she last take the breast?"

"Just before you came," Mrs. Claypole said. "But she did not eat much."

I nodded. A waning appetite was not a good sign, but at least she had eaten something. "When the soup is ready, eat as much as you can and then see if Deborah will suck. If she does, the barley may cool her humors and break the fever."

"We should pray as well," Mr. Claypole said.

Mrs. Claypole lay the child in her lap, and the three of us joined hands, praying in turn. I begged God for His mercy in these perilous hours, begged Him not to rob any mother of her child. By the time we finished, Deborah had fallen asleep, and soon after the maid came with the soup. Mrs. Claypole drank it down and closed her eyes. In a few moments, she, too, was asleep.

Mr. Claypole touched my shoulder and nodded to the chamber door. I joined him outside.

"You must tell me the truth," he said.

"There is nothing to tell you that you don't know," I replied. "The fever is serious. If it does not break soon, I will not be able to save her."

Mr. Claypole took shallow breaths, trying to control the panic within. "When will we know?" he asked. "When will it be too late?"

"We will know one way or the other by morning."

Mr. Claypole nodded, and we returned to his wife's bedside. The maidservant brought bread and cheese for our supper, and after that Mr. Claypole and I sat in silence. When Deborah whimpered, I picked her up and soothed her back to sleep. I held her for hours after that, praying for her survival and for Elizabeth's safe return. I told myself that both would be safe, that the girl's fever would break, and Elizabeth would find her way home. Perhaps Elizabeth had thought better of her adventure and returned to Pontrilas. Perhaps after leaving Pontrilas, she had fallen in with a trustworthy crowd and had come to London with them. Perhaps Martha had found her, and the two of them were now waiting in our parlor, wondering where *I* could be.

When night fell, Mrs. Claypole woke with a start. She looked wildly about for Deborah, her eyes wide with fear.

"She is here," I said.

"How is she?" Mrs. Claypole asked.

"The fever has not broken, but she has slept," I said. "And that is no small thing. You should see if she will eat."

Mrs. Claypole took the child and offered her breast. I said a prayer of thanks when Deborah began to suck. That she ate was hardly a guarantee that she would live, but it would have boded ill if she had refused. When she had finished, I anointed her once again with oil and gave her back to her mother. "Now we wait," I said.

The nighttime hours passed with agonizing slowness. Mr. Claypole slept in his chair, while I lay with Mrs. Claypole, the child between us.

I woke with a start to a woman's weeping, and found Mrs. Claypole holding her daughter to her chest. "She—she—is cold."

I fought back tears of my own as I took the child in my arms. I put my wrist to her forehead and began to laugh despite myself. "She is not cold," I said. "Her fever is broken, and she is sleeping." Deborah opened her eyes and began to cry. "See? She is hungry."

Mrs. Claypole began to laugh as well and shook her husband's knee to wake him. "She is well," she cried. "She is well."

Deborah ate and went back to sleep. With the fever broken there was little left for me to do, so I packed my valise. I wondered what news—if any—awaited me at home.

"Will you not stay for breakfast?" Mrs. Claypole asked. "It is the least we can offer."

"I am afraid I cannot," I said. "I have business I must attend to. I will send Martha back this afternoon to check on both of you."

As I neared my home, Watling Street seemed no different than on any other morning, but I knew in mere moments I might learn that my daughter had died. I begged God for strength and started up the stairs.

Chapter 24

I'd not yet reached the door when it flew open and a figure trailing bright red hair flew across the threshold and into my arms.

It took perhaps half an hour for Martha and Tom to pry Elizabeth and me apart, and half as long again for me to stop crying. When Will returned it all started again: laughter, tears, the demands that Elizabeth tell her story, and my halfhearted reprimands for what she'd done and the worry she'd caused us. With far too little food in our apartment, the five of us retreated to a victualing house for breakfast, and there Elizabeth told her story.

"Getting here was as easy as could be," Elizabeth insisted. "I rode in a farmer's cart from Pontrilas to Hereford—people make the journey every day. I spent a cold night in a hayloft, but I'd brought a blanket, so it wasn't too bad."

Tom—not knowing Elizabeth as the rest of us did—stared in open-mouthed wonder. "You just wrapped yourself in a blanket and went to sleep?" he asked.

"Well, I didn't sleep much," Elizabeth admitted. "But what else was I to do?" I had introduced Tom as Will's master—in what work, I did not say—thinking she could wait to hear the news that he soon would be her stepfather.

"Well, you might have stayed in Pontrilas," I said. Nobody heard me.

"And how did you come to London?" Martha asked. She had made the same journey in her youth, but she had not been quite so young, nor had she been alone.

"That was no trouble, either," Elizabeth said. "I waited until just before Hereford's market day to leave Pontrilas, for I knew the town would be crowded with people going to London. I went to the market and looked for someone traveling east."

"You approached strangers and asked if they would take you to London?" Tom asked. "Just like that?"

Elizabeth shrugged. "Not just anyone. I only talked to widows and men who had their wives with them. I thought they would be less likely to cause me trouble. And if someone did . . ." Elizabeth reached into her apron and produced a knife.

"Elizabeth!" Tom and I gasped together, while Martha and Will laughed.

"Would you have had me travel alone and unarmed?" she asked.

"I would have had you stay in Pontrilas," I said, but once again nobody heard me.

"And when you found someone, what did you tell them?" Will asked.

"The truth." Elizabeth laughed. "That my mother was in London and she had sent for me."

I started to interrupt, but Elizabeth held up her hand. "It *was* true, Ma. You had sent the letter to Hannah a few days before I left."

"You did not know I had sent it," I pointed out.

Elizabeth shrugged as if this detail were of no import, and continued her tale. "In the end I traveled with a cloth merchant's widow. She had two servants with her, so we were safe enough. Once we came to London I walked to St. Paul's. It was easy enough to find. Then I asked directions to the Cheap, and then to Watling Street. Once I'd found that, I could hardly miss the sign you'd hung up. And that was that. The gold paint is lovely, by the way."

By now we'd finished our meal and wandered onto Cheapside Street. We spent the rest of the day walking through the Cheap showing Elizabeth the Great Conduit, St. Mary-le-Bow, and other landmarks that would help her find her way around. Tom and Will started back to the Horned Bull, while Martha and I returned to Watling Street. As we climbed the stairs to our tenement, Elizabeth fell silent and furrowed her brow, clearly deep in thought. By the time we reached our door, she'd come to some sort of conclusion. She whirled on Martha and me, her eyes ablaze.

"Just what have the two of you been doing here?"

Martha and I looked at her in astonishment. "What do you mean?" I managed.

"First you send your silks and fine linens back to Pontrilas with no explanation. Then I find you living in this . . . this . . ." She gestured at our rooms at a loss for words adequate to describe them. She shook her head. "You are not suddenly poor, so you must be over the shoes in some strange business. I demand to know what it is."

Martha and I began to laugh at the same time, and I embraced Elizabeth. "Very well. We will tell you everything."

Over the course of the evening Martha and I told Elizabeth of our work for Cromwell, my betrothal to Tom, and our plans to move together into a larger house. She was, of course, entranced by our work as spies, and pleased with London, having taken a liking both to Tom and the Cheap.

"I'm glad you found someone else to love," she said just before she went to sleep.

With Elizabeth's arrival, the apartment on Watling Street became far too small. We borrowed a bed from Katherine, but the only place to put it was in the parlor. While Martha and I had become used to sharing a room, Elizabeth chafed at the idea that her chamber also would serve as the kitchen, dining room, and parlor. When Will sat on the edge of her bed as if it were just another piece of furniture, she chased him off it with a broom and a few choice words.

Luckily, the tenants in the house I had found agreed to depart early, and within a fortnight we moved from our tenement to the house further down the street. More room meant more work, of course, and I took on a maidservant named Susan Oliver to help with the cooking and cleaning. The sign Martha and I had hung over Mrs. Evelyn's door came with us, of course, and soon we'd settled in quite nicely.

For her part, Elizabeth began to frequent Katherine Chidley's shop, and within weeks the two of them were as closely knit as any gossips in London. Katherine had only the one living son, and Elizabeth's arrival gave her the chance to mother a girl. Elizabeth claimed that she enjoyed the needlework, but it soon became clear that she and Katherine spent as much time talking about politics as they did sewing coats.

"How is it," Elizabeth asked me one morning over bread and cheese, "that you sought a license from a bishop for your midwifery?" The edge in her voice made clear that she was not asking a question, but preparing to make a speech. She continued without waiting for my response. "Was the Archbishop of York well versed in the art of midwifery? That would make him a rare man indeed, don't you think?"

"*Someone* has been spending rather too much time with Katherine Chidley," I murmured.

"Or perhaps the Archbishop bore children himself, and learned the art that way," Elizabeth continued. "But that would be no less rare. They say the world is full of marvels, but what could be more marvelous that a bishop in travail?"

When I did not take the bait, Elizabeth chose a more direct route. "Why would you beg a bishop's permission to do the work of a midwife? What does a bishop know of a woman's travail?"

"It is a complicated thing," I said.

Elizabeth stared at me, feigning innocence and waiting for me to explain myself.

"It would not be mete for just any woman to serve as a midwife," I said at last. "She must be respectable, of good reputation, and ready-handed in the work. When Rebecca Hooke showed her malicious nature, the Archbishop took her license and York's mothers were better for it."

"But it was the Archbishop who gave her a license in the first place," Elizabeth pointed out. "And Katherine Chidley is a fine midwife, but she has no license. And neither does Martha."

"Ah, but with the bishops out, neither Katherine nor Martha *can* take a license," I said triumphantly.

"So there are hundreds of unlicensed midwives in London, and thousands more in the country, yet women are giving birth just as they always have. That is a wonder indeed." Elizabeth took a satisfied bite of her bread.

Despite Elizabeth's arrival and the readiness with which she took to life in the Cheap, I could not forget Daniel Chidley's death and the ensuing violence. Abraham Walker no longer haunted my dreams, but in unguarded moments my thoughts went to him, to Enoch Harrison, and to the assassin that Mr. Marlowe had tortured and hanged. Could these deaths truly be the last? I did not believe it, but weeks passed, and England remained free from both rebellion and invasion. I wondered if somehow we truly had foiled a Royalist rising. I did not believe that Marlowe's prisoner had told the truth about the powder, but it seemed possible—even likely—that he and Walker had been at the heart of the scheme. If that was the case, their deaths would have caused the plot to collapse or inspired their comrades to rethink their plan. And with each day, this hope grew stronger.

And so I contented myself with a more ordinary life, or at least one free of plots and murders. Tom and I made the final plans for our marriage, which we intended to solemnize that summer. We'd hoped to marry earlier, but Tom's sister in Lancashire begged him to wait until the roads became passable so she could attend, and he would not deny her. To my great pleasure, Martha and Will announced that they would marry on the same day.

Curiously enough, even as Martha, Elizabeth, and I settled into a routine free of chaos and discord, Katherine Chidley's life became more tumultuous. The spark for the change came when Parliament ordered the arrest of the chief Levellers in England for sedition and treason. In March, Cromwell sent hundreds of soldiers throughout the city, scooping up men like John Lilburne, William Walwyn, and Richard Overton. According to Tom, Cromwell had said that the only way to deal with the Levellers was, in his words, *to break them into pieces.*

Mr. Marlowe, of course, sent notes demanding any news I might hear of a Leveller rising, and in every case I told him the truth. The Levellers responded to the arrests of their leaders as they always had: not with violence, but with books and petitions. I also told him—since it was no secret—that Katherine led this charge against Cromwell's tyranny. (I did not call it that, of course, but neither did I see the benefit in arresting men for mere words.) Katherine attended more meetings than ever, carried petitions throughout the city collecting thousands of signatures, and even wrote petitions of her own, each one demanding their leaders' release and an end to Parliament's arbitrary rule.

With London's waters so troubled, I was not surprised when I came home one afternoon to find Tom and Martha waiting for me in the parlor. They both wore their coats, ready for a hurried departure.

"Mr. Marlowe has summoned me?" I asked. "This is a happy day indeed."

When neither Tom nor Martha smiled, I began to worry.

"It is about Mr. Marlowe," Tom said. "But he did not summon you."

"What do you mean?"

"He's been murdered," Tom replied. "And it seems to be the same man who killed Daniel Chidley and Enoch Harrison."

I stood in silence and tried to make sense of Tom's words. "Mr. Marlowe is murdered?" I said at last.

Tom nodded. "A stiletto to the heart, with no other wounds."

I spent a moment trying to imagine what this murder could mean, but was entirely overwhelmed by the possibilities and the dangers.

"Take me to the body," I said.

Chapter 25

"When he did not come to the Tower this morning I sent a guard to rouse him," Tom said. We were walking south and east, in the general direction of the Tower. "He was back within minutes, pale and shaking. Mr. Marlowe's door was unlocked, and his body was inside."

"What did you do then?" I asked.

"Locked the guard in my office so nobody else would find out about Mr. Marlowe's death," Tom said, "and sent Will to guard Mr. Marlowe's apartment until I found you and Martha."

We came to a modest building northwest of the Tower, and Tom led us up a set of stairs where Will waited.

"Have you been inside?" Tom asked.

"Aye," Will said. "It is as we were told. His body is in the parlor." Will opened the door and the four of us stepped into Marlowe's rooms.

Marlowe lay on the floor, arms and legs splayed wide. The handle of a knife protruded from his chest. Martha and I crossed to the body and bent over for a closer examination. I looked first at

Marlowe's face. His eyebrows were raised as if he'd just heard some interesting news, and his mouth was slightly open in an *O* of surprise. Martha lifted his chin, and we saw that his neck had none of the bruises we'd found on Daniel Chidley.

I had never even imagined how Mr. Marlowe lived, but I was nevertheless struck by how utterly ordinary his apartment was. The furniture was better than the pieces Martha and I had purchased for our tenement, but not so fine as what I'd owned when I was a gentlewoman. For a man who had held remarkable power, he lived in an unremarkable fashion.

Martha looked to the knife handle. It was made of wood, and unadorned except for a small rose carved on each side. Martha took the handle between her thumb and forefinger and wriggled it back and forth. "It could be the same knife that killed Daniel Chidley and Enoch Harrison," she said. "It has the same narrow blade."

"And just the one wound," I added. "It must be the same killer."

"If so, why did he leave the weapon behind?" Will asked.

"Pull it out," Martha said.

"What do you mean?"

"Come over here and pull it out of his chest."

Will grasped the knife and gave it a tug. Marlowe's body jerked, but the knife remained in place. "It's stuck," he said.

"Aye," Martha replied. "It's caught between his ribs. The murderer would have had a devil of a time getting it out. If he were in a hurry it might not have been worth the trouble. There are other knives in London."

"How could this be?" Tom asked. "Abraham Walker is dead and buried. Could there be *two* assassins in London who kill in such a fashion?"

We stared at Marlowe's body for a time, hoping to make sense of this strange turn of events. And then I knew what had happened.

"It never was Walker," I said.

"What do you mean?" Martha asked. "He killed the Harrisons' servants, nearly killed the two of us, and cracked Katherine Chidley's skull. You heard him admit to Margaret that he had killed her father. You can't think he was innocent."

"I have no doubt that he was a black-hearted killer, and would have murdered the lot of us without a moment's hesitation," I said. "But he did not kill Daniel Chidley, and while he might have been there when Enoch Harrison died, he did not wield the knife."

The blood had run from Tom's face. "How can you know that?"

"Walker's choice of weapons," I said.

All three looked at me in confusion.

"Tell me, Martha," I said. "When Abraham Walker came to kill Margaret Harrison, what was the first weapon he used?"

"Pistols," Martha replied, and in an instant her face lit up. "If he were skilled enough with a stiletto to kill Daniel Chidley and Enoch Harrison, why did he bring pistols and a cudgel to kill Margaret Harrison?"

"Exactly," I said. "A knife would have been far quieter, but it takes skill that Abraham Walker did not have."

Tom's eyes darted between Martha and me. "You are saying that the assassin is still out there."

"Aye," I said. "But it's worse than that. Why would he kill Marlowe now? We were sure of Walker's guilt and called off the hunt. If the murderer had kept his knife sheathed, we'd never have known we were wrong."

Tom thought for a moment and then cursed. "The plot is not

yet foiled. Walker's death stopped nothing. The rebellion could begin at any moment. Blood of Christ."

I nodded and surveyed the room. "Did Mr. Marlowe keep any papers here? Anything that could tell us what plots he suspected?"

"It would be unusual," Tom replied. "He rarely left the Tower except to sleep, and I never saw him bring papers with him."

A quick search of the apartment confirmed this—Marlowe had neither papers nor letters. "They might have been burned," Martha said, pointing at the hearth. "The ashes are cold, but so is Marlowe's body."

Tom growled in frustration. "I will return to the Tower and search Mr. Marlowe's papers. Will, you stay here for now. I'll send some men for the body."

"And us?" I asked.

"I don't know." Tom sighed. "Figure out what we missed. There has to be something. We must find the killer before his plot is launched."

Tom left, closing the door behind him. When the latch clicked shut, Martha crossed and examined it.

"Look here," she said. Will and I joined her at the door. "That's a good lock, and he's got a second one that can't be opened from the outside."

"Marlowe let the killer in," Will said.

"He must have known him," Martha said.

"Known him and trusted him," I said. "He would not have let a stranger or an enemy take him unawares. But who could it be?"

I returned to the men we'd suspected from the start—the Leveller Jeremiah Goodkey, the Royalist Charles Owen, even Lorenzo Bacca. Would Marlowe have been foolish enough to let *any* of these men into his apartment? I could not imagine him doing so, but that left only one possibility: The killer was someone we'd not yet considered.

With nothing more to do at Marlowe's apartment, Martha and I bid Will farewell and started back to the Cheap.

"Will we tell Katherine Chidley?" Martha asked.

I am ashamed to admit that the question hadn't even occurred to me. "Tell her that the man who murdered her husband is still alive and well?"

"And that he has killed yet again," Martha added.

In truth this was no easy question. We both knew that Abraham Walker's death had offered Katherine a measure of peace. While she still missed Daniel, the aching was less each day, and her constant work with the Levellers had helped her to embrace her widowhood. What would happen to the new life that she had built for herself if she learned that Walker had not killed Daniel, and that his murderer was still walking free?

"Not yet," I replied. "We should not trouble her until we discover who really killed Daniel." While I believed this was the right decision, I did not like the prospect of lying to our gossip yet again. Martha nodded, but she was no more pleased than I at our decision. With that settled we returned to the question of who could have killed Marlowe. To our mutual frustration, we made no progress. It simply seemed incredible that Marlowe would let anyone he suspected of murder get so close to him.

"If he would not let an enemy or a stranger into his rooms, it must have been a friend," Martha said.

"Charles Owen suggested that one of Marlowe's men killed Daniel," I said. "Perhaps he was right. Perhaps the killer was one of Marlowe's own spies. I will ask Tom; he knew Mr. Marlowe's business better than anyone."

As soon as I said the words, a most disquieting thought reared up in my head. Could Tom be behind the murders? As a soldier, he was certainly skilled in the art of killing, and he knew that Mr. Marlowe's death would cancel my debt to him, freeing us both. And, most damningly, he certainly could have convinced Mr. Marlowe to open his door.

Martha had kept her eyes on the street before us or else I am quite sure she would have seen the fear in my face. I told myself that Tom was no murderer and pushed the thought as far from my mind as I could.

"Let us go to the Nag's Head for supper," I said. I hoped that the commotion there would drown my suspicions.

When we arrived, we found the tavern busier than any beehive, as people—mostly women, I noticed—flowed in and out by the dozens. We shouldered our way through the crowd and found Katherine at the center of all the activity. She strode among the tables overseeing a group of women, including Elizabeth, who were busily copying some kind of letter. As soon as one of the scribblers finished, someone in the crowd would take the paper and dash out the door. With each finished letter, Katherine would shout encouragement to the rest of the writers.

"There you are!" Katherine cried when she saw us. Her eyes shone with excitement, and I knew that I could not tell her that Daniel's murderer might still be alive. "I am glad you are here."

"What is happening?" I asked.

"It is not what is happening, it is what is *going* to happen." She thrust one of the letters into my hands. "Tomorrow we Leveller women will march on Parliament by the thousands. We will climb the stairs of St. Stephen's Chapel and present our petition to the Speaker of the House of Commons. We will show these tyrants that they that they cannot arrest good men without cause. We will show them that we will be heard whether they like it or not, and that their tyranny will not stand. Read it—you will see."

I looked down at Katherine's petition. I can only imagine the look of surprise that spread over my face, not least because it was in Elizabeth's hand. While it began ordinarily enough—it claimed to be a "humble petition from many well-affected women of London"—it quickly ventured into fantastical realms.

> *We women are assured of our creation in God's image and also of a share in the freedoms of the Commonwealth of England. Thus we cannot but grieve that we appear so despicable in your eyes, as to be thought unworthy to represent our grievances to this honorable House.*
>
> *Have women not an equal interest in those liberties and securities contained in the good laws of the land? Are women's lives, liberties, or goods to be taken from us more than from men, except by due process of law and conviction?*

"You are going to take this to Parliament?" I asked. I could not quite believe it.

"Of course," Katherine said. "For my sake, and yours, and Elizabeth's as well. The liberties of England are due to *all* the English, not just the wealthy, and not just the men. If we women want the freedoms that are ours by birthright, we will have to take them for ourselves, for this Parliament will never give them to us willingly. Women and men must be equal in the eyes of the law."

"When will you go to Westminster?" I asked.

"Tomorrow morning," Katherine said with a laugh. "We are sending notices throughout the city: to Westminster, to Southwark, everywhere. We women will march on Parliament together. There will be thousands of us."

Not for the first time, I marveled at Katherine's audacity. I could not imagine what manner of world we would have if Katherine's vision came to be, but I could see that she would not be stayed. One of the other women called for Katherine, and after bidding us farewell she returned to the business of petitioning Parliament.

Elizabeth crossed to my side, and I knew her question even before she asked it.

"No," I said. "You may not."

"Please!" Elizabeth cried out. "I will be with Katherine and among friends. And I've never been to Westminster."

"Absolutely not," I said. "Who can know how Cromwell will react to such a provocation? I will not have you arrested."

"Provocation?" Elizabeth asked. "When did petitioning Parliament become a provocation? It is a liberty, not sedition."

"It is too dangerous."

"Very well," Elizabeth said, but what she meant was, *We will continue this discussion later.*

With no hope of finding our supper among such a crowd, Martha and I returned home and dined on what food we had there.

When Elizabeth came home I readied myself for a second skirmish over the march on Parliament. When she went to bed without even asking, I did not know whether to be thankful or suspicious. She had traveled from Pontrilas to London without my leave; why would she not walk a few miles to Westminster? I resolved to watch her closely the next morning lest she slip away.

That night as I drifted to sleep, I wondered what fate awaited Katherine and her fanciful dreams for England. I could not imagine Parliament would grant all—or any—of her demands. I only hoped that she would not frighten them so badly that they would clap her in irons and send her to the Tower.

• • •

It was not yet daylight when Martha and I awoke to a pounding on our door. I arrived downstairs before our maidservant, Susan, and as I reached for the lock a vision of Mr. Marlowe's corpse leaped into my mind.

"Who is it?" I called through the door.

Lorenzo Bacca's deep laugh answered my question. "You are grown more careful, Mrs. Hodgson. I commend you for that, but it is only me."

"Why have you come?" Martha had joined me at the door. I said a prayer of thanks that Elizabeth was still abed.

"Why are you so suspicious?" the Italian asked.

"Tell us what you want," I demanded.

"I am here for Jane Owen. She has begun her travail and sent me to find you," Bacca said. "Why will you not open the door? Is something wrong?"

Martha retrieved a fire iron from the hearth and stepped to the side of the door. She nodded at me, and with one motion I pulled open the door and stepped back. Bacca stood in the hall, his silks resplendent even in the guttering light afforded by his lantern.

"Open your cloak," I said. "Show me your belt."

Bacca raised an eyebrow and allowed a smile to creep across his lips. "And a good morning to you, as well," he said.

I stared at him, and after a moment his smile faded. "Very well," he said, and pulled back his cloak. As I expected, he wore a knife on his belt. It had a long, thin blade, ideal for slipping in between a man's ribs and killing him in an instant.

"Put the knife on the ground," I said.

"What is it?" Bacca asked. He now sounded worried. "What has happened?" When I did not answer, he put the knife on the ground and tapped it toward me with his toe.

I scooped up the knife and stepped back. I stared at the polished bone handle and ornate gold band that graced the pommel. It was entirely unlike the knife that had killed Mr. Marlowe.

"What has happened?" Bacca asked again.

"A . . . friend was murdered," I said. "And we do not know what the murderer intends to do next. I fear we are in danger."

"If you are in danger, it is not from me," Bacca said. "I promise you that."

I looked down at Bacca's knife and made a decision.

"Will you take us to Jane Owen's?" I asked, handing him his knife.

"Why so trusting?" he asked. "I could be lying."

"I saw the knife that killed our friend," I said. "You'd have choked him to death before you condescended to use such a blade."

Bacca laughed as he sheathed his weapon. "That is the only reason? Well, I suppose it will have to do."

"How long has she been in travail?" Martha asked as she stepped into sight. She still held the fire iron at the ready.

"Ah, there you are!" Bacca said. "I imagine if I'd tried to come inside without an invitation I would have caught the iron in my ear. Well done."

"The travail?" Martha asked again.

Bacca shrugged. "Long enough to need a midwife, I suppose. I do not pretend to comprehend women's business. I just did what Mrs. Owen asked of me, and that was to summon you."

"I'll gather what we need," I said. "Martha, tell Susan where we are going. And tell her to keep a close watch on Elizabeth. I fear she will try to join Katherine's march despite my warning."

A few minutes later, the three of us were winding our way through the darkened streets toward the Crown.

Chapter 26

When Martha, Lorenzo Bacca, and I neared the Crown, Bacca led us around a corner to a comfortable and well-appointed house. We entered without knocking and found Charles Owen and a few of his friends sitting in the parlor talking softly. He glanced up when we entered. When he recognized us his eyes bulged and he leaped to his feet; I took an involuntary step backward, suddenly thankful for Bacca's presence.

Owen glanced at his friends and regained himself. "You must be Jane's midwives," he said. "Welcome."

"Thank you," I replied. None of the men seemed to have noticed Owen's initial reaction. "She is upstairs?"

"Aye, but before you go up, could I have a word in private?"

I glanced at Bacca, who nodded slightly. "I will stay near."

Martha and I followed Owen into the kitchen. As soon as the door closed, his anger at our presence had returned in full force. "How is it," Owen asked through his teeth, "that of all the midwives in London, my wife settled on you? Do you know the trouble you caused the last time you came? You accused me of murdering

Daniel Chidley, and nearly convinced my friends that I work for Cromwell. And now you are back?"

"We'll offer no apologies for hunting Daniel's murderer," Martha replied. "And if you suffered a mild inconvenience for it, you'll get no sympathy from us."

"Three men died, and you are still living," I said. "Some men would be grateful."

Owen took a breath and made a visible effort to calm himself. "None of this tells me how you came to be here," he said at last. "Are you truly here as midwives?"

"Your wife sent for us, and we came," I said. "You can ask her yourself."

"And why would you help her if you think I consort with rebels?"

"If favoring the King were a crime, half of England would be hanged," I said. "You've broken no laws, so we'll cause you no trouble."

"We are here for your wife, not for you," Martha added. "Every mother deserves a good midwife, whether she favors the King, Parliament, or no government at all."

Owen stared at her for a moment, weighing her words. "I will speak to Jane. If you are telling the truth, I will not keep you from her. Wait here."

A few minutes later, a maidservant appeared. "Mr. Owen asked me to take you to my mistress."

Martha and I followed the girl out of the kitchen. As we passed through the parlor, Owen glanced at us but made no sign that we were anything other than strangers he'd just met.

We found Jane Owen in good spirits, talking amiably with half a dozen gossips who had come to attend her. Jane smiled when we entered and motioned us to her side.

"How is your travail?" I asked after we embraced.

"It is my first one, so I cannot say for sure." She laughed with delight at the thought. "But it is not too severe, so I will not complain."

I felt her belly through her shift, and found that the child was still high in her matrix. She was early in her travail. With nothing to be done at that moment, Martha and I settled in to better acquaint ourselves with Jane and her gossips. I found her to be as delightful as any mother I'd delivered since coming to London. She was kind to her friends and exceptionally quick of mind. I could not help wondering if she might someday take up the art of midwifery. Since Martha had come into her own, I soon would need a new deputy. I resolved to raise the question once I had delivered her.

Around sunrise I anointed my hands with oil and lay Jane on the bed. The neck of her matrix remained closed, which meant that her final travail was still some time away. I sent Martha to another chamber to get some rest, and then rejoined the gossips in their conversation.

A few hours after Martha had gone to sleep, we heard the sound of voices outside, as if a crowd had gathered beneath Jane's window. Within minutes the noise had grown so great that it roused Martha, and she joined us in looking out the window.

My mouth fell open at the sight that greeted us. Hundreds—nay, thousands—of women had filled the street and were marching together. They had sprigs of sage in their hats and sea-green ribbons pinned to their aprons. It could only be Katherine's crowd, bound for Parliament. I marveled at their numbers and—for the barest of moments—wondered if they might somehow sway Parliament in their favor. If the rule of kings could be overthrown, why not the rule of men?

Just before I turned away, I saw a blaze of red hair among the throng of women. I caught my breath and looked more closely. It was Elizabeth, of course.

Martha saw her as well. "I cannot say I'm surprised," she said with a laugh. "If she can escape Pontrilas and come to London on her own, slipping out of the house and going to Katherine's would be no challenge at all."

In a few moments, Elizabeth passed us by. I said a prayer for her safety. "Do not worry," Martha said. "She has done far more dangerous things than this."

"I know," I said. "But a mother cannot help worrying."

By now a handful of Jane's friends had joined us at the window to marvel at the crowd below.

"It is a strange thing to see women petitioning," one of the gossips commented.

"No less strange than cutting off the King's head," another replied. "These are the times we live in."

Once the crowd had passed I let the curtain fall back into place. At that moment the chamber door burst open and Charles Owen entered. The gossips immediately began squawking at the intrusion, but Owen paid them no mind. He crossed to Jane and took her hands.

"It is time," he said. "Today is the day."

I stared in wonder when Jane burst into tears. She wrapped her arms around Charles's neck and buried her face in his chest. The women stopped their protests and watched in silence. What could this mean?

"Jane, I must go." Charles spoke with such sorrow I could feel his pain in my own heart. With all the gentleness of a mother wrapping her child in swaddling clothes, Charles pulled away Jane's arms and stepped back. "I love you."

Jane tried to reply but could only choke back a sob.

Charles took a deep breath, turned away from his wife, and walked out of the room. From the look on his face it appeared that each step caused him more pain than I'd felt since my children died.

When the door shut, Jane fell to her knees and buried her face in her hands. Her sobs filled the room, shaking us all to our bones. The gossips gathered around and lifted her to her feet, offering what comfort they could. They had no more idea what had happened than I did, but they knew Jane needed them.

Perhaps it was Jane's grief that drove matters forward, but within the hour Jane's travail began in earnest. Martha and I together delivered Jane of a beautiful boy. While Martha swaddled the child, I saw to Jane and sent one of the gossips for her breakfast. She returned with a plate of bread, cheese, and roast fowl. When I handed the plate to Jane my eyes fell upon the knife that the gossip had brought.

The only marking on the wood handle was a delicately carved rose.

I counted it a miracle that I did not cry aloud or drop the plate in Jane's lap. I glanced at Jane, wondering if she had seen my reaction. To my relief she was more intent on her meal than her midwife.

Once Jane was fully occupied by her breakfast I pulled Martha to the side. "Come with me," I murmured.

Martha nodded and we slipped out of the chamber and descended the stairs.

"Come to the kitchen," I said. "You must see this." We followed the smell of roast meats and found a maidservant cleaning dishes. I plunged my hand into the tub of water and retrieved the forks and knives from the bottom.

I stared in dismay at what I found. None of the knives resembled the one I'd seen on Jane's plate.

"What is it?" Martha asked.

"The knife that the gossip brought with Jane's dinner was the twin of the one that killed Marlowe. It had the same carved rose."

"A carved rose?" the maidservant asked. "That must have come from the Crown. Mrs. Owen favors the roses. All the knives have them on their handles."

"Do you have any others?" I asked.

The maid opened a drawer and produced a thin-bladed knife, perfect for boning a fowl—or for slipping between a man's ribs.

"Charles Owen killed them," Martha breathed. "But where is he now?"

My mind returned to Jane and Charles's tearful farewell. I realized then that Charles's resignation and calm resembled that of a man who knew that death was near and unavoidable. And Jane's sorrowful acceptance was that of a woman who knew she would soon be widowed.

"Some kind of plot is underway," I said. "And Charles Owen does not expect to survive it." I tried desperately to recall some detail that might have escaped my notice, something that would tell us where Charles had gone, but could think of nothing.

"We have to ask Jane," Martha said.

I nodded. It would pain me to press her, but if our suspicions were correct we did not have another choice. We returned to Jane's chamber to find her nursing her son. She looked up when we entered.

"There you are. Come see—he is eating well, I think." The child was indeed nursing with great enthusiasm.

"He is named Charles after his father," one of the gossips volunteered.

At this Jane's eyes filled with tears.

I could tell then that she knew where her husband had gone, and that she did not expect him to return. "Where is he, Jane?" I asked.

Jane's eyes snapped to mine, her sorrow replaced by fright and anger. "What do you mean?"

"Where is your husband? What is he planning to do?"

Jane's face turned as hard as stone. "Who are you?"

"Where is Charles?" I asked again. "You must tell us. We can save him."

Jane clapped her mouth shut and regarded us through half-lidded eyes. "You are the midwife who killed Abraham," she said at last. "Bacca brought one of Cromwell's spies into my chamber? He and I will have to talk about this."

"Tell us where your husband has gone," Martha said. "Do not deprive your son of a father."

Jane's thin smile was as cold as the north wind. "Do not lie to me. Even if you were to find him, my son would never see his father. Charles would be clapped up in the Tower until the day he was hanged. I have no reason to tell you anything, and with Charles already gone, nothing can make me. Perhaps your master is brutal enough to rack a woman a few hours after she gives birth, but even then you would be too late."

Martha swore a most foul oath.

"If it is any consolation," Jane said, "you will know when Charles has finished his work. All of London will know. Now, be gone, both of you."

I glanced at Martha. I knew that every minute we spent interrogating Jane would be wasted, and I did not think we had many minutes to spare.

"Follow me," Martha said. "I have an idea." Martha and I left the chamber and she led me to a room at the back of the house. It held a desk and a low bed where Martha must have slept while she awaited Jane's travail. A small chest secured with a heavy iron lock sat next to the bed.

"Do you have your picklock?" I asked. "Can you open it?"

"I don't, and we haven't time," Martha said. She retrieved a fire poker from the hearth and threaded it through the hasp of the lock. She stood and twisted it with all her strength. The chest's iron studs groaned but held fast. "Help me," Martha said through her teeth.

I took hold of the poker and the two of us pulled together. With a shriek the staple tore free from the chest. The lock—still secured—fell to the floor.

"Now that's a good lock," Martha said with a smile.

We lifted the lid to find a sheaf of papers and a leather bag full of coins. Martha emptied the bag on the bed and whistled as the money piled up. "There is a lot of money to be made in keeping a tavern," she said.

A flash of red from among the papers caught my eye. I pulled out a silk rope with a beautifully tied knot in the middle of it. Martha and I immediately recognized it as a twin to the one we'd found on Abraham Walker's body.

"This proves Charles is a spy," Martha said. "But we still must find him."

I handed half the papers to Martha. "Start reading."

It turned out that the reading would not take us long at all, for nearly every letter had been composed in a cypher. I supposed someone at the Tower might have the time to figure out what the symbols meant, but we did not.

"Here, what's this?" Martha asked. "Last summer, Charles Owen rented a house in Westminster."

"Let me see." The paper was nothing more than an agreement between Charles Owen and one George Moody to rent a home described as *near to the chapel now called St. Mary Undercroft.*

"That's next to St. Stephen's Chapel," I said. "That's where Parliament meets."

"Why would he rent a house in Westminster?" she asked. "It is miles from here."

I sat on the bed and closed my eyes. I knew we had the pieces to solve the puzzle. We just had to see how they fit together.

"Jane Owen told us that all of London would know when Charles finished his work," Martha said.

My eyes snapped open. "Gunpowder and Guy Fawkes," I said. "Charles Owen intends to blow up Parliament."

"And that's where Elizabeth and Katherine have gone."

Martha and I ran pell-mell down Bread Street toward the river. Neither of us spoke, entirely intent on the task before us. When we reached the Salt Wharf, I raced to the water's edge and started waving frantically to the wherries. Within seconds a strong young man guided his boat toward us. I threw myself in and Martha followed close behind.

"Westminster," I said. "And you must hurry."

The lad bent his back to the oars and began to pull us upriver. God smiled on us that day, for he rowed with a rising tide and in a few moments we seemed to be flying. But what an agony sitting in the wherry was, unable to do anything except gaze at the riverside mansions as we rowed past.

"Are you with those Leveller women?" our driver asked between strokes. "I've never seen so many women in one place. I can't say I ever want to see such a thing again."

"We're not with them," I said. "We have other business with Parliament."

The lad shook his head in wonder. "This is a curious world the rebels have fashioned. These women are marching, and you have business before Parliament. What is next? Will we be ruled by women?"

When Martha and I ignored his affront the boatman shrugged and began to sing in time with his rowing.

"Will we arrive in time?" Martha asked.

"I don't know." I fought back the panic that clawed at my throat, screaming for release. "If all he needs to do is light the fuse, then we might not. If he has other work to do beforehand—perhaps."

"He does not intend to escape," Martha said.

"No. He will die with all of Parliament. But in a hundred years, he will be no less famous than Guy Fawkes."

The journey to Westminster seemed to last an eternity, but in truth it could not have been more than a few minutes. "Will the Whitehall Stairs be close enough?" the boatman asked.

"Yes," I snapped. "Just get us ashore."

As we approached the stairs I could see the crowd of women still streaming toward St. Stephen's Chapel, where the Commons met. "If he sets off the gunpowder now he will kill more Leveller women than Parliament men," I said.

"What the Christ do you mean by that?" Our boatman had stopped rowing and now stared at us in horror.

"Nothing," I said. "Just get us ashore and row downriver as fast as you can. Get away from here."

A few moments later, Martha and I were running up the steps and straight into the crowd of women.

"Which house is it?" Martha cried out. We could see the entrance to St. Stephen's Chapel in the distance. A line of soldiers stood before the doors, keeping the women from entering the hall.

I shook my head, not knowing whether to scream or weep. "It must be one side or the other, left or right."

Martha looked around us and spotted a sergeant of the trained bands. He stood in an alley, watching the crowd as it flowed past. "You there," she shouted. "Which way is St. Mary Undercroft?"

He looked at her suspiciously. "Why do you want to know? Are you here with this lot?"

I approached the sergeant. He was a tall, thin man, with bright blue eyes and a close-cropped beard. I remembered that I was a gentlewoman by birth and a midwife by profession, and I summoned every bit of my authority. I hooked my fingers around the collar of the sergeant's coat and looked him in the eyes. "Sergeant, what is your name?"

"Hirst," he replied. "Why? What is it?"

"There is a plot afoot to blow up the Parliament," I said. "The gunpowder is in a house next to St. Mary Undercroft—cartloads of it. If we don't find it, Parliament will be destroyed, thousands will die, and another war will begin. We need your help."

He stared at me in horror. "You are serious."

"Never more," I said.

"Follow me." Sergeant Hirst turned toward St. Stephen's Chapel and started pushing his way through the crowd. Along the way he shouted for his men, and soon Martha and I had an entire squad of soldiers surrounding us.

"There is the chapel," the guard said, pointing. "But which house is it?"

I looked again at the letter we'd found in Owen's office. "It just says it is near the chapel." I wanted to scream in frustration, but I found strange comfort in the knowledge that if the gunpowder exploded now, I would be among the dead. Better that than to lose Elizabeth and keep on living.

"Then we'll search them all," the sergeant said. He turned to the men who had joined us. "We are looking for a man who intends to blow up the Commons," he announced. "He is in one of these houses. Go in twos, pound on every door. If nobody answers kick it in. We are looking for . . ." He turned to me. "Who are we looking for?"

I described Charles Owen as best I could. "Be very careful. He has killed three men with a knife and has no expectation of living out the day. He will kill you without a moment's hesitation."

"Go, now!" the sergeant shouted. The men dispersed and soon the street was filled with their shouts and the sound of doors crashing open if the owners were slow in answering.

"What about that one?" Martha asked. One house had not yet been searched, and none of the watch were nearby.

"We'll do it," Sergeant Hirst said. "The three of us."

We approached the door, and Sergeant Hirst pounded on it with a closed fist. While we waited, I went to a window and tried to peer in, but it was covered with a heavy black curtain. I could see nothing at all. Sergeant Hirst knocked again.

"We haven't time," I said. I picked up a cobblestone and hurled it through the window. I reached in and pulled the curtain aside. The room was filled with small barrels of gunpowder.

"Oh God," I moaned. "This is it. This is the house."

Chapter 27

To his credit, Sergeant Hirst did not hesitate. He stepped back, raised his foot, and delivered a terrific blow to the door. The wood around the knob splintered, and the door flew open. Martha and I charged in with Sergeant Hirst close behind. The room we entered had been emptied of all furniture but filled from wall to wall with barrels of gunpowder. Owen had stacked them against the far wall, from floor to ceiling. I could not imagine the damage that would come if Owen succeeded in his scheme. We had the gunpowder, but where was Owen?

"Upstairs," Martha said. "He must be there."

We dashed up a set of stairs and ran to the back of the house. Like the rooms below, the upper chamber was filled with gunpowder, but we also found Charles Owen. He was hunched over the hearth trying desperately to light a fire among the wood shavings and kindling. He cried out in frustration when he heard us enter the room.

Sergeant Hirst stepped forward and drew a brace of pistols from his belt. "Stand up slowly. It is over."

"He may have a knife," I warned.

"I've no knife," Owen said. He turned to face us. True to his word, his hands were empty save the flint and steel he'd been using a moment before. He dropped those and stared for a moment at the sergeant's pistols.

"I'll get help," Martha said. She dashed down the stairs, and I could hear her shouting for the rest of the guards.

A strange smile crossed Owen's face, and in an instant I knew why. "Sergeant Hirst, you cannot fire your pistols near so much powder," I said.

Charles Owen took that as his cue. He drew a knife from beneath his coat and with a dreadful scream leaped toward the sergeant.

Sergeant Hirst dropped his pistols, more willing to die than to fire them and risk killing us all. He raised his arm just in time to block what would surely have been a killing blow, but Owen's knife cut through fabric and flesh. Blood splashed across them both, and the sergeant cried out in pain. Owen raised his knife again, and Sergeant Hirst threw himself forward, hoping to knock Owen to the ground before he could strike.

But Owen was too quick. He dodged to the side and delivered a terrific blow to the back of Sergeant Hirst's head. He fell to the ground and lay still. Now it was just Owen and me.

My eyes locked with Owen's, and we both heard the sound of men shouting downstairs. There would be no time for him to start a fire using flint and steel. That left only Sergeant Hirst's pistols. Owen dropped his knife and we dove for them simultaneously, clawing and grappling for purchase; I was desperate to live, while he hoped to die.

He seized one pistol by the butt, and his finger sought the trigger. I grabbed the barrel and wrenched it forward. It slipped out of his blood-smeared hands, and I hurled it toward the stairs. It clattered down, leaving one pistol in the room, but in the confusion neither of us knew where it had gone.

With a victorious cry, Owen threw himself forward and—too late!—I saw the pistol peeking from behind a barrel of powder. We both were moments from death. He turned the pistol toward the powder and tried to pull back the cock, his bloody thumb slipping once, twice. I looked above him and saw another barrel tottering on its edge. I leaped forward and gave it a final push. It landed on his extended arm and the pistol fell from his hand. Owen's scream, equal parts pain and frustration, filled the room. I stepped forward and took the pistol for myself.

Moments later, half a dozen members of the watch thundered up the stairs. Two saw to Sergeant Hirst, while the rest bound Owen's hands. They showed no sympathy for his ruined arm. Another sergeant appeared, his eyes wide at how close we had come to ruination.

"I am Sergeant Willoughby," he said. "The men told me what you said to Sergeant Hirst. I could hardly believe it, but it was true."

I nodded. "He meant to kill us all."

Sergeant Willoughby kicked Owen in the stomach and searched his pockets. He found a few coins and then produced a third red silk cord. He stared at it in puzzlement for a moment. "What is this?"

"It is another sign of his guilt, as if it were needed," I said. "The plotters carried them so they could know each other." I took the cord and put it in my apron. "I will bring this to the Tower. The jury will want to see it before they pass judgment."

The sergeant nodded. "Should we take him straight to the Tower, too?"

"Aye," I said. "Send him by boat. There is a Colonel Reynolds there. He will lead the questioning."

Sergeant Willoughby nodded to the soldiers. "Go on. She just saved your lives and all of Westminster. You should do as she says."

"Thank you, Sergeant," I said.

"Would you care to explain how you came to know about all this?" Sergeant Willoughby gestured at the barrels of powder lining the walls.

"It is a long story," I replied. "And not one I can tell right now. Perhaps another time."

Martha and I excused ourselves and made our way back to the river, where we found a wherry to take us to the Tower. When we arrived, we found the guards waiting for us. They led us through the maze of towers and halls until we reached the White Tower. Will was waiting outside.

"Martha, Aunt Bridget!" Will cried when he saw us. He crossed the last few yards between us and took Martha in his arms, hugging her fiercely. "The guards told us what happened. The house was filled with gunpowder?"

"Barrels of it," I replied. "The carnage would have been . . ." I closed my eyes and imagined the aftermath if Owen had sparked a flame: thousands dead, Parliament destroyed, a new civil war begun. And if the explosion had started a fire, who knew how much of London would have burned?

I shook my head to chase away such visions. "Is Charles Owen here?"

"Aye. They brought him in through the Traitors' Gate, and straight to a cell. Colonel Reynolds started questioning him as soon as the jailor had him in irons. He expected you would come and asked you to wait in Mr. Marlowe's office."

Martha and I followed Will into the Tower. Once we were

settled, we told him of our day's adventures. When we'd finished, Will shook his head in wonder.

"My God, if you'd arrived in Westminster just a few minutes later . . . Parliament destroyed, Cromwell likely killed, the Leveller women slaughtered in the street. It would have been like nothing England has ever seen."

"Aye," I said. "It was a damnably close thing."

Some hours later, as the sun disappeared behind the Tower wall, there came a knock at the door and Tom entered.

"I don't think you need to knock." Will laughed. "It will likely be your office soon enough."

Tom smiled thinly. "An old habit." He looked to me and his smile broadened. He took a few hesitant steps in my direction before remembering that we were not alone. After such a harrowing day, I too wished to feel his arms around me, but knew it was neither the time nor the place.

"Thank God all of you are safe," Tom said. "I still cannot fathom how close you—and all England—came to disaster."

"What did you learn?" Will asked. "Did he confess?"

Tom nodded. "Given he was caught with flint and steel in hand, he could hardly claim innocence. He says he killed Daniel Chidley, Enoch Harrison, *and* Mr. Marlowe. His only regret is sending Abraham Walker to kill Margaret Harrison. *I should have done that myself,* he said."

"Remarkable," I said. "Did he tell you who his comrades were?"

"He gave us a few names, but says that they fled to France this morning. He was the one chosen to stay behind, light the powder, and die a martyr's death. They drew lots."

"And his wife?" Martha asked. "What of her?"

Tom sighed heavily. "He says she knew nothing of the plot, and we've no proof to the contrary. I will send some men for her in the morning, but unless she volunteers for the hangman's dance nothing will come of it."

"Such is the nature of the law," I said.

"I am sorry to do this," Tom said. "But Will and I must return to business. Once we have chased down all of Owen's accomplices—at least those still in England—the four of us will dine together. I should like to hear just how you discovered the plot when Mr. Marlowe and all his spies could not."

I told Tom that I understood, and a few minutes later Martha and I were walking back to the Cheap.

"Jane Owen knew about her husband's plan," Martha said. "She told us that herself."

"Aye, she did," I replied. "But I do not see what good would come out of exposing her. She would hang for the crime of keeping her husband's secrets, and her child would be an orphan. And a newborn deprived of his mother would likely die within weeks. I have no interest in sending one of my mothers to the gallows and then burying her child, simply because she married a Royalist."

Martha nodded. "I suppose you are right."

Dinner that night was exceedingly strange, as Elizabeth had returned from the march on Parliament buzzing like a bee in springtime. I knew she wanted to tell us about all she had seen, but because she'd gone without my permission she could not say a word. I, of course, could not tell her that I knew of her disobedience or of how close she had come to death at Charles Owen's hands.

As I prepared for bed I reached into my apron and discovered the red silk cord we had found in Owen's pocket. I had meant to give it to Tom, but by the time we'd arrived at the Tower, it had slipped from my mind. I told myself that in light of Owen's confession it did not matter, but something about it troubled me.

I lay in bed for hours, unable to sleep. I knew we had missed something vital, but could not figure out what it was. Martha knocked softly on my door, and I bid her enter.

"You cannot sleep?" I asked.

"No," she said. She crossed the room and sat on the edge of my bed. "There is one question that bothers me still: How did Charles Owen get into Mr. Marlowe's apartment?"

"What do you mean?"

"We discounted Owen's guilt because Marlowe would never have let him get so close. We thought the murderer had to be someone that he trusted, or at least someone he did not see as a danger. Were we wrong about that?"

"I don't know," I said. "But there is something else that puzzles me as well." I reached to the table next to my bed and picked up the silk cord. "Why did Charles Owen have two cords?"

"Two cords?"

"We found one in the chest at his house, and a second in his pocket when we caught him. Why did he need them both?"

I knew the answer as soon as I asked the question.

"Jane Owen," Martha and I said together.

"Marlowe would not have been afraid of a woman, especially one who was with child," I said. "And if she was a part of the plot she would have needed a cord of her own."

"She is the one," Martha said. "She killed them all."

As Martha and I hurried toward the Owens' home, I asked myself what I intended to do. I had said that I did not wish to see Jane hang for merely knowing of her husband's treason, but what of the murders she had done? What of the hundreds who would have died if Charles Owen had managed to kindle a fire? I neither wanted her to go free, nor to see her son made an orphan.

We found the Owens' house dark and stood outside gazing up at the windows. The guttering light of our lantern threw mad shadows on the street.

"Should we send for help?" Martha asked. "If she killed Mr. Marlowe—and the others as well—it would be wise."

"Aye, it would. But I want to see this through to the end. And we will be on our guard in a way that the others were not, for we know how dangerous she is." I stepped forward to try the door handle. To my surprise the door opened at my touch. It had been neither latched nor locked.

Martha and I exchanged a glance. Only a madwoman would leave her door unlocked at night.

We slipped into the Owens' parlor and peered into the darkness. The silence was suffocating. "Something is wrong," I said.

Martha crossed to the hearth and poked at the ashes. "Nobody bothered to bank the fire," she whispered. "They just let it burn itself out." We continued into the kitchen and found the same thing—no signs of trouble except for the dead, cold hearth.

We climbed the stairs as quietly as we could, but each creak sounded as loud as a dying man's scream. The door to Jane's chamber was open. It was here that we finally saw signs of what had happened. Jane's clothes chests lay open, their contents left in disarray. The layette that Jane's gossips had brought for little Charles was missing, and there was no sign of the swaddling clothes I had given her. Jane had fled.

"What now?" Martha asked. In the darkness her voice seemed unnaturally loud.

"Let us look in the back room," I said.

We ventured down the hall. I was not surprised to find that the cyphered papers had disappeared, as had the pile of coins we'd left sitting on the bed. The only thing that remained was the red silk ribbon, which Jane had carefully laid upon the bed, as if bidding us farewell.

"I suppose she didn't want to be caught with that on her person," I said.

"We should send word to the Tower," Martha replied.

"Yes," I said. "But I do not think Jane Owen will be found easily. I imagine she joined her comrades in fleeing to the Continent."

"On the day she gave birth?"

"What choice did she have? If she tarried, she risked hanging alongside her husband, making her son an orphan before he'd spoken his first words. Which of us would have done anything different?"

Martha nodded. "Let us go home. We can send a letter to the Tower from there."

When we turned the corner from the Owens' house I noticed a dim glow from inside the Crown. I put my hand on Martha's arm and pointed.

"You don't think it's Jane, do you?"

"I don't know who else it could be," I said. I pushed on the tavern door and—like the Owens'—it opened to my touch. The room was lit by a single lantern and the dying coals in the hearth. A nearly empty bottle of wine sat on the table next to the lantern.

"Lady Hodgson!" Lorenzo Bacca's voice frightened me so badly I had to swallow a scream.

"Jesus," Martha hissed. "Are you mad?"

"I am sorry—I did not mean to startle you." Bacca stepped out from behind the bar. "I went for another bottle of wine. Will the two of you join me? I'll get more glasses."

"Where is Mrs. Owen?" I asked, ignoring the offer.

"You are too late for that," Bacca replied. "She left not ten minutes after you raced off after her husband."

"Where did she go?"

Bacca shrugged. "France? The Netherlands? Ireland? Scotland? Perhaps even America. If her goal is to avoid hanging for treason, anywhere that is not England would suit her needs. She has money enough to go wherever she pleases and buy some secrecy along the way."

"How do you know all this?" Martha asked.

"I have eyes and ears, don't I? In the last week half the Royalist agents in London fled to France, so I knew something was afoot. Then Jane Owen's gossips told the neighborhood about her husband's intrusion into her delivery room, and the even stranger conversation you two had with her. It was not hard to figure out the rest." Bacca paused for a moment. "There is one other thing I should show you."

"What is it?" I asked. "If you mean the silk knot, we already found it."

Bacca knitted his brow in confusion. "No, it is not that. Far from it, in fact. Follow me." He picked up the lantern and led us through the kitchen to a small closet. He opened the door to reveal a man's body, curled up on the floor, his hands bound behind him. He was clearly dead, and had been for some hours.

"Jane did this?" I asked.

"Lord, no," Bacca replied. "I did. Jane hired him to kill all three of us. Me for bringing you into her chamber, and you two for foiling their plot to blow up Parliament. He made the mistake of coming for me first."

"How do you know all this?" I felt myself growing dizzy, and I wished I'd accepted the glass of wine he'd offered earlier.

Bacca laughed. "I asked him. He knew he had seen his last sunrise, so he had no reason to lie. Paid assassins are not known for their loyalty when things go wrong."

"And then you killed him?" I asked.

"If I hadn't, he would have killed me," Bacca said. "And the two of you as well."

"Are we still in danger?" I asked. "Are there others?"

"I do not think so," Bacca said. "Before I killed him, I made him write to one of Mrs. Owen's friends in France saying he'd killed the three of us. Unless she returns to London and stumbles across us at the market, Mrs. Owen will think we are all dead." Bacca closed the door, and we returned to the dining room.

"But with all this confusion and danger," Bacca continued, "I think it would be prudent for me to find a new profession. I fear I have become too old and too tenderhearted for the life of a spy."

"What will you do?" Martha asked.

Bacca looked around the room and a smile played across his lips. "It appears that the Crown is in need of a new owner. Perhaps I will take up the work of a tavern-keeper."

I laughed. "So London agrees with you?"

"More so than the hanging that awaits me in Italy," Bacca said. "After so many years I've even grown used to the winters. Yes, I think I will stay.

"But what of you?" he asked. "With the plot ended and Mr. Marlowe dead, you are free to return to the country, are you not?"

"I suppose I am." It was true, of course, and I was surprised that the thought had never occurred to me. But was my home in Pontrilas truly my home? Or was the Cheap my home? "Come to think of it, I will accept that glass of wine."

Chapter 28

The next morning I sent a boy with a letter to Tom saying that Martha and I would be visiting. After breakfast we made our way through the city to the Tower. Will was waiting at the gate.

"You'll find Colonel Reynolds in a black humor," he warned us as we made our way to the heart of the castle.

"Let me guess why," I said. "Jane Owen has disappeared, and you have no idea where she went."

Will stopped and stared at me. "How did you know?"

"It's even worse than you think," I said. "I'll tell you and Tom together."

"If you have worse news than that, I'm not sure I want to be there," Will said. When we reached Mr. Marlowe's office (it was hard not to think of it that way), Will knocked twice and we entered. Tom sat behind the desk, leafing through a sheaf of papers, frustration etched into his brow.

But the smile that crossed his face when he saw that I'd come warmed my heart. Tom rounded the desk and embraced me.

"I fear I do not have much time to talk," he said. "Jane Owen has disappeared from her home, and we must find her."

"You won't," I said.

"What do you mean?" Tom asked. "How do you know?"

"She's fled England," I said. "But that is not all."

Tom stared at me for a moment and realized the seriousness of my news. "Tell me."

"Charles Owen lied about the murders. He didn't commit them, not all of them anyway. Jane killed Mr. Marlowe."

"That can't be right," Will said. "She is a woman and was with child."

"That's how she got into Mr. Marlowe's apartment," Martha said. "He never would have opened the door for a man, especially Charles Owen. But a young woman who was with child? He never would have seen the danger, not until the knife was already between his ribs."

"What about Daniel Chidley and Enoch Harrison?" Tom asked.

"I don't know," I said. "Only the Owens can say for sure. But once again, where Daniel Chidley and Enoch Harrison might have suspected a man, Jane could get close enough to do whatever she pleased."

Tom sighed. "I will ask Owen, but if he's lied this long, I doubt he'll suddenly decide to tell the truth." Tom paused for a moment. "Are you sure it was her? Do you have any proof?"

"There are these." I removed the two silk knots from my apron. "We found one in a locked chest at the Owens'. Charles Owen had the other when he was taken by the watch."

Tom took the cord. "They are the same as the one that Abraham Walker carried."

"Aye," I said. "I should have realized it as soon as we found the second one in Owen's pocket, but I too was blinded by Jane's sex."

"And the fact that she fled can only be a sign of guilt," Martha said. "A mother who flees on the day she gives birth must be very frightened of something."

Tom nodded. "So I allowed a murderess with a newborn in her arms to escape from my grasp? That will inspire confidence in the Council, I should think."

We stood in silence for a moment.

Tom looked up at me. "Oh, we did make one discovery of note, and it makes your case for Jane Owen's guilt all the stronger. She was Abraham Walker's sister. Charles Owen and Abraham Walker were brothers through Jane."

Such news was unexpected, but after the events of the last two days I could hardly say I was surprised. "A family of spies," I said.

"Aye," Tom said. "It is also how they were able to escape Mr. Marlowe's investigations. I can't tell you how many men Mr. Marlowe had hidden in among the Royalists, but he never knew of this plot."

"He would have had to marry into it," Martha said. "And as a result they came within a few minutes of destroying all of Westminster."

"That also explains Jane's farewell gift to me," I said.

"What do you mean?" Tom asked.

"Before she fled, Jane Owen paid a man to murder me and Martha. She wanted revenge, it seems."

Tom looked to Will. "Gather a squad of men." He turned back to me. "Who is he? We will take him today and keep you safe."

"Tom, it is fine," I said. "Lorenzo Bacca ensured my safety. The assassin will not trouble us. And with Cromwell's spies on her trail, Jane Owen is in no position to pursue revenge. I am safe enough."

"I do not like it," Tom said.

"I would be disappointed if you did," I replied. "But you must not worry."

Tom sighed heavily. "Very well. But right now, Will and I must return to business. Will the two of you join us for dinner tomorrow? We can meet at the Horned Bull and walk to a victualing house that is more agreeable."

"Very well," I said. "Tomorrow it is." I crossed the room, kissed him lightly on the cheek, and slipped out with Martha close behind.

When the next afternoon came, so too did a boy with a letter. It was short, simply asking Martha and me to meet Tom and Will at the Tower rather than the Horned Bull.

"It seems dinner will have to wait," Martha said. "I wonder why."

"Perhaps he captured Jane Owen," I replied. "It could be anything." But the truth was that from the moment the letter arrived, I felt a growing sense of unease. I told myself I was imagining the worst when I should hope for the best, but such pleasant thoughts failed to cheer me. By the time we departed for the Tower, I was utterly convinced the happiness that had seemed within our grasp was slipping away before my eyes.

My suspicion became a certainty when we arrived at the Tower gate and saw Will's ashen face.

"Will, what is it?" Martha and I asked at the same time.

"Colonel Reynolds will tell you." He could barely choke back his tears, and I began to weep, though I did not know why.

"Will, you must tell me," Martha said.

Will shook his head. "Come with me."

We followed Will to the White Tower and into Tom's office. He sat at the desk, slumped down in his chair, staring vacantly out the window. He glanced at us when we entered and rose to his feet.

"Tom, what has happened?"

"Will and I are going to Ireland," he said. He turned to the window, unable to meet my gaze. "Cromwell will take the army there very soon, and we are to help prepare the way."

I think Tom continued to speak, but all I could hear was the sound of blood rushing in my ears and the thundering of my battered, broken heart. He turned to face me, clearly awaiting some kind of reply, but I had no words.

"Ireland?" Martha's voice seemed to come from a great distance. "For how long?"

"As long as we are told," Tom replied. "Queen Elizabeth's war lasted nearly ten years."

"I thought you would have Mr. Marlowe's place." My voice sounded both petulant and sad. "I thought you would be here in London."

"As did I," Tom said. "But in war nothing is certain."

"Will Marlowe's successor inherit us along with this office?" Martha asked.

Tom shook his head. "I've already seen that he won't. I burned all the papers relating to the murders and gunpowder, and I sent a letter to Sergeant—now Lieutenant—Hirst, commending him on single-handedly stopping Owen's plot. The only others who know of your role in this business are Will, me, and the Owens. Will and I will hold our tongues, and the Owens will be dead or fled soon enough. You are free."

The problem, of course, was that I had no interest in my freedom. I wanted to be Tom's and for him to be mine, on that day and forever. This was too much for me to bear. I found my way to a chair and sat, overwhelmed by the outrages that Dame Fortune had seen fit to inflict upon us.

"When will you leave?" Martha asked.

"On the morrow. Cromwell wishes to put down the rebellion as quickly as possible."

I could not control the sorrow that welled up in my chest. I opened my mouth to cry and curse, but only a thin moan emerged. Tom sat and took me in his arms, while Will embraced Martha. Tom wept, whispered to me of his love, and swore that he would return. All too soon, Martha and I found ourselves outside the Tower walls, retracing our steps to the Cheap. The brilliant sunshine could not penetrate the sorrow that enveloped us, and we clung to each other like sailors drowning in a foreign sea.

The next day, Tom and Will were gone.

Martha, Elizabeth, and I responded to Tom and Will's departure much the same way I had responded to the death of my children. We visited mothers approaching their travail, saw that the children we delivered were doing well, and sought out new women for clients. In short, we did everything we could to keep from thinking about what we had lost. Of course it did not work, for sorrow cannot be so easily chased away. The only cure for grief is the passage of time. In these dark weeks, Elizabeth began to accompany us on our journeys, and I began to teach her the art of midwifing. I had long intended to do this, and had thought that such lessons would bring me great joy. But under the circumstances, they were merely a salve for a terrible wound.

Tom and Will had been gone for less than a month when my maid, Susan, roused me from a deep sleep. "There is a girl here for you."

"Is someone in travail?" I climbed out of bed and began to dress.

Susan hesitated before responding. "Katherine Chidley has died."

I stared at Susan, one sleeve on, one sleeve off. "Died? How?"

"I don't know. The girl might."

"Wake Martha," I said.

Downstairs I found one of Katherine's maidservants weeping in the parlor.

"What has happened?" I asked.

"Last night. After supper she went to her chamber. She said she was going to read and write before she went to bed. I was in the garret when I heard a crash from downstairs. I found her next to her bed."

Martha joined us, sorrow already etched into her face. "Is it true?"

"It seems so," I said, and began to weep. I wondered that God would rob me of Tom and Will, and just a few days later strike down the best gossip I had in London.

"What happened to her?" Martha asked the maid.

"When I came to her room, she was having a most terrible fit. Blood ran from her nose like I'd never seen. It was awful. We called for a physician, but by the time he came . . ." She shook her head.

I dried my eyes as best I could. "I will tell Elizabeth," I said. "Katherine's body is at her house?"

The girl wiped her nose on her sleeve and nodded.

"We will be there soon."

I went to Elizabeth's chamber and woke her as gently as I could, for there would be no softening the blow that I was about to deliver. She knew something was wrong as soon as she saw my face.

"Katherine Chidley has died," I said.

Elizabeth stared at me, her mouth slightly open, refusing to believe the news and waiting for me to take it back. When I did not, she closed her eyes, trying in vain to hold back the tears. I wrapped my arms around her, and we wept for the death of our friend.

"Martha and I are going to the body now," I said. "You can come with us, or wait until morning."

Elizabeth sat up. "I will dress now."

By the time Martha, Elizabeth, and I arrived at Katherine's house, word of her death had spread throughout the Cheap. Her body had been wrapped in linen and laid out on a table in her shop. A dozen people stood around her, speaking softly. I recognized some from the Nag's Head, others from Watling Street, and there were a few I'd never met. The crowd continued to grow until it flowed upstairs into Katherine's parlor and out onto the street. Martha, Elizabeth, and I drifted among the mourners, still unable to believe our friend was gone. Elizabeth clung to Martha and me as if she were afraid of losing one of us as well.

When morning came, people brought bread and cheese, and Jeremiah Goodkey arrived with a barrel of ale, but by then the crowd was so great it was clear that one would not be enough. I began to talk with other mourners and found them as motley a bunch as I'd ever hope to encounter. There were Levellers, of course, still talking politics, continuing their usual arguments, despite the presence of Katherine's corpse. I thought she would approve. Alongside these were mothers whom Katherine had served, including a woman who told me that Katherine had delivered two generations of her family. Neighbors came, and the parish churchwardens, and finally a squad of soldiers. They said Katherine's son was in the north minding the Scottish border. A letter had been sent, but he would not hear of his mother's death for days or even weeks.

The godly came by the dozens, and with them their minister, Mr. Snodgrass. They prayed for a time, and we all joined them. After, Mr. Snodgrass delivered a sermon, reminding us all that death was near and that we must repent of our sins and turn to God. And then the godly joined with us in the drinking and mourning. It was a fine and fitting farewell for one of the most remarkable women I'd ever met.

That night, after Elizabeth had gone to bed, Martha and I sat in the dining room with a bottle of wine between us. We drank in silence for a glass or two.

"She was not like most women," I said after a time.

Martha laughed. "To say the least. Midwife to the Cheap, spy for Cromwell, provocator for the Levellers."

"Scourge of the bishops," I continued, "vindicator of Grace Ramsden, and avenger of her husband. Her tombstone would read like a book."

"What do you think killed her?" Martha asked. "Was it Abraham Walker's blow to her head?"

"It could be," I said. "Probably. But we'll never know for sure."

"How is it that such a good woman should die at the hands of such a cruel man? He intended to murder his lover, and with her his own child."

"You know as well as I that this is the way of the world. All we can do is fight the tide. After all, that is what Katherine did." I paused for a moment and recalled the sight of thousands of women marching past Jane Owen's window on their way to Parliament. "If it *was* that blow, you could say that Katherine survived her own murder by nearly half a year, and led ten thousand women to Westminster in the interim. *That* is a deed worth remembering."

Martha offered a sad smile. "Aye, it is. We could add that to her stone."

For several weeks after Will and Tom left for Ireland, we received no news, nor did we expect to. Indeed, fighting first broke out much closer to home when a handful of Levellers in the army mutinied. They demanded back pay as well as the right to choose their own officers. My heart leaped when I learned of a third grievance: They refused to go to Ireland. If the army would not go, would Tom and Will return? To my sorrow, Cromwell and his generals made short work of the rising. They paid the common soldiers their wages and arrested their leaders. While most of the rebels were pardoned, one was shot by a squad of men in St. Paul's Churchyard. A few weeks later, the army departed.

To our relief, letters from Ireland began to arrive soon after this, usually in pairs, one for Martha and one for me. Tom said little of the army's bloody work subjugating the rebels, for which I was grateful. Rather, he professed his enduring love, and said he was counting the days until we married. Such letters warmed my heart, but also left me in a melancholy state, for I missed him terribly. Will's letters were of a similar nature and had similar effects on Martha's humors. We found ourselves bound even more closely in this curious concoction of happiness and sorrow.

As autumn approached and the weather began to cool, our lives turned yet again. Martha and I had spent the day visiting new mothers, offering both advice and care, when we happened to pass by the Crown. I had no intention of stopping, but a voice called out to us through the open door.

"Mrs. Hodgson, come in, come in!" It was Lorenzo Bacca, of course.

I glanced at Martha, and a smile danced across her lips. She nodded, and we stepped inside to find the tables full and the ale flowing freely. Bacca chased two customers from a small table and sat down with us.

"You will have ale?" he asked. "I prefer wine, of course, but I have a brewer who is a magician." Without awaiting a response, he signaled to the tapster, who brought cups of ale for Martha and me.

"The business of running a tavern seems to agree with you," I said.

Bacca laughed. "It does indeed. It is not quite so exciting as the work of a spy, but it is far less dangerous. Just ask your friend Charles Owen." Owen, of course, had been hanged as a traitor as soon as it became clear that he could not—or would not—disclose his wife's whereabouts.

"So you have abandoned the spying entirely?"

Bacca raised an eyebrow and smiled darkly. "Such work is hard to abandon entirely," he replied. "It will follow you wherever you go. But I am not in any one man's service. I trade in whatever information men seek. It is remarkable what you can learn if you simply keep your ears open."

Perhaps it was because of the quality—and strength—of the ale, but after a time, I felt bold enough to ask Bacca a question that had been troubling me ever since Jane's travail.

"It was not mere chance that you suggested Martha and me as midwives to Jane Owen," I said. "Nor was it our skill in the craft."

Bacca smiled. "I wondered when you might realize that."

"Tell me what happened," I said.

"I suppose I can trust you not to betray me to the Royalists." Bacca leaned forward in a conspiratorial fashion. "I knew Owen had stolen the gunpowder, but I thought it was for an ordinary rebellion. I did not think it would amount to much, and it was none of my business, so I did not trouble myself."

"What changed your mind?" Martha asked.

"I nearly made the same mistake as Cromwell's spies. There was talk of the gunpowder, but nobody spoke of raising troops to use it. That was when I realized that what mattered most were the things that the Royalists *weren't* saying."

"If they had no soldiers, there could be no rising," I said.

"And if they weren't going to use the gunpowder for a rebellion . . . ," Martha said.

"It could only be for a spectacular attack on the city itself," said Bacca. "I had no stomach for such a thing, but I could hardly intervene on my own."

"So you pressed the two of us into service," Martha said.

"And you performed admirably," Bacca said with a laugh. "You saved the Parliament, the city, and perhaps the nation. Nobody knows your names, but you are heroes all the same."

"Pour us another ale," I said. "We are heroes, after all."

From that day, Martha and I came to the Crown more and more, often with Elizabeth in tow. The ale was every bit as fine as Bacca had promised, and he was always glad to see us. Elizabeth became entranced with his strange manner of speech and fantastic tales of life in Italy and beyond, some of which might have been true. It was a strange thing, I admit, but very soon Bacca, Martha, Elizabeth, and I became friends.

And so it was that Martha and I were in the Crown when a maid sought us out.

"Are you Mrs. Hodgson?" she asked. The fear in her eyes set me on edge in an instant.

"I am," I said, rising to my feet. "What is the matter?"

"It is my sister," she replied before bursting into tears.

I took her hand and eased her into a chair at our table. "All will be well," I said. "Tell me where she is, and I will see that she is delivered safe."

"That is the problem." The girl looked at me with red-rimmed eyes. "I don't know where she is. She is missing, and none will help me find her."

I glanced at Martha and saw the familiar set of her jaw.

"We will help," I said. "Tell me what happened."

Author's Note

While literacy rates rose dramatically during the early modern period, England of the seventeenth century was as much an oral culture as a written one. News was spread and history remembered as much through song as prose. In chapters ten and fourteen I have adapted two songs for a modern audience. The first, about Guy Fawkes and the Gunpowder Plot, is from a 1626 book, *A Song or Story for the Lasting Remembrance of Divers Famous Works Which God Hath Done in Our Time.* The second, a satire on the Rump Parliament, appears to come from *The Anarchic; or, the Blest Reformation Since 1640.* This poem has been reprinted several times, including in *Rump: Or an Exact Collection of the Choycest Poems and Songs Relating to the Late Times* (1662). Katherine Chidley's petition is based on a longer petition that Leveller women brought to Parliament in 1649.

As strange as it seems, the curious pregnancy of Grace Ramsden is also based on fact. I know some readers will read this note before the book, so I won't give anything away, but the records of the case (and thousands of others!) are available online. Visit the Old Bailey Proceedings Online (www.oldbaileyonline.org), and search for reference number *t16770601-6*.